CAMP KINROSS

HOLLY LOUISE PERRY

PERRY LANE
——Press——

Don't be a Carly Simon song.

First paperback edition July 2022

Book design by Dean McKeever

(Everything I Do) I Do It For You

ISBN 979-8-9864356–1-9 (paperback)

ISBN 979-8-9864356-0-2 (e-book)

www.perrylanepress.com

To Squish and Jake, with love

prying parents. A black and gray plaid couch with pilling fabric and cigarette burns was crammed between stacks of plastic bins labeled "Christmas" and "Glassware—FRAGILE!" A relegated TV sat on a particle board nightstand with a brass painted drawer handle. The VCR balanced precariously on top of the TV. Board games with broken boxes were piled in the corner: Clue, Sorry! Life, PayDay, Battleship, Go to the Head of the Class. Tom dropped the movie on two plastic milk crates pushed together—a makeshift coffee table. The screen door slammed upstairs.

Maggie, in a V-neck tee and cutoffs, kicked off her shoes at the door and ran her fingers through her damp, shoulder-length brown hair. She dropped a paper bag on the counter.

"Hungry?" asked Tom, emerging from the cellar. "I'm making dogs and mac 'n' cheese."

"Dinner of champions," smirked Maggie.

"If you think this is bad, wait until we're stuck at camp," scoffed Tom.

She pretended to gag and grabbed cups out of a cabinet. "Want some water?"

"Yeah, thanks," said Tom. He chopped the hot dogs and dumped them into the cheesy pot.

"I bought some penny candy at Cams for us," she said, motioning to the bag on the counter. "We should probably stock up before we go to camp—use it as leverage to buy our way to the cool kids table."

"I couldn't care less about that," said Tom.

"No kidding," said Maggie, rolling her eyes.

They took their dinner down into the cool, dank hangout and dug into their meals. As Tom scraped the last of his mac and cheese from his bowl, the phone rang. He set down his dish and walked over to the wall near the washing machine to answer it.

"Hello? Hey, man, what's up… Yeah, no, I dunno, man, I was just gonna chill. Yeah, she's here—hey, don't be a dumbass. What's that? He has what? Really? Hang on."

He covered the receiver with his hand. Maggie turned and looked at him bemused.

"Wanna ride to Beakman's Plaza before we watch *Wayne's World*? It's Harvey, and he says Smitty has 'grand plans' for a bottle rocket. He says we can't miss it."

She rolled her eyes. "Fine, yeah, let's go."

"Yeah, Harvey, we're on our way."

Maggie skewered her remaining chunks of hot dog with her fork and carried their bowls upstairs.

"I left my bike at home," she said, pulling on her Chucks.

"That's fine. I fixed my pegs the other day. You can ride on those."

"Cool. I can't imagine what stupidity Smitty has planned this time."

Tom grinned. "Right? Think he'll get arrested while we're away at camp?"

"Probably, knowing our luck," Maggie sighed dramatically.

"He'll never learn."

Tom pulled the front door closed and hid his house key under a rock by the steps. He went to the side of the house to get his bike. Maggie waited until he had his balance, then stepped up onto the back pegs. She held on to his shoulders, and Tom pedaled into the twilight descending over the small town of Bradford.

2

They pulled into a dilapidated strip mall. Beakman's Plaza once housed a diner, a thrift store, and a lawn care supply store; now all that resided there was litter pushed up against the sidewalk and a barbershop—its faded red and blue pole the only swirling sign of life. Tom rode to the back of the building, where two rows of parking spaces were encased by a rusty chain-link fence. Beyond it was a field of crabgrass, where they could barely make out shadows of mischief.

Maggie hopped off the bike and Tom leaned it against the fence. They ducked through the jagged hole cut into it and walked onto the field.

"Taahhmmaay!" bellowed a gravelly voice from a large figure, arms stretched high into the sky like it was Christmas morning. Maggie smirked watching annoyance spread across Tom's face.

"This was probably a mistake," Tom muttered.

"No way," argued Maggie, thoughtfully chewing on a gummy worm. "We can't pass on an opportunity that could make Smitty look like even more of a moron."

Ahead of them, their friends Smitty, Harvey, and Kyle stood around a cardboard box filled with projectiles and cans of beer.

"Hey, guys," said Tom, sizing up the box. "Where'd you get those?"

"The fireworks?" asked Smitty, casually throwing his arm in a "what's behind door number two?" motion toward the box.

"You truly are the ringmaster in a circus full of idiots," said Maggie.

"M'lady!" replied Smitty, bowing.

"We found them at the playground after the Fourth of July, like always. You know how it is—the college kids home for the summer wind up drinking too much and leave a ton of shit lying around."

"They leave those, too?" said Tom, motioning to the beer.

"Nah, I ripped those from my older brother," chimed in Kyle, absentmindedly picking at a zit on his forehead. "He's throwing a party this weekend while my parents are out of town. He's going to beat the shit out of me when he finds out I stole them, but it'll be worth it." He laughed nervously.

"I bet." Maggie grinned. "Peachie O, anyone?" she asked, offering her bag of candy to them; they obliged.

"So what fresh hell have you boys cooked up tonight? Gonna try to blow up the school again with another M-80, Harvey?" she asked.

"How'd you know about that?" Harvey's eyes narrowed.

Maggie shrugged.

"That was the scariest shit, dude. I'm not even kidding. I had no idea it had that kind of power. I threw it out the second-story bathroom window, near Miss Heller's classroom. It sounded like the school had been bombed! And it was so friggin' tiny—the size of my thumb!"

"You're lucky you didn't get caught, man. That'll get you expelled," said Kyle, reaching for a beer.

"I know, I know. You assholes better never say anything to anyone…" His eyes narrowed. "Especially you, Smitty."

"Why you gotta single me out like that, huh? Don't even!"

I'm so freaking loyal—you don't even know!" yelled Smitty.

"C'mon, you know you have a big mouth, Smitty." Tom laughed. "And I doubt anyone saw you, Harvey."

Smitty started swinging at Tom, but Tom bobbed and weaved around him. Smitty teetered on one foot, lost momentum and focus. He slowly spun over to the cardboard box.

"Who wants a beer?" he sang. He leaned over the box, but then dropped to a knee from exhaustion. He handed out cans, regardless of who actually wanted one.

"So, what's the plan—to light off these fireworks?" asked Tom, cracking the tab on his beer.

"Well, yes," said Harvey, "after…"

"After what?" Tom pressed.

"After Smitty shoots a bottle rocket out of his ass."

Maggie spit out a mouthful of beer. Smitty grinned, raising his eyebrows repeatedly.

"You're kidding, right?" she said, laughing and wiping her face with the back of her hand.

"No, ma'am. Do you want to, uh, do the honors?" he said, motioning to his backside, his balled up fist moving back and forth.

"There's not enough money in the world,"said Maggie.

"Oh, come on! Don't make one of these guys do it. They'll just jam it in. I need a woman's…touch."

Maggie threw her half-empty can at Smitty's head, full force. It caught him square in the shoulder.

"Ouch, Jesus! What was that for?"

"Don't be gross," she replied, and walked to the box to get a new can of beer.

"Okay, okay, fine, sorry," said Smitty, rubbing his shoulder. "Harvey will do it."

"Pass," said Harvey. "Kyle can wedge it in there. I'll light it."

"Where are you going to do it?" asked Tom.

"Here—don't you think?" asked Smitty, surveying the field.

"Have you considered the trajectory? You can't just bend over and fire it out—it'll be... anticlimactic. You need to be propped up or something," sputtered Maggie.

"What about one of those rocks over there? You could just bend over it…" said Harvey, stifling giggles.

"No, screw that. I'm going to get into a downward dog position and you'll light it. It will fly out of my ass and light up this field like the goddamned Sherman house Christmas lights on Maple Street!"

"Their electric bill has to be astronomical," commented Kyle.

"Let's get on with it. We have a movie to watch," said Maggie.

"Oh, a 'movie' to 'watch,' huh?" Smitty smirked, making exaggerated air quotes.

"Seriously, right now? I have another can of beer I can waste," replied Maggie, holding her arm in a throwing motion.

"You guys never did mention how Noah's party was." Smitty cocked his head. "I heard there was some drama around Spin the Bottle?"

Maggie turned away.

Tom cleared his throat and looked at his watch. "Better set up the launchpad before the cops patrol through here. They come by at what—eight thirty p.m. and ten p.m.?"

"Typically, yeah. All right, let's do this," said Smitty, looking around to make sure the coast was clear. Kyle put down his beer and rummaged through the box to find a bottle rocket. He tossed a lighter to Harvey.

"Jesus, a regular lighter? Why didn't you bring one of those grill lighters—you know, the long ones? I don't want to get up near his hairy ass to light this thing! He might go up in flames!"

"How far do you think the bottle rocket needs to go in, exactly?" asked Smitty angrily.

"This may as well be a book of matches," retorted Harvey.

"I have serious questions about the physics of this," added Maggie.

Tom laughed and crushed his beer can with his foot; it made a satisfying crunch. "Yeah, Smitty, this is pretty fucking stupid, even for you. What if it doesn't work and you explode or some shit?" he asked.

Maggie doubled over laughing, hitting Tom in the chest on her way down.

Smitty shotgunned the last beer and dropped trou. "Boys," he said, raising his empty can to them and twirling his other hand through the air, "if I explode into a million fleshy bits and rain down over this shitty small town, then it was a pleasure to serve with you." He knelt down and assumed the position, slapping at a mosquito that landed on his thigh. Tension mounted as Kyle and Harvey circled Smitty, trying to figure out the proper angle. Tom stood to the side, offering advice, but mostly words of caution. Kyle snickered nervously. Harvey got down on his knees and faced Smitty. "Any final words?"

Smitty, grimacing in his state of discomfort, wiped the newly formed beads of sweat away from his brow and bared his teeth. "Fire in the hole."

Harvey flicked the lighter to life. The bouncing glow created dancing shadows around the clearing. He leaned in and held the flame to the firework. It ignited, the orange embers projecting an ambient glow onto Smitty's exposed backside.

Giggling, Maggie said, "Hey wait, guys, that doesn't look like the right end. The fat end of the firework should be pointed up."

"What? WHAT?" yelled Smitty, his eyes darting around in a full-blown fit of panic. But it was too late. Sparks began to fly out of the bottom of the firework, signaling the lit fuse had almost reached its ignition point.

"She's kidding, man!" roared Tom.

They all took a step away from Smitty, without taking their eyes off his posterior.

"Don't, uh, clench too hard, or it won't fly," snickered Harvey.

This brought about a whole new round of snickering.

"Guys, do you think this will actually even wor—" started Kyle, but he had his answer before he finished his sentence. A whine shot past them through the air. They turned their heads in the darkness, following the firework's Doppler effect. Then silence, followed by a brisk pop. A green ball of light exploded a few hundred feet away. Harvey, Kyle, and Tom all ran toward the light hooting and hollering. Maggie tossed back her head, gasping for air between laughs, and jogged to catch up with them.

"Guys! Hey, guys, did it work? I didn't see it. Did it work?!" yelled Smitty, throwing the remnants of the bottle rocket on the ground and quickly jostling his shorts back up around his waist. He ran ahead of Maggie to catch up with the others.

"Smitty, you're a legend, man! You're a batshit crazy legend!" squawked Kyle as Smitty came barreling toward them.

"I cannot believe that worked!" said Harvey, high-fiving Smitty as he panted to a halt. He threw his arms around Tom's and Kyle's necks and let loose a drunken, guttural laugh.

"I'm the king of the world!" he shouted at the stars as they walked back to the box of fireworks.

"What now?" asked Kyle. "We're out of beverages."

"What now? We're going to light off the rest of these fireworks!" said Smitty.

"When do you guys get shipped off to camp, anyway?" asked Harvey, turning to Tom and Maggie.

"Couple of days," said Tom.

"Bum rap," Harvey replied.

"Yeah, pretty much," agreed Maggie. "Hey, Tom, what time is it? I gotta be home by midnight tonight."

Tom checked his watch. "Guys, we're gonna take off—we rented *Wayne's World*."

"Party time, excellent!" said Harvey, casually high-fiving them.

"See you clowns later," said Smitty.

Maggie grabbed a Roman candle from the box and walked over to Smitty.

"I hereby dub thee Smitty, King of the Firework Fools," she said, tapping his shoulders with the explosive. Never one to pass on a theatrical invitation, Smitty knelt solemnly and bowed his head. Maggie laughed. She tossed the Roman candle to him and said, "Maybe you should try launching this one next."

Smitty stood up and flicked his middle finger at her.

"Don't do anything else stupid while we're gone," said Maggie.

"No promises!" yelled Smitty, tossing the box of fireworks up into the sky. They rained down, hitting Harvey and Kyle in the head.

"Jesus Christ, Smitty, what's wrong with you? How are we going to find them now, huh? With that piece of shit lighter you brought with you?" Harvey chased Smitty in circles. Smitty laughed maniacally and dodged near blows to his body.

"Later, guys," said Tom.

Maggie giggled all the way back to Tom's bike. She threw her arms around Tom's chest and hopped up onto the pegs. "That was ridiculous," she said.

"That guy is going to get seriously hurt one of these days," said Tom, shaking his head incredulously.

"Classic Smitty," Maggie said, rolling her eyes.

"Classic Smitty," agreed Tom. He stood up on his bike and pedaled them into the night.

3

Maggie propped her feet up on the milk crate, her head still swimming slightly from the evening's shenanigans. Tom flopped down onto the couch, tossing the VCR and TV remotes on the cushion next to him. Their bodies sank closer together into the worn crevices of the cushions. Tom shifted his leg and Maggie rested her head on his shoulder. It was always like this.

"You pack yet?" Maggie asked.

"Nah, how about you?" said Tom.

"Nope."

"I don't know. I'd rather just hang around here. My mom was like, 'This will be good for you, Thomas, you'll be doing things!' Typical parent garbage."

"Yeah, my parents said pretty much the same thing. 'You'll be making lifelong memories! It's a rite of passage!' If it's such a rite of passage, then why are they forcing us to go to summer camp now, at the age of fifteen? We're too old for this. It's weird."

"Exactly. I bet they just want us out of the house so they can bone."

"Probably," Maggie giggled.

Bradford didn't have much to offer kids in the sweltering

summer months, apart from two overcrowded ponds, a few ball fields of burned grass, and a McDonald's just beyond the one stoplight in town. This summer, Maggie's parents had fanned a camp brochure at her, promising engaging experiences to "last a lifetime." Three uniformed campers in navy polos and khaki shorts had beamed from the flier—a blonde pigtailed girl with hands on hips and a fixated smile; a freckled girl with mousy straight brown hair, doubled over in laughter; and a robust redheaded boy with beaming eyes, readying an archery bow. "Camp Kinross: fun for all time!"

Tom's parents had done the same. It was weird, this sudden parental interest in shipping their kids to Vermont, but the fees were unusually low, and deposit checks had been mailed.

"It's going to take forever to get there, too—what, like, six hours?" said Maggie.

"Something like that. At least our parents agreed to carpool," said Tom, reaching for the bag of candy. He balanced it on their touching legs.

"Let's start planning our escape," said Maggie. "I have no interest in braiding hair and making bracelets for a week. I think I'd rather watch Smitty do something stupid."

"Yeah, no kidding—it kinda feels like a death sentence."

They turned their attention to Wayne and Garth's futile attempt to play street hockey. Before long, Tom heard Maggie's rhythmic breathing that he had become accustomed to over the years—she was always fast asleep by the end of whatever movie they watched. Her arm draped over his, her body curled toward him. Tom let the credits run while his mind shifted to Smitty's snide remark about Noah's party.

Noah's parents had been out of town, and what was supposed to be a chill night playing cards turned into half the school showing up with booze and the desire to get some. Tom and Maggie found themselves buzzed, sitting in a big circle of their classmates with an empty bottle of Heineken spinning in the middle. Before he knew what was happening, it was Maggie's turn to spin it. He stared at it, mesmerized by the green blur against the wooden floor. Maybe it will spin forever—maybe she won't have to kiss any of these idiots, he thought. As the bottle slowed, his heart rate increased. What if it landed on him? He looked at Maggie, who bit her lower lip and watched the bottle intently. The bottle slowed, its neck seemingly stretching toward Tom in its final rotation. Before it stopped spinning, he quickly stood up and muttered, "I gotta take a piss." He didn't look back at Maggie or the rest of the group. He ignored the drunken, squealing protests of not being allowed to leave the circle while the bottle was spinning. And after the party, Maggie and Tom acted like nothing had happened.

He leaned his head into hers and sighed. If he had kissed her that night, it would have ruined everything. It would have made things weird. No, it was better this way. Except now they were being shipped off to some stupid camp in Vermont, and who knows who she'd meet or what would happen there.

Maggie sleepily shifted closer to Tom, her cheek pressing into his arm. The VCR clicked while the TV flickered black and white. Staring at its monochromatic glow, he couldn't help but think that going to summer camp was a complete waste of time.

4

Tom and Maggie swapped mix tapes on their Walkmen to survive the tedious ride to camp. Tom's dad grumbled to himself while driving along route 89 and the winding roads of rural Vermont. After what seemed like an eternity of being trapped in the car, they arrived. A simple painted wooden sign read "Camp Kinross, Next Right" on the side of the road. A barely visible dirt driveway cowered under majestically tall pines. Bits of blue sky and sunlight snuck through to kiss the underbrush enshrined by the towering trees.

The driveway seemed endless. The smell of honeysuckle hung heavy in the air. Tom's eyes jumped over each tree they passed. He thought he saw an animal out of the corner of his eye—a deer? No, too big. A wolf or coyote? Maybe.

But it had been slinking low to the ground. Weird.

Maggie wrapped her headphones around her Walkman and shoved it into her backpack. She looked at Tom with a raised eyebrow as if to say, "You ready for this?" He returned the look with a pained smile.

A short man with thick rimmed glasses stood in the middle of the parking lot, holding a clipboard and a click counter. His nasally voice repeated, "Girls through the left arches! Boys through the right arches please! No—nonono, your other left, dear—yes, this way. Keep it moving! Keep it moving!" Click, click, click went the counter.

Tom and Maggie watched as others filed through the appropriate wooden arches welcoming them to Camp Kinross. Maggie turned to Tom's dad and gave him a brief hug. "Bye, Mr. Dunne, thanks for the ride!"

Tom's dad straightened himself, cleared his throat, and stammered, "Yes, well, er, have a good time. Call if you need anything." He gave Tom a squeeze on the shoulder and a pat on the back that left him coughing.

"Well...here we go!" said Maggie with fake excitement.

"Yep. Guess I'll see you?" Tom stepped in to give her a hug, but he was interrupted by a tap on the shoulder.

"Excuse me, yes, hi, hello—and you are?" said Mr. Clipboard. Click, click.

"Uh, Tom, Tom Dunne. You?"

"I am...busy, but you can call me Neal. *Counselor* Neal."

"Okay, Double O Seven," said Tom.

"Huh?" said Neal, confused and annoyed. Click.

"Never mind. Uh, how can I help you, Neal?"

"*Counselor* Neal. And you, Tommy, can help me by shuffling over through the boys' arch. Yes, yes, move it along. Let's go. Atta boy." Neal wrapped his arm around Tom's shoulder and herded him away from Maggie. Tom looked back at her with raised eyebrows. She smirked and threw him a little wave as he walked off.

Maggie stepped over gnarled tree roots and jagged rocks along the path, and listened as the other girls chirped their excitement around her. The path led to a clearing lined with tall grass and fuzzy pine trees. It had rows of logs—an outdoor theater. The center aisle stopped at a large tree stump. The base of it showed some signs of rot, but the trunk itself was freshly sanded. A smooth sheen highlighted the bumps and knots around it. It wasn't a clean break—lightning had probably struck it at one time. Its uneven bark fingers pointed accusingly to the sky. A creepy pulpit, thought Maggie. She shuddered.

A bright "WELCOME CAMPERS!" banner snapped in the breeze above the trunk. Next to the podium, Maggie watched a woman and man murmur to each other. The woman dangled a megaphone by her waist. Maggie's eyes drifted across the crowd, searching for her only familiar face in the sea of boys filing into the rows. She found Tom seated next to a chubby kid with a bowl haircut and wire-rimmed glasses; he appeared lost in thought. The megaphone squawked to life.

"Please find a seat as quickly as possible! We have a lot to cover! Thank you! Take a seat please!" As more and more campers piled in, the joyful screams, fake wrestling matches, and arm punches continued.

"Campers, I implore you to take a seat—we must get on with it! Sit!" the woman yelled into the megaphone.

The din of high fives, butt slaps, belly laughs, secret handshakes, and chants drowned out the megaphone.

"SILENCE!" shrieked the woman. Her face contorted into grotesque lines of impatience. The entire clearing immediately went still, as if all the campers were playing a giant game of freeze tag, and the woman had caught them at the same time with her shrill cry. Her face quickly softened into a broad smile. "If you could all quietly find a seat, we are ready to welcome you to Camp Kinross!"

At this, the clearing erupted in cheers, whoops, and whistles. The woman looked to the man next to her, her eyes shining, and nodded her approval. She turned to the audience and patted the air with her hands to settle the campers once more.

"Campers, it is my pleasure to welcome you to Camp Kinross! Whether you're a newbie just getting your feet wet for the first time in Lake Aeternus, or if you're an old pro at Manhunt, we want to let you know that this is your summer.

You are unique and powerful in your own way—you are here to explore your strengths and embrace your weaknesses! You have full control of your destiny!"

Her speech was met with a few sniggers in the crowd, but she was fully prepared for them.

"I know, I know, it sounds a little corny, but it's true! This is the ultimate camp experience. Think of your favorite movie about summer camp. What do you love about it? The camaraderie? We have that! The rustic adventure? We have that! The summer romance? We may even have a little of that!"

A boy jumped up and shouted, "Aw, yeah!" and was answered by infectious giggles.

The woman wagged a disciplining finger at him, then smiled warmly. "We are better than those movies, though, because we are *real*. We are here to help you live out this dream. The only complaint that we receive year after year is that a week just isn't long enough! Now, for those of you who don't know me, I'm Head Counselor Kate, and this is Head Counselor Greg," she said, motioning to the man beside her. "And with that, I leave it to Greg to go over the rules."

The girls' side of the camp breathed a collective sigh when Greg stepped to the podium; he resembled the Ken doll that most of them had recently outgrown.

"Hello, campers! Hello, ladies!" he said.

Maggie looked around skeptically at the jittery girls wringing their hands and fanning flushed faces.

"At Camp Kinross, we have a few rules." He was met with boos but pressed on. "I know, I know, but it's the only way this place will run like a well-oiled machine, and it's the only way we make this summer the dream experience that Head Counselor Kate just promised you!"

"So hear me out," Greg continued. "They're not bad. They're actually pretty simple to remember. Are you ready?" He paused for effect, scanning the crowd.

"Rule number one: No boys in the girls' cabins; no girls in the boys' cabins." He was met with more boos, but raised his arms in a "nothing-you-can-do, I-don't-make-the-rules" shrug. His tone then changed into one of all business.

"Rule number two: No campers are allowed to be out of their cabin once the evening bell has rung. Also, you may not leave your cabin in the morning until the morning bell has rung."

Kate interrupted. "There are things in these woods that you cannot even fatho—"

"Now, now, Kate, no need to scare them on the first day! She's kidding! She's kidding!" Greg laughed with a little too much gusto, while giving Kate side-eye. He looked around and continued, "Just know that this is a very important rule, and if you break it, you will face immediate expulsion. No chances!" He paused again, letting the severity sink in.

"Rule number three: HAVE FUN!" said Greg.

Smiles crept onto campers' faces as they fidgeted in anticipation.

"You'll find your bunk assignments posted on a bulletin board over by the cabins. Girls, you'll be walking down this path over here to get to yours—on the other side of the Mess Hall," said Greg, pointing. "Guys, you'll be walking along the path to your left to your cabins."

The campers clambered to their feet. The boys snuck glances at the girls, who were still staring at Head Counselor Greg.

Tom overheard two campers nearby.

"Hey, Paxton, have you seen anyone else from back home yet?" asked one camper.

"Nah, but I heard that Caitlyn Myers was coming," said the other with a wry grin, "and coming…and coming!"

"No shit," said the first camper, laughing.

"You from around here?" Tom's eavesdropping was interrupted by the chubby kid with the bowl cut now walking next to him.

"Nope, Boston—south of Boston," said Tom, distracted.

"Ah, Beantown!" he replied, eyes lighting up with recognition.

Tom fanned away a mosquito. "No one calls it that."

"Right, well, I'm Bunsen Jones. Pleasure!" The camper stretched out his hand eagerly.

Tom raised an eyebrow and shook his hand reluctantly. "Bunsen? Like the burner?"

"Indeed! But most people call me Jonesy."

"Uh, nice to meet you, Jonesy."

The line of campers stopped abruptly. Counselor Greg motioned everyone to gather around. Five cabins formed a semicircle in a well-manicured clearing. A flag blew in the breeze, and a weathered bulletin board stood off to the side, as if to educate the passersby to some historical exhibit or battlefield. In front of each cabin stood a college-aged counselor, poised with tight lips and hands at parade rest.

"Okay, gents, here's your home for the next week," said Greg. "Your bunk assignments are posted over there, but before you get settled in, let's meet your counselors! We have Neal, Barry, James, Doug, and Mark!"

Each counselor stepped forward and offered a nod or casual flick of the wrist in acknowledgment.

"These guys will explain the nuts and bolts of Camp Kinross to you, keep you on schedule, and help you out if you find yourself in a jam. All right, have at it!" Greg motioned like an air traffic controller to the bulletin board.

Tom maneuvered around eager campers muscling for a glimpse at the bunk assignments. He squinted at the yellow lined paper, scanning for his name, and then walked toward the cabin with a wooden number "2" next to the door.

"'Sup, man," Counselor Mark stood next to the steps and held out his hand for a low five. "Welcome to Camp Kinross." The screen door bleated like a dying sheep, its rusted springs exhausted from years of repetition.

The cabin was straight out of a Hollywood set. Beds lined each wall, with a small dresser in between. On top of the army-green bedding lay a neatly stacked pile of clothes—two pairs of gray shorts, two navy-blue polos, swim trunks, khakis, drawstring shorts, a few navy-blue T-shirts, socks, and underwear. A small card with the name "Tom" in simple handwriting crowned the pile of clothes.

"So weird," muttered Tom, "why did we even pack clothes?" He looked around the rest of the cabin. A few of the beds looked lived in—probably kids sent for the whole summer, Tom surmised. At the back of the cabin was a doorway with a curtain partially open. Tom saw the foot of a bed, and what looked like a Soundgarden poster on the wall. The screen door slapped shut as other campers filed in.

"Hey, guys, hope you're settling in okay," said Mark, leaning his head through the screen door. "Dinner's in ten, so get into your new threads and do what you gotta do. We head out for the Mess Hall in a few." He entered the cabin and moved toward the curtained doorway.

"Is that you back there? Where do you sleep?" asked Tom as he walked by.

Mark narrowed his eyes, leaned in, and whispered, "I don't." He winked and passed through the curtain.

One of the guys closest to Tom overheard his conversation and let out a sympathetic laugh. "First time at Kinross, eh? I'm Alex." He reached over the bed to shake hands.

"Yeah, first time at any camp, actually," said Tom, pulling the polo over his head.

"No way!" Alex laughed, running his fingers through his dark hair.

"I know, right? Yeah, it's the same for my friend Maggie— she's here, too. Both our parents thought we needed to get out, experience things or whatever." He cringed at his honesty.

"Truth be told, no better place," said Alex, brushing the front of his shirt straight.

"Yeah?" said Tom, waiting for the punchline.

"I've been coming here for three summers now. They made me a Lifer, actually—there are a few of us kicking around here." He motioned around the room. "Germ is the one with the headphones around his neck—he's really into music. Corey is the one tossing the tennis ball over there—he can be broody, but he'd take a bullet for you. Ryan is pretty cool—sometimes too cool for school—but a good guy. And Joey is, well…Joey. You'll see."

"When did they make you a Lifer?"

"A few summers ago. Becky's been here a little longer, I think. Kinross is pretty sweet—we've got contests, archery, campfires, and the girls, oh God, the girls…"

"Ha, really?" said Tom, blinking.

"All I'm saying is, with this kind of setup, you have a lot of opportunities to 'connect' with the girls. I'm telling you, dude, you're gonna want to stay all summer."

"Doubt it."

"Yo, Joey, Ryan—you guys ready?" Alex called across the room. He rapped his knuckles on the wooden wall. "Good to go, Mark!" he said.

Counselor Mark emerged from behind the curtain with a fresh polo, slicked back hair, and a taunting smile. "All right, let's hit it," he said.

5

The Mess Hall sat in the woods between the boys' and girls' cabins of Camp Kinross. It was a low, wide structure that showed obvious signs of overuse. Painted a matte red-brown, it was meant to be an inviting chestnut hue in the drab wooded area, but instead looked like someone dumped a bunch of melted burnt-sienna crayons all over the building.

In front of it was an old well with a thick cement lid to prevent campers from falling in. Above the well hung an oversized, foreboding bell with a rope attached to its pendulum.

The smell of overcooked peas, meatloaf, and a heavy cloud of bleachy steam wafted through the Mess Hall. Lining one of the walls were two rectangular folding tables holding several yellow drink coolers and stacks of clear plastic cups. Tom grabbed the empty seat next to his new bunkmate, Jonesy, unsure of the protocol for getting food. He scanned the festive atmosphere for Maggie. He found her sitting on the outskirts of the cafeteria, the warm light bouncing off her flushed face. She wore a placid smile that Tom immediately recognized as the face she made when she was bored, but being polite. He grinned.

Counselor Kate stood on a milk crate and blew a whistle

repeatedly. "Campers! Settle down, please! Thank you! Welcome to the Mess Hall! I hope you're all hungry, because our wonderful kitchen staff, headed up by the world famous chef Forrest Pemberton—we all affectionately refer to him as 'Woody'—has cooked up a delicious classic to welcome you to Camp Kinross! Form a line over to my right—no, don't all jump at once. There's plenty for everyone. And the bug juice is over there," she said, pointing to the coolers.

Tom shuffled his way through the line. A server jiggled mashed potatoes from a serving spoon and then ladled thin gravy over a lump of gray meat. Tom balanced his tray of food on the edge of the beverage table while dispensing a cup of bug juice. He carried the plastic cup between his teeth to where the rest of his cabin was sitting. The cherry-red liquid sloshed back and forth, staining a pink mustache on his upper lip.

"Why didn't you just put the cup on your tray?" commented Jonesy, baffled.

Tom ignored him. "Why's it called bug juice, anyway?" he asked, pulling in his chair and looking around at the others.

"Oh, I'll tell you why," smirked Joey. "Legend has it that there used to be a batshit-crazy serial killer. He went around to all of the insane asylums in New England, slipping inside under the cover of night, and hacking off one or two poor, unfortunate souls. He'd siphon their blood with a small hose and store it in twist-tied plastic baggies. Once he built up a decent supply of human juice, he started visiting camp Mess Halls all over the area. While everyone was asleep, he'd fill the drink coolers with some of his blood from the psychos, mix it with the Kool-Aid powder and water, and then leave. Next morning, the kitchen staff just assumed the juice was made the night before—no big deal, nice to have one of the four thousand pain-in-the-ass jobs already done. Sickest part is—the campers loved the juice: they drank it right up. Guzzled it. Demanded more! It was gone before lunch. But after a day or so, kids started getting sick. Not throwing up or shitting their pants, but like, weird sick. Their eyes started to bulge. All of them—like big bullfrog eyes—bugging out of their head."

"Bug juice!" guessed Jonesy.

Alex rolled his eyes.

"Exactly," continued Joey, soaking up the attention. "And then it was like their eye sockets just couldn't take it anymore—their eyeballs popped right out of their heads. The blood from the looney bin had turned all of the campers mental—just out of their minds mental!"

"That's gross, dude," said Germ, pushing a piece of meatloaf around his plate.

"That's bullshit. It would've been in the papers," said Corey through a mouthful of potato.

"Nah, I'm telling you, it happened. My neighbor's aunt, her brother was one of the counselors who worked at one of the first camps that reopened after the whole incident. They shut down every camp in New England for like, years, trying to catch that guy."

"And they never did?" asked Jonesy, furrowing his brow.

"No idea. I just know what I was told. I mean, they had to catch him, right?"

"Nah, bug juice gets its name because it's so damn sweet and delicious, the bugs bust through the weak-ass mesh screens of the Mess Hall just to get a taste," said Ryan.

"Or because they puree bug guts and—" started Joey.

"Give it a rest, Joey," said Alex, throwing a dinner roll at him.

"Cheers!" said Joey, holding up a plastic cup to his smirking lips.

Choking down a bite of the mushy meat, Tom swallowed hard and said, "So what's next—when do we start activities or whatever?"

"They basically rotate each cabin through all of the

activities for the week. They pair us up with a girls' cabin—the girls usually get all bent because we are better than them at the physical activities, but you know, it's all part of their game," mused Joey.

"You're a pig, Joe," commented Germ.

"Is there a competition, or talent show, or something at the end of the week?" asked Jonesy.

"You could say that," said Ryan, lifting an eyebrow.

"Kinross sort of operates on a survival of the fittest mentality," continued Alex.

Tom and Jonesy exchanged hesitant looks.

"No! No, what I mean is that the more you embrace camp culture, the more fun you have, and the more fun you have, the better the chance you'll get tapped."

"Tapped?" said Corey. "Now we're part of a goddamned camp secret society, Alex?"

"I like to think of it like that," shrugged Joey. "For us—the Lifers—we started out just like you guys. Parents signed us up for a week, and when the week was almost over, we were tapped. Head Counselor Greg came to each of our cabins in the middle of the night and had us go through initiation. He praised us in his goofy game show voice and said that we had an opportunity to stay on for the rest of the summer, free of charge. He had personally called each of our parents to get their okays, and they all basically said, yeah fine, whatever."

"He told us it was our choice to stay—we were free to leave—we weren't prisoners or anything!" added Alex. "But he really believed in us to make this camp successful. He said he would be disappointed if we didn't embrace our potential to show other campers their—what did he call it, Ry?"

"Their inner vision," recited Ryan, "a way to stretch beyond the ego and to live successfully in a utopian environment—temporarily—filled with all the nostalgia and the innocence that is so precious in these formative years. Or some bullshit like that."

"Huh," said Tom. He wiped his mouth and eyed his untouched bug juice.

"Yeah, pretty heavy stuff, especially for three a.m. or whatever time he dragged us out of bed to initiate us. But it made sense. One of those moments when you think 'Yeah, okay, maybe I do have some influence—I'll stay here instead of going back to my boring suburban town in western Connecticut,'" said Joey.

"Do you think anyone has ever turned Greg down?" asked Germ.

"Ummm, maybe one kid? Two? Did Slater turn him down, Alex?"

"Yeah, I think so," said Alex. "But his parents just came to pick him up the next day. No big deal."

Tom glanced across the Mess Hall. Metal chair legs scraped across the sticky linoleum. He watched Maggie pick up her tray and maneuver to the dish drop-off conveyor belt. Tom pushed back his chair and said, "I gotta go—see you guys back at the cabin." He weaved between the chairs and caught up with her.

He tapped her on the shoulder. "Hey, how's it going?"

"Oh gosh, Tom, you scared me! Listen, we should talk. This place is kind of—"

"Shh, Maggie, not here. We need to find a better place. But yeah, I know. It's not…right. And the guys in my cabin just told me…well…we have to talk."

"Okay. But how? When?"

"I'm not sure."

Woody appeared at the window to receive dishes. He stared at Tom's full cup of red liquid on his tray to be thrown out and muttered, "If you know what's good for you, you won't drink that."

"Wait, what?" asked Tom, but Woody had already walked away. Tom and Maggie exchanged glances, but before they could say anything more, Counselor Kate was at the entryway to the Mess Hall, announcing that dinner was wrapping up and that campers should head back to their cabins before the night bell rang.

6

Archery—the quintessential summer camp rite of passage. Pillowy primary colored targets rested on weathered easels standing in tall grass. Crickets sang their morning hymns, and dew clung to blades of grass on the recently mowed field. The earth smelled freshly laundered. Campers rubbed the sleep from their eyes and opened their mouths in contagious silent roars, despite having already eaten breakfast.

Tom couldn't shake the weirdness from the night before—the crazy urban legends that had morphed into intense conversation. Maybe that's what people love about the whole camp thing, he thought.

"Morning, campers! Who's ready to have some good ol' archery fun?" Counselor Mark stood next to a pretty, lithe counselor with blonde hair and tanned skin. "Counselor Mary and I will show you the ropes—er—bows, and after a few practice rounds, we'll break into teams and have a friendly competition! Form a line at each tree stump and start firing." He pointed with an arrow to three tree stumps that sat several hundred yards away from the targets.

Murmurs of encouragement echoed through the air for those sending arrows into the ground, while "Great bid, Lucy!" and "Atta boy, Germ!" were awarded for direct hits.

Tom's first sleeve of arrows sailed over, around, and beneath the target. At one point, his arrow grazed the outer white circle, but only nicked it before sailing out to pasture.

Mark made his way over to Tom. He put his arm on his shoulder, as Tom readied to fire his bow again. "You're overthinking it, man," he said calmly. "Shut out everyone else around you, and focus on what you want the most." His voice lowered to a whisper. "You want to hit that target. You need to hit that target. You want to drive that arrow through the heart of that target and watch it bleed out the other end. Northing's stopping you, but you. Let it go and just do it. Now!"

Tom instantly released his fingers from the arrow. The feathers whistled through the air. Bull's-eye. Tom dropped his bow, stunned. The silence lasted only a moment, before the archery field erupted into a raucous celebration. Tom grinned, astonished. The Cabin Two guys high-fived each other, and the girls grinned, trying to make eye contact with the fleeting champion.

"Awesome. That was awesome. I knew you had it in you," said Mark, a coy smile forming on his lips as he moved on to help the next camper.

7

Waiting on stragglers, Counselor Kate yanked on the bell's rope to signify lunchtime. Her gaze was stoic, set far beyond the carousing campers making their way into the Mess Hall. It went past the pines, into the depths of the woods.

Tom's bunkmates set up shop at the table they had eaten at the previous night, their spirits jovial.

"I had no idea archery was so much fun," said Tom.

"Yeah, that was really incredible, I can't believe how much we all improved from when we first picked up the bows," chirped Jonesy.

Alex flashed a knowing smile and added, "What did I tell ya?"

"The way you hit that bull's-eye three times today—no question, dude, ridiculous," added Joey.

"Thanks, man," said Tom. The beginnings of camaraderie seeped in. "Cheers," he said, raising his cup of bug juice to the table and downing it in one gulp.

"What do we do after lunch?" asked Jonesy.

The Lifers all replied at once, "Swim."

"Yeah, they'll have you pass a quick test to make sure you know how to tread water and at least doggie paddle," said Corey, poking his empty paper cup with his fork. "The lake is pretty sweet, though."

"And so are the girls," Joey drawled with a wink.

"Joey talks a big game," replied Alex.

"That's not the only thing that's big," retorted Joey.

"You just lob 'em in for him, Alex," said Ryan, shaking his head.

"Let's go back and change," said Alex, ignoring Ryan. He jammed the last bite of hot dog into his mouth and pushed back in his chair.

Tom carried his tray over to the conveyor. Woody was chopping onions—two ten-pound bags of the potent vegetable sat on the metal prep table.

"No one loves that job, hey, Woody?" Tom offered, setting his tray down.

"Spare me your sob story, kid," replied Woody without looking up from his knife. Tears from the onions streamed down his face.

Tom shook his head and turned, bumping into Maggie on his way out of the Mess Hall.

"Oh, hey—hey! How was your morning?" he asked cheerfully.

Maggie raised an eyebrow and grinned cautiously.

"It was pretty good? We went boating—kayaks, canoes, the whole bit. We raced at the end—that was kinda fun, I guess. How about you? What did you guys do?"

"Oh, man, Mags, it was so cool. We had archery, and we all really sucked at the beginning, but then we were all pretty awesome by the end!"

"You're awfully peppy. Yeah, that's how it felt with the rowing stuff—weird. Hey, so what did you want to, you know"—she dropped her voice to a whisper—"talk about from last night?"

"Oh, nothing, nothing—I was being stupid," said Tom, laughing a little. "Today has been great though, and next we have swimming, I think."

"No, really, I mean, there are a few girls in my cabin who seem—"

Tom cut her off. "Mags, it's fine. We're just new. There are Lifers in my cabin, too. They're cool, and pretty fun to listen to. I think we're just not used to doing things like this, being around people like this. Maybe it's like riding a bicycle or whatever. Once you get the hang of it…"

Maggie scrunched up her face in pained protest, as if Tom had ripped a mystery meat fart that she couldn't escape.

"Really, I think it's going to be fine. Don't worry. See you at the lake?" He grinned.

"Sure, yeah, see ya…" said Maggie, her voice trailing after him.

8

Early afternoon clouds moved in over Camp Kinross. The counselors speculated about potential rain headed their way and strategized on the best way to keep campers occupied if and when the skies opened up.

Lake Aeternus was a giant ink splotch dropped in the middle of the camp. The swimming area had an L-shaped dock jutting into the water, where a few life-saving rings lay along the walkway. To the right of the main dock floated a square wooden platform with a water slide; farther out was another one with a diving board.

The beach was overwrought with weeds along the edges. The intrusive earthy scent of fresh water, mixed with the aggressive use of sunscreen and the humidity of an impending rain made the beach smell like a teenage rainforest. Girls clustered on the beach, giggling and surreptitiously scoping out boys from the safety of their unnecessary sunglasses. Their navy-blue one-piece bathing suits were tied halter-style behind their necks, with a flirty ruching between the breasts. A few girls were walking along the edge of the lake, kicking water at each other and shriek laughing; beads of water hesitated before sliding down their freshly shaven legs.

The guys of Cabin Two tossed their towels by the lone lifeguard chair on the beach and moved toward the lake in pack formation. Tom saw Maggie sitting across the beach on a towel, propped up on her arms talking to a few girls he presumed to be her bunkmates.

"Here we are," said Alex, surveying the water.

"What's it called again—Lake Artemis?" asked Jonesy.

"Lake Aeternus," corrected Corey. "It's Latin or some shit for 'eternal.'"

"Yeah, there's some lore about kids swimming in it and living forever," Alex said, winking.

"Name doesn't exactly roll off the tongue," said Tom.

"Exactly! That's why we call it Lake Anus instead. Much easier on the tongue, isn't it?" smirked Joey.

"Ignore him," replied Alex, swatting at Joey.

"Anyway, some guys like to charge into the water, all William Wallace style," Ryan explained to the newbies. "They think it's funny—'Hey, look at me, I'm a laugh! Water!' Don't be that guy."

"Yeah, there's always collateral damage when you do that—girls on the periphery—and then they go back and tell the rest of their cabin that you're the asshole who messed up their hair or makeup or whatever. You don't want that kind of black mark," added Germ.

Jonesy and Joey trailed behind, gawking at a group of girls laying out their towels on the beach.

"So…what then?" asked Tom.

"Our usual play is that we're all business walking to the water; don't even give them the time of day. The last thing they need is the satisfaction of knowing you're checking them out as you thump past them through the sand," said Alex.

"Yeah, and then once you're in the water, you can check them out more discreetly. You know, throw a glance, catch her eye. If she's brave enough, she'll coax one of her sidekicks to go into the water with her. And then it's on," said Joey.

"Unless you're Joey, in which case you slither around until you can sting one into submission," said Ryan. They all laughed as Ryan shielded himself from Joey's swinging arm.

"Sometimes we get out here and sit on the dock if no one's claimed it yet. The girls will sometimes inch their way over, or play some fake game of tossing a hat, or headband, or something. It just happens to be thrown near where we're sitting, or beyond the dock, so someone gets to be a hero," said Alex.

"It's all a ruse," sang Joey, smiling and nodding to a girl at the far end of the dock. She returned a "not in this lifetime" look and slipped into the water.

A few campers were by the diving board, but most were on the beach or dipping their toes at the edge of the water. Counselor Neal walked with purpose down the dock. Instead of his clicking counter, he swung a red megaphone in hand. It whined as he pressed the button to speak into it.

"All right campers," his nasally voice cracked through the speaker, "if this is your first time at Kinross, come over this way so you can take a swim test and get it over with." He motioned to the left side of the L-shaped dock.

"Form a line on the dock—yup, all the way to the end. Yep, there you go. Great."

New campers queued all the way to the end of the dock, snaking around towels and water bottles lying on the beach.

"We'll be testing on the left side of the dock. The rest of you, you know the drill—have at it," he said in a bored tone.

On his whistle, Neal instructed new campers to jump into the lake, tread water for two minutes, and then swim around the outside of the dock to rejoin the others on the opposite side.

Tom jumped into the water and sputtered as he resurfaced. He pedaled his legs and waved his hands back and forth with sudden determination. He didn't just want to pass the test—

he wanted to be good. He wanted the same accolades he received during archery that morning. For a fleeting moment he wanted to out-tread the others, to be the best survivor.

"Okay, great job—now swim around to the other side," said Neal automatically, chewing on the back of a number two pencil. Tom swam around, dejected at the lack of attention, until he heard Neal say, "Hey, you—what's your name?"

"Tom, Tom Dunne."

"Good form out there, Dunne." Neal made a notation on his clipboard.

"Thanks!" He flicked his wet hair back and grinned.

Tom rejoined the rest of Cabin Two, and they floated over to the far right of the swimming area. Two girls moved slowly through the water toward them, batting their eyes and flashing half smiles before looking away and stifling giggles of contrived embarrassment.

"Oh shit, it's Becky," Joey said in a hushed tone.

"Looks like she has a new friend," concurred Ryan.

"Hello, ladies! Are you enjoying this lovely swim?" hollered Jonesy, gesturing a little too grandly at the expanse of the lake. Alex hit him in the chest with his forearm, which made two girls floating in tubes nearby giggle. Jonesy reddened.

"I'm just, uh, gonna go jump off a bridge—er—dock. I'll be back," muttered Jonesy.

"Oh boy," said Joey, watching as he swam over to the side of it.

"He's going to double down?" said Germ, half in awe, half incredulous.

Jonesy hoisted his legs one at a time onto the dock, as if he were lifting baked hams onto the checkout belt at the grocery store. After this minor miracle, he placed his wire-rimmed glasses on the side of the dock and regained some of the confidence he lost in front of the girls. He grinned at Cabin

Two; they were staring at him in the way anyone watches an astonishing act of stupidity. He waved his hands wildly with a "Look, Ma, I'm on TV!" hysteria, launched himself from the wooden planks, squeezed his stubby arms around his shins while airborne, and plummeted into the depths of Lake Aeternus. A water mushroom cloud bloomed, sending shock waves through the entire swimming area.

"Jesus," said Tom, shaking his head.

When Jonesy resurfaced, his shit-eating grin turned to panic—all of the girls in the aftershock zone were hurling insults and not so flirtatious splashes of retaliation at him. "Jerk!" they cried, their previously blown-out hair now wet and stringy. Though the lake was cold, his face flushed.

"What a tool," Ryan laughed.

Alex and the others turned their attention back to Becky, who had finally sidled up to them with her new friend.

"Hey, Becky," said Alex. Something lingered in the silence between his hello and her name.

"Hi, Alex," replied Becky simply. She turned to the others. "Hi, boys. I'm Becky." She flashed them a dazzling smile while her eyes quickly assessed the new campers.

"What brings you over this way, Parker?" said Ryan, his tone cold and uninterested.

"Well," said Becky, prolonging the word in a thoughtful singsong voice, "this is Liv. She's new here, and she's my little—"

"Pet?" interjected Ryan.

"Cool it," warned Alex.

Becky looked at her manicured nails, ignoring the insult. "She's my new little friend—"

"You mean protégé," challenged Ryan.

"Dude, take a chill pill," said Alex.

"It's fine, Alex, honestly. I'm a big girl! I can handle him—but thank you," said Becky, tossing her wavy blonde hair over her shoulder.

"Couldn't handle me last summer, though, could ya?" smirked Ryan.

Alex pushed his tightening fists underwater.

"Oh, as if!" scoffed Becky. "Anyway, Liv wanted to meet some of the nicer boys here, but asked to be introduced to this one in particular. I said sure! But then silly little me realized that I didn't know him yet. What's your name?" She motioned to Tom.

"Uh, Tom. Dunne. Hey," said Tom, looking down, then away.

Liv pushed a piece of her straight brown hair behind her ear, and smiled before letting out a simple, "Hi."

Becky watched this exchange with amusement. "Nice to meet you, Tommy," she said. She paid no mind to Jonesy and Joey, who were gawking at the camp-issued bathing suit clinging for dear life to her well-developed figure. "Maybe we'll see you at dinner, then. Come along, Liv."

"Nice to meet you," said Liv. She glanced over her shoulder once and sheepishly grinned as they walked back to the beach.

"Dude, stay away," Ryan said to Tom.

"What's your problem, man?" said Alex through gritted teeth. The others stood waist deep in the uncomfortable silence that followed.

"What's my problem? My problem?" said Ryan, his voice raised. On the shore, they spotted Counselor Mark stand up and walk from the beach to the water.

Tom watched the fiery-eyed friction of the two Lifers, but his mind kept circling back to Liv. Her olive skin—she looked soft, without any hard muscular angles jutting out. Her lips had a natural purse to them, and her dark eyes were round and kind. His daydream vanished when Mark intervened.

"Everything cool here?"

"Sure," said Alex, his eyes fixed on Ryan.

"Ryan?" said Mark.

"Yeah, fine," said Ryan through gritted teeth.

"Good. Let it go. You're only hurting yourselves and your potential. You guys good?" asked Mark, turning to the rest of Cabin Two. They nodded.

Jonesy turned to Tom. "That's one way to diffuse a situation, I guess," he said.

But Tom only murmured an absentminded acknowledgment—his head had already drifted back to the clouds.

9

After the beach, the campers mixed up the seating in the Mess Hall. Maggie apologized as she pushed in front of two campers, motioning that Tom was holding her a spot in line to get food.

"Hey! Thanks so much!" she exaggerated, glancing quickly at the two annoyed faces staring back at her.

"Huh?" said Tom, not registering what had happened. "Hey, what's up, Mags?"

"Hey! Did you enjoy swim? Did you see that clown who cannonballed? Apparently the girls of Cabin Three were less than pleased with this 'Jonesy' from your cabin," she said in amusement.

"Wow, that actually happens." Tom laughed.

"What does?"

"Girls blacklisting guys or whatever."

"I guess. I don't know. All I know is that they are pissed and want blood. It's pretty ridiculous."

"Funny," said Tom, sliding his tray toward the chicken patty station.

"Wanna grab a table?" Maggie asked eagerly.

Tom scanned the room and caught Alex's eye. He motioned for Tom to make his way over to where he was sitting. Becky slid into a seat across from Alex and next to her was Liv.

"Eh, I promised Alex I'd eat with him tonight. Maybe, later, okay?" said Tom.

"Oh, yeah, okay, sure," said Maggie, dropping her shoulders and pulling her tray away from the food line.

Maggie navigated to a table in the back where some of her bunkmates were already eating. She looked to the left and saw Tom grin as he sat across from the blonde bombshell and her pretty sidekick—both from her cabin. Slowly it dawned on her. Tom had blown her off.

Too busy glaring at the unfolding scene, she didn't see the spilled bug juice on the floor in front of her. Her foot slipped in the puddle and bumped into a chair sticking out in the aisle. Her tray flipped over and came crashing down onto the floor, sending her juice cup airborne. An immediate hush fell over the Mess Hall, followed by the obligatory sniggering klutz applause.

"Oh, go fuck yourselves," Maggie muttered, picking up a soggy chicken patty bun and dropping it onto her tray. She looked up and met two bright brown, laughing eyes. Something sparked inside her. She grinned. He raised his eyebrows and looked down at his lap; bug juice dripped down his legs. It suddenly dawned on her what had happened, and she winced through an apologetic smile.

"Oh shoot! I'm really sorry—I didn't mean to—can I buy you new shorts at the camp store or something? Is there a camp store? There's always a camp store in the movies, and they said this would be like the movies, right?" rambled Maggie.

"Nah, it's fine," he said, sopping up the red liquid with a few paper napkins. "I was hoping to get eaten alive tonight on the walk back to my cabin, so you did me a favor. I'm Ryan."

"Well, in that case, you're welcome," she retorted, shooting him a half grin through reddened cheeks. There was something familiar about him, something she couldn't place. Her heart stuttered. She piled the rest of the spilled food on her tray. "I'm Maggie."

"Hey, wanna get out of here, Maggie? I have some food back in my cabin—these guys can be such assholes."

"Yeah, sure," she said. "Wait—is it okay if I—I mean, are we going to get in trouble?"

"If you're lucky." Ryan grinned. "No, we're fine, as long as we sit outside."

"You seem pretty familiar with this rule," said Maggie, smirking.

"Ha, guilty. But I gotta get away from all of this tonight," said Ryan, glaring at Alex's table.

"Same," said Maggie, following his gaze. "Let's go."

Ryan pushed his chair backward, the metal scraping loudly against the linoleum, and picked up his tray. The clatter resonated through the Mess Hall. Tom looked up from his table, his stomach pinching as he watched Ryan and Maggie clear their trays and walk out together.

**

Frantically rushing toward the Mess Hall, Jonesy bumped into Maggie and Ryan outside near the bell.

"What's up, man? You all right?" asked Ryan.

"No, I'm not," he moaned. "I can't find my glasses! Have you seen them? They're metal. I've been everywhere! I thought maybe I left them in the cabin after swim, but they aren't anywhere!" He tugged at the knotted bracelet on his wrist with his teeth. "I don't know what I'm going to do—I don't have a spare! My parents are going to kill me!"

"No one's going to mess with your specs, Jonesy. I'm sure they'll turn up." Ryan patted him on the shoulder.

"Yeah, maybe let your counselor know?" added Maggie.

"Yeah, yeah," said Jonesy, his mind elsewhere. "I need to get some food before they close the Mess Hall."

"Least you won't be able to see what you're eating," Ryan joked.

"Right," he croaked.

"Hey! Did you check the beach? I mean, with your whole cannonball thing earlier, do you think you left them somewhere out that way?" asked Maggie.

Jonesy paused a moment, then brightened. "Wait—yes! I think they might be on the dock! Wow, thank you! Yes! I took them off before I jumped in. Thank you—er—"

"Maggie."

"Maggie. Maggie! You're Tom's friend from home, right?" said Jonesy.

"Yeah," Maggie winced, trying to gauge Ryan's reaction in her peripheral vision.

"Great—I'm gonna grab some food and then go look down on the dock. Thanks again, guys!" Jonesy said. He skipped toward the Mess Hall.

"Hey, Jonesy!" called Ryan. He hesitated for a moment, then continued. "Make sure you're back before the night bell rings, okay, man?"

"Sure, sure!" he called out, reaching the doors.

"Do they really kick people out for breaking that rule? You're a Lifer, I take it," said Maggie as they resumed their walk to the boys' side of camp.

Ryan sighed and glanced around to see if anyone was within earshot. "Yeah, it's pretty harsh." He switched into an overexuberant mocking voice. "But the reason this place 'runs like a well-oiled machine' is because of its rules.'"

"Makes sense, I guess," said Maggie, laughing.

"Yeah," said Ryan. Ahead, they saw the warm glow from the porch lamp hanging above the door of Cabin Two. "I don't think he's going to make it back, though."

"Really? Couldn't he just let your counselor know? They

seem pretty reasonable."

"The counselors always defer to Greg and Kate, and it's a zero tolerance policy. Plus he showboated big time today at the lake. That won't win him any favors."

"I see."

"He should just wait until tomorrow morning, but he won't," said Ryan, shrugging and kicking a rock next to the front steps of the cabin.

"Did you guys grow up together or something? Sounds like you know him pretty well."

"Nah, I just...know his type, that's all." Changing the subject, Ryan said, "I'm just going to run in and grab some new shorts. Wait here, okay?"

"Sure," said Maggie. She sat down on the front steps and watched glow bugs pulse light into the darkness. The spark she felt in the Mess Hall was still there, quietly crackling away inside her chest. Crickets sang their rhythmic night songs; a faint howl could be heard in the distance. Maggie shivered, despite the humidity in the air. After a moment, Ryan reappeared in clean khaki shorts, two Snickers bars in hand.

"Want one?" he asked, sitting down beside her.

"Wait—this is the 'food' you had back in your cabin?" she asked, bemused.

"Is it not food?" he asked innocently.

"I mean, it is, technically?" She grinned and grabbed the candy bar out of his hand.

"Easy there, tiger." He laughed.

"Shut up." She grinned, shoving his arm. They sat in the quiet, watching the fireflies bob in the clearing.

"So when did you start coming to this camp?" she asked.

Ryan freed some caramel from his teeth with his tongue before replying.

"Dunno, really, it's a little hazy. It was a few years ago, I think? The first summer I came here was incredible; I had the time of my life. The activities, the leadership—even the food was great. Arm in arm, swaying around a campfire kind of friendships," he said.

"And the girls," added Maggie, thoughtfully chewing. Ryan gave her a sheepish shrug, then lowered his voice.

"It was perfect. And then, I don't know, it's still great. It really is. But I'm always chasing that feeling of the first summer."

"I get that," she said.

"Yeah, it's just—it's different now. There are things that go on here—it's—I don't know. It's just best if you put your head down and try to enjoy yourself. Better to not think about it too much."

"What do you mean?" Maggie said, shifting in her uneasiness.

"Oh, uh, nothing. It's just hard for me to not compare everything to the old days, I guess."

"The old days? Next you'll be yelling at kids to get off your lawn." She laughed.

"Damn kids and their music," he smirked.

"Well," she said, crumpling up the wrapper and stuffing it into her pocket, "I hope you're able to catch that feeling again."

"I got a hell of a lot closer tonight," he said, looking at her from the corner of his eye.

The spark ignited. Maggie's face burned.

"I better walk you back now—the bell's gonna ring soon." He stepped back into the cabin, grabbed his flashlight, and reappeared on the steps.

On their way back to the Mess Hall, they passed Becky, Liv, Alex, Tom, and the rest of the guys from Cabin Two. Ryan and Alex regarded one another, their earlier feud having subsided some. Maggie threw a casual wave and "Hey" at Tom, and kept walking with Ryan. Tom furrowed his brow slightly and shook his head before saying hi back.

"Wait, did you see Jonesy with them back there?" Maggie

asked Ryan. They turned around and scanned the dispersing group.

"No, I didn't. Hey—think you can make it from here?" Ryan asked. He looked at his bunkmates and then back at Maggie. Gaggles of girls swarmed outside the Mess Hall, feeling their way through the darkness to the path leading back to their cabins.

"Yeah, of course. Thanks for—for that," she stammered, motioning to the Mess Hall. She pushed her hair behind her ears and looked at Ryan with the slightest grin. "And for the 'food.'"

"The pleasure was all mine. See you tomorrow, then?"

"Yeah, sounds good. 'Night," she said, turning toward the path. Moths attacked the floodlight above the entryway of the Mess Hall. Counselor Kate was sitting on top of a picnic table. She narrowed her eyes at Maggie, then glanced at her watch. "Hurry up, the bell's about to ring," she said flatly.

"Yes, going!" Maggie hurried toward the path. She was flustered by the course of the night's events. She was still pissed at Tom blowing her off. They were best friends—even if another girl was involved, that was a terrible way to treat her. She was mortified that she drew so much attention to herself in the cafeteria, and even more so for caring about it in the first place. Tom probably laughed at her, too. She softened. She would have probably laughed at him—it had been funny, after all. And if it hadn't happened, she wouldn't have met Ryan. Ryan, with his floppy hair and shining eyes, brash banter and contagious demeanor. What was it about him? She reached into her pocket and pulled out the candy bar wrapper. She ran her fingers over it and grinned. See you tomorrow, then.

10

Ryan stared at the ceiling, listening to squeaking bunks and rattling breaths as the guys of Cabin Two fell under the spell of sleep. He replayed the day in his head, fast-forwarding to the part where he had met Maggie. The door had appeared for her, instantly. In the two years it had been showing up off and on in his mind, it had never happened that quickly, and never when he had been in the presence of the person. He reached under his pillow, pulled out a notebook, and scribbled something down.

The door had first shown up one night a few years ago, randomly, right there on his dream screen. He initially didn't know what to make of it. He had been a lucid dreamer since he was six years old; his sisters used to make fun of him at the breakfast table. His mother would ask if he had nice dreams the night before, and he would reply with something like, "I was in the ocean without a boat, but then I fixed it by adding a boat, and a nearby island to explore." His sisters would giggle and ask if he created girls in his dreams, too, and would then run screaming from the table when Ryan knocked his chair backwards to chase after them.

This was different, though. He had a basic grasp on his lucid dreaming, but ever since the door's arrival, he hadn't been able to figure out how or why it inhabited his subconscious. What triggered it? He tried to trace clues through his waking life, but that proved to be a dead end. It was, after all, an unassuming door—like any other closed door—that sometimes sat in his mind, off to the side, while his sleeping imagination exploded in Technicolor.

At one point, he thought maybe he should try opening it. His chance arrived when the door had appeared while dreaming about Corey. It was the summer Penny went missing at camp. So, he opened it, and walked into what appeared to be Corey's subconscious.

Afterwards, it took some convincing—a lot of convincing—to get him on board, but Corey's desperation to get to the bottom of what happened to Penny won out. By using the subconscious door, Ryan and Corey pieced together their memories of her. But with her disappearance, all they had were a few clues and conjecture.

And then there were the more recent visions of an unspeakable evil, which seemed to manifest out of thin air.

His mind suddenly flashed white. Maggie stood near a rock, facing the darkness. White lights spun around in front of her. I barely even know her, but it's going to be her? How does she fit into all of this? Is there something unique about her, like with me? He squeezed his eyes shut tight and shook his head. He opened them and saw the wooden grooves of the cabin's ceiling. His heartbeat slowed. What if one of these times he can't get out of it? He wiped his forehead and inhaled deeply. With Maggie, the door showed up while he was awake, which bothered him.

Even though they had only just met, he knew what he had to do. He didn't like it—it felt like an invasion of the worst kind. Would this mess everything up? Would this fix everything? He blew air toward the ceiling and closed his eyes again. He pictured Maggie's profile, sitting on the cabin steps with him, her eyes trailing the glow bugs.

With this thought, the door immediately appeared. He reached for the knob and twisted. He hesitated a moment at the threshold, before stepping through and boarding what appeared to be a train headed for the sea.

11

As the prior day's onset of clouds had foreshadowed, the next day of camp brought rain. Water hammered against the roof of Cabin Two like rhythmic construction workers driving countless nails through the ceiling. Tom caught his breath, blinking. He had just awoke from a horrible dream. Wiping his forehead, he lay back down and stared at the ceiling, relieved he was nowhere near the lake of blood that had just inhabited his mind during sleep. That was pretty messed up, he thought. Where did it even come from?

The others gradually came to life, making guttural noises as they reached for stray socks and sweatshirts.

"Up and at 'em!" said Counselor Mark through a yawn. "It sucks to have to tell you this, but I may as well do it now—you're going to hear it in a few minutes anyway. Last night, we lost one of your bunkmates."

A confused murmur ran through the cabin as the campers looked around.

Tom's heart quickened. His thoughts must have been transparent on his face, because Mark followed up with, "No, no, he's not 'lost.' We had to send Jonesy packing. He was out past the night bell. Sorry, guys, but breaking that rule is the real deal."

"Wait—you sent him home in the middle of the night?" asked Corey.

Germ tapped his empty bunk. "How'd you get all of his stuff?"

Mark rolled his eyes. "You guys sleep like logs, you know that? And you all snore, which is annoying. Anyway, yeah, he's gone. He left early—before six a.m. I...saw him off. He said to say bye and sorry he couldn't say it himself."

"Did he give a reason?" asked Ryan.

"Yeah, he said he was looking for his glasses, but you know how it is, Ry, he should have just let us know—we could've found them first thing this morning."

"Yeah, no one's going to steal glasses. He came into the Mess Hall rambling about them last night," said Alex.

"We tried to tell him to calm down, but he wasn't having it. I guess he's one of those guys who gets an idea in his head and refuses to hear anything else," said Joey.

"That's too bad," said Tom. "He seemed like a decent enough guy. Did you guys find his glasses?"

"Yup, they were on the dock, perfectly fine, when they caught him by the beach," said Mark. "Okay, enough of this. Let's go get some grub. Look alive. You're all still here, and today is going to be a blast."

"What are we doing today?" asked Germ.

"Boating!" said Mark, holding the door for the campers to file out.

12

The Mess Hall was more subdued than the previous day. The air carried a muggy aroma of maple syrup and cinnamon. The guys of Cabin Two sat down at their usual table. Tom sliced through a piece of French toast with his fork, then chewed it critically. He stared at the empty seat across from him. Jonesy's seat. A manicured hand suddenly grabbed the top of the chair and dragged it backward.

"Mind if we join you, boys?" asked Becky with an innocent smirk. Liv stood to the side of her and gave a sheepish grin and then looked away.

"Free country," muttered Ryan.

"Sure, pull up a chair," said Alex, motioning to Liv between bites.

"Oh, Ry, did you have a bad night? Didn't get the results you wanted with the new girl you're trying to hook up with?" teased Becky. "Poor guy, I heard all about it."

"Leave it," said Alex, looking from Becky to Ryan, and then to Tom.

"Nah, she's great. We have great chemistry," said Ryan.

Becky let out an audible scoff. Tom choked on his orange juice.

"Easy there, pal," said Germ, patting Tom on the back.

"Funny," continued Becky, "I could've sworn I saw Tommy with her at orientation." She turned her predatory gaze toward Tom. "Are you two going out?"

Tom cleared his throat. "Nah, we just grew up together. It's cool." He glanced at Liv and gave her a weak smile.

"Looks like you have his blessing, Ry," snorted Joey.

Ryan ignored him and looked across the Mess Hall. Maggie stared out the window, pushing French toast crusts around on her plate, while an overzealous girl with pigtails talked at her. He turned back to his food and finished it quickly. When he stood to clear his plate, he saw that Maggie was readying herself to leave as well. "Later, clowns," he said as he walked to return his tray.

***

He found Maggie outside, standing by the bell.

"Go ahead, ring it!" he said.

Startled, Maggie turned, then laughed. "You ring it, hotshot."

"No chance. I've seen what happens when someone rings it who isn't supposed to."

"And what's that?"

"Counselor Kate throws you into well, where you rot with the other dumbass campers for all eternity," he said, shrugging.

"Shut up, she does not."

"Swear."

"You're lying."

"Try it!"

Maggie laughed. They weaved their way between the trees outside of the Mess Hall, unaware of the sky's drizzle dampening their clothes.

"So, sleep all right?" he said.

"I guess. I mean, I had a really weird dream, but it's

probably nerves," she said. "Also, a girl in our cabin was kicked out last night, apparently. We found out this morning. I feel bad."

"Yeah? What did she do?"

"I guess she tried to sneak over to one of the boys' cabins."

"Rookie mistake."

"I can't believe they're so strict here—not even a warning! I mean, isn't that the classic camp move—sneaking out after dark to meet up with a guy or girl?" she posed.

"Yeah, you're right—it's harsh. But I think...I think they probably have their reasons."

"Hmm," said Maggie, unconvinced.

"You better think twice before sneaking out to see me," said Ryan, grinning.

"In your dreams," she retorted, rolling her eyes.

"What activity do you have today?" he asked. The Mess Hall started to empty; the wooded area grew congested with milling campers waiting to start their day.

"I think we're headed to the Art House," she said, unenthused.

"Don't eat the paste."

"I might have to after that breakfast. What activity do you have?"

"We're boating, I think."

"Even in the rain?"

"Yeah, I think so. Hey—is Becky in your cabin—blonde hair?"

"Yup. Cabin Three. She's a Lifer, right? Loves herself a little too much?" said Maggie.

"Yeah, that's her," he said, laughing. "Well, listen—just don't get on her bad side, okay?"

"I barely talk to her," said Maggie.

"Good, you don't want to mix with her. Trust me. She's toxic," said Ryan. "If you want to survive, share nothing with her."

"Survive?" Maggie laughed. "Can I really commit more of a social suicide at camp than dropping my tray in the cafeteria?"

"Ha, yeah, true. I'm just saying. I think she already has a mark against you because her new pet Liv is into your boy Tom."

Maggie blushed. "He's not my—it's not like that, really, but—"

"And now you're talking to me, and she and I had a thing a summer ago."

"Ah," said Maggie. Her voice trailed off as her heart fell.

Ryan detected the change in tone and added, "Let's grab lunch together, yeah? I want to hear about this dream you had."

"All right," she said, brightening.

13

"Okay, two to a canoe. Grab a paddle, untie, and then head northeast toward that hill over there," said Mark, pointing across the lake to a green mass in the distance.

Alex looked at Tom and grinned. "Wanna pair?" he said.

"Yeah, sure," said Tom, looking uneasy.

"All righty then! Let's take that one at the end." Alex pointed.

They each picked up an oar lying on the dock. The water seal had started to peel, giving the paddles a weathered, honey color. Germ and Ryan climbed into the canoe beside them. Tom held his breath and pushed the paddle under the water, tensing as he lifted it for the first time. Water dripped off the end, but nothing more. He breathed a sigh of relief.

Alex watched with interest. "You okay, man? Never been in a canoe before either?"

"Nah, I'm fine. Just had a crazy dream last night—the lake turned to blood." He laughed at how ridiculous it sounded. Alex's eyes grew dark for a split second, before twinkling with delight.

"Are you kidding me? What a trip! You must have been subconsciously worried about boating today, huh?" he said.

"Yeah, it was something."

"Imagine that—a lake of blood. Jesus. That's some twisted psyche you're rocking there," he marveled. The morning drizzle had transformed into a misty sprinkle. Fog brewed on the surface of the lake.

"Yeah. So what do we do when we reach the other side of the lake?" Tom said, changing the subject. Alex didn't seem to hear him.

"I mean, I guess when you think about it, the entire planet is soaked in blood. All of the blood people mop up or dispose of has to go somewhere. It doesn't just vanish into thin air."

"Dude, come on, I just ate," said Tom, his face souring.

"All the wars, the decay—it's a liquid commodity, really."

"Dude!"

"I'm just saying," said Alex, casually dipping his oar into the lake.

"So what's your deal with Becky, anyway? And Ryan?" asked Tom, trying to change the subject.

"Well, I guess it was your classic love triangle. She was with him at the start of last summer, then one night he was sick—food poisoning—and we started chatting during a Bonfire Night. Then we just kind of became, I don't know, a thing. Unofficially, though. Ryan's okay with it for the most part. I don't think he was ever really into her to begin with."

"Is she a Lifer?"

"Yeah, she's been here longer than both me and Ryan. Few summers, I think. Seems like her friend is into you," he commented.

"Maybe. Who knows," said Tom.

"You should go for it," said Alex.

"Yeah?"

"Why not? She's hot. Pretty shy, though. Bonfire Night is later tonight; you should make a move," Alex said, shrugging.

"What's Bonfire Night?" Tom asked.

"Just what it sounds like—a bonfire, s'mores, music. Basically it's a big beach party."

"But it seems like the counselors don't want you to really get with—"

"Nah," Alex said, cutting him off. "It's not like that. They just don't want you out past the bell curfew. They definitely want us to be…social. Trust me."

"Why can't we be out past curfew though? Seems so strict—"

"What is this, Lord of the Flies? Society needs rules, Tom. There's an intricate order to everything we do. You take that away, you have chaos. Chaos ultimately breeds extinction."

"Do you always talk like this?"

"Just paddle, dipshit, and think about it."

14

The Art House wasn't much bigger than the cabins. A large square table sat in the middle of the open room; bright pine walls were decorated like a proud parent's refrigerator, displaying projects by ghosts of campers past—watercolors, murals, macrame, finger paints, intricate string patterns woven through Popsicle sticks. Repurposed soup cans filled with markers, scissors, and glue sticks lined the ledge under the panoramic window, looking out into the dense, wet woods.

Counselor Hannah casually flipped through an overstuffed binder on the desk adjacent to the table.

"Hello, my little pretties! Today…today we are going to express our truest selves through art. And today's theme is near and dear to my heart. Friendship! It's synonymous with looooove. You can't have a friendship without looooove. It just…is. Think of someone who you treasure—yes, yes, think of the one who sets your heart afire. The one who engages your spirit—your counterpoint. And if you don't have one yet, well…use your heartbreak to create art!" Hannah tossed a rainbow of bunched up string onto the table. The campers gingerly reached for colors.

"What the hell was that?" said Maggie under her breath.

"Right?" giggled the girl next to her. "I don't think we've officially met. I'm Beth. I think my bunk is next to yours."

"Hey, yeah, I think you're right—I'm Maggie. What are we supposed to do with these?" she asked, holding up the packets of thread.

"Friendship bracelets?" guessed Beth, lifting her chin toward the binder that Hannah had moved to the table, illustrating an intricate knot pattern.

"Ah, got it," said Maggie.

"First time here?" asked Beth.

"Yeah, you?"

"Yeah, at this camp," said Beth, reaching for scissors to trim the string. "I've been to a few others, but this one is supposed to be pretty good."

Across the table, Becky's eyes narrowed on Maggie, a lioness ready to pounce on her prey. She cleared her throat loudly. Maggie looked up.

"So, Margie, how are you connected to our friend Tommy—are you his sister? Second cousin?"

"It's Maggie. Why?"

"Oh!" exclaimed Becky, her laughter arcing. "No real reason. I'm just doing my due diligence on his availability, that's all."

"My dad says 'due diligence,'" muttered Beth.

"I'm sorry, who are you?" replied Becky. Beth shook her head and focused on her knots. "Well, Margie—is he...available, or isn't he?"

"Why don't you ask him yourself?" challenged Maggie. Ryan's warning about steering clear from Becky suddenly popped into her head. She quickly added, "I'm sure he would love to know he has admirers."

"Admirer," corrected Becky. "My lovely Liv here is...smitten."

"You have my blessing," replied Maggie. Liv reddened and glanced at Becky, whose permagrin hadn't wavered since the beginning of their exchange.

"Wonderful." Becky clapped her hands together as if dusting away an unpleasant housekeeping task. "Oh, wait! There is one more teensy little thing we have to discuss."

Maggie looked across the table with her eyebrow raised ever so slightly. "What? Do you want my bunk or something—fine, take it—I don't ca—"

"No, no, no, no, no, silly!" Becky's shrill fake laughter staccatoed against the Art House walls. "I already have the best bunk, obviously. No, we need to discuss Ryan."

Now it was Maggie's turn to redden. She recalled the vision of Becky swishing by the two of them the night before, a haughty frozen smile plastered across her shiny face. Was there a hint of jealousy?

"What about him?" said Maggie, pushing past her embarrassment, her voice cool and even. After all, she and Ryan weren't a thing. They were barely even friends. And yet, there was that spark, though she couldn't pinpoint what it was, or where it came from. She looped a piece of green string around a blue one and knotted it.

Becky cleared her throat. "I think it would be in your best interest to stay away from Ryan. He's trouble. He's a player, and honestly he doesn't belong at Kinross. Girl to girl."

"Seems a bit judgy," remarked Beth.

"I've been coming to this camp a long time, and yes, he and I have a brief, regrettable history, as you may or may not know. Trust me, you don't want to walk down that path."

"Thanks," said Maggie, "but I can handle myself."

"Oh! I don't doubt that—look at you, with your ragged footwear and angsty forehead." Her laughter now pierced through Maggie's skull. "It's just that…I'm not so sure you can handle him."

Maggie's anger boiled. Her palms started to sweat, and she felt her temperature rising. She stared at Becky's impish face. "And why's that?"

Becky's eyes twinkled with delight. "You'll find out soon enough."

"Well, my pretties, it's time to leave this creative respite and head to the food factory! You can bring your bracelets and finish them later when you have some downtime." Hannah sashayed through the room, putting away art supplies.

The campers packed up the strings and scissors and left the Art House. Becky and Liv walked ahead of the rest of the cabin. Maggie let out a deep sigh and looked at the ground as she walked. A few more days, she thought, and this will be all over. Beth caught up with her.

"Do we really have to share a cabin with that she-devil for the rest of the week?" said Beth.

"Right? I don't know what her problem is. She hasn't said a word to me from Day One—Day One! But then she saw me walking with that guy Ryan last night, and now she's throwing sugary veiled threats at me like poison cupcakes," said Maggie.

"She's threatened by you, that's for sure. Or, at the very least, territorial."

"She makes it sound like she runs the camp."

"Maybe she's just looking out for her lapdog."

"Yeah, maybe. But why bring up Ryan?"

"Who is this Ryan guy, anyway?"

"Just another guy in my friend Tom's cabin. He seems cool," said Maggie.

"Huh," said Beth, her comment hanging in the misty, humid air. They walked for a moment without saying anything.

"I mean, he's not even my type—he's funny, but he's pretty crass. Plus it seems like he's dated loads of girls. I don't need that. Okay, he's hot, but we're here for what—a week? What's the point…"

"How very pragmatic of you." Beth laughed, pushing a

sapling branch out of their way. They emerged from the path at the Mess Hall clearing. Through the screen doors, Maggie could see Becky's blonde head bobbing through the lunch line.

A hand reached out and tugged Maggie's shoulder backward. She let out a yelp, and Beth turned to her, alarmed.

"Hey!"

"Agh! Ryan, you—you! You jerk! Who does that!" squawked Maggie, shoving him into the bushes. Ryan laughed and bounced back.

"Hey, I'm Ryan," he said, flashing a toothy smirk at Beth.

"Beth, Ryan. Ryan, Beth," said Maggie through gritted teeth.

Ryan shook her shoulder, grinning. "Someone's on edge, huh? Worried about an encore performance in the Mess Hall?"

"Wait, last night—was that…" started Beth.

"That was nothing, forget it," said Maggie, walking ahead of them, her face reddening.

"We're just messing around," said Ryan, jogging ahead to grab the door to the Mess Hall.

"I just had a run-in with that evil Barbie doll during arts and crafts and—"

Ryan cut her off, by leaning into her shoulder and murmuring, "Not so loud, Mags."

"What? Why? What do I care about this stupid social cir—" said Maggie, her voice raising a decibel.

"Seriously, stop," said Ryan.

Maggie rolled her eyes but dropped it. The three of them grabbed trays and queued at the serving station. Woody dished out leafy greens with tongs and raised an eyebrow as they came through.

"Salad?" he barked at Maggie.

"Sure, thanks," replied Maggie, taking her plate back from Woody. He paused a moment, looking directly at her.

"I have a hunch about you," he muttered.

"What?" Maggie said, her face souring.

Woody didn't break his gaze with her but slowly walked backward. He reached for the volume knob on the beat-up kitchen radio. Ryan let out an uncomfortable laugh; Beth's face was paralyzed with a sympathetic smile. Woody twisted the knob all the way to the right. The haunting vocals of Simon and Garfunkel's The Sounds of Silence crooned through the static.

He dropped his eyes and walked back to the serving spot. Maggie shivered and blinked a few times. "Well, that seemed totally normal," she said.

"Right? Weird," agreed Beth.

The three of them pulled their trays away from the line and made their way over to an empty table near the windows.

"So," said Ryan, lowering his voice, "tell me about this dream you had."

"Uh, where do I start..." said Maggie, looking warily out the window.

15

She was in a city. A stifling city. It wasn't like summer in the suburbs, granting moments of reprieve—a cool breath of air drifting over the nape of a neck or weaving through bare toes propped up on a porch. No, this was the city, and a relentless one. One where the heat engulfs everything and everyone the second an air-conditioned train is disembarked. Sweat instantly seeped from her pores and soaked through her already damp dress. Her makeup melted down her face. Showers and air conditioners could only provide a temporary relief in this type of weather. Like a needy girlfriend, the heat of the city was always there, outside, waiting to smother. But when Maggie stepped off the train, she was no longer in the city. She was at the sea.

The street led to a boardwalk that had a haunting charm of yesteryear. A little girl skipped by with a lollipop in her mouth. An elderly couple hobbled over the weathered boards, pointing out memories of summers past from underneath a sun umbrella. Maggie walked, unsure of where she was going. She automatically moved toward a noise. Clickety-clack, clickety-clack, followed by a whoosh and shrieks. She looked up. A wooden roller coaster thundered against the brilliant blue sky. She wiped sweat from her brow.

And then she saw him. Ryan.

He was leaning against a metal fence underneath the roller coaster. The rattling din of the amusement above muffled his hello. His smile burned out the sun. She said, "Hey," and hugged him—it seemed like the making of something that was bound to resonate. What that something was exactly, she didn't quite yet know. They descended on the amusements, a world bursting with roller-coaster rides, bumper cars, and music floating across the sea breeze. They walked along a pier; fishermen with salty beards baited their lines, while con artists in rickety lawn chairs played three card monty—the tangy scent of chum and body odor engulfing the dock. The setting sun over the island was a living postcard.

They took the train back to the city, and their conversation turned to arcade games.

"I love Ms. Pac-Man. My sister had a ridiculous high score growing up—I forget what it was, but it was impossible to beat," Ryan reminisced.

"I could beat it. I'm wicked good," Maggie said, shrugging.

"I doubt it."

"I bet I could beat you."

"I doubt that, too."

"Let's go play! Find me an arcade. There must be an machine somewhere in this city—let's go play right now!" she insisted, not wanting the day to end for all of the world.

"Next time," he said.

She couldn't stop her legs from standing and moving toward the exit doors. She was getting off the train. He remained.

"Come with me?" she tried to ask, but no words came out. She threw him a sheepish smile and tried to say it louder— surely that would do the trick.

"Come WITH ME!"

No luck. Her smile fell, and anxiety set in as the doors of the train snapped shut to separate them. She banged on the window where he was sitting. He looked on, smiling and mouthing something she couldn't understand. Burning hot tears streamed down her cheeks. The train was pulling away—she was losing him forever. The station started to melt into itself, an oozy blackness seeped through her consciousness.

"Ryan! Ryan! Please come back!"

Through her hot tears, she saw his figure standing at the emergency exit of the last train car. Her eyes zoomed in, and she could read his lips saying, "I can't, Maggie—I'm sorry."

She spun around, looking for a stairwell to street level. Her body felt like it was ablaze, despite her inability to move. Maybe she could run to the next stop and somehow get there before he arrived. But the train station was gone. It was night; she was now back at camp, standing in front of the bell. There weren't any other campers outside. It must be past curfew, she surmised. And then her senses were assaulted with rapid fire. A dense white light shot silently out of the well, into the sky as far as the eye could see. Her fingertips burned like fiery coals. The white light morphed into a jubilant tornado, swarming with black and white birds. From somewhere within the vortex came invisible, bloodcurdling screams.

16

"Maggie?" Ryan shook her arm a little. "You okay? You drifted out on us for a second there."

"Huh? What? Yeah, I'm okay, thanks. So, anyway, that was my dream," she continued, intentionally leaving out the entire portion involving Ryan. "It was really messed up."

"Did you try to touch the light or the birds?" asked Beth.

Ryan cut off Maggie before she could answer.

"I wouldn't tell anyone else about this," he cautioned.

"Why?" asked Beth, smirking a little. "Is a shrieking tornado of light something Maggie should seriously be worried about?"

"No, no," said Ryan, thinking quickly. "It's just that, well, given her previous performance she probably doesn't want to draw anymore unwanted attention in the Mess Hall."

"Oh, shut up!" said Maggie, shoving him.

"Incoming," warned Beth.

They looked up from their conversation to see Becky closing in on their table, Liv trailing in her shadow. Maggie looked past her and caught Tom's gaze directed toward them. She scowled and turned back at the sound of Becky's sugary voice.

"How's your latest pet project, Ry? All's well?" smirked

Becky.

"I should be asking you the same thing," retorted Ryan, nodding at Liv. "Does she speak, or are you not allowing that yet?"

"I have always enjoyed your charm," she pursed her lips into an air kiss.

"Is there a reason you're here?" said Maggie, her voice flat.

"You ought to mind your manners, Margie," said Becky coolly.

"You're right, my sincerest apologies! To what do we owe this pleasure, your highness?" Maggie replied.

Beth choked on her water. Ryan kicked Maggie under the table and shot her a warning glance.

"Ow! Jesus!" yelped Maggie.

"You better watch it," threatened Becky. She turned to Ryan and said, "There's a Lifer meeting at three p.m. And remember, you can't bring your baggage."

"Anything else?" asked Ryan, disinterested.

Becky huffed and spun around with her tray. "Come on, Liv, let's go sit with Tommy and the other boys." Liv shuffled behind her, offering an apologetic half smile to the three of them.

"You don't have to buy into her crap, you know!" Ryan called out after Liv, but the message was lost in the din of scraping dishes and sliding chairs. "God, she's so fucking terrible."

"What the hell was that for?" said Maggie, bending down to rub her shin.

"You'll thank me someday," he said, shrugging.

"Sure I will."

"I don't get why we have to walk on pins and needles around her like she's Cleopatra," said Beth, trying to distract Maggie from throwing eye daggers at Ryan.

"Yeah, no kidding. Can you explain that one?" asked Maggie, not breaking her gaze.

"It's complicated," said Ryan, unblinking.

"Does her family own the camp or something? Are her parents in politics?"

"Beats me."

"Stop being so evasive! You want me to play your game of kissing her ass, then you need to tell me why. I don't subscribe to this social hierarchy nonsense," said Maggie.

"Yes, you do. Everyone does. It's inescapable. Even by saying you don't subscribe to it makes you a part of the hierarchy. Everyone fits on the food chain."

"Isn't it a food web now?"

"Whatever. And next, Pluto won't be a planet," said Ryan, twisting his straw wrapper around his fingers.

"Your point?" sighed Maggie.

Beth watched the conversation pinball with interest.

"My point is that every creature on the food chain—web, whatever—has predators and prey. There are the hunters and the hunted. If you're not careful, no matter what your station is, you're fucked. It applies to the animal kingdom and it applies to social circles. Even social circles at camp."

"Deep," Beth said, rolling her eyes.

"I still think it's ridiculous. How much trouble could she get me into—either she makes me commit some sort of social suicide, which I'm pretty sure I already accomplished on my own, or she gets me kicked out of camp. Big deal, I'll just spend the rest of my boring summer watching *Rocky Horror Picture Show* and eating mac and cheese."

"Listen," said Ryan, leaning over his tray while pushing his chair back to stand up, "I know we only just met, but you have to trust me. At least, for now. You'll get it eventually, but for right now, you just gotta stop antagonizing her. Please."

"What's in it for me?" challenged Maggie.

"I'll let you keep talking to me," Ryan said with a wink. He took his tray to the conveyor belt.

"Lucky me," groaned Maggie through gritted teeth,

fighting back a smile.

17

Tom saw Becky's mouth moving but nothing was coming out. She's sort of better this way, he thought, muted, and with less of that fake sugary ooze that normally spews out of her. But none of this mattered, because as long as Becky was yammering on about whatever, he could keep sneaking glances across the table at Liv. He noticed that the polo shirt she wore had two buttons unfastened. Yesterday it was only one. Did she do this intentionally? He envisioned her thin silhouette against the lake, the glow of the fire bouncing off her tan skin.

"Right, Tom?"

"Huh?" replied Tom, shaking away the fuzzy anticipation of Bonfire Night. Corey, Germ, and Joey stared at him for a moment before unloading.

"Ahyup, earth to Tom, come in, Tom, over!"

"No, no, wait, I have a better on—"

"Wait, wait, I've got it—this is ground control to Major Tom!" serenaded Joey, reaching his arm across the table.

"Haha nice one, Joe," Germ reached out for a high five.

Becky cleared her throat to regain the floor. "I was just explaining to Liv that tonight is Bonfire Night—we need to make plans to get there early to get a good spot. We don't need Amy from Cabin Four claiming our area, like she did last week. Don't you think that would be nice, Tommy?"

"Oh, yeah, yes. Cool," replied Tom, punching Germ in the arm.

"Hey, what'd I do?" Germ replied, punching him back.

"See you boys later," said Becky as she and Liv stood up to clear their trays.

"Me Tom, you Liv," grunted Joey.

Tom lunged across the table, spilling two cups of bug juice into Joey's lap.

"Thanks a lot, asshole!" yelled Joey, his lap soaked with red.

"Looks like you need to visit the bathroom," chided Tom, gaining confidence with Corey and Germ's laughter.

"Hey, Joe, why you so pissy?" Germ laughed.

"Yeah, Joey—that time of the month already?" asked Corey.

"I hate you guys," muttered Joey, knocking his chair back and storming off.

"That's just the PMS talking!" Tom hollered after him, which fueled a whole new bout of laughter.

"Nice one, man, that was really funny." Tom felt two hands on his shoulders.

"Oh hey, Alex, when did you get here? Lunch is almost over."

"Where were you, man?" asked Germ.

"Greg needed help dragging some of the canoes on shore. Hey, guys, we have a meeting in a little bit anyway," said Alex.

"What kind of a meeting?" asked Tom.

"What is this, twenty questions? It's a Lifer meeting, that's all. How to encourage new campers, yada yada yada."

"You just yada yada'd camp philosophy, man, how dare you?" accused Corey, feigning shock.

"I'll yada yada your face in a minute," retorted Alex.

"Do it!" exclaimed Corey.

"I'll catch up with you jokers later. Bonfire Night, right?" said Alex.

"Absolutely," said Tom. Alex gave him a go-get-'em tiger shoulder rub and walked off. Tom turned to Germ and said, "This Bonfire Night is all the rage, huh?"

"Dude. Yes."

18

The post-lunch air was buzzing with anticipation, and all afternoon activities had been postponed to prepare for Bonfire Night. Ryan jumped off the front step of his cabin and crossed the clearing toward the Rec Hall.

"Ryan! Hey! Hang on!" called out Alex, jogging across the grass. Ryan kept walking.

"Dude, hey, we have to sort this out. Come on, we cannot go to this meeting with conflict, or you know what they'll do," Alex pressed.

"There's nothing to sort out. It's fine. We're fine."

"Nope. They'll know. They always know."

"It's too trivial. They won't care. Stop."

"You stop!" said Alex, falling in line with Ryan's quickening pace. Ryan stopped in his tracks and glared at Alex.

"What? Is it Becky? Is that wh—" started Alex.

"I don't give two shits about her—come on. She's awful. You can have her."

Alex winced. "Then what—is it the new pledges?" He lowered his voice. Ryan glanced around.

"I just think whatever is going on, it's getting out of hand. I mean, the number of campers being booted is..." Ryan whispered.

"Dude, I know. Yeah, I've been having those thoughts, too, but they said that type of thinking will happen from time to time, and we can't indulge it."

"I know, I know, but there's something different about this week—I'm worried."

"It'll be fine, buddy, just wait and see." Alex slapped Ryan on the back as they wound around the outside of the Rec Hall. Beyond it lay a path that navigated to a dense wooded area with a small circular clearing. Severed tree stumps were arranged like a miniature Stonehenge. Most of the other Lifers had already arrived and were sitting on the ground in a semicircle; behind them stood the counselors. In the middle of the circle was a bench, where Head Counselors Greg and Kate sat, ready to begin. Ryan swallowed his hesitation and sat near Counselor Mark.

"Lifers, welcome," Kate said, smiling. Her voice spread over the circle. "Corvus oculum corvi non eruit," she chanted.

"Corvus oculum corvi non eruit," they echoed back.

"Wonderful, thank you. Now, let's just have a quick little recap—any issues to report? Things to keep on the radar?"

Across from Ryan, Becky cleared her throat and leaned forward.

"Becks, have anything for us?" asked Greg, rubbing his hands together. A big smile emerged on his face.

She pursed her lips and raised her eyebrow slightly at Ryan.

"Don't," mouthed Ryan.

Becky turned to Greg, a satisfied smirk on her lips, and said, "Oh no, sorry, Counselor Greg, I just had a tickle in my throat, that's all."

"Ah, okay," replied Greg, his smile souring.

"Anyone else?" asked Kate, a twinge of impatience sneaking through her request.

"Guys," interjected Greg, "I know I don't have to remind

you of how important this information is for us to procure. You guys have done such a kickass job in the past, and you know that. So please, let's keep up the streak. You are part of something so much bigger—you're cultivating an experience that Hollywood can't even capture in the movies!"

Ryan looked over at Alex, who was busy tracing lines with his eyes up and down Becky's spindly crossed legs. None of the Lifers seemed to be particularly concerned or motivated to contribute to the meeting.

"And," continued Greg, his face darkening, "I don't have to remind you how lucky you are to be in the position you're in. You were chosen. Don't make us regret that decision."

"Don't make us unchoose you!" added Kate, exasperated.

"Now, now, Kate," he said, laughing heartily. "We'd never unchoose any of you. We couldn't, even if we wanted to."

"But we can make your life hell," said Kate, her eyes turning wild, pointing to no one, everyone.

A Lifer from Cabin Four spoke up. "Yeah, I guess I have something."

"Go ahead, Brice. What's going on?" asked Greg.

"Yeah, that camper Pete—some call him Petee—he's uh, well…" He hesitated.

"Go on," pressed Kate.

"Well, he's been bragging about how he's going to sneak off with Cara and get into, uh, her pants during Bonfire Night."

Greg exchanged a look with Kate. Kate walked slowly over to where Brice was sitting, and squatted down, facing him. Brice blinked twice, their noses almost touching.

"You're sure about this?" she whispered.

"Uh, pretty sure," said Brice, his peripheral vision scouting out the other Lifers for a reaction.

"Thank you," she hissed, staring directly into his eyes. She stood up and backed away. "Thank you, Brice!" she proclaimed louder. "Looks like someone is taking his role at

Kinross seriously."

"Now, tonight is Bonfire Night for this camp session—let's make it one they'll never forget! And don't forget that charming Lifer hospitality, m'kay?" said Greg.

"Meeting adjourned!" snapped Kate. Becky stood up and shot one more triumphant smirk at Ryan before threading her arm around Alex.

Mark approached Ryan, his hand in the air waiting to accept a casual high five. "Hey, Ry, how's it going?"

"It's all right, man, you?"

"Good, man, all good here," said Mark. They made their way back toward camp. "I've seen you hanging with that newbie—she cool?"

"Maggie? Yeah, she's all right." He shrugged. "Think she's hung up on that other kid, though—Tom? They grew up together or something. But yeah, she's a cool girl."

"Gotcha," said Mark. "That's cool, man, good to see you getting out there."

"Oh, no, it's not like that with her, but yeah okay," said Ryan, clearing his throat.

"Not yet, anyway." Mark winked. He slapped Ryan on the shoulder and jogged off. "See you back at the bunk—I gotta go check in at the Infirmary."

"Later," called Ryan. Mark's words swirled in his head. "Not yet, anyway." Did Mark see something he couldn't? She was a cool girl. In another life, they'd be perfect for each other. He had never felt so comfortable with someone so quickly. It was as if he'd known her his whole life—the way she gave him shit right back, the way she didn't flinch when he was close to her. He thought of the night they sat on the cabin steps, shoulders nearly touching, watching the glow bugs floating in the field in front of them. It was unexpected, this feeling that made him nostalgic for something he couldn't quite place. And now, it was impossible to erase the potential of Mark's words, "Not yet, anyway." In those three little words he was instantly consumed by a curse that he suspected would forever expand like fractals. A curse that, deep down, he was okay with having. Her.

19

The girls of Cabin Three huddled around the small mirror that hung in the hallway leading back to Counselor Hannah's quarters.

"I wish I had something better to wear! I'm over this uniform already!"

"Can I use that green eyeshadow?"

"You just have to work the outfit—there's plenty you can do with it."

"Where's my elastic? Who took it?"

"Don't bump me! I'm doing my eyeliner! God!"

"How can I fix this outfit? Seriously, look at it. Total frumpfest."

"Do you think Pete will be game tonight?"

"You just have to hike up the shorts, cuff them, and pin the polo back tight—hey, does anyone have an extra safety pin?"

"Aren't we going to get yelled at if we do that?"

"I'm a Lifer, sweetie, it's fine. I wouldn't say it was fine if it wasn't!"

"What about these front buttons?"

"That all depends on what you're going for…"

"Or who!"

"You're such a slut, Stacey!"

"I am not!"

"Anyway, I don't know how you haven't heard of the three-button rule, but you have to pin your polo. That's the only way it works."

"Okay, okay, what is it? Tell me!"

"Three buttons means you're intentionally being unattainable—you're basically asking for a challenge. Two buttons is classic, you'll either end up making out with someone, or crying in the corner. One button is usually used when you have your eye on a particular guy—like, if you know you're going to be around him, and only him. Not buttoning any buttons is reserved for girls who'll spread their legs for any old thing, and we steer clear of that in Cabin Three."

"But having someone unbutton those buttons is a whole other story!"

"What the fuck, Stacey, are you in heat or something? Jesus!"

"I'm just making a point! Where's that candy apple lipstick?"

"So pin it like this? And I'll go…two buttons, then?"

"Ahhhhh, someone wants to mess around with Petee!"

"Oh also, pull your boobs up and out of your bra some—like this. It'll give them more oomph—polos are not forgiving, regardless of the number of buttons you can unbutton."

"Which Petee will be taking care of!"

"Shut up, I doubt it. He's kinda dense."

"Oh, Cara, please. Here, take a few strands of your hair from the front and let them outline your face. There. That's better."

"That works!"

"How do you even, like, mess around on Bonfire Night? We're all sitting by a bright fire, so…"

"Sweetie, have you looked around? We're surrounded by woods!"

"And they just let you go into them? Unsupervised?"
"Don't you think the counselors are preoccupied, too?"
"Really?"
"Oh, honey."

20

The bonfire's bright glow bounced off the trees as campers emerged from the trails to the lake. Well-worn logs were positioned around the blazing pile of flammable debris. Coolers of bug juice were clustered at the base of the dock, and bowls of snacks were balanced on various pieces of nature along the beach. A boombox crooned chart toppers from the fifties and sixties. Off to the right, counselors sat in lawn chairs, murmuring to one another while watching the campers arrive.

Mark ushered Cabin Two guys onto the beach with an "Enjoy the night, fellas!" before he veered off to join the other counselors.

"So this is Bonfire Night," said Tom. He walked alongside Joey and Germ, while Alex, Ryan, and Corey pulled up the rear.

"Sure is!" replied Joey. "And if you know what's good for you, you'll hunt down that doe-eyed piece of tail and get her near the lake to, you know—"

"Um, I don't actually know," replied Tom.

"Don't encourage him, please don't encourage him," implored Corey.

"You know," Joey said, clearing his throat, readying

himself for a grand delivery, "you want to take her near the lake to GET. HER. WET. Get it? Because it's a lake? And—" He was interrupted by a slap upside the head.

"Jesus, what the hell, Alex—I'm just messing around!"

"Your asinine comments aren't a good look for us tonight. Maybe if you shut your trap you'll actually get some action with a real live girl," said Alex.

"Thanks, Dad," muttered Joey. He broke off from the group and walked around to the other side of the fire.

"I'd still like to know who made him a Lifer," said Alex, shaking his head.

"Eh, lay off him. He has a purpose just like everyone else," said Ryan.

"Please," said Alex dismissively.

The guys sat down on a log with their backs to the counselors.

"Hey, guys, I've wanted to ask you about that," interrupted Tom. "How do you become a Lifer? Like, what do you have to do?"

"You have to be chosen. You have to make them see the desire—that you are willing to go above and beyond to make your camp experience the best camp experience possible. When they see that, they know they can channel it into a contagion for other campers," said Alex, staring into the fire.

"Contagion? Like a disease?" asked Tom, shifting uneasily on the log.

"Ha, no, no," said Alex quickly. Ryan shot Alex a warning glance. "What I meant was they can use your enthusiasm and positivity and make it contagious, so that others have a great time, too."

"And why would they want to do that? What happens when you have a camp full of Lifers?"

"It's not like that," said Ryan quickly. "It's all about their...business model. I mean, even Lifers eventually age out of camp."

"Unless they become counselors," said Corey.

"I guess that makes sense," said Tom.

"Speaking of that, Tommy, I overheard a few counselors drop your name earlier. Think you may be on the right track," said Alex, grinning.

"Really?" Tom perked up.

"Yeah, something about how you're dedicated and coachable, that campers seem to like talking to you, or some shit," replied Alex.

"Hey, that's cool, but I don't think I've actually talk—" said Tom.

"Speaking of talking, now's your chance. Here comes Liv," said Alex. He patted him on the shoulder. Tom nervously ran his fingers through his hair, watching her walk toward them.

***

Maggie scanned the crowd and caught Ryan's eye over the outlier flames of the bonfire. She quickly turned back to the conversation consuming her bunkmates.

"So, do you think Petee is really going to go for it?" asked Cara, fidgeting with her already perfectly tucked polo.

"He'd be a fool not to," commented Lily, pulling on her piece of Bubble Yum.

"I just don't want to get in trouble, with all of these rules," said Cara, her eyes darting to the fire, then back to the conversation.

"Pete is a big boy. He can take care of himself," said Becky flatly. She watched as Liv walked over toward the boys of Cabin Two. "Excuse me, girls, I need to get to work myself." She sauntered past the fire.

Maggie turned to Beth. "I thought she'd never leave."

"No kidding. Hey, maybe now your friend Ryan will come over and talk to you."

"What? No, I doubt that—it's not a thing, I swear—it's

just—"

"I should rephrase that," interrupted Beth. "Hey, now your friend Ryan is coming over to talk to you."

"Wait, what?" said Maggie. Beth turned to pretend to be engrossed with Cara's dilemma.

"Hey, Mags," said Ryan.

"Oh, hey! You're calling me 'Mags' now, huh?"

"Yeah, I thought it was time."

"Time?" Maggie twitched.

"Yeah, it's been what—a couple days? I thought I'd take it to the next level."

"Jokes on you. Maggie is already a nickname."

"Ahh, okay, so are you an expat?"

"An ex what?"

"Did your family live in England? Big Margaret Thatcher fans?"

"Yes, no. Well, yes to Thatcher, actually, no to England. They're just massive Anglophiles. It's so weird."

"It's not that weird. Have you heard the music coming out of the UK?"

"It's my parents."

"Parents can be cool."

"Growing up, they gave me Digestives instead of Oreos and Dairy Milks instead of Hershey bars..."

"And diabetes?"

"Funny."

"I know. Okay then, Margaret, how abou—"

"Nope, you're not my dad."

"Thank God for that."

"Ew."

Ryan laughed, the fire making his eyes twinkle. "All right, Magpie it is. So what's the good word—want to go—"

"Into the woods where you have a 'secret location' that nobody knows about, where we can 'just talk'?" retorted Maggie.

"You wish. Nah, I thought we could 'just talk' over on the docks. Let's go."

"Oh, yeah, all right," said Maggie, swallowing a pang of dejection.

"Come on," smirked Ryan, bumping into her shoulder to prod her along.

Maggie turned and flashed apologetic eyes at Beth, who shooed her away. They scuffed their feet through the sand and hopped onto the dock, sitting cross-legged a few feet away from the coolers. Across the beach, Maggie saw Tom cozied up next to Liv, while Joey sloshed bug juice all over the place, entertaining the group with some sort of theatrical narrative. She turned her attention to the water lapping against the dock.

"So what's the deal with this place, anyway?" she asked.

"You're meddling with powers you can't possibly comprehend."

"Oh, okay, Indy."

"It was Marcus Brody who said that actually, not Indiana Jones."

"Okay, nerd."

Ryan turned to face her, his eyes dark and intense, but not unkind.

"All will be revealed in due time. I promise."

"Well, that's not at all vague and a little creepy."

"Yeah. Sorry. It's just"—he lowered his voice—"there's a lot I can't say. But I will. You just have to trust me. Can you trust me?"

"I guess."

Ryan continued to look hard at her.

"Yes, yes, I can, okay? We've known each other for less than a week, but sure. I'll go against my gut and blindly trust a stranger."

"Stranger. That's funny."

"Why's that funny?"

Ryan changed the subject. "So, tell me something about you. Where are you from?"

"Oh you know, Anytown, USA, where there's one stoplight, seven pizza joints, and mostly nothing to do."

"Ah yes, Anytown, I've heard of it. The goal is to get out before the clock strikes midnight and you turn into a townie forever, right?"

"Basically. The library is pretty great, though."

"Yeah?"

"Yeah, it has all of these little nooks and crannies you can hide in to get lost in a book."

"Your library is inside a Thomas' English muffin?"

"Shut up. So, are you from the city or something?"

"Or something."

"Your mysteries know no bounds," said Maggie, rolling her eyes.

"All part of the charm."

"Right. Clearly what won Becky over," she challenged.

"Becky…that's not quite the sordid history you're imagining."

"I'm not imagin—"

"She's the longest Lifer here—one of the first. She likes to think she owns the place." He lowered his voice to a murmur and leaned toward Maggie. "She kisses up to Greg and Kate, and they value her over any of the other Lifers. She can't be trusted—she wields an awful amount of power."

"Yeah, but that doesn't explain—"

"She's power hungry, and what she wants, she usually gets. She cherry picks her protégés, and she thinks guys are a disposable commodity. She's terrible. But she hasn't always been this way."

"You knew her before?"

"Yeah. At the beginning of last summer she was self-absorbed and annoying and everything, but bearable. Then, there was this whole thing, and afterward she became the nightmare you get to experience every day."

There was a lull in the conversation. Maggie watched the bonfire crackle into the sky and remembered watching the fireflies with him again. She didn't ask him to elaborate on "this whole thing" that happened with Becky, for fear of him giving her that look again. She stretched out her legs and balanced her Chucks on the surface of the water. Her shoelace dipped into the lake. Ryan stared ahead.

"Anyway," he continued, "it is what it is. Things aren't always what they seem in life, right? But I think it's going to be different this summer."

"Why's that?"

"Because you're going to save the camp."

"What?"

"We gotta go. We've been out here too long."

"I'm going to what?"

"I hope I've cured your homesickness." Ryan stood up and made for the beach. Maggie scrambled to follow, not understanding a single thing that had just transpired.

"Huh? I'm not homesick, you weirdo! Hey, Ryan, wait up!"

Ryan turned halfway and gave Maggie a low wave, before rejoining his bunkmates by the fire. Maggie walked over to a log where Beth was fixated on the flames licking the sky. She sat down in a huff.

"That kid is impossible to read, Beth! First he banters, then he's serious, then sincere, then abrupt like we just completed a business transaction—what the hell!"

Beth continued to look at the fire.

"That's weird, right? Am I way off in thinking that?"

Beth continued to stare, unaware.

"Uh, Beth?" Maggie nudged her. Beth immediately snapped out of her trance. "Oh, hey! How long have you been sitting there?"

"Um, a minute or so. Are you okay?"

"Yeah, I just had the strangest thoughts in my head, that's

all."

"Really? Like what?"

"Eh, nothing. Forget it," said Beth. She stood up with her empty plastic cup and looked for a trash can.

"It's okay, you can talk to me. What were they?"

"Not now. Besides, you're meddling with powers you can't possibly comprehend," Beth said, laughing as she headed back to the cabin.

Maggie's ears bristled at hearing the phrase again. She was certain Beth hadn't been in earshot when Ryan said this to her on the dock.

***

Bravado aside, it took Pete a good forty-five minutes to warm up to the idea of trying to actually make a move on Cara. He was new to camp and didn't know which rules were truly enforced or how much of the envelope a camper could push. When he finally found his nerve, Cara was sitting by the fire with Amy and Stacey, sulking.

He got right to it. "Uh, hey, Cara! Wanna go for a walk? I know this spot..."

Cara's face flushed in the firelight. She jumped to her feet.

"Yeah, okay, cool," she replied, a smile curling in the corners of her lips.

She walked close to Pete, where the beach met the woods for a while. He turned and stopped her.

"Okay, so wait here for like five minutes, then meet me by the tree diagonal from the bell near the Mess Hall. We should be discreet!"

Cara groaned. "Petee, there are like a thousand trees diagonal from the bell. I thought you said you had a—"

"Yeah, yeah, you'll see it, trust me—it's the one with the hollowed out part at the bottom. It's big!"

"That's what she said."

"Huh?"

"Nothing, Petee. Fine. Okay. Go. Ugh!"

Pete grinned at her, then ran off into the woods. Cara rolled her eyes and looked around, self-conscious that people were watching her.

And they were. The counselors were looking right at her, but they were also interested in the path Pete weaved through the trees back toward the Mess Hall.

Two of the counselors slipped away from their lawn chairs and headed for the woods. Their migration went unnoticed to Cara, giddy with adrenaline at the possibility of getting some.

She stepped into the woods, whispering "Petee? Petee!" every so often, scanning the bottom of each tree for a hollow opening.

"Petee! Where are you?" she rasped. "Ugh, this is just so typical," she muttered to herself. She swatted the mosquitos whining in her ears. The earth was still damp from the earlier rain. Cara's foot slid sideways on some leaves. She caught herself from falling over a slippery root. Driven by sex, she plodded frantically through cobwebs and wet underbrush. She glanced around and saw the bell in the distance. "Okay, so maybe this way," she said, turning around.

A twig cracked behind her.

She froze.

A hand covered her mouth to muffle her screams.

***

There was a warmth inside Tom, and it wasn't from the blazing fire. Liv leaned into him and made hushed observations about campers and the ongoings of Bonfire Night, and he found himself laughing quietly along with her. She was close, so close that he could smell her shampooed hair. Was it witch hazel? Something floral? Pert Plus? It didn't matter. Tom was overcome by it all. How had he never been to camp before? It was actually magical. You could never have a night like this back in Bradford, not even on the Third of July, when the neighboring town lit tons of bonfires along the beach. He couldn't place the feeling. It was bigger than high school camaraderie, and more thrilling than bottoming out on the first drop of the Coney Island Cyclone.

He looked around. Ryan and Germ were sitting off to the side, flicking their fingers at hovering June bugs, their voices low in conversation. Maybe they were talking about Maggie. A twang of jealousy pinched at him, but quickly subsided. Good for her, he thought, sipping on his third cup of bug juice. She should get out there, shouldn't she? Being stuck in Bradford your whole life can make you blind to the rest of the world. You find the best you can within that bubble, and make do until you can bust out. No hard feelings, right? It was unrealistic to think that the two of them would be inseparable forever. But then, if he didn't care, why did he pretend to use the bathroom during Spin the Bottle at Noah's party?

Alex interrupted his thoughts.

"Great night," he said.

"Yeah, you were right. We're pretty much living the dream."

"Told ya."

Joey, drunk on bug juice, flopped into the sand and moved his arms and legs across it frantically. The juice stained his lips, giving him a maniacal smile.

"Come make a sand angel with me, baby!" he called out to a female camper walking by.

Becky, sitting with one leg draped over Alex's lap, kicked sand at him with the other. "Pig," she chided, but the spirit of the night had softened her—a disapproving grin curled up around the edge of her lips.

"What! We're young and full of life!" he cried, sitting up and falling forward onto his knees, his hand pressed emphatically to his heart. "We're invincible with this nectar from the gods!" He raised his cup. "Drink!"

Liv looked at Tom, laughter in her eyes. Alex made a "why not" face, and Becky wiped sand from the bottom of her cup. Corey put his head down and raised his glass. Leaning forward, Ryan and Germ stretched their arms toward the rest of them.

"A toast!" exclaimed Joey, his eyes wild with mischief and drunken adoration.

"A toast!" they all repeated, giggling.

"To the best years of our lives! To the best summer ever! To our glorified purpose! To this bonfire! To the newbies! To our miraculous youth! To this goddamned bug juice!" At that, Joey toppled over, spilling drink all over the sand. Liv hung her head, laughing. Becky rolled her eyes. Tom grinned. Ryan and Germ shook their heads.

"Cheers!" they said as they laughed and emptied their plastic cups.

21

Maggie sat on a car seat, but it wasn't in a car. She squinted her eyes, trying to make them adjust to the darkness. Rock music blared from somewhere. Gritty walls were smattered with paraphernalia from Detroit. She noticed a go-go dancer in the window, her vapid eyes rolling into the back of her head as she swayed to the music. A line of people snaked around the bar, waiting for the bathroom.

"They're all just waiting to bang."

Her eyes focused on the seat across from her—Ryan again.

"What? No. No way."

"No, really," he insisted. "Just watch—check out how many people go in there when the next person comes out. I'll bet it's not one."

Maggie grinned in disbelief and turned to watch the door. Several moments passed before a guy emerged, motioning an apology for destroying the toilet.

"Oh, gross!" exclaimed Maggie.

"Keep watching." Ryan grinned and pointed ahead.

She turned back, and sure enough, a muscular guy with tattoos pulled in the voluptuous blonde beside him and shut the door.

"That's allowed? How are they not getting tossed out of

this place?"

"Beats me," he said, shrugging. "Are you going to tell that guy he can't do that?"

"Good point," she replied.

Ryan picked up a lit votive candle on the table between them and balanced it on Maggie's knee. Maggie looked up, quizzical, and put it back on the table. Ryan did it again.

Maggie returned the votive to its place. His hand brushed up against hers. He did it again—a game.

"Stop! You're going to light me on fire!" she exclaimed, laughing a little.

"Come on, baby, light my fire," sang Ryan.

Maggie rolled her eyes.

"Hey, I gotta take a piss, and I'm sure as hell not waiting in that line. I'll be right back," said Ryan, standing abruptly.

"Wait, what if you can't get back into this place?" asked Maggie, noticing a queue outside through the window.

"I'll be fine," he replied, and walked toward the door.

She watched him walk away, fidgeting in her seat. In a corner booth, a twenty-first birthday party was in full swing. The birthday girl wore a crooked tiara and had squeezed into a royal-blue sequined dress that her legs forgot she was wearing. "This is the best night everrrrrrr!" she slurred. Against the wall, a pinball machine chimed for a crowd of leather-clad bikers surrounding it.

Maggie turned back to the door, waiting to see Ryan's bright eyes once more. She looked again at the go-go dancer, but she was no longer dancing in the window. Through the crowd waiting to be served at the bar, the dancer reappeared, walking toward Maggie. Her once vapid expression had transformed into a grotesque Edvard Munch skeletal yawn. In each hand she held two severed arms by the wrists, dripping with blood. A blinding white light shot from her eye sockets.

Maggie looked around, horrified. Was no one else seeing

this? The crowd was closing in, forming a circle around her and the wraithlike nightmare. She looked past the crowd. Her eyes panicked. Tears burned down her cheeks.

She heard banging on the window glass.

"Ryan!" Maggie shrieked. "Save me! Please! I'm trapped!"

The circle around her tightened.

Her throat started to close up.

"Ryan!" she tried screaming. Anxiety seared through her body. She looked again and couldn't see him.

The go-go dancer was an arm's length from her. She hissed, making the detached limbs clap their deadened hands. A scorching heat burned in Maggie's fingertips.

A crash. Shards of glass sprayed everywhere. A metal trash can from the street was lodged into the side of the bar, knocking several people unconscious. Ryan shoved through the crowd and grabbed Maggie's hand. He drew her close.

"Close your eyes," he whispered.

She could feel his breath in her hair. Without questioning, she shut them and squeezed his hand. A bright white flash made her instinctively turn her head into his shoulder. Ryan grabbed her by the waist. Her feet instinctively ran. Her heart was in her throat.

She opened her eyes. Sweat poured down her temples.

It was another sunny morning at Camp Kinross.

22

"Up and at 'em, boys," Mark said, yawning and running his hand through his hair. "We don't want to be late for waffle day at the Mess Hall—Woody won't make extra batter for stragglers."

"Mmm, Woody's batter." Joey chuckled from under his covers.

"Not gonna land any ladies with that quality material," said Mark, throwing a football at Joey's bed.

The cabin slowly came to life, crawling from blankets, emerging from hoods of sweatshirts, and staggering like teenage zombies to the toilet. Alex threw his arms in the air for a space-consuming stretch, landing his hands on Tom's shoulders.

"Great night, huh, buddy?"

"Yeah," replied Tom, blinking. "Really good."

"Joey, get your ass up!" said Alex, picking up the football and again throwing it at the lump of blankets on the bed.

A barely audible groan was returned, along with a middle finger from the limb hanging off the side of the bed.

"C'mon, Joey, let's go!" yelled Mark, ushering the rest of the bunk toward the door.

The smell of waffles lured the sleepy campers into a

delicious trance as they approached the Mess Hall.

"Oh my God, I love waffle day," said Corey, perking up. Ryan, Alex, and Germ mumbled their agreement.

There was an unusual energy in the Mess Hall that morning. Campers had their heads on a swivel and spoke in hushed voices.

"I'll find out what the deal is," said Alex. He sidled up to one of the girls on line for breakfast. "Hey, Amy, what's going on—why does everyone in the Mess Hall seem spooked?"

Amy pushed a stray piece of hair behind her ear and blushed. "Huh? Oh, I don't know, Alex," she said, sneaking a glance at him while sliding her tray down the line.

"Amy," cooed Alex, "tell me. Tell me, tell me, tell me! What's up? Why is everyone acting so freaking weird in here? It's cool—I'm not going to tell anyone. My cabin got here late. Don't leave me out!"

"Well," Amy hesitated.

"Yeah?" Alex persisted.

"People are all freaked out because there's a rumor that Petee was kicked out last night for trying to hook up with Cara."

"Okay, yeah, well, he shouldn't have been flaunting that all over camp—"

"It's not just that. Cara didn't make it back to her bunk last night, either. But no one knows if she was officially kicked out or not, so there's all this speculation."

"If they were caught messing around, they'd both be kicked out. That's obvious," said Alex.

"But that's what everyone doesn't get. It seems like that sort of thing is allowed sometimes? I mean, the whole point of Bonfire Night?"

"Amy, Amy, Amy," said Alex, rolling his eyes, "do you think Greg and Kate really want a teenage pregnancy on their hands? Get with it."

"Still, though—all of the Lifers have been saying the

counselors are pretty lax about campers hooking up."

"Two waffles, thanks, Woody," said Alex.

Amy picked up a fork from the utensil bin and turned to Alex. "It just seems weird, and Christine was saying it would be impossible for Petee to leave so quickly, too, because he's from Pennsylvania."

"Ahhh, yes, right, that would be hard, wouldn't it... Except that there's a camp van, and usually if the counselors can't get the parents to come right away, one of them drives the camper directly home or meets the parents halfway."

"Oh," said Amy. Her face fell while processing the information.

"Yeah, feel free to spin that into the rumor mill, 'kay?" Alex chirped, his left hand patting her shoulder.

"Verdict?" asked Germ through a mouthful of waffle.

"Apparently, everyone is skittish because of the whole Pete and Cara thing from last night—I think they were probably bounced," Alex replied, sitting down.

"'Course they were bounced. What craziness have the newbies cooked up this time?" said Joey. He took a giant bite of cantaloupe, its juice dripping out of the corners of his mouth.

"Oh, the usual conspiracy theories," said Alex.

"Really?" prodded Ryan.

"Yeah, you know, the 'logistical impossibilities'—like this is the only camp in the world that doesn't have an exit plan for derelicts," said Alex.

Tom listened with interest. "Well, it does seem like there are some mixed messages on the social stuff," he offered.

"Gotta learn to walk before you can run, Tommy," replied Alex. "You can't just hatch a plan to get laid in the woods on the third day. Pete was a moron."

"Attention, campers! Good morning!" Counselor Kate stood at the front of the Mess Hall, sweater draped around her bony shoulders, clipboard in hand. She gave a frozen smile to the waffle-filled audience.

"I'm sure you all have some questions about some of the things that have been going on at Kinross over the last few days."

A wave of murmurs washed over the room.

"Now, I know some of you newer campers may be confused as to how we run things here at camp. Greg and I are more than happy to address these issues with you on an individual basis, or you can go to your bunk counselor for clarification. But given the recent events, Greg and I both feel it's necessary to address all of you right now. Greg?"

Greg, tight-lipped, stepped forward, his tan arms folded across his chest.

"Oh shit," whispered Germ.

Ryan looked across the cafeteria and saw Maggie looking down at her plate, pushing a piece of waffle back and forth in a puddle of syrup. Look up, he thought. Look up or he's going to single you out. Look up, Maggie. Look up! As if on cue, Maggie sighed and put her fork at the top of her plate, her eyes shifting to Greg.

"He looks mad," whispered Tom.

"Shh," hissed Alex and Joey.

The crackle of Woody's radio was barely audible from the kitchen. Greg waited until the clink of utensils had ceased. His eyes honed in on an oblivious camper across the room, yammering away to the person sitting next to him.

"I'll wait, Mr. Murphy! …I'll wait," said Greg.

The camper sat up straight. "Oh! Sorry...sir."

"That's fine, Mr. Murphy, you're not wasting my time. You're wasting yours," replied Greg coolly, "and if I'm being honest, it's not just cutting into your activity time, but also your whole experience here at Camp Kinross.

When you waste your time on what-if scenarios that have no footing, you're opening yourself up to a world of anxiety, and ultimately ruining your camp potential. Not to mention everyone else's. Anxiety is a sickness, a parasitic glutton that feeds on vulnerable minds and fallacies that are then, in turn, woven into mediocre 'camp lore.' Camp Kinross has never tolerated the sort of slanderous exchanges that have been churning the past few days, nor do we plan to now.

In three days we've sent home five campers. I'll say that number again: five. That's the highest number we've ever sent packing in one summer, let alone one week!"

"I only counted four," said Corey under his breath to Ryan.

"This is unacceptable," Greg continued. "You're here to experience some of the finest days of your formative years. But that does not mean that it's a free pass for a week of debauchery."

Kate spoke up. "Given the past few days, Counselor Greg and I have decided that we are canceling today's scheduled activities and taking you on a hike at neighboring mountain, Mount Kinross. Woody woke up extra early this morning and packed brown bag lunches for everyone.

This needs to be sorted out—now. Not just these big things, but also all of the internal squabbling that has been going on. Don't think we haven't noticed. We have to get back to nature. Back to the source of life. Erase the toxicity. A full day outdoors is just the remedy."

"Finish up your breakfast, then hit your bunks to grab a sweatshirt. We leave in fifteen minutes—buses will be in the driveway," said Greg.

Campers clamored to clear their trays and get out of the Mess Hall. Ryan made his way through the crowd to find Maggie, who was tossing a crumpled napkin into the trash. "Sit with me on the bus," he said, and then walked away before Maggie could turn to say hi to him.

23

Two old school buses idled in the main parking lot; the same lot that just a few days ago had been packed with vehicles and cheerful parents seeing their kids off to camp.

"Wanna sit together?" Beth and Maggie stood next to one of the buses with the other campers, waiting for instruction from the counselors.

"Eh, sure—I mean, well—" Maggie stretched her face into a frown.

"Oh, what—Ryan?" asked Beth, slightly put out.

"He said, 'Sit with me,' during the mass exodus from the Mess Hall, before I could even say anything! But I had another one of those messed up dreams, so I kinda want to tell him about it?"

"Oh, okay. I'll sit behind you, I guess," said Beth.

"Thanks, sorry," said Maggie, grateful for not having to explain any further. "I'll fill you in later."

"Cool," said Beth.

Maggie spied Tom over near the arches leading down to where they initially had orientation. She walked over and gave him a nudge.

"Having fun?" she asked.

"Yeah, definitely. You?"

"Yeah, so far, so good."

"You ready for this hike?" he asked, glancing at her beat-up sneakers.

"I mean, I doubt I could outrun one of Smitty's bottle rockets, but yeah, I'll be fine," Maggie said, grinning.

"Yeah, that seems like years ago, huh?" Tom's eyes glazed over. He looked around and shifted uneasily.

"Dude, are you okay? Should I not be talking to you? You're acting weird."

"I'm fine, Mags."

Maggie furrowed her brow. "You don't seem fine. Am I messing things up for you and that girl? I can leave—"

"Really, stop, Mom. I'm good," Tom insisted.

Maggie recoiled from the sting of Tom's comment.

"Okay, cool. Yeah, sorry, have fun!" It was trying to hold on to a fistful of sand at the beach. She was losing him. She didn't know what was worse—that he was slipping away, or that she wasn't as upset about it as she thought she should be.

She turned away and caught sight of Ryan coming across the clearing. Maggie walked back to Beth, and the three of them boarded the same bus.

"Everyone get on a bus and find a seat. Let's go!" yelled Mark from the driver's seat. He motioned impatiently to stragglers still hanging around outside.

Maggie slid into a seat in the middle of the bus, and Ryan moved in next to her. He looked around. Alex and the rest of Cabin Two had taken over the back of the bus, along with Becky, Liv, and a couple of other girls from Cabin Three. Alex winked and gave him a grin. Ryan half smiled before facing forward.

"Ready to get into the great outdoors?" He elbowed Maggie.

"I thought we already were in the great outdoors," she replied.

"No chance," he said. "Get ready."

"The counselors were pretty riled, eh?"

"Yup. I've only seen that kind of wrath one other time since I've been a Lifer. But the 'punishment' was swimming laps for hours."

"You're lying."

"I'm not."

"They can't do that."

"Are you going to tell them they can't do that?" Ryan shrugged.

Maggie shivered, his words echoing from her latest dream.

The bus roared to life. Mark turned the steering wheel with concerted effort. They rumbled down the dirt road exiting camp. Maggie stared out the window. The woods were spacious. Gnats and dragonflies swirled in the sunlight cutting through the shade created by regal pines. Maggie spied a few opossums skulking around some shrubbery. That's odd, thought Maggie. Weren't opossums nocturnal?

The bus bounced over rocks and potholes. Kate walked down the aisle, taking a headcount and tossing lunch bags onto campers' laps. She raised an eyebrow at Maggie and Ryan before moving on. Ryan returned a sheepish grin.

"Hey, so I wanted to tell you, I had another—" started Maggie.

"Not...now," Ryan said under his breath.

"Ugh, I'm so sick of this secrec—"

He cut her off again before she could finish. "I don't think you want to be the next camper to go missing, do you?"

Maggie's eyes widened for a moment at the word "missing" and then turned back to the window. Missing? They were sent home, weren't they? And why did he want her to sit with him on the bus, only to keep quiet?

After what seemed like an endless ride on the divided highway, the bus turned onto another dirt road and pulled into a small parking lot.

"Popular place," said Maggie, noting the empty lot. An

uneasiness set in when she noticed the absence of trail maps and hiking signage. A lone narrow trailhead started between two parking lot barriers, then disappeared into the woods. Maggie raised her eyebrows.

"What's the matter Colonel Sanders...chicken?" Ryan said, smirking.

"We won't be combing the desert here, that's for sure," Maggie retorted, looking around.

Ryan grinned. "Nope."

The campers filed off the buses and stood in a semicircle, unsure of the next move. The underbrush was thicker at the base of Mount Kinross than the woods they were familiar with at camp.

"Ah yes, this is just what we need. I can feel it in my bones!" said Kate, breathing heavily and looking upward with a satisfied smile. Greg tugged on his ankle to stretch out his hamstring and nodded in agreement.

"Limber up, kiddos, we don't want anyone spraining anything!" he pepped.

"Seems like he's in a better mood," Liv whispered to Tom.

"Yeah, he does. Those campers were idiots, and now we have to suffer the consequences," said Tom, looking down at his own worn down Chucks.

"Might not be so bad," replied Liv. "I mean, we get to hang out all day, so..." Her voice trailed off and she flashed him a little grin before looking away. Electricity shot through Tom. He ran his fingers through his hair and looked the other way, fearing that everyone standing nearby could see the sudden charge emanating from him.

***

The campers trudged among the trees of Mount Kinross for what seemed like hours. Maggie breathed heavy, but was determined to keep pace with Beth, Ryan, and the rest of the group. Mark and Kate wove their way through the campers, offering verbal nuggets of encouragement like "You're doing great!" when campers lost their balance or tripped over a bulging tree root.

Maggie paused to wipe sweat from her brow. Up ahead, a narrow ditch was filled halfway with murky water; it wasn't terribly deep, but required a good jump to clear it. The sides of the crevice sloped downward into a "V" shape. Each camper hopped the stagnant water effortlessly and kept hiking.

Ryan leapt across with ease but turned back when he heard a yelp. Maggie faltered as she tried to scramble up the sloping side of the ditch. He rushed over to the side of it and held out his hand to pull her up. She grabbed his hand gratefully and climbed out of the ditch. At his touch, a shock wave shot through her body. An instant connection. His skin felt so familiar. What would his hands feel like all over her? Her already flushed face burned at the thought.

"Thanks," she stammered.

Ryan half grinned and turned back toward the trail.

"Everything hunky-dory back there, you two? Should I call Counselor Kate?" asked Becky, her eyes full of mocking concern. She put her hands on her hips and turned, looking ahead for Kate. "It's really no troub—"

"We're good," replied Ryan.

"You're such a Boy Scout, Ry, always looking to help those who are helpless," Becky replied, patting his back.

"Where's Alex?" Ryan replied.

"Are you trying to get rid of me?" she asked, pouting.

"Hi, guys! Great day for a hike, right?" said Kate, making her way through a side path to where the three of them stood. "Becky, Ryan, why don't you run on ahead and keep the other newbies company? Some of them are starting to fade. I'll keep—" She paused, searching for a name.

"Maggie."

"Yes, thank you. I'll keep Maggie company back here. Run along!" shooed Kate.

Maggie saw a split second of wariness in Ryan's eyes before he flashed a smile at Kate and replied, "Okay, cool, see ya!"

They took off in a light jog to catch up with the others. Maggie tried to keep track of everything that had just happened: Becky's spite, Counselor Kate manifesting out of nowhere, the warning she thought she saw in Ryan's eyes, the leftover buzzy electricity in her fingertips from touching his hand. She wanted to be alone with that particular thought— to play it on a loop to see if she could detect any sort of sign that he felt what she had felt, too. But instead, she had to walk a conversational tightrope with Kate, while Mount Kinross tried to knock her on her face.

"So, Maggie—I've seen you around a bit, but we haven't really connected—you are very interesting to me," started Kate.

"Me? Oh. Thanks? I'm not sure why?"

"Relax, Maggie, this isn't an interrogation. I promise. I don't bite!" She laughed. "I'm here to answer any of your questions, no matter how crazy they may be. It's a lot—camp, that is—especially if you've never been."

"Wait, how do you know I've never—"

"Oh, it's one of the questions on the application. We try to check in on the first timers to make sure everything is going okay. It's kind of fantastic that you've never been to camp, and that Kinross is your first experience! Nothing will ever compare to this week. I'm not trying to brag. It's just the truth. You'll never go to another camp like this." They arrived at the tree line. Kate stopped walking and turned to Maggie.

"Look," she said, "I know that social circles aren't your thing. I can tell. I get it. I was like you."

At this Maggie raised her eyebrows.

"No, really!" Kate insisted. "I think that's why I've noticed you more than the other first timers. I see a lot of me—a lot of who I once was—in you. And honestly, I think the clique crap is just that. Please don't let Becky get to you."

"Oh, I'm not—"

"But she does get to you. I know her type, and she would have annoyed the shit out of me back when I was your age. Honestly, she still does sometimes."

Maggie laughed, her guard softening. "Thanks," she said. "It's pretty hard to explain that to people. Everyone is so caught up in it, you know?"

"I know. And people like that, sure they have their reign, but it never lasts. Don't let the negativity from all of that influence you. You are infinite. Your potential is infinite. And if you want something—" Kate paused to look ahead to the trail Ryan and Becky were climbing, and looked back at Maggie before continuing. "You need to go for it. Never let go of something—or someone—that you believe in." Her eyes clouded over for a moment, but then she quickly blinked it away.

"Well, it's complicated—" Maggie started.

"No, it's not," snapped Kate. "You can break everything down into small, solvable problems. I'm quite certain you'll figure it out. C'mon, let's catch up to the others. We're almost at the summit."

Kate led Maggie up the last bit of trail. At the summit, everyone was putting on their sweatshirts and rummaging through lunch bags. Maggie found Ryan and Beth sitting against a boulder. The view was vast and beautiful. A sea of muted emerald trees ebbed and flowed over the smaller adjoining peaks. The valley below was speckled with red and white—barns and silos—and bright patches of green farm life.

"Whatup, speedy?" teased Ryan.

"Funny," replied Maggie.

"How was your hike with Kate?" asked Beth, her voice

lowered.

"Oh, it was fine," said Maggie. "It actually wasn't as bad as I thought it would be."

Ryan rubbed his neck and looked directly at Maggie.

"What did she talk about?" he asked.

"Hm? Oh, just my potential at camp, and to not let the social circle stuff drive me crazy."

"Huh."

"What?"

"Nothing, it sounds like she's interested in you becoming a Lifer. Weird, because she's never really talked to you until today."

"Thanks for the vote of confidence, pal," huffed Maggie.

"You're welcome."

"Ugh."

"We've only been here for a few days," Beth pointed out. "Do they pick Lifers this early?"

"Sometimes, I guess?" replied Ryan.

"Hey," Beth interrupted, looking around. "Have you guys seen that girl Stacey, from our cabin? I don't think she's here."

"What?" said Maggie.

"She was here earlier—I passed her on the hike—but I don't see her now."

Maggie stopped chewing her peanut butter and jelly sandwich. "How can that be?" she asked.

Ryan leaned forward, brushing against Maggie. A new wave of electricity buzzed through her.

"Are you sure she didn't somehow get left behind? Or maybe she's around here somewhere?" said Ryan, looking behind them.

"I don't think so. I mean, she hangs out with the Cabin Four girls a lot," Beth replied, pointing to a group standing in a close-knit circle, their heads on a nervous swivel.

"Something's not right," said Maggie, biting her lip. She looked at Ryan, startled to catch him looking right at her.

"What?" she asked, a little too loudly.

"What? Nothing," he stammered. "Yeah, something's up. I'll go talk to Greg." He stood up abruptly, dusting the dirt off his shorts, and walked over to Greg. Maggie and Beth stole glances at their interaction. After a few moments, Ryan walked back, and Greg made his way to the group of perplexed campers.

"Greg's, uh, on it. He said she twisted her ankle during the hike, and that Hannah took her back to camp."

"Weird that they didn't tell her friends, though, right?" commented Beth.

"Beats me," replied Ryan, sitting back down.

This time, noticed Maggie, he was sitting ever so slightly closer to her. The buzzing commenced.

24

They were walking near a river with cups of ice cream in their hands. The sky was a brilliant blue, and the warm breezy air held the crisp promise of a perfect spring day. Crocuses pushed their way through the still thawing soil. As they walked, they casually marveled at the misplaced wildlife—an oversize brassy turtle lounging on the riverbank, a seal rolling through the golden water. Insects busied themselves with meaningless missions, darting between rays of sunlight slicing through the water.

They stopped walking to take in the scenery, standing side by side in a comfortable quiet. Ryan balanced on a rock next to her, at the edge of the river. Maggie looked up. His eyes met hers. In their held gaze, something unspoken, unsure. Something innocent. Hopeful. Pretenses dissipated. Kiss him, just kiss him, she thought, scraping the bottom of her ice-cream cup, looking for a morsel of courage. He turned and looked out over the river. "One day, this will all look different, Mags," he said.

She had missed her chance.

"It's really nice here; I don't want to leave," she said.

"Yeah," he replied. "C'mon." He leaned into her shoulder and kept moving. Maggie turned to follow him, but her foot was stuck. She looked down. Something dark and hard had caught her sneaker. A tree root, she thought. She tried to slide her foot out from underneath it. It was trapped. She glanced up. Ryan was already fifty feet ahead of her.

"Ryan! Hey! Wait up!" she tried to call. No sound came out of her mouth. Her heart quickened. A beady-eyed opossum meandered toward her, its snout sniffing the ground. "Ryan!" she yelled, but again, nothing. Another root grew out of the ground and wrapped around her other ankle. Maggie wobbled to stay upright. She shrieked as the sinewy marsupial neared.

"Ryan!" she screamed, but the sound was lodged in the back of her throat. Hot tears streamed down her face. Ryan was now a few hundred feet away from her, but wasn't turning around.

Her throat tightened. The opossum was at her feet now.

It sniffed and rubbed its snout on the sides of her mud-caked sneakers. It's cordlike tail whipped back and forth.

Maggie watched in horror. The more the tail whipped, the longer it grew.

It coiled around Maggie's ankles.

It strangled her calves, thighs.

She desperately fought to unravel her body with her arms, not yet tethered by the nightmare.

Her fear exploded into to white-hot anger. Tears slid down her cheeks like candle wax, scorching her skin. Anger seared through her veins as the opossum gnawed on her sneakers. Its jaw clicked with determination. The animal's beady marble eyes fell out of its head and rolled onto the ground. A white light burst from the hollow sockets. Its tail continued to wrap around Maggie's torso.

Something inside her snapped.

Her tears hissed as they came into contact with the grass at her feet.

A burning erupted from her chest.

White specks of light came out of her fingertips and whirred around her hands.

An ear-splitting scream followed.

A flash of blinding light, then everything went black.

When she came to, Ryan was sitting on the ground next to her, his fingers barely touching hers. "You've got this," he said.

Maggie looked at him with confusion before it came rushing back to her. She looked around for signs of the twisting appendage that had wrapped itself around her body. There wasn't a trace of it, the opossum, or the tree roots. A pile of smoldering ash was scattered on the riverbank.

"What happened to me? I—I screamed for you!" she cried.

"I'm not always going to be able to save you," he replied quietly.

"Huh? What? Why not? I thought we were—I thought this was—" Maggie stammered, getting to her feet.

"It has to be you, Magpie," he said.

"What does that mean, huh? I was almost killed by a freak opossum and you're choosing now to be cagey with me?" she screamed.

"You wouldn't have been killed—there's more to you than you think," he said.

"You don't know that!" she replied.

"Actually, I do," he said. "You're dreaming."

"What?

"Wake up," he said simply.

Maggie blinked. She was in bed, her sheets soaked with sweat. She leaned over the side of her bed.

On the floor, arranged neatly, were her clean sneakers.

25

"Rise and shine, sleepyheads!" Counselor Hannah sang to the girls of Cabin Three.

Maggie blinked and pulled her blanket over her face. "Five more minutes," she mumbled.

Her legs proved to be a sore souvenir from yesterday's hike. Her mind drifted to the previous day's events—Kate's talk, Ryan's hand. She landed on the latter for a moment, a groggy half grin appearing and then disappearing. A familiar saccharine voice dripped down the walls of the cabin. Becky and Liv were standing at the mirror in the hall by the bathroom, adding the finishing touches to their faces.

"That's such great news, Liv! You have him right where you want him!" cooed Becky.

Maggie rolled her eyes and grabbed her shorts and polo from her dresser.

"Now," Becky continued, "we need to start grooming you to become a Lifer. I'll put in a good word. Lord knows he's going to want to be one after yesterday, if you know what I mean!" Liv giggled, watching Becky blot her lips with a piece of folded-up toilet paper. Blowing an air kiss goodbye to the mirror, she turned on her heel and said, "One thing's for certain: I don't think you have to worry about her anymore."

Unprovoked, Maggie grabbed her shampoo and towel, and slid past them to the bathroom. She thought she heard a barely audible "hmph!" but something in her mind kept telling her to stand down. It wasn't like Maggie to let stuff roll off her shoulders, especially the passive-aggressive exchange that Becky had just tried to initiate. But something in her head steered her away from it and kept saying, "Stay calm, focus. It's nothing."

When she finished showering, the rest of the girls, including Beth, had already left for breakfast. Maggie jammed her blistered feet into her chucks and hobbled out the cabin door.

Maggie looked up to see Ryan sitting on top of a rock. He gave her a slight nod. She walked toward him like they had been meeting like this for years.

Ryan hopped down. "What's up, Magpie—how'd you sleep?"

"Do you even know what a magpie is?" she bantered.

"Yeah, it's what they make humble pie out of, right?" he smirked, acknowledging her hobbled walk.

"Yeah, blisters are really funny. And I think what you're thinking of is eating crow," she shot back.

"I'd rather eat waffles," he said, grinning.

"I'm going to need a coffee if we're going to continue this way," she replied, looking into the woods so he wouldn't catch her smiling.

"Keep up," he said. They walked in silence for a minute, before he broke it.

"So, how was your morning? Anything eventful?"

Maggie turned and narrowed her eyes. "No," she said slowly. "Why?"

"Easy, tiger. I was sitting on the rock waiting for you, when Becky and Liv left for the Mess Hall, that's all. Becky was all worked up about something."

"Oh, well yeah," replied Maggie, relaxing. "I think she was

trying to get me going first thing this morning, but I just kept telling myself to—"

"Stay calm?" Ryan offered.

"Yes," Maggie answered slowly, her eyes narrowing again. "That, and to focus, because it's nothing. It's not worth it."

"Nice, it worked."

"What? What are you—"

"No, I mean, it's nice that it worked for you. A lot of people can't clear their heads and switch gears like that so quickly. That's pretty cool."

"Uh, okay... Anyway, yeah, so maybe Counselor Kate's pep talk helped," she said. Up ahead, the bell and the Mess Hall came into focus.

"Who knows," he replied.

"Yeah, whatever. So what do we do today?" she said, changing the subject.

"Beats me. Community Service Day is tomorrow, I think. My guess is more activities, followed by a game night maybe?"

Maggie bit her lower lip and waited, but Ryan didn't say anything more. Still rattled and frustrated by her dream, but not wanting to reveal her subconscious affections, she recounted as much as she could to Ryan.

"It's pretty messed up—I wonder why I keep having these crazy dreams."

"And that's it? There wasn't anything else?"

Maggie thought she saw something flash across his eyes. There's no way he could know, she thought, dismissing it immediately.

"Why don't you seem phased by any of this? You're just like, 'Oh, no big deal.' It's only a dream about a freaking opossum with a tail trying to squeeze me to death, and a go-go dancer attacking me with dead arms! But you don't care."

"Eh, I've heard worse," he said, shrugging.

"Of course you have," retorted Maggie. She couldn't help

but be drawn to him, but the way he kept everything so close to the vest annoyed the shit out of her.

When they reached the Mess Hall, Ryan grabbed the door handle and held it open for Maggie. "Thanks," she replied, "I'm going to find Beth—did you want, I mean—where are you—uh..."

"Yeah, I'm headed this way." He nodded to where his cabin mates were eating. "But I'll see you on the field." Ryan smiled.

"Field?" Maggie winced.

"Our cabin is playing your cabin in flag football after lunch," Ryan said, grinning.

"Super," she replied, and made her way to the food queue. In line, she felt a tap on her arm and turned.

"Oh, uh, hey, Counselor Kate, what's up?"

"You can just call me Kate, Maggie." She smiled. "I don't want to hold you up, but I was hoping you could help me out."

"Yeah, sure, I can try?" replied Maggie. She stepped out of the way of a camper reaching for a tray.

"Great. Okay, so at the end of each session of camp, we throw a little party, or dance—call it what you want. Anyway, we usually need some help picking out the music, and I thought you might be perfect for the job."

"Really? Wouldn't that kid who always has headphones around his neck be better?"

"Who, Germaine? He's made a few in the past, but I thought it might be up your alley, too."

"Oh, well, yeah, sure, but I only brought a few mix tapes with me?"

"Don't even worry about that. We have crates full of old records, and equipment and blank tapes so you can record the order of songs however you want."

Maggie paused, thinking it over. "That...that actually sounds like fun."

"Oh, good! I knew you'd be into it. Okay, well I'll have Counselor Adah show you where all the stuff is after breakfast—it's in a closet in the Rec Hall. You can work on it all morning, but take a break after lunch to play flag football with your cabin, and then you can get back at it—does that sound good? The dance is about three hours long; I'd come up with four hours of music to be safe. Are you sure you don't mind missing a few activities to do this?"

"No, no, that's fine. I'm in," Maggie said, grinning.

"Excellent, I'll leave you to your breakfast. And, Maggie?" Kate smiled. "Thank you." She spun around and strolled across the room to the counselors' dining corner.

Maggie glanced at the hot-food line and opted for the cereal bar. She filled her bowl with cinnamon Life, grabbed a milk carton from the mini fridge, and found Beth sitting alone by the window on the far side of the Mess Hall.

"Hey!" said Maggie, swirling her spoon through the deteriorating sugary grains.

"Hey," replied Beth, looking out the window.

"You okay?" continued Maggie. "I hope you don't think I was ditching you or anything with Ryan, I just—" Beth turned away from the window and looked at Maggie.

"No, it's not that. That's fine. Stacey never came back from the hike."

Maggie leaned across the table and whispered, "What? How do you know?"

"I ended up walking with another girl from our bunk to breakfast this morning, and she told me. She waited up forever last night, but Stacey never came to bed. This morning, all of her stuff was gone."

"What exactly did she say?" said Maggie, letting her spoon sink into the milky residue.

"She said," Beth started, "that she asked Kate and Greg, and they said Stacey had to go home because her ankle was much worse than they thought. So after the Infirmary, they had her parents meet her at the hospital."

"Okay," said Maggie slowly, "that makes sense, I guess. But it's still pretty weird that this many people have been 'sent home' and the week isn't halfway over."

"That's not even the weird part."

Maggie paused mid-bite and looked at Beth.

"She heard from her other friend in Cabin Four that Stacey was actually from New Jersey. There's no way her parents could have made it up here in that time span."

"What about the van I heard about? I guess they can drive campers home or meet the parents halfway, if their parents can't come right away?"

"I don't know. It doesn't sound right. Hannah was in our cabin this morning. Everyone was at dinner last night, you know? Why hasn't Hannah mentioned it to us? Where do they park this van? Have you ever seen it? Plus they said her parents came to get her," she hissed.

"No, I haven't seen it. You're right. That's all pretty weird. But I also haven't seen the Rec Hall, which apparently is a thing somewhere around here. And oh! Counselor Kate wants me to pick out music for the dance at the end of the week," commented Maggie.

"Dance?" Beth winced.

"Yup. So no pressure there." Maggie rolled her eyes.

"Not like anyone will be left at camp, at this rate," replied Beth.

"Yeah, really. I mean, I want to think it's all just a bunch of spooky camp lore to rile up the newbies, but I see what you're saying. When you look at the hard facts, it doesn't make any sense," said Maggie.

"Right. Anyway, we should keep our eyes open. Maybe we should tell Ryan, too," said Beth.

"Oh, yeah, maybe," Maggie replied. "He didn't exactly want to eat with us this morning, though. I don't know what his deal is. Maybe we can meet up with him at lunch."

"Yeah, okay," said Beth, sliding her chair backward. "I have to run back to our cabin before morning activities. I'll see you later."

"Later," said Maggie.

She scanned the Mess Hall looking for Counselor Adah. Her eyes fell on Tom's table, where all of Cabin Two was laughing and jockeying for position to look at some indiscernible mushy gray concoction on Joey's plate. "Eat it, eat it," they chanted, pounding their fists on the table. Tom was right in the middle of it all, but stealing glances at Liv, who was sitting across from him.

Something simmered in Maggie. She clenched her fists under the table. This is not how the summer was supposed to go, she thought. That's fine if he wants to be around some other girl, but Tom was the last person on earth to buy into the petty vapidness of a popularity contest. He listened to The Clash and Radiohead for God's sake. This isn't him, she told herself over and over again. Her eyes narrowed. She thought of every mean girl she'd ever encountered back at home. Every girl who memorized Cosmopolitan from cover to cover, but had no idea who F. Scott Fitzgerald was. Every girl who showered Maggie with insults in her own daily ticker tape parade of misery. Tom was too smart to buy into this crap, this crowd. It sickened her, to see him so blithe around such stupidity—stupidity they would have mocked for hours back at home. But they weren't home. They were two hundred miles from home.

Hot anger coursed through her veins. She squeezed her eyes shut, to abate the burning throughout her body. Please let something good come from this, she thought, because I don't know how much more I can take. She really hoped someone or something was listening.

26

The Rec Hall was an oversized living room straight out of 1974. A large, wrap-around couch hugged the far corner of the room. Three wide stripes of brown, yellow, and orange were painted around all four walls, just under the windowsills. Several mismatched cushioned chairs were scattered around the outskirts of the room. In the corner closest to the entrance lived an overgrown fern in a sunken wicker basket. The linoleum floor was pockmarked and worn. Leaning stacks of folding chairs lined the walls, except near a wooden door with "JANITOR" stenciled on it.

"So, this is where the magic happens?" commented Maggie, looking doubtful. She crossed the room with Adah.

"Yep," sighed Adah. "And this...is the Lab." She swung open the door to the janitor's closet and tugged on a dangling string from the ceiling. The bare light bulb flickered as it swung back and forth. The room was small; the walls were lined with dusty metal shelves, holding plastic milk crates stuffed with records, cassettes, and a few CDs. A whiff of mildew exhaled into the Rec Hall.

Maggie scrunched her nose. "The...Lab? I think you meant the place where music goes to die."

"Don't be too put off by it—there's some cool stuff buried

in these crates. You just have to find it." Adah winked.

"We'll see," retorted Maggie. "So I just pick out some records and then play them at the dance?"

"No, you make a mixtape—there are a bunch of blank tapes in one of these crates."

"I'm happy to just play the records straight—"

"We want you to be able to dance, too!"

Maggie winced at her enthusiasm.

"So, you good? Don't forget to come up for air," said Adah.

"Got it. Thanks."

Maggie turned back to the closet. She flexed her fingers; they tingled with the anticipation of going in blind to create a mix for the dance. She grabbed one of the couch cushions and carried it into the Lab.

On one of the shelves in the closet sat an old record player and boombox. A pair of giant over-ear headphones, strangled by its long black cord, were in the crate next to the turntable, along with some blank cassette tapes. Maggie moved to the next crate filled with records—there had to be twenty or so— and lugged it to her cushion. She flipped through the stack, her thumbs grazing the ends of ABBA and Springsteen records. She paused when she landed on Tommy James and the Shondells' *Crimson and Clover*. She coaxed the vinyl disc from the sleeve and examined the silky smooth black surface for scratches. She then sized up the relic record player.

"Here's hoping," she mumbled, and slipped the vinyl onto the turntable. With the precision of a surgeon, Maggie guided the stylus to the very edge of the record and heard the clunk-clunk of the needle drop. She leaned backward, elbows propped on the couch cushion, pulled the headphones over her ears, and closed her eyes.

God, this song, thought Maggie. Tommy James's smooth voice had a way of instantly infecting you. It's the kind of song that seeps through your skin and owns you. It's beyond infectious; it's dangerous. Something about the tremolo effect of the guitar, something about the way the repetition builds before fading, something about the magic between the notes—it has the power to change the course of someone's life. She had always believed this to be true, from the very first time she heard it at the impressionable age of twelve. She was lying on her living room floor with her head next to her boombox, listening to the Top 500 on Oldies 103.3.

This song would be best during one of those barely moving slow dances, she decided. The serious ones you see in movies, when two people really want to be together, but the fates and directors won't allow it...except for that one dance. During that three and a half minutes, the rest of the world freeze frames, and their dance becomes everything.

This song had to go on the mix.

Maggie sighed and lifted the record from the turntable and returned it to its sleeve.

She made piles and wrote her picks on a napkin with a chewed up Bic pen, both of which she found on the floor near a peeling piece of tile. In addition to Tommy James and the Shondells, her "yes" pile after the first crate included The Beatles' *Please Please Me*, the *Footloose* soundtrack, and U2's *Achtung Baby*.

"Why can't these be in some kind of order?" she groaned, pushing a crate back onto a shelf.

"You have a better chance of discovering something when there's no order," replied a gruff voice. Maggie dropped *Automatic for the People* and spun around.

"Woody! I, uh, Kate said I could be in here—it's for the dance—the music, I mean—" she stammered.

"Yeah. Don't break anything," he replied, and turned to leave.

"Wait—is this, is the Lab—how did this all get here?" she asked.

Woody turned back and stared at her. "I don't know what you mean by 'lab,' but yeah, some of it is mine."

"Wow, so you're like, really into music then," she surmised.

"Am I?" He looked over his shoulder for a moment, then returned his gaze to her and pointed at the floor. "That your list?"

"Uh, yeah."

Woody motioned for her to hand it to him. Maggie cringed, her hasty first pass of selections being exposed to someone so soon. He scanned the napkin and then held it back out to her.

"Add some Billy Joel."

"Oh—you think? But, uh, which one? Like 'Uptown Girl'?"

Woody scoffed. "'We Didn't Start the Fire.'"

"But that's not really a dance song..."

"Think about it," he said.

"I'm not sure what you are getting at," she frowned.

"My hunches aren't usually wrong, kid," replied Woody, shaking his head as he left.

"What's with this place?" Maggie muttered. She slid another crate back into place and rummaged around until she found a red-and-black cassette jammed into its case. She examined it for a minute, shrugged, and slid the tape into its slot in the tape deck. She repositioned the headphones over her ears and pressed play. Cheering and classic eighties synth filled her ears. Her foot automatically started tapping along to Billy Joel's methodical retelling of US headlines and cultural significances.

Her thoughts returned to Woody's request for the song. Why would he want this played? And hunch? What hunch does he have? So it's a glorified history lesson, big deal. Ugh, whatever, she thought, and added it to her list. Maybe some try-hard camper will show off by singing along loudly to prove to everyone that they know all the words.

By lunchtime, Maggie had over an hour's worth of songs scrawled on both sides of the napkin. Outside the Rec Hall, she took a few steps into the sunshine, but stopped when something shiny caught her eye. She walked over to the glint, knelt down, and brushed away the pine needles around it. Wire-rimmed glasses. One of the lenses had popped out, and the other was cracked. The frame was completely warped— no—mangled. "No, these can't be," whispered Maggie. She picked up the glasses and examined them. Were they Jonesy's? The temple tips were caked in something dark— what she hoped was mud. Her stomach churned. She shoved the glasses in her pocket, took a deep breath, and walked toward the Mess Hall.

27

Inside, Maggie scanned the crowd for Ryan. He was at Cabin Two's usual table, his back to her. She walked with purpose over to it and tapped him on the shoulder.

"Look, Ryan, your girlfriend is here!" sang Joey.

Maggie reddened. Ryan threw a tater tot at Joey's head and turned to look at her.

"Uh, hey, what's up?" said Ryan coolly.

"Can I talk to you for a sec? I have something to show you," she said, ignoring Joey.

"I bet she does!" exclaimed Joey.

"Save it, clown," sneered Maggie.

The retort drew "oohs" from the rest of the table. Maggie glanced quickly at Tom, who immediately looked away. Right, of course he's not going to stick up for me sitting with this group of meatheads, she thought, because that would make too much sense. Rage simmered inside her. She turned her attention back to Ryan.

"I found something tha—" Maggie started again.

"That's great. I'm sure it's cool. I'll see you later, okay?" said Ryan, brushing her off.

"Sounds like a date!" interjected Joey, popping the tater tot Ryan threw at him into his mouth.

"Forget it." She shoved her hands in her pockets and stormed away, spotting Beth at their usual table by the window.

***

Ryan ran his fingers through his hair as he watched her walk away. "Joey," he said, rubbing his eyes. "Why do you gotta be such a dick, huh? Seriously, dude."

"What? What'd I say?" replied Joey, flecks of tater tot flying out of his mouth as he spoke.

Ryan gave him a hard look, then switched his attention to Tom. "And you're just gonna let Joey shit all over your friend like that? Just to keep in good with a Lifer?"

"No, I, she had it, it's fi—" said Tom, caught off guard by his accusation.

"That's sad, man. Really sad." Ryan scraped his chair backward against the linoleum floor and stormed off.

Outside, he stood near the bell, watching campers file out of the Mess Hall. After a while, Maggie appeared, alongside Beth. Her eyes briefly met Ryan's, before she veered to the right to avoid walking near him.

"Hey! Hey, Maggie! Wait! Hey—I can explain," Ryan littered qualifiers in her footpath.

Maggie stopped and turned to face him. "You can explain? You can explain! Okay, then, explain to me why I'm supposed to trust you—'Just trust me,' he says! 'All will be revealed,' he says!" She turned to Beth, incredulous, and then swung back to face him. "So I said, 'Okay, Maggie, trust him, it's fine—he won't hurt you. He won't treat you like garbage, because you hardly know him, but he seems like a decent human being!' And then, when I have something really important to show you—" Ryan winced, but she continued, "What do you do? You blow me off in front of your stupid friends! So, sure, go ahead, explain away!"

"I was a jerk. I'm sorry, okay? But I don't know how to make you understand that we cannot talk about this stuff in the open. You can't just come barging into the Mess Hall with some 'discovery' that could upend the camp! There are eyes and ears everywhere."

"Right, I'm supposed to just drink the Kool-Aid. No wait, the bug juice. But without any real explanation," she retorted.

"Yeah." Beth lowered her voice as two counselors walked by them. "How are we going to figure out what is happening behind the scenes if we don't know the whole story?"

"Because there is no 'whole story,'" said Ryan. "No one knows it." They moved through the woods toward the flag football field. "Most everything is speculation; there's no physical proof that anything sinister is actually happening at Kinross, but...honestly? This place is evil."

"Yeah, okay." Beth laughed.

"It is. Truly, deep-seeded evil. But no one knows what it is, or how it came to be, when it happens, why it happens, or how to stop it."

"Okay, hotshot, so how do you know all of this stuff then?" asked Maggie.

"I'm—I'm not exactly sure. Let's call it a hunch," Ryan replied. His eyes pleaded with her to believe him.

"You sound crazy. You know that, right?" said Beth.

"Shit," said Maggie, staring at Ryan. She reached into her pocket and pulled out the glasses. Her hand shook slightly. "Well, this might be some physical proof."

Ryan took the frame in his hand and closed his eyes. "Jonesy." He opened them again and searched Maggie's face.

"Wait, how do you know they were his?" asked Beth.

"I don't for sure," he said quickly. "But they look like something he'd wear."

Beth and Maggie exchanged skeptical glances.

"The way they're messed up, it doesn't look right. It doesn't look like they just fell off his face and someone happened to step on them," said Maggie.

"Right, and Mark said his glasses were fine when he got kicked out of camp. 'Perfect condition.'" Ryan felt the metal rims between his fingers. He examined the caked temple tips. "I think—I think this is blood. This isn't good," he said, shifting uncomfortably. He looked directly at Maggie.

"What's not?" said Maggie.

"We need more time to figure this out. You're going to have to become a Lifer. Both of you are," he said, nodding at them.

"But that means…" started Maggie, swallowing the realization like a mouthful of expired milk.

"Yup. You're going to have to get in good with Becky," sighed Ryan.

"No chance," she replied. "We'll find another way. Kate said I don't even have to worry about her."

"Right, I get that, but if she has a problem with you, she'll vocalize it day and night, until the counselors can't take it anymore. They aren't going to want to deal with her for the rest of the summer."

"He has a point," agreed Beth.

"And the best way to get to her is—" said Ryan.

"Tom," resigned Maggie.

"Exactly," said Ryan.

"So, what do we do now?" asked Beth.

They stopped walking. Ryan scanned the trees and ran his fingers through his hair.

"Hmm, how about this: Maggie, you try to get in with the she-devil using your Tom intel as bait. Beth, keep your eyes and ears open—eavesdrop on the counselors, chat up Woody—do whatever you can to get info on the campers who have 'left,' but make sure not to put out a concerned vibe. I'll try to recruit another Lifer to help us. We're going to need numbers if we're going to blow this thing wide open. And if anyone has any messed up dreams or whatever, we'll hash them out over breakfast. Everyone's still groggy. It won't draw as much attention. Cool?"

"Oh, so all is forgiven then, just like that?" huffed Maggie.

"Yeah, pretty much," replied Ryan, his eyes dancing.

28

Tom stood in a grassy clearing with Velcro flags hanging from his waist. Though the boys of Cabin Two were paired against the girls of Cabin Three, Mark and Hannah mixed the campers with the intent of a fair game.

"This oughta be good," griped Maggie. She looked across the field at Tom, who was stealing glances at Liv. Suppressing a gag, she caught Ryan's eye. He winked at her. Her face soured, more than when she ate a black cherry Warhead. Becky witnessed the exchange and snickered.

Maggie buried her disgust and used the opportunity to casually move closer to Becky. "Hey, Becky, so, uh, you were right—Ryan is kinda annoying."

Becky stood at the center of the field, with Liv not far behind. She looked at Maggie. "Told ya," she said, her nose in the air. "Maybe listen to me next time."

"Yeah, yeah, sure," Maggie pressed on. "Hey, uh, I know we got off to a bad start, but, like, thank you for giving me that heads-up, even though I didn't believe you. If you like, want any, uh, information on Tom"—she swung the conversation toward Liv—"I'm happy to help. Really."

"Oh, sweetie, Liv is doing just fine. Aren't you, Livey?" cooed Becky.

Well, at least I tried, thought Maggie.

"Uh, thanks," replied Liv, smiling a little.

Joey snuck up behind Corey and snatched the football out of his hands. He ran around the field laughing maniacally like a streaker on Superbowl Sunday.

"Dammit, Joey, we haven't even started yet," huffed Mark, rolling his eyes at Hannah before taking off to chase after him. He tackled Joey to the ground and grabbed at the football.

"From my cold dead hands!" screamed Joey, wrestling Mark onto his back.

"We can make that happen, pal!" said Mark.

Maggie shot a look at Ryan, who quickly looked away. Mark sideswiped Joey's legs out from underneath him. Joey face-planted onto Mark's chest. The ball came loose. Mark rolled away from Joey and stood up, shoving Joey to the side. Alex picked up the loose ball and tossed it to Mark, who was dusting off his shirt.

"Hey, I thought this was flag football, Coach!" whined Joey, shaking pine needles out of his hair and falling back into line. A jug of bug juice balanced on a tree stump at the side of the field, a stack of plastic cups standing at attention beside it. "Can I get a drink before we start?" He panted.

"No drinks! Get back on the field! Are we ready or what?" yelled Mark. A mumbled response incited Mark to repeat, "I said, are we ready to play or what?!"

"Game on!" answered Tom, clapping his hands together.

Maggie leaned toward Liv and said, "Quick, yell, 'Car!'"

"Huh?" replied Liv.

"Just do it, trust me. It's from *Wayne's World*," urged Maggie.

"Car!" yelled Liv.

Tom's face broke into a disbelieving grin.

Liv turned to Maggie and grinned. "Hey, thanks for that!"

"Sure thing," replied Maggie. Becky eyed her cautiously.

Mark tossed the ball back to Alex, who kicked off to the

other team. The game went as most teenage co-ed matches typically go: equal parts showboating and teasing. Guys feigned clumsiness as they reached for the flags around the girls' waists; girls shrieked while being chased—any excuse to touch one another. Tom grabbed Liv around the waist in an attempt to make her miss a catch. "Hey, no fair! Ref!" she squealed.

"You gotta grab the flags, Tom," commented Ryan. He shoved by him to get to the line of scrimmage.

"Yeah, I know," said Tom, his voice changing from jovial to abrasive.

Alex tossed the ball to Tom and said, "Hey, Tom, why don't you QB this one?"

"Okay," he said, jogging to the center of the field. "Set, hut!" He ran backward, waiting for his teammates to run their routes.

"Tom, I'm open!" yelled Maggie, wide open and running down the grassy field. He ignored her and instead saw Becky in the far left corner. The football spiraled through the air. She caught it easily and ran to the end zone.

"Touchdown!" yelled Hannah, throwing both arms up to the sky.

Tom looked at Liv with a sheepish grin. She laughed and shook her head. Maggie turned away at the sight of this.

"Great pass, Tommy!" squealed Becky as she circled back for a high-five.

"Thanks! Couldn't have done it without you," he replied, slapping her hand.

"Nice teamwork, guys," commented Mark. "Okay, take a break. Get some juice."

"Yeah, way to go," muttered Ryan as he brushed by Tom and Alex.

"Hey, man, what's your problem?" said Alex.

"Nothing," Ryan replied as he kept walking. Maggie was standing to the side of the field, grabbing a stitch in her side.

He stood in front of her, clenching his jaw.

"Uh, are you okay?" she asked, raising an eyebrow. "You look… tense."

"It's nothing."

"Sure it is."

"Your boy is a dick," he replied.

"First of all, he's not 'my' boy, and second, I thought we were trying to keep a low profile? I thought I was supposed to be the difficult one," she smirked.

"He's an idiot. He's completely unaware of what he's doing," he said.

"It's really not a big deal. He's just doing his own thing?" offered Maggie.

"I see the way you look at him—he shouldn't do this to you—not even giving you the time of day, it's obnoxious," said Ryan. He kicked a clump of grass with his foot.

"No, it's not like that with us," said Maggie, hesitating, "Yeah, we grew up together, so I know him really, really well. I know that he'll only eat bananas if he can dip them into Skippy peanut butter. I know that he watches The Breakfast Club when he's depressed. He leaves his window unlocked year round so if my parents start fighting I can have a place to sleep. Stuff like that. It's not that I care about the Liv thing, or him ignoring me," she said, motioning to the rest of them standing around the cooler. "What bothers me is how he's selling out. He'd never subscribe to any of this back at home. It's weird seeing him act this way." They paused to watch Tom throw back another cup of bug juice, laughing at Becky's reenactment of the touchdown.

"Yeah," said Ryan, "but you have this connection with him. You always will. You can't just write him off."

"Yeah, I guess I'm sort of stuck with him, but I'm not like, into him like that, or anything," she said. "I just hate watching him go from the coolest—I mean—one of the coolest guys I know, to some sort of all-American douchebag who falls all over himself to impress some precious flower. He likes The Clash for God's sake."

"It happens, I guess," commented Ryan.

"It's gotta be the bug juice, right?" she joked.

"Beats me. Only one way to find out." He smiled darkly. "Thirsty?"

"Funny," she said, punching him in the arm.

He looked away, failing to hide his grin.

29

Maggie found everything as she had left it earlier in the Lab. She dragged a crate from the back of the room over to her cushion and started flipping through more records. Johnny Cash, Tom Petty, The Verve—Tom would love this place, she thought. A wave of bitterness laced with regret consumed her. Why did she help Liv during flag football? And how could her best friend dismiss her like she hadn't been a part of his life for the past fifteen years? He was better than that, wasn't he? At home, they were inseparable—was the town of Bradford so small that all it took was being away from it for a week to completely write off everything they had? Maggie's mother always said you never keep your high school friends forever—maybe one or two if you're lucky. That seemed unfathomable. Could this be the beginning of the weeding out process, only starting with her closest friend?

She mulled over Ryan's comments. Maybe she did have feelings for Tom. Maybe that's what was causing her throat to close up every time he saw her talking to Liv. But no—no! It was Tom for crying out loud. Tom, who lost a bet to Smitty and had to skinny dip in murky Baker's Pond one night last summer. Tom, who sulked for the rest of the day if Kay's Omelette Shop was out of their squishy diner bagels—the

147

kind that stuck to your teeth when you took a bite. Tom, who thinks hot dogs and mac and cheese make a complete meal. Tom, who would argue straight up through the apocalypse that U2 will never produce an album better than *Achtung Baby*. No, the thought of liking him in that way was absolutely and unequivocally ridiculous.

Her thoughts paused when she came across a dusty copy of The Doors' self-titled 1967 release, tucked in the back of the crate. "Oh, no way," she mumbled, carefully guiding the record out of the sleeve.

She felt more paper in the sleeve. The inserts were in it, too, after all this time? This must be worth a fortune, she thought. She coaxed the contents out of the cover, excited to check out what sort of liner notes the band included. What fell out instead was a small envelope. It wasn't sealed; the flap had been pushed inside itself.

"Weird," Maggie said aloud. She hesitated, unsure of whether she should open the envelope. If this was Woody's collection, the envelope probably belonged to him. If he wanted something to be hidden, there's a good chance that he didn't want her, or anyone else, to find it. And who in their right mind would want to be on the bad side of the person in charge of all the camp meals? Maggie looked around the Lab. She leaned backward on her cushion and stretched out through the doorway into the Rec Hall, looking for any signs of life. Satisfied the coast was clear, she sat up and returned her attention to the envelope. Biting her lower lip, she unfolded the flap and pulled out a few yellowed newspaper clippings. She gazed at them without really looking at them, absentmindedly shuffling them like playing cards. It took a minute for her brain to process the information in her hands. Then her stomach bottomed out.

A creaking outside the Lab startled her. Her breath quickened. She shoved the clippings back into the envelope and hid them under her cushion. She turned back to the crate and pulled out a KC and the Sunshine Band LP, pretending to read the back.

"Knock, knock!" a cheery voice called out. "How's it going in here?"

Maggie looked up and smiled at Kate. "Oh, pretty good, thanks! This is a crazy collection!" She nodded at the record in her lap.

"I know, right?" Kate laughed. "Yeah, it's sort of a hodgepodge graveyard of music from former staff."

Maggie's eyes widened.

"You know, stuff no one wanted anymore?" offered Kate.

"Yeah, but there's actually a lot of good stuff in here. You just have to dig," replied Maggie.

"I knew I had made a good decision putting you in charge of this." Kate smiled, surveying the closet. "So what do you have so far?"

"I'm almost done," said Maggie, steadying her shaking hand to give Kate the playlist. Kate looked it over. Maggie glanced down, not wanting to see the reaction to her selections.

"Maggie, I have to say," said Kate slowly, "that this list is, well…perfect. It's phenomenal!"

"You think?" mumbled Maggie.

"No, I mean it. Dance aside—hell, camp aside—this is a killer mix. I knew I picked the right person for the job."

"Cool! Uh, thanks," replied Maggie, half grinning.

"You have no idea what I've had to deal with in previous summers," said Kate, shaking her head.

"I do, actually," said Maggie, letting out a little laugh. "I listened to a few of the tapes the other 'DJs' made…and well…you've had some pretty interesting dances."

"Tell me about it," said Kate, rolling her eyes. "I'll never forget the time a camper queued Janet Jackson's 'Again' three times in a row. By the end of the third play, campers were yelling, 'Again! Again!' It was madness."

"That sounds like a nightmare."

Kate nodded, laughing. "Well, it looks like you're all set—why don't we walk back to the cabins so you can get ready for dinner?"

Maggie shifted on the cushion, hoping that she slid the envelope completely under it. "Oh, I was just going to test the tapes again before dinner, if that's okay? I want to make sure they recorded properly, and that they won't jam in the camp stereo."

"Nonsense, Maggie, you've done incredible work. Let's get you out of this dusty closet and find some food. You can wrap up tomorrow night, after Community Service Day."

"Are you sure? I mean, I've made a mess. There's vinyl everywhere."

"Totally sure. No one will ruin your piles. Let's go."

"Okay." Maggie reluctantly stood up and glanced down at the floor, praying the corner of the envelope wasn't sticking out.

Kate switched off the lights and together they exited the Rec Hall.

"Maggie, I wanted to talk to you, too."

Maggie stepped over a rock in their path and glanced sideways at Kate. "Sure, what's up?"

"Well, it's two things, really. The first thing, and I know it's a shot in the dark, but…I wanted to personally ask you if you'd want to be a Lifer here at Camp Kinross."

They walked in silence for a moment.

"It would be pretty cool, for sure. But I thought…well, I thought I had to be in tight with more Lifers to even be considered? I mean, they either don't know me or don't particularly care for me," said Maggie.

"I understand what you're getting at. But the Lifers aren't the deciders, Maggie. They don't own your fate—you do. You determine what you want in life—it rests wholly on your shoulders, and no one else's. And normally I'd say, yeah, sometimes the other Lifers can impact a decision for a new Lifer to be initiated. But that's only if we're on the fence about them. With you, we definitely aren't. You would be the single greatest addition to our ranks because you are incredibly real. You're cool, you're selfless, and you're accepting—"

"Selfless?" Maggie laughed.

"You are!" said Kate, nudging Maggie with her shoulder. "I heard what you did for Liv earlier today during flag football. *Wayne's World*? Game on? Car?"

"Wait, how did you—"

"Counselor Hannah saw the whole thing. We see more than you think, Maggie. And I don't mean that in a creepy way. It's just that sometimes campers are so wrapped up in this world—your own world—that you can't see what we see. It's a product of your age. You can't see the forest through the trees." Kate laughed.

"Yeah, I was just trying to get in with Becky and them," admitted Maggie.

"Because you want to be a Lifer—and that's great! Anyway, that leads me to my next point," said Kate. They navigated a winding path leading to the clearing for the girls' cabins. Kate stopped and held Maggie's arm, stopping her, too.

"It's not a matter of choosing," said Kate, looking hard at her.

"Choosing?" asked Maggie.

"Ryan or Tom," she said simply.

"Oh, I, uh, well—it's not like that," stammered Maggie.

"Stop it. Stop being embarrassed, and stop beating yourself up over them. Do you think that you can only have one love in a lifetime? How ridiculous does that sound—you're only allotted one person, out of all the people, to connect with during your fleeting time on Earth, and that's that? That's rubbish."

"But I'm not in lo—"

"Look. It's not for me to judge. I just wanted to tell you, don't limit yourself. And don't get caught in the morality of it all, either, or it will eat away at you, until you're nothing but a pile of bones. Things change. People change. Circumstances change. People die. But the most important thing is to not let others rule your world. To thine own self be true, and all that. You can't choose who you fall in love with. It just happens. It sneaks up on you. It blindsides you. And it always comes back to that age-old certainty—the heart wants what the heart wants."

"Woah, yeah, okay," said Maggie, her face flush in the dark.

"Also, for the record, I see the way he looks at you," Kate knowingly grinned and elbowed Maggie.

"He? Who?"

"Ryan."

"What? No...we're just—"

"Forest through the trees," reminded Kate. "Now run along and get ready for dinner. Oh, and so about being a Lifer? You're in then?"

"Oh, right," said Maggie, smiling. "Um, yeah, okay."

"Excellent," beamed Kate.

30

"Draw four, dipshit. The color is...blue." Germ laughed, tossing down a wild card onto the pile of played Uno cards.

Joey grumbled, "Oh, come on!" and kept drawing. "You know I haven't had blue this whole game. You're just being a dick—"

"How could I even see your cards? You're sitting across from me!" insisted Germ.

"You kidding me right now?" started Joey. "I leaned forward to get that Cheeto that fell!"

"Don't drop it next time," said Corey, lying on his bunk, throwing a tennis ball against the ceiling.

"Unbelievable," sighed Joey. He finally pulled a blue deuce from the deck and slapped it on top of the discard pile.

"Your turn, Tom," prodded Alex.

"Oh, I thought we were taking a break while Joey pulled every card but blue," smirked Tom.

"At least he can pull something," said Ryan from behind a notebook in his corner bunk.

"Hey, Corey, give me that ball," replied Joey, irritated.

"Sorry, man, I would, but it's not blue."

"Speaking of blue balls, how's it going with Liv, there, Tommy?" Joey challenged.

"So far, so good," Tom said, shrugging.

"Reverse, your turn, Tom," said Alex.

"Dance is coming up in two days," said Germ.

"Yeah, what's the deal with that, anyway?" asked Tom.

The Lifers stopped what they were doing and looked at Tom in disbelief.

"What's the deal? What's the deal?!" exclaimed Joey. "The deal is that all bets are off at the dance. It's like the end of every fucking camp movie you've ever seen!"

"Yeah," added Alex, "it's a highway jammed with broken heroes on a last chance power drive."

"It's a Springsteen song?" asked Tom, bemused.

"It's that moment when desperation collides with desire to make some lasting camp memories. It's electric," added Corey.

"Uno," said Alex.

"Typical," replied Joey.

"We gotta get through Community Service Day, first," said Corey.

The screen door to their cabin squeaked open, and Counselor Mark waltzed through, catching Corey's ball midair.

"What's up, fellas? Almost ready for dinner? Who's winning?" He tossed the ball back to Corey.

"Not Joey," Ryan said, grinning.

"Uno," said Alex, tossing his card onto the heaping pile. He leaned backward, and stretching his arms to the sky, said, "Nice game, boys."

"Hey, Ryan, can I talk to you for a sec?" asked Mark, motioning him to come back into his room.

"Yeah?" said Ryan, throwing his notebook onto his bed. He stood up and followed Mark to his room.

"Hey," said Mark, lowering his voice. "I gotta talk to you about the flag football thing."

"I figured. I'm sorry. I didn't think—"

"No, that's fine, man. It's all good. You're not in trouble. But where did that hostility come from?"

"Eh, I don't know—Tom bugs me…"

"Yeah, that's what I wanted to know. I'm only asking because he's up for being a Lifer, so I wanted to know if there was anything we might not be seeing, that we should take into account before we induct him."

"Oh, nah, he's fine. He's just being kind of shitty to his friend from home."

"Do you think it's intentional?"

"I doubt it," replied Ryan.

"Right, right. Is it that girl you've been hanging with? What's her name—Maggie?"

"Yeah. She's cool."

"Yeah, I just came from our staff meeting," said Mark, lowering his voice even more. "Kate actually talked to her separately. She's going to be a Lifer, and she's already agreed. I thought you'd want to know."

"Really?"

"Yeah." Mark grinned, staring intently at Ryan.

"Oh, uh, that's cool. Hey, Mark? What's our community service tomorrow?" asked Ryan.

"I think some of you are going in town with some of the Cabin Three girls. Why? What's up?" said Mark, grinning more.

"Well, I was, uh, wondering…" Ryan hesitated. "Any chance you could pull some strings so I can get library duty with her? She's mentioned that she loves libraries, and, well, with the dance coming up and all…"

"Look at you, guy! I've never seen you like this over another camper. Yeah, I'll see what I can do, but no promises. Kate was pleased about whatever influence you've had on her, so it shouldn't be too difficult. Just lay off Tom, okay?"

"Yeah, sure, no problem."

"Better go get ready—we leave for dinner in five."

Ryan closed his eyes, and a kaleidoscope of images flashed through his mind. He cycled through the pictures until he came to the scene of her, in a grassy field rife with wildflowers at twilight, the scent of honeysuckle consuming. Her sundress flapped in the breeze; she was running. His heart skipped a beat, and he quickly blinked his eyes open to dismiss it all.

His thoughts climbed over one another like a never-ending Escher painting. How could she invade his life like this, in such a short period of time? He had never met anyone like her. It was like they had known each other their whole lives. They had a chemistry that not even Marie Curie could explain. Was it Camp Kinross? Were its charms finally affecting him, after all this time? And why hadn't this happened with the loads of other girls that he had hung out with during past summers? It certainly never happened with any of them, or with Becky.

Ryan's gut suddenly tightened as a new image and subsequent revelation entered his mind. A wall of fire and white light. Wet ground. A sickening, smacking noise. Screams. A searing pain in his forehead, then darkness. It was in that moment, standing in his cabin waiting to leave for dinner, that he realized he would never be able to really be with her, no matter how much either of them wanted it. And she was never going to understand.

31

The Mess Hall was buzzing with the rehashing of the day's activities and the banter of fast-formed, but well-seasoned friendships. Despite it only being several days into camp, the Kinross camaraderie was infectious; with every gulp of bug juice came a carefree confidence that was impossible to achieve in any regular school cafeteria. Maybe it was the warm lighting of the Mess Hall, or Woody's scratchy soundtrack playing through the tinny kitchen radio. Whatever it was, the ingredients were measured perfectly for serving a big helping of future nostalgia.

Ryan slid into a seat next to Maggie at their usual table by the window.

"Hey, guys," he said casually. Beth slid her tray over to make room for his.

"Hi," said Maggie slowly.

Beth stared at her, her eyes bugging out of her head. She chewed her food quickly.

"Tell him!" she hissed, prodding her fork in the air at Maggie, still rapidly chewing a piece of dry chicken.

"Um, a lot has happened in the last two hours, I guess?" Maggie lowered her voice. She turned to Ryan; his eyes were keenly focused on her, causing her to stammer.

"So I went to the room—the music room—no—the room for making out—I mean making the music for the dance, ugh, talk much!" She paused, exasperated. She looked away from Ryan and took a deep breath to start over.

"So I went to the Lab, where I'm picking out music for the dance, and I found something." She looked back at Ryan. His dark brown eyes were both stunning and unnerving. She blinked and shook her head a little. "Well, I think I found something. I'm not sure."

"What did you find?" asked Ryan. He took a sip of water and wiped his mouth with a paper napkin, not breaking their gaze.

"I was going through Woody's old records—" Her eyes lit up, and her voice started to rise.

"Shh," Beth reminded her.

"Right, right." Maggie nodded and lowered her voice again. "So I'm going through Woody's old records, and I came across The Doors self-titled album."

"Arguably their best," interjected Ryan.

"Right? Tom's always yelling about it being *Strange Days*, but it's definitely their self-titled—it has to be," exclaimed Maggie. "Anyway, this record is basically in mint condition, so I pulled it out of its sleeve to see if the inserts were in there…"

"And…" prompted Beth.

"And they were!"

"And?!" scoffed Beth.

"And also an envelope fell out with random newspaper clippings in it."

"Okay, so let's see them," said Ryan, eyes wide, leaning in.

"That's the thing," sighed Maggie. "Just as I found it, I heard a noise, so I had to shove it under the cushion I was sitting on because Kate came in."

"Shit," said Ryan.

"I know," sighed Maggie, defeated.

"So what were the clippings? That's where you left off when Ryan sat down," said Beth.

"I didn't get a great look at them—they were weird. One was a missing girl, I think—Penelope something? Another was about some local history of some sort. Lore maybe? I didn't get to read that one. The one that freaked me out was an article about opossum overpopulation. Remember my dream? Why am I dreaming about opossums, and then finding an article about them? There were handwritten dates on each of the articles, but I can't remember what those were, either."

Ryan played hockey with a stray pea on his plate. Beth looked out the window nervously, as if one of the wily creatures was lurking beneath it.

"Yeah, so that's about it. Oh, and Kate asked me to be a Lifer."

Ryan dropped his fork. "Really?" he said in disbelief. Maggie threw her dinner roll at him.

"Are you so shocked, so amazed, that I would get asked to be a Lifer—that you momentarily couldn't control your silverware?" she huffed.

"Basically," he said, his eyes twinkling.

"Ugh."

"So what do you think it all means?" asked Beth, cutting through the friction.

"Well," said Ryan, taking a bite out of the roll that Maggie had hurled at him, "I think we need to get back into the Lab, as soon as possible. We need to get that envelope, especially before someone else does."

"But who hid it to begin with?" questioned Beth.

"Maybe a camper from a previous week? I've listened to a few mix tapes made by other campers for the dance. I imagine they did exactly what I've been doing. I mean, who else has access to that room?" said Maggie, turning to Ryan.

"Beats me. It's mostly Woody's collection, isn't it? So

maybe him? I'm pretty sure most counselors just dump their old music in there, along with stuff that parents have donated to the camp and whatnot. Plus confiscated tunes from campers—things like that. That envelope could've come from anywhere, or anyone."

"Or maybe it's just a weird coincidence?" offered Beth. "Maybe you dreamed about opossums because you saw the article."

"No, no, I had the dream last night, and only just found the articles this afternoon," said Maggie, drumming her fingers on the table.

"Ah, right," said Beth.

"We gotta get into the Lab. We gotta get the envelope, and then we'll see if any of the stuff checks out at the local library," said Ryan.

Maggie grinned sarcastically. "Oh, right, okay, I'll just go ask Greg if I can have a pass to the nonexistent camp library. Sure."

Ryan grinned back. "Tomorrow is Community Service Day."

"Yeah, but we don't know our assignments yet," replied Beth.

"I guess we'll have to come up with something better if that doesn't pan out," said Ryan, grinning knowingly.

"You are just—just the worst sometimes, you know that?" said Maggie, growling in frustration.

"Thank you!" he replied cheerily.

"How do we get back into the Lab tonight?" asked Beth.

"It can't be tonight. I don't think—dinner is almost over, and there's no way we'd make it back before curfew," said Ryan, his face switching gears to serious. "No, it'll have to be early tomorrow morning."

"That seems sketchy, too," said Maggie.

"What choice do we have?" argued Beth.

"Wait! I know!" Maggie's eyes lit up. "What if I go talk to

Woody? Maybe he can help us out. He did come in one day while I was working on my mix. He seemed to take an interest in it. He wanted me to add a song for him."

"Woah, why didn't you tell us before?" asked Ryan, furrowing his brow.

"It seemed unimportant at the time? He's such a weird guy. I thought he was just off-kilter or something," replied Maggie.

"What song did he want you to add?" asked Beth. The campers from nearby tables began to clear their trays.

"'We Didn't Start the Fire' by Billy Joel," cringed Maggie.

"I can sing that entire song," said Beth.

Maggie and Ryan stared at her.

"What? I can!"

"Huh," said Ryan. "Okay, well, that's interesting—about Woody, I mean. I still think we need to get into that room first thing in the morning. Just tell Hannah you left something in there by mistake last night. Take Beth with you, so she doesn't think you're wandering around camp looking to get with some guy or something. I'll meet you here at breakfast."

Maggie's stomach churned. Maybe it was the tepid, underseasoned chicken, maybe it was the hasty plan they hatched in five minutes—a plan that could ruin her chances at becoming a Lifer, where she could spend the rest of the summer hanging out with Ryan. Something like this could potentially get them kicked out of camp...or worse. She swallowed the burning in her throat and said, "Okay. Beth?"

Beth hesitated. "We could get into real trouble if we mess this up," she said.

"Yeah," agreed Ryan. "But we have to do this."

They both looked at Beth.

She blinked and sighed. "Okay, I'm in."

32

"All right, pretties, lights out!" sang Hannah, standing in the doorway of the cabin with her hand on the light switch. The minty freshness of toothpaste drifted through the room. Maggie pulled on her sleep shorts and slipped into bed. She looked over at Beth in the bunk next to her and raised her eyebrows. Beth nodded reluctantly and motioned with her chin to Maggie's wrist. Maggie nodded in agreement, looked down, and frowned. She quickly jammed her hand under her blanket and rolled her bracelet carefully up her wrist and over her knuckles. Her fingers passed over the familiar knots. Tom.

A few summers ago, Tom's parents had whisked him away to Myrtle Beach for three weeks. He came home raving about all the mini golf he played, while his dad golfed at various country clubs the whole time. He told wild stories involving hundreds of hardcore, leather-strapped bikers who rode down the strip for Bike Week. While Tom pushed quarters into Mortal Kombat at the local arcade, he watched a fight between two bikers break out over a game of Skee-Ball. The rest of their gang looked on, eating soft-serve twists. While away, he also visited a plantation, picked up skim boarding pretty quick, and never saw an alligator…thankfully.

When he came home in early August, he and Maggie were

sitting on his front steps overlooking a cranberry bog. He took out a baby blue, teal, and white macrame bracelet and handed it to her.

"Here, I found this in a cool record shop down there. You would've loved it, Mags—vinyl from floor to ceiling. Anyway, there was a little dish at the cash register with these in it."

She took the bracelet and half smiled. "This is cool...but you didn't get me a record?!" she joked.

"That would have been a pain in the ass to transport! I went on our third day there—I wasn't gonna lug *Abbey Road* all over South Carolina for three weeks and keep it in whatever pristine condition you would've insisted." He laughed.

"Lazy," she replied, hitting him in the arm.

"Yeah, okay, I'll take it back then—I'll find someone who will—" he replied.

"Nope, I'm putting it on right now." She struggled at wrapping it around her wrist.

"You can't tie it with your teeth. You'll ruin it," he said matter-of-factly. "Here, let me do it."

The sun drooped behind the pine trees, making their tips look like silhouetted mascara brushes. A breeze dried the damp perspiration on their foreheads. Tom pulled tight the second knot.

Maggie looked up at him. "This is really cool, thanks—I'll never take it off."

"Yeah, it'd be pretty impossible after the knots I just tied." He laughed. She looked back down at the knots.

"Oh my god, how many did you tie?" Her eyes widened.

"Shut it. Wanna go watch a movie or something?"

"Yeah, sure."

Maggie stared at the cabin ceiling. She held the bracelet in her right hand, running her fingers around it under her covers. Hannah switched off the light, and darkness fell over the girls of Cabin Three. Maggie's eyes welled up. She shoved

the bracelet underneath her pillow and turned onto her side
to sleep.

33

She was transported to someplace small—a room. In the corner, a clock radio blinked 2:00 a.m. A bag of goldfish crackers and a board game sat on top of a wooden table hugging a wall. She heard a yawn and turned around. Ryan.

"What is this place? What are we doing here?" she asked.

"Huh?" he said, rubbing his eyes. "What are you talking about?"

"Where are we?"

"You said you wanted to play Scrabble, so let's get on with it. What do you want to listen to?" he asked, standing up from a couch and walking over to the clock radio in the corner. He turned on the radio and looked expectantly at Maggie.

"Uh, I dunno, whatever you want," replied Maggie, looking around the room for more clues, more understanding.

"Am I dreaming?" she asked.

"Nope, this is the real thing, baby," he slurred, smirking.

"Don't be gross," she remarked.

"You just lob 'em, and I hit 'em out of the park," he remarked. He turned the radio dial on the clock. The haunting pleasantness of Michael Stipe's voice filled the room.

"Oooh, R.E.M., great tune," said Maggie.

"I know," retorted Ryan.

"Ugh, let's just play. It's so late," said Maggie.

"You're the one who insisted on playing—I'm ready to sleep," Ryan yawned.

They set up the Scrabble board, placing tiles in their trays. Ryan took a handful of goldfish and offered her the bag. Maggie reached into it, and Ryan's eyes went wide with horror.

"What?" she asked, bemused.

"Don't just reach into the bag like an animal!" He took the bag from her and said, "Here, hold out your hands…"

"I'm not a two-year-old," she replied.

"Said the girl who just stuffed her whole hand in the bag!"

"Oh shut up. Fine, I'm ready for my snack!" she patronized, holding out her cupped hands. He dumped some crackers into her palms.

"If you're good you can have more," he smirked.

"Thanks, Dad."

"Go first," he said, nodding to the game board.

"Are we playing with a timer? Do we have a diction—"

"Just play," he said, rolling his eyes.

They took turns trying to outwit one another with triple word scores and argued the validity of obscure two-letter words.

"That's always that whole thing with this game—do you go for the word that makes you look really clever, or do you play exclusively for the points?" he posited.

"Stop, you're trying to mess with my concentration!" She rubbed her eyes and rested her chin on her hand. "Break, twenty-two points." She smiled, satisfied.

She studied Ryan's face while he took his turn. His intelligence was mesmerizing. Their banter was childlike, but calculated. There was an ever-present electricity between them—whirling electrons that she couldn't get to short circuit, even if she wanted to. Did his foot just slide on top of hers? Did he realize it was there, or did he think it was the bar connected to the table? The rush of adrenaline whipped her stomach into a tizzy, which only proved to be a further distraction.

He rearranged his letters on the tray.

"Come on, Ryan, go already…" she whined. Another R.E.M. song played. "Hey, that's weird—does your clock radio only play R.E.M songs?"

"Shh," he replied, tapping his fingers on his temples. After another minute, he looked up at her, his dark eyes somehow both expressive and hidden. It was like he was looking directly into her mind.

"What?" she asked, shifting in her seat. She was careful, however, not to move her foot. If he kissed her tonight, she thought, she wouldn't stop him. She was transfixed.

Ryan looked back down at his letters and slowly started to place tiles on the board. W.

Then he used the "e" from her "break."

Then he placed an "n" next to it.

Next a "d."

Then an "i."

Then a "g."

"'Wendig?' You're kidding, right? 'Winding,' yes. 'Wedding,' yes. 'Windy,' sure. But 'wendig' is definitely not a word. Did you flunk spelling in grammar school? Because that would explain this," she taunted.

"I wasn't done," he said calmly.

He then placed an "o" after the "g."

"Uhhh," said Maggie, still perplexed, staring at the board.

"Wendigo. Sixteen points," he said, looking back up at her, his eyes even darker.

"What the hell is that—I call bullshit," Maggie insisted. She looked at Ryan; an uneasiness replaced the buzzy electricity and consumed her by the second.

"Wendigo, Magpie," he repeated.

"Yeah, I get it—but I don't think it's a word."

"It is. Wendigo. If you remember nothing else from this, remember wendigo. Please, you have to."

Maggie stared at the board, concentrating on his letters. She looked back at him. He was blurry—a shadow of himself. The radio in the corner sped up R.E.M.'s "Electrolite" to triple time. Maggie looked at the clock—it was spinning off the shelf. She turned back to the table. Ryan was barely discernible—a mist. The Scrabble board levitated from the table, tiles flying through the air and ricocheting off the walls of the room. Maggie screamed. The ceiling cracked open; above, a giant black vortex loomed with streaks of white light splintering it. A deafening pain coursed through her body. Around the outside of the vortex spun hundreds of cawing birds.

"STOP!" Maggie yelled, her throat hot with bile. Her fingers felt like they had been dipped into a deep fryer. White light spun like hundreds of fireflies swarming around her hands. She screamed and squeezed her eyes tight. When she opened them, blood was all over the table, dripping from the Scrabble board onto the floor. Ryan was gone. The vortex was gone. Everything was silent. She looked at the game board. Three giant slashes ran through it. The hair on the back of her neck prickled. She turned around. Inches from her face was a horned horror with translucent, sagging skin. Its oversized mouth was crowded with razor-sharp teeth, each the size of a boomerang. It dripped blood and oozed green puss.

"Wake up!" she yelled at herself. The monster cocked its head. Puss spilled onto her shoulders as it unhinged its jaw farther—ready to snap shut around her neck.

"Wake up!" she demanded.

"Wake up, Maggie!" a voice commanded.

She bolted upright in her bed. A flashlight shined in her eyes. She squinted. "What? What's going on? Where am I?" Maggie asked.

"You were tossing and turning like a lunatic," Counselor Kate said, laughing quietly. "Come on. It's time for your Lifer initiation."

34

"I thought we couldn't leave our bunks after the night bell rang?" Maggie wiped the sleep from her eyes.

"You're with me. It's fine. Now get your shoes on and let's go," said Kate.

Beside her stood Liv and a girl she didn't recognize. Maggie grabbed her hooded sweatshirt and pulled on her Chucks.

Adrenaline pulsed through her veins. What were they going to make her do—slice their hands open to become blood sisters? Swallow goldfish whole? Sleep in a coffin? Fry like bacon? Her imagination sprinted through hazing scenarios—she had read plenty of books on secret societies and could recite *Dazed and Confused* by heart. Hopefully, this initiation didn't involve Ben Affleck's "FAH Q" paddle.

They stepped out of the cabin and into the night. Maggie shivered; there was a chill in the air, mixed with the uncertainty of their final destination, and the unsettling knowledge of the campers who were no longer at camp for breaking curfew. They stepped gingerly through the wet grass and weaved through the trees down the path that led to the camp entrance. In the small clearing ahead, another counselor stood waiting, a wide grin on her face.

"Girls, have you met Counselor Delilah?" Kate offered.

"Hi," the girls said in unison.

Delilah rubbed her hands together in front of her face, her eyes gleaming. "Are you ready to become a part of something super amazing? Eeek, I'm so excited for you! You don't even know how great this is going to be!"

The girls looked at one another. Maggie ran her hand through her hair and looked at Liv, who sent a weak smile back.

"Okay, girls, follow us," said Kate. They walked over to where they were all first welcomed to camp. The jagged tree stump was visible in the moonlight, fresh sap dripping down its sides like sticky tears. Delilah motioned for them to take a seat on the ground. Maggie and Liv sat, but the other girl hesitated. "It's wet, though."

"Is she serious?" Delilah asked Kate in disbelief.

Kate cleared her throat and turned to the camper, her face amused. "Now, June, if you want to be a Lifer, you're going to have to get past that. Becoming a Lifer is more than just getting to hang out at camp all summer. It's more than being a good influence on the other campers. It's also about becoming one with nature, and finding where and how you fit into this life."

"You should be so lucky," chided Delilah, "that the grass lets you sit on it. It regenerates year after year and lets us walk around on it and sit on it. It provides us with a truly beautiful aesthetic—in some ways I think it could be at the very foundation of nature. It has such a humble existence, and yet without it, we just might not exist."

June opened her mouth to argue, but thought better of it and promptly sat down. Maggie's eyes widened at the exchange. The conversation was received in delayed transmission to her brain, still heavy with sleep and the swirling nightmare that engulfed her not twenty minutes ago.

They didn't dare speak; their breath puffed silently into the dark air.

"Girls," started Kate. "First, thank you for being standout campers in your own unique way. You are truly exceptional, and I speak for everyone at Camp Kinross when I say that it has been an honor to have you here this week. You have brought intrinsic value to our establishment, and for that we are eternally grateful."

Maggie swallowed hard. Having someone eternally grateful to a fifteen-year-old seemed paradoxical to the whole concept of being a teenager.

"We don't pick Lifers every week of camp, either," interjected Delilah. "And to have three from one session is especially rare. Congratulations."

The girls looked at one another and exchanged sheepish smiles. Kate stood up and slowly paced back and forth in front of them.

"You're probably wondering what the actual initiation is," she said, looking at each of them. They nodded.

"Don't worry. It's nothing sinister, so you can stop looking at me with those deer in the headlight eyes!" Kate laughed, a little too loudly. "No, really, it's not bad. It truly isn't. We teach you a little Latin, go over your main objectives as a Lifer, and we take a drop of blood from you. We'll walk to the Infirmary and Counselor Eve will draw it from you."

"Blood?" Liv blurted.

"It'll be fine, I promise."

"Why do you need our blood?" Maggie's eyes widened.

"You don't have to become a Lifer, we're not going to force it on you or anything," said Delilah, grinning. "But if you accept, you get to stay the rest of the summer, and there are a few other, uh, perks."

Kate jumped in. "Well, we can save all that for later. It's just a little blood, that's all. It's part of the paperwork the state requires from us when we let kids stay all summer. Like a fingerprint, sort of. Are you ladies in, or what? Maggie?"

Maggie hesitated a moment. "Yeah," she said slowly. Ryan's words about needing to become a Lifer so they could solve this thing echoed in her head. "Yes, I'm in," she replied.

"Liv?"

"I…I guess so. Yes."

"June?" Delilah prompted.

"Well, I don't—it's just that—well, I mean the whole summer is a long time—it's not that I don't want this, I do, but…" June hugged her knees.

Kate exchanged a look with Delilah. Maggie caught Delilah running her tongue over the edge of her teeth, while maintaining a sympathetic smile.

"That's totally fine, June. Don't sweat it. We are thrilled you even considered it," said Kate.

"Can I just have, like, a day to think it over?"

"Eh, I'm afraid not." Kate frowned. "We have these procedures in place and do things a certain way on certain nights—it's now or never."

"Um, well…thank you so much? But I think I'm okay for now. I really appreciate the offer, though!" June replied, smiling as best she could with Kate and Delilah staring at her. "Um, do I still get to stay at camp for the rest of the week?"

"Of course!" said Kate graciously. "Delilah, will you take June back to her cabin? I'll go over the rest with Liv and Maggie."

"You got it," said Delilah. "Let's get you some sleep." She ushered June to stand up, and together they found their way back to the wooded path.

"I had a feeling about her," sighed Kate.

"What do you mean?" asked Maggie.

"Well, I was on the fence about her for a few days, whether or not she was Lifer material. I went against the nagging feeling in my stomach and invited her anyway. That should really be the first rule of being a Lifer—always go with your gut," Kate replied. She looked hard at Maggie and Liv.

"Were you, uh, on the fence with us?" asked Liv.

"Oh, God no. I knew about you two from day one. I have a knack for spotting Lifers. And you'll both be interested to know that Tom is being initiated right now, too."

Maggie and Liv exchanged uncomfortable glances and looked away.

Sensing the tension, Kate said, "You're Lifers now. You have to put all that aside. Understand? It's not worth it. It doesn't benefit you, or the camp. Got it?"

"Got it," said Liv.

"Yeah, okay," agreed Maggie.

A distant high-pitched scream echoed through the forest. Maggie and Liv sat up, shooting worried looks at Kate.

"What the hell was that?" asked Maggie, fidgeting with her fingers.

"Ah, so sorry, I should have warned you. There's a murderer on the loose."

The girls' eyes widened.

"Kidding! I'm kidding! Gosh, you guys are easily spooked! No, we have a fisher cat problem around here."

"Fisher cat?" Liv crossed her arms across her chest to keep warm.

"It's like a weasel, but way more vicious. It shrieks when it feels threatened and sounds like a girl getting murdered, doesn't it? Or what you would think that would sound like. Normally they hunt smaller stuff—rabbits, mice—but the population has gotten out of control over the past few years. Three years ago, we had an incident with a camper, which is one of the reasons why we have the bell curfew."

"Funny, I heard something about an opossum problem," added Maggie quickly.

"Yeah, we basically have a woodland creature problem, but that's nature for you." Kate said dismissively. "Okay, you girls ready to learn your Lifer objectives and have some blood drawn?"

"Sure," answered Maggie, still trying to process the information about the fisher cat. Why did they only hear it just now, right after June left? Was it a coincidence? She made a mental note to tell Ryan and Beth at breakfast.

"Okay, here goes." Kate cleared her throat. "The objectives of being a Lifer. Objective one: always look for ways to maximize your potential, to be your best. Live your best life at camp. Engage in every moment. Make other campers envious—not in an obnoxious way—but through encouragement. Show them that they can have what you have. It's infectious, and not only does it contribute to Kinross philosophy, it allows you to grow in unimaginable ways. You have the Kool-Aid, and you want other people to drink it."

"Or bug juice," said Liv. Maggie stopped herself from rolling her eyes.

Kate chuckled. "Yes, very good, Liv. So yeah, you genuinely want campers to be drawn to what you have, but not for your own personal gain. It's a shift in self that has to happen. This is what you're working toward."

As if reading Maggie's thoughts, Kate continued. "Yes, a lot of Lifers struggle with this: they get caught up with the power they wield within their social stratosphere. It's understandable—they're only human! You don't acquire superpowers once you become a Lifer, unfortunately. But you do have the tools to spin your destiny in a strong and compelling way."

She continued. "Lifer objective two: As a Lifer, you are our eyes and ears. You're in the trenches. And while we 100 percent condone campers having the best summer of their lives, we have a zero tolerance policy for anything that will compromise the purity of what we are trying to achieve here."

"Purity?" asked Maggie.

"Yes, purity. We are providing the most wholesome adolescent experience in New England. Hell, maybe the whole country! We cannot have it sullied by a few brazen kids who want to take advantage of the system, by messing with our rules and pushing the boundaries."

"Okay, I get that, but then why do Lifers say things like, 'Oh, just wait until the dance—all bets are off—that's the night to make memories.'" Maggie furrowed her brow.

"It's a bit of a fine line, I'll give you that," agreed Kate. "We just don't want the line crossed. We don't need any teen pregnancies on our hands. We don't need an aerosol can to accidentally blow out a camper's eye, just because they thought it would be a good idea to sneak into the Mess Hall and try whip-its for the first time. But we do encourage more than your average camp, as far as teenage freedoms. We want you to have that kiss outside the Rec Hall after the dance! We want you to be able to joke and play pranks on one another! We want you to have those classic movie moments, but without permanent consequences. You can get 'some,' just not 'all,' you know?"

"Yeah." Maggie leaned back onto her hands, thinking. Maybe she wasn't confident enough when she was with Ryan. Maybe she should go for it, even if the potential rejection scared her more than her subconscious dream screen that's been playing out each night. Now that she was a Lifer, she had a little more time to gauge it, anyway.

"So, yeah, that's about it. Any other questions? Liv?"

"It sounds great." She smiled. "Do we stay in the same bunks the whole summer? Do we call home to tell our parents?"

"Yes and no. I know it seems strange to have so many Lifers bunking in the same cabin, but sometimes it happens that way. It's not a big deal to us—you see enough of the other campers in your activities and at the Mess Hall—we don't worry about the high concentration. Plus it's good to have you guys together—Lifers need encouragement, too. And no, we call your parents for you, and if there's any issue on their end, we let you know—there usually isn't. Parents love their free time, no offense."

"Right," said Liv.

"Okay, so you know the basics, the goals, your general responsibilities. To sum it up, we want you to have the most fun you can have without going off the rails. And if you slip up once, we are usually more forgiving with the Lifers than with the regular campers—we've invested a lot of time and energy into your potential. Don't worry. You two will be fine. Let's go get that blood drawn, then I'll take you girls back to your bunk."

35

The Infirmary resided in a small hut, just beyond the Mess Hall. It wasn't a bastion of newness or order, but it was clean enough. The roof was an uneven pile of dilapidated shingles, and the screen door swung askew on a single squeaky hinge. Inside, medical supplies were haphazardly shoved onto shelves: boxes of overflowing gauze, hydrogen peroxide, a few IV bags, half-torn open boxes of Band-Aids, rubbing alcohol, tweezers, packaged syringes. A stethoscope was draped around a rusty nail hammered into the wall behind a sea-foam green metal desk. Two Mess Hall chairs sat in the corners of the room. A small bookshelf resided under the sole window, where a wilting, viney houseplant lived out its last moments.

"This place has seen better days," said Maggie under her breath. Rummaging could be heard from a hidden alcove. Kate rapped her knuckles on the door trim and sang out, "Knock, knock!"

The rummaging stopped and out popped a bug-eyed waif of a woman with dull, wavy brown hair and oversize metal-rimmed glasses.

"Kate! Oh good, you're here. The boys just finished, and I was digging out the last of my syringes. I just can't seem to find them." She frantically scanned a basket filled with shiny instruments. Maggie cleared her throat and motioned to one of the shelves on the wall.

"Oh, right, yes, thank you! And you are?"

"Maggie," Kate interjected, "and this is Liv. Girls, this is Counselor Eve. Thank you for fitting us in so late, Eve, as always."

"Of course, of course, of course," said Eve with a dismissive wave. "It's an honor to be able to do this! You know, being a part of something so big—"

"Indeed," said Kate, cutting her off. "Who's up first?"

"I'll go," said Maggie. "Unless you want to go first, Liv?"

"No, thanks." Liv reluctantly stepped away from Eve. Maggie turned to her. Though they were standing under a cool fluorescent light, the color had drained from Liv's face. She looked down and shook her head.

"I don't do so well with blood."

"Blood? Oh, dear girl, don't worry about that," assured Eve. "You won't have to see a thing. Besides, this is far better than the alternative, if you get what I mean."

"No, I'm not sure I under—"

"Maggie, why don't you have a seat over here." Kate ushered her to a corner chair. "And, Liv, why don't you look out the Infirmary door to preoccupy your mind." Maggie picked up a pile of newspapers from the chair she was told to sit on and glanced briefly at the top headline. It read "Abbottsville Husband and Wife Missing—Police Baffled." She scanned it for a date. Last year. She placed the stack of papers on the floor and sat down. Her muscles tightened when the pinch of the needle pierced her arm. She watched Liv staring out the door. Did she just shudder?

"Okie dokie, honey, you're all set. Hold the gauze on it for a minute. I'll put a piece of tape over it—I just have to find it." Her eyes darted around the room like two Mexican jumping beans desperately trying to take flight.

"Liv, you're up," said Kate, motioning Maggie to stand over next to her. Liv looked whiter than a ghost.

"Are you sure you're okay?" asked Maggie, holding the gauze tight on her arm. "I can, uh, hold your hand or something, to get you through it?"

"Thanks, I think I'm good." Liv swallowed hard and squeezed her eyes shut.

"How about we learn our Latin mantra while Liv finishes up—to take her mind off it?" Kate smiled.

"Good idea," said Maggie.

"Okay, here it is. 'Corvus oculum corvi non eruit,'" said Kate, looking from Liv to Maggie. "Say it with me, 'Corvus—oculum—corvi—non—eruit.'"

The girls stumbled through the pronunciation, but after a few tries, both were riding without training wheels.

"What does it mean?" asked Maggie. "My high school doesn't offer Latin."

"Literally, it translates to 'a crow will not pull out the eye of another crow.' But basically it means unequivocal solidarity. At all costs. You're completely loyal and in it till the end. You will eat, sleep, and breathe this. Live it. It encapsulates everything we stand for at Kinross."

Liv wobbled as she stood up from the chair. Eve gathered the dark red vials and made a little notation on each one.

"I'll just, um, I'll take care of these, Kate. You girls are all set."

"Great, thank you, Eve," said Kate. "Come along, girls, you can still catch a few hours of sleep before the morning bell."

Maggie and Liv shuffled out of the Infirmary into the low sitting fog in the woods. When they reached their cabin, Kate carefully opened the screen door to avoid its audible announcement. "Good night, Lifers," she whispered with a grin. "See you in the morning!"

She ducked out, closed the door slowly, and disappeared into the night.

Maggie stepped on the heel of her shoe to slide it off. A hand caught her arm. She turned. Liv's face was as white as it had been before her blood was drawn. "What is it?" whispered Maggie, not wanting to wake anyone, especially Becky or Hannah.

"I—I saw something. Something in the woods." Liv pressed against the wall to stop her hand from shaking. "I didn't believe it—don't believe it. But whatever it was, it was—not right. It was terrifying."

Maggie put her hands on Liv's shoulders. "What was it? What did you see?"

"You—you don't think I'm crazy? I mean, I know you don't like me, but—"

"Just tell me what you saw," insisted Maggie.

"I—I'm not sure. But it was tall. And fast. I couldn't really make it out, but I know that it—it—it saw us." Liv bit her nails.

"How do you know that?"

"Because for a split second, I saw a head—or what I thought might be a head. I saw teeth. A mouth. It was big. But I only saw it because it turned away. It had been facing the—the—the Infirmary."

"And you're sure it wasn't a bear or some other creature?"

"It wasn't. There's no way—"

"Jesus. Okay. Well, I guess you're in this with us now, too."

"In what?" Liv rocked back and forth on her heels.

"We'll talk tomorrow, okay? I mean, I guess we can always be friends under the guise of both being new Lifers, and well, Tom," Maggie thought out loud.

Liv ignored her. "Maggie, what if it comes—"

"We can't worry about that right now. What we need to do is—"

"Maggie, they have our blood! What if it smelled it and—" she spiraled.

"Stop it! We'll talk tomorrow. God only knows what time

it is right now. Everything is more terrifying in the middle of the night. We'll find a way to hash it out in the morning, okay?"

"Okay," hesitated Liv. She stood in between the beds, staring through the unlocked screen door.

"Night," whispered Maggie, sitting down on her bunk. She pulled off her hooded sweatshirt, and after briefly replaying the plan that she was supposed to hatch in a few short hours, collapsed into her pillow.

36

The morning bell rang. Chickadees twittered amongst the scrub trees between the girls cabins. Beth was already pulling on her sneakers, while the other girls groaned and flipped over, looking for more sleep under their pillows. Maggie yawned and sat up. Glancing around, her eyes landed on Liv's bed —she was out cold.

Maggie swung her feet to the floor and reached for her clothes. Her polo and shorts were piled next to her bed like a rumpled accordion. She reached under her pillow and took out Tom's bracelet. She shoved it into her pocket, looked at Beth, and nodded. They crept down the little hall to the back of the cabin, and into Hannah's room.

Hannah's walls were covered in easel paper with painted inspirational quotes, like "Try to be a rainbow in someone else's cloud" and "A ship is always safe at shore, but that's not what it's built for." Dried forest flowers hung over the sides of dusty mason jars, cluttered on top of her bookshelf and nightstand. Her dresser housed a collection of essential oils and a small Tibetan flag. A dusty, sun stained picture of Hannah with two other counselors was taped to her mirror. It looked like it had been taken years ago; they looked much younger, happier.

Beth and Maggie exchanged looks. Maggie leaned over the end of Hannah's bed and shook her foot. Hannah haphazardly kicked under her blanket, rolled over, and continued to sleep. Maggie shook her foot again.

"Hmm? Everything okay?" Hannah lifted her hanging arm—it had fallen off the bed during her slumber - and rubbed her face.

"Hannah? It's Maggie."

"You okay? You can sleep for twenty more minutes you know," yawned Hannah, rolling over again.

"I haven't gotten much sleep," whispered Maggie, "See, I lost my bracelet. I think it may have fallen off in the Lab."

"The wha…" Hannah asked.

"Oh, sorry—the Rec Hall - I'm making the mix for the dance, remember? Anyway, my wrist got caught on one of the crates and I think it broke off or something—is it okay if I go look for it quickly before breakfast?"

"Uhh," Hannah rubbed.

"I'll take Beth with me, and we'll head straight to the Mess Hall after, I promise."

"Did you get initiated last night?"

"Yeah."

"Did the morning bell ring yet?"

"Yep."

"Okay, fine, yes, just stop talking. Take Beth," yawned Hannah, and pulled the covers back over her face.

The girls left Hannah's room and tiptoed out of the cabin. The grass was fresh with dew. Translucent insects zipped happily through the air. Beth and Maggie scurried down the paths of pine needles to get to the Rec Hall, barely saying anything to one another. They didn't encounter anyone on their way, and fortunately the Rec Hall door was unlocked.

"I doubt they lock anything around here," commented Beth. They carefully wiped their feet at the door and moved across the Rec Hall. Maggie opened the door to the Lab and gasped.

The room was completely clean. Her cushion had been returned to the couch. All of the record crates had been returned to their proper spots on the metal shelving. The pile of Maggie's music picks, along with the tape that she created, were stacked neatly next to the stereo.

"Oh, shit!" she exclaimed, spinning around.

"What?" asked Beth, looking around for something unusual.

"No, no, no!" Maggie wailed. "This isn't how I left this place the other night, when Kate insisted that I leave with her! You know, before I could stash the envelope!"

"Oh, man—do you think?"

"I don't know what to think. Shit, if Kate found that envelope - I don't even —I mean, she initiated me last night, so she would have known-"

"Oh, well congrats to that, I guess," muttered Beth. "Looks like I'm going home at the end of the week."

"Maybe I can talk to Kate about you? She seems reasonable, and one of the other girls who was tapped turned it down. But if we don't find that envelope, I'm definitely screwed. Let's look around here. Quick, help me—maybe it's in another record sleeve."

They combed through records, opening up each and peeking down into it looking for a white envelope. After about ten minutes Beth sneezed and said, "I don't think it's here."

"Shit, shit, shit!" Maggie looked around the room, as if the envelope might manifest out of thin air; as if someone might have conveniently taped it to the back of the Lab's door for her to pick up at a later date.

"We better head over to breakfast," resigned Beth.

"Wait!" Maggie stopped searching as an idea flashed over her widening eyes.

"What?" asked Beth.

"That's it! We have to get to breakfast! We can ask Woody!"

"Woody, of all people, won't want to talk to us right before the breakfast rush. Besides, he bristles anytime any camper directly interacts with him."

"I know, but we have to try! If he put this room back together, that means he has the envelope, or he did something with it."

"Yeah, but Maggie, what if he isn't on our side?"

"We have to take that chance."

"Do we, though? He feeds us."

"True, but I think it's worth a shot—we gotta get over there before the other campers start arriving. Come on!"

They ran out of the Rec Hall.

"Maggie, wait!" Beth huffed, as they reached the clearing before the Mess Hall.

"Huh? What?" Maggie tugged at the bottom of her shirt. In the distance she could make out campers heading towards the Mess Hall.

"Your bracelet—put on your bracelet. Our cover story!"

"Oh, right, thanks," said Maggie, and removed the bracelet from her pocket and forced it over her wrist. They caught their breath as they walked up to the Mess Hall doors.

The aroma of bacon and scrambled eggs slapped them in the face. The Mess Hall was empty, except for Woody and his assistant, who cracked eggs into a giant metal mixing bowl. They wandered over to the food service window. Woody busied himself making hamburger patties by grabbing chunks of ground beef from a large metal bowl, and methodically flattening them between both palms. His assistant whisked the egg yolks with an unusual amount of zeal, droplets of yolk flying through the air.

Maggie coughed. "Um—Woody?"

Not looking up from his patty production, Woody barked, "Mess Hall isn't open yet —run along."

"Yes, right, we know," Maggie spoke quickly. "It's just that we have something to ask you."

"No special orders, kid," replied Woody, stacking another burger on top of a prep tray. The tower of patties leaned precariously into one another.

"Oh, no, it's nothing like that," Maggie went on. "We wanted to talk to you about The Lab? And the music for the dance? You see—"

"Hey Curtis, go check the drink jugs, will ya? Leave the eggs, you've beat them enough." Curtis put down the whisk and slouched out of the kitchen. When he was out of earshot, Woody looked up at Maggie and Beth and grunted, "I'm not sure how I can help you with your dance."

"It's not that, Woody, see-" Maggie's voice became an exasperated whisper. She could hear laughter in the not so far off distance. "See, I left something in the Lab the other night, something I found—an envelope—and now it's gone, and the room is totally clean. I need to find it. Can you help us? "

Woody blinked twice, staring through Maggie and Beth. Beth nudged Maggie's arm.

"Look," Maggie continued, "if you know what I'm talking about, please help us. I think something big is—"

"It's not my fault you didn't clean up after yourself."

"What?"

They stood in silence, staring at each other. Woody slapped another patty down on the prep tray. The girls flinched.

"So you aren't going to help us then?" Maggie's palms started to sweat. A heat seared across her forehead.

"I didn't say that," said Woody evenly. He glanced over at the Mess Hall door. Campers were milling just outside of it.

"Okay, so, uh, what then? You will help us?" Beth whispered. The screen door slammed behind the first campers entering the Mess Hall.

"Definitely, maybe," said Woody deliberately. He carried the metal bowl with pink crumbs of meat to the sink. Maggie thought she saw the corners of his mouth twitch upwards.

She tipped her head backwards and blew air out of her mouth as she turned away. "You've got to be kidding me!"

"What the hell does that even mean?" asked Beth. They grabbed some water and made their way to their usual table.

"I don't even know," replied Maggie, rubbing her head. She pulled out her chair and plopped down, propping her head up with her hand. She perked up a little when she saw Ryan walking through the Mess Hall doors.

"Oh man, I have so much to tell you two about last night," Maggie said.

Having secured their table, they both returned to the food line to get breakfast. Maggie gave Ryan a sleepy smile as their paths crossed. He grimaced in return, and went to sit down at their table. In line, Maggie felt a tap on her shoulder. She leaned back and looked over her right shoulder.

"Oh, hey Tom," she said, dropping silverware on her tray.

"Hey, you! How's it going, huh? Things great? You look a little -"

"Tired, yeah, thanks. You're peppy."

"Are you tired for the same reasons I'm tired?" he raised his eyebrows several times and punched her lightly in the arm.

"Oh god, Tom, it's too early for euphemisms," she said, moving her tray along the line.

"Ha ha, no, Mags, that's funny. I mean, were you up late, too, for..." he leaned into her ear, "initiation?"

"If I tell you, I'll have to kill you," she said flatly.

"Oh Mags, always such a jokester. So you were!" he exclaimed, taking a plate of well done bacon and scrambled eggs.

Maggie stopped and faced Tom. "'Jokester'? Tom, do you even hear yourself? Who are you right now?" she hissed.

"What's your problem, Mags?"

"Sorry, I'm just really tired, that's all," said Maggie, backpedaling. "Yeah I was tapped. I need a coffee—why can't they serve coffee here?"

"No idea, but I hear you. Alright, I'll catch you later," Tom meandered over to his usual table. Maggie shook her head and sighed.

When she arrived back at their table, she found Beth recounting what they didn't find at the Lab, and their interaction with Woody.

"It's weird, though, right?" reiterated Beth.

"Yeah, he's pretty cryptic, If he was trying to help you, he was very careful with the words he chose. Morning, Magpie," he said, grinning around his orange juice straw.

"Hey," said Maggie, rubbing her eyes.

"So what did he say specifically?" asked Ryan.

"I asked if he would help us and he said 'definitely possibly' or some weird word contradiction like that," said Maggie, crunching on a piece of bacon.

"No, it was something else, but close to that," interjected Beth.

"He may have been giving us a clue or something—think," Ryan urged.

"Uh…" stalled Maggie, "It was something like 'sure maybe,' or —"

"That's it!" Beth exclaimed, "He said, 'definitely maybe.' But I don't see how that does us any good."

"Hmm, maybe it's a catchphrase in a movie," said Ryan.

"Or a book?" offered Beth.

"Wait," said Maggie, swallowing a mouthful of egg. "Woody is an audiophile, right? If it's anything, it's probably music-related. Like a lyric or something."

"Good call," agreed Ryan. He narrowed his eyes in concentration, flicking through the cataloged music in his mind.

"Did you catch what was playing on his radio this morning?" asked Beth.

"It was turned down too low, I think it was Keane or Oasis

or something," said Maggie.

"That's it," said Ryan, slapping his palm on the table. "I knew that I knew it! I'm surprised you two don't." He smirked in victory.

"What?" said Maggie and Beth in unison.

"I said maaaaybe..." sang Ryan, smirking.

"Oh my god," said Maggie. "Oasis! *Definitely Maybe*! He was definitely trying to tell us something!"

"'He was *definitely* trying to tell us something? You dork," smirked Ryan.

"Oh shut up. And I know who Oasis is—I love them. I'm just beyond tired," remarked Maggie.

"It's cool, we know who the real fans are," he shrugged.

"Okay hot shot, so what is he trying to tell us?" retorted Maggie.

"Who am I, Keanu Reeves? That's your job," replied Ryan.

"Maybe there's an Oasis record in the Lab?" said Beth.

"I don't remember seeing one," said Maggie, rubbing her forehead, "And I'm not sure if I'm going to get another chance to go back before the dance. Today is Community Service day, right? We'll be gone all day."

"Yeah, but I bet Kate will let you go over early before the dance, to make sure everything is prepped," said Ryan. "Also, I think I may have another Lifer we can ally with—Corey."

"You make it sound like we are going to war," said Beth.

"We may as well be, we don't know what we're up against," replied Ryan.

"Wait, wait," said Maggie, holding up her hand while taking a sip of water. "I have more information."

"Really?" asked Beth.

"Go on," said Ryan.

"Well, first, I had another insane dream. It was right before Kate woke me up for initiation last night. There were a ton of black birds flying around this dark tornado. But it wasn't a regular looking tornado. I don't know—it was more sinister."

"Do you remember anything else about it? Anything at all?" asked Ryan.

Something in the tone of Ryan's voice jolted her memory. "Yes, actually," she said, but then stopped herself short. She couldn't tell Ryan she was dreaming about him—she couldn't let him have that kind of leverage on her.

"I was playing Scrabble and… a word appeared on the board. WENDIGO. And then the ceiling of the room blew off and hell flew in."

"What is 'wendigo'— I've never heard that word in my life," said Beth.

"Me either, I sure hope you challenged that one," winked Ryan. Maggie stared at him. How could he say the most fitting things for something he had absolutely no idea about?

"Yeah, I dunno what it is. It's probably nothing," said Maggie, desperately trying to dismiss the blush creeping up her cheeks.

"This is good stuff. If one of us lands library duty today for community service, we can hit the books," said Ryan,

"There's more," Maggie put her elbows on the table and leaned in towards them.

"More to the dream?" asked Beth.

"Yea—No! No, not more to the dream," Maggie replied, flustered. Ryan swirled his straw around in his orange juice dregs. Was he grinning? "No, the other thing that happened—Liv was tapped last night."

"Seriously? Her?" asked Beth.

"Yeah, I know, but whatever, that isn't the point. Last night three girls were tapped, but one declined."

"Oh," said Ryan, shifting in his seat.

"Yeah, so then this other counselor allegedly took her back to her cabin, and Kate took Liv and I to the Infirmary to have our blood drawn or catalogued or whatever the hell it is they do with it—it wasn't clear, but I wasn't about to ask. When it was my turn, Liv looked out the door because she can't handle needles. But when we got back to our cabin she looked terrified. She said she saw something in the woods. And she said that 'something' was watching the Infirmary, and it was tall, and fast, and oh! Before we walked to the infirmary, we heard a blood curdling scream, but Kate said it was a fisher cat?" Maggie took a deep breath. "Yeah, so that's all I've got."

"Oh, wow." Beth anxiously twisted her napkin around her finger.

"Okay, before you spiral out, let me just say in Kate's defense, there is a huge fisher cat problem, and most likely an opossum problem. The other thing is, let's say for the sake of argument that Liv saw one of those animals in the tree, staring at her. It's the middle of the night, you were both woken from dead sleeps, people can see weird shit that isn't real," said Ryan.

"You don't believe me," Maggie pinched the bridge of her nose and rubbed her eyes.

"No, I didn't say that. I'm saying we need to look at every angle. What's the big picture? The end game? We need more evidence before we can come out blazing with accusations. We'd be kicked out of camp faster than Joey gets a hard on when any female walks by."

"Ew," said Beth. Ryan grinned, then turned back to Maggie.

"Who was the other recruit—the one who declined?" he asked.

"Some girl named June," said Maggie. She scanned around the Mess Hall, now a full house of hungry campers. "I don't see her, though. They wouldn't have sent her home, right? They said she could stay for the rest of the week."

"I don't know," said Ryan, distracted. He pulled his tray towards him and stood up.

"Where are you going?" asked Beth, incredulous.

"I gotta go. I gotta talk to Corey. Here's hoping we get library duty," said Ryan, giving them a tight smile.

"Fingers crossed!" Maggie rolled her eyes.

"I don't get him," said Beth.

"Tell me about it," replied Maggie.

"Seriously, though, what's his deal? Is he trying to spin this stuff in our heads? And why doesn't he sit with his friends anymore? I don't care, but it's weird. I thought that Lifers had an unbreakable bond. Seems weird he branched out."

"No idea," said Maggie, twisting her fork in a bit of cold scrambled egg. "I don't get what any of these things mean— the weird occurrences of missing campers that were 'sent home', my messed up dreams, the overpopulation of creepy woodland creatures, Woody, the articles from the Lab—it's not adding up. Something is going on here, but I just can't put it together." She squeezed her fists in frustration.

"Yeah, I know what you're saying," said Beth. "At least you get to stay the summer to figure it out."

"Oh please, I'd rather not. I guess some parts are cool, but this place creeps me out."

"Which parts—the Ryan parts?" Beth grinned.

"I'm leaving," Maggie rose from her seat.

They cleared their trays and left the Mess Hall. Outside, a crowd had gathered around the small bulletin board affixed to the side of the Mess Hall's entrance.

"Hey, don't push! You guys need to take turns! Find your bunk number and name, and your community service will be next to it. Then get out of the way so others can see—let's go guys! Move it along!" yelled Mark.

Maggie and Beth shuffled to the front of the crowd. Maggie drew an imaginary line in the air to connect her name to her assigned community service assignment. Library Assistance. She quickly looked at the Cabin Two Boys list and saw Ryan's name. She grinned and looked down before fighting through the stream of campers angling to see where they were placed. Scrawled next to his name was also Library Assistance.

37

"So what did Beth land for community service?" asked Ryan. He and Maggie stood side by side in front of a cart, organizing books to be reshelved.

"Um, something to do with keeping the elderly company, I think?" replied Maggie, squinting at a book spine. "Is this a B or an eight?"

"Eight, I think. Ah, she landed Pinegrove duty. It's not so bad there. Mostly a bunch of old people playing cribbage and rummy-o, looking for new ears to listen to their 'when I was your age' stories."

"Right," said Maggie, painfully aware of Beth's buffering absence from their small group. "I wonder why she didn't get library duty with us, though."

"Well, they can't exactly play favorites," said Ryan. He held up a copy of *Forty-Five Easy Alternatives to Indoor Plumbing* like he was holding someone else's used tissue. "Who in their right mind would borrow this one?"

She looked at his book and made a face after pausing to read the title, then busied herself with the lower portion of the cart. "And yet we were both conveniently assigned to the library."

"You should be so lucky." He elbowed her in the ribs.

"Hardly. Don't flatter yourself," she retorted, shoving him back to his section with her shoulder. "Hey, way to create your own Dewey decimal system there, buddy." She pointed to a stack of books in disarray on his cart.

"Calm yourself. I haven't gotten to those yet. Besides, it doesn't matter. You just have to get them sort of close. People can figure it out once they're in the right section of the library."

"Patrons," she corrected. "Library patrons can figure it out, and a little bit of me just died."

"Nerd alert," he said. "You're telling me that it's too difficult to look a few books over once you're in the general vicinity of what you're looking for? How else will you ever discover anything new, unexpectedly?"

"My library back home is like that. Things are never where they're supposed to be. It's a nightmare. You can't honestly tell me shelvers are doing it for the *exploration of literature*, I mean, come on."

"You can't prove it." Ryan grinned.

"You can't win this one."

"I think I just did."

Maggie shook her head. "Okay, well, I'm going to go take these books and shelve them properly, I don't care what you say. You can just sit here and pretend to fulfill your community service duties."

"Nah, I have to help you," he said, standing up.

"Nope I'm perfectly capable of—"

"We need to do some…'research in the stacks,' anyway."

"Oh, is that what you're calling it? 'Research?' You're such a dork." She dragged the squeaky cart down the main aisle of shelves.

The library wasn't big; the camp's neighboring town, Abbotsville, had no more than five thousand residents. The building looked more like a cozy house than a stately beacon of knowledge. It had the unmistakable musty sweet scent of old books and broken-in furniture. The carpet was an undetectable color, well-trodden by countless feet over the years. Pipe railings lined the wooden staircase that twisted up to the second floor, where several offices served as binding repair and cataloging stations. Plants and African violets adorned the windowsills. There were three sublevels on the first floor, each lowering just a few steps; a small ramp ran parallel next to them. There seemed to be endless nooks and crannies; the shelves were initially symmetrical, but each one veered off into its own little alcove. A few small tables were pushed to the back of the first floor, against a big picture window overlooking a dell behind the library. The card catalog stood prominently at the front of the library next to the circulation desk. The librarian looked over her glasses at the squeaking cart with a disapproving glare.

"Seriously though, we have to look up a few things," said Ryan, lowering his voice.

"That's going to be tricky, don't you think?" whispered Maggie. They walked by a balding man sitting in an oversized chair reading a gardening book. Maggie pushed the cart down the ramp and headed toward the 390s. They turned down a tight aisle and both kneeled to grab a few books to reshelve.

"Ooh, I love this book," said Maggie, waving a misplaced paperback copy of *The Great Gatsby* at Ryan.

"It's fine," Ryan said, shrugging.

"Fine?" implored Maggie. "It's not fine. It's a masterpiece! The writing is brilliant! The parties, the opulence, the unrequited love, the struggle with amoral values—"

"Daisy was a superficial bitch who wanted it both ways."

"What? No way! She was trapped!"

"She wasn't trapped; if she really loved Gatsby, she would've left Buchanan for him. She loved Buchanan's money more."

"I don't think she cared about the money, but yeah, she was

pretty careless with Gatsby's heart. I think she knew she messed up—that's what makes it so brilliant," Maggie put the book on the cart.

"Speaking of, think this helped whoever took it out?" Ryan held up *How to Make It Work With Your Spouse Before Using the D-Word*.

"When was it checked out? Check the tag," Maggie said, grinning.

"Three days ago," said Ryan, raising an eyebrow.

"I'd say probably not," Maggie laughed. She stood on her tiptoes to shelve *The Marvelous Psychology of Mice*.

"People are into the weirdest shit," said Ryan.

"No kidding. Speaking of weird shit, how are we going to find out what a wendigo is?"

"Beats me. I guess we start at the beginning of the nonfiction section?"

"Yeah, sounds good." Maggie pulled the cart out from the aisle and dragged it to the 000s. She traced her fingers along the spines of each book, row by row, mumbling the titles. Ryan stood next to her scanning the shelf below.

"*Mythical Beasts, Local Folklore, An Unusual History of Vermont, Nightmare Monsters and How to Destroy Them*. These all look like winners."

"I know." Ryan laughed. He leaned over Maggie, his arm slowly brushing hers as he reached for *An Unusual History of Vermont*. "This could be interesting."

"Maybe this, too?" said Maggie, flustered. She grabbed *Nightmare Monsters and How to Destroy Them* a little too quickly. The books leaning up against it flopped onto their backs, disrupting the quiet.

"Easy there, killer." Ryan laughed. "Here, put those on the cart, and we'll go to the other end of the library to look at them, away from the eyes—"

"Ahem," a throat cleared. "Can you please make a better effort to keep quiet? The last time I checked, this is a *library*."

The librarian folded her arms across her chest.

"Yes, yes, sorry!" exclaimed Maggie. Ryan cringed.

"Shhh! Whisper!" she hissed, muttering all the way back to her desk.

"You're kind of a nightmare for someone who loves libraries," said Ryan.

"Well, this book should really help you out then," smirked Maggie, tapping *Nightmare Monsters and How to Destroy Them*.

"Let's hope so," said Ryan, swiping a piece of scrap paper and golf pencil as they passed one of the tables.

The back of the library was deserted. Maggie parked the cart and carried their books to the end of the aisle. They sat down on the floor and flipped through the pages.

"Let's check out the history book first," said Ryan, moving closer to Maggie until their legs barely touched. Her pulse quickened.

"Yeah, I guess we should check the index first, to see if 'wendigo' is listed."

"Unlikely, but okay," agreed Ryan.

Maggie flipped to the back of the book. "Hmm, Waterbury, witches, Woodford State Park—yup, you were right."

"Try, Kinross," he suggested.

"Okay, um, K, it must be on the previous page," said Maggie, her finger scrolling down the page.

"Here it is," said Ryan, pointing to the lower portion of the page. His finger grazed hers. "'*Kinross, Former Township.*'"

"Former?" questioned Maggie. "That's weird."

"Page one hundred and four."

"Okay." She flipped to the page and took a deep breath. At the top of the page was an old photo of a decaying building. Ryan leaned in close to her to read over her shoulder.

There's a rich and unusual history surrounding the former township of Kinross. Nestled in Vermont's Green Mountains, the area has always had an issue with maintaining a steady population, dating all the way back to the 1790 census of thirty-four inhabitants.

Prior to 1790, the Abenaki Indian tribe resided within the area, though not on nearby Mount Kinross, which they always believed to be simultaneously cursed and a sacred place where the four winds met. During the Revolutionary War, the Abenaki fought alongside with the British, and as a result, in 1776 they migrated into Canada, as the state of Vermont denied them their homeland.

Following this, settlers of Kinross struggled with growth, until after the Civil War, when the surrounding townships tried to take advantage of the mountain's timber resources. In 1872, growth necessitated a railroad system to cross Mount Kinross. Sawmills, housing, and several kilns were constructed to turn timber into charcoal.

By the 1880s, however, the mountain had been cleared of nearly all of its mature trees. The small town's economy suffered, despite an attempt to transform worker housing into a resort-like setting for travelers. The Kinross population dwindled in the early twentieth century, hitting a low of seven residents in 1937, when legislation passed to unincorporate the town. It has since been deemed a ghost town, save for the sixty acres of land that was transformed into a summer camp for teens. Kinross is also often linked to the Bennington Triangle in local folklore.

"Huh," said Maggie, looking at Ryan out of the corner of her eye. Her mind churned over the information as she scanned the page again. "So the Abenaki tribe believed that the land our camp is on was cursed? What do you think the Bennington Triangle is?"

"I've heard some stories from locals," said Ryan.

"How have you heard stories from locals?" challenged Maggie. "No one has even lived near our camp for hundreds of years! Save for a mountain man here and there."

"Vermont kids who come to camp—kids from the north, like Barre or Burlington—most kids from the state end up mentioning it when they come here."

"Kate and Greg must love that." Maggie rolled her eyes.

"Yup. But anyway, it's all urban legend shit. Our camp is

supposedly located in part of this paranormal triangle. Maybe that's why the Abenaki thought it was cursed. There are always rumors of Big Foot roaming the mountain, weird smells in the woods, people disappearing..."

"Disappearing people?" An alarm sounded in Maggie's mind. "I'm pretty sure one of those newspaper clippings I saw in the Lab was a missing person article. A Penelope?"

"That was probably about Penny—Corey's girl. People go missing all the time in the world, though, Maggie, it's pretty hard to pinpoint it to something supernatural. The real die hard Triangle conspiracy theorists insist that when all of these Bennington Triangle people went missing, it was at a certain time of year—the winter—and they were all wearing jean jackets—weird stuff like that."

"Huh. Let's see if this book says anything about it, anyway."

"Okay."

Maggie skimmed the index and turned to page eighty-six. A topographical map of Kinross with precisely aligned seismic readings filled the left-hand page.

The Bennington Triangle is a nickname coined by author Joseph A. Citro to denote the southwestern part of Vermont where more than ten people disappeared between 1920 and 1950. It is also regarded as a vibrant area for paranormal activity, including Big Foot and other beast sightings, UFO activity, and a common place to witness strange lights, noises, and sounds. Local folklore suggests that the Native Americans regarded Mount Kinross as cursed and avoided it, except to bury their dead.

The Triangle is also known for having unexplainable unruly and catastrophic storms, as well as unusual weather patterns at a moment's notice. Though there are hiking trails throughout the area, outdoor enthusiasts are cautioned to prepare for the worst when traveling through Kinross, even on the most serene seeming days.

Coincidentally, this is not the only paranormal Triangle situated in New England. Kinross has been linked to a sister Triangle in

Massachusetts, the Hockomock Triangle, with similar lore.

"Oh my god," said Maggie, pressing her hand onto the page.

"What?" asked Ryan, looking up from the book.

"Hockomock—the Hockomock Triangle! I know that place! It's a few towns over from my hometown—Bradford." A shiver ran down her spine.

"Really? That's crazy. Uh, you okay?" he said, acknowledging the look of horror on her face.

"Yeah, I'm just—okay, so like, reading all of this stuff, yeah, it's creepy—the weird paranormal rumors, the cursed mountain that we hiked the other day—that doesn't totally bother me, because I'm so removed from it. 1800s, old wives' tales—it's spooky but that's it. But this…" she said, tapping the word Hockomock on the page, "this puts it into perspective. No one goes near this place where I'm from."

"Really? Not even you?" Ryan grinned.

"Nope. Idiots go there. Idiots go there and they don't come back," said Maggie. "Our friend Smitty won't even go near it, and he shot a bottle rocket out of his ass. Hockomock is Native American derivative as well, but the lore revolves around a swamp, not a mountain."

"It's probably just a coincidence because they're both triangles and they both have weird paranormal shit surrounding them," replied Ryan, shrugging.

"You can't be serious right now."

"You have to give rationality the benefit of the doubt, Mags; even urban legends can have a powerful grip on the smartest people."

"Ugh, stop!" said Maggie, throwing her hands in the air. "Then how do you explain my messed up dreams, huh?"

"I'm not saying weird stuff isn't going on. I'm just saying that we can't prove it…yet."

"Fine, so how do we prove it?"

"We keep researching." Ryan opened *Nightmare Monsters*

and How to Destroy Them. Maggie sighed and fanned through the rest of *An Unusual History of Vermont,* looking for anything else that could explain the geographical abnormality. She leafed through the pages, but stopped at a chapter titled "Northeastern Indigenous Lore." She scanned the page, then murmured, "Hey, Ryan, look at this."

Widely dismissed as superstition and local folklore, many tribes, such as the Chippewa, Iroquois, Abenaki, Cayuga, and Algonquin have always believed the act of cannibalism to be a contemptible offense, and a direct gateway to the realm of evil. In the early days of these tribes, it was taught that to eat the flesh of another human being, even in moments of extreme desperation, is abhorrent and would anger the spirits so greatly that it could transform the wrongdoer into an unstoppable, horrific creature that could wreak havoc on the tribe and surrounding areas, for allowing such barbarism to occur in the first place.

"Do you think the 'unstoppable, horrific creature' referenced could be a 'wendigo'?" Maggie tapped her pencil on the book.

"Beats me. Let's see if it's in this monster book," replied Ryan. "Hey, check this out—this is weird. Some of the pages at the end are missing. See?"

Ryan's fingers traced the perforated remnants. He looked at Maggie.

"Yeah, probably some overzealous kid who's really into werewolves." Maggie shrugged. She pointed to something in the index and brushed Ryan's fingers while trying to turn the page. Electricity shot through her.

"I don't know. Four pages? That's a very specific number."

"I'm just being rational," mocked Maggie.

Ryan flipped to the index. "Maybe if I look—" He moved his fingers closer to Maggie's lingering hand on the page.

"Hey, bookworms! No sitting on the job," whispered a voice from the end of the row.

Ryan and Maggie sat up straight. It was Mark. Maggie

grabbed the books and shoved them onto the cart before Mark could see the titles.

"I'm kidding, but the bus will be here in five, so wrap it up. I'm running across the street to grab a coffee." Mark winked at Ryan.

"Can I get one?" asked Maggie.

"Ha, nice try," laughed Mark as he turned to leave.

Ryan grinned and said, "Okay, we'll be out in a sec."

"What are we going to do now?" whispered Maggie. "That wasn't nearly enough time!"

They pushed the cart into the main aisle and left it to the side.

"Well, you're a Lifer now—maybe we'll land library duty again next week? You better, uh, say something to her before we go." He motioned to the librarian, whose hawkish eyes honed in on their approach.

"Right, okay," said Maggie. She walked up to the checkout desk and whispered, "Thank you for having us! I'm really sorry about the noise earlier."

The librarian let out a "Hmph" and returned to her crossword puzzle.

Ryan and Maggie pushed through the double doors and into the sunlight. The sky was scattered with pillowy clouds. They sat on the curb shaded by a large maple tree. Crabgrass grew through the cracks in the pavement. Across the street, a faded hardware store sign creaked in the breeze. An elderly couple exited a nearby diner with concerted effort and hobbled to their red Oldsmobile parked on the street.

"So, what's your story, anyway?" asked Maggie. She picked up a twig and methodically snapped it into smaller pieces.

"What do you mean?" asked Ryan, examining the laces on his sneakers.

"Where are you from? What's your town like? What do you listen to besides Oasis? What do you want to do when you're out of school?" asked Maggie.

"What is this, twenty questions?" He stole a glance at her and smirked.

"Maybe," replied Maggie.

"I was born in Pennsylvania, but then my parents moved me and my sisters to upstate New York when I was about ten. The town we live in now is pretty nice. It's probably like Anytown, USA, you know, where you're from."

"Probably."

"There's a cool diner on Main Street, though. It's old school. Green-tiled floors, maroon booths, a picture menu up on the wall—it's straight out of old New York. We like to go there and hang out until they kick us out."

"Sounds cool," said Maggie.

"Yeah, it is. The guy who owns it keeps it open until one in the morning because there's nothing else for kids to do in our town. It's supposed to keep us out of trouble."

"Define trouble," challenged Maggie.

"Smoking weed in abandoned parking lots?"

"You're such a rebel."

"You love it." He grinned.

They sat in silence for a moment. Maggie tossed the bits of stick she had broken and looked down the road.

"Hey, I should probably tell you something," said Ryan, aligning his toes with one of the cracks in the pavement.

"What's that?" She turned to look at him. Their eyes met for a moment, before Maggie quickly became engrossed with an ant journeying to a nearby sand mound.

"Well, see, I have this thing…" started Ryan. A rumbling could be heard in the distance. The Camp Kinross bus was cresting over the hill at the other end of Main Street.

"A thing? What thing?"

"Well, it's something you're not going to believe. And then when you do believe me, you're gonna be pissed."

"What, you have a girlfriend or something? Listen, I—"

The bus ambled down Main Street, its brakes wheezing at an intersection stoplight.

"No, it's nothing like that."

"Jail time? You *are* a rebel!" Maggie raised her eyebrows.

"You wish," replied Ryan, turning over the words in his head, hoping they'd reveal themselves like the answer to a Wheel of Fortune puzzle.

"I'm pretty sure I'm not going to be pissed, whatever it is," said Maggie, standing up as the bus pulled over in front of the library.

"Yeah, forget it, no big deal. It's just, uh, family stuff," said Ryan.

"Everyone has that." Maggie shrugged, walking through the collapsible doorway and up the bus stairs.

"Right," sighed Ryan, watching her board the bus.

38

"Hey, aren't you Maggie's friend from home?"

Beth and Tom stood in the lobby of Pinegrove Rehab and Nursing, a facility straddling the towns of Abbottsville and Southfield. It was a ubiquitous brick medical building, aesthetics last updated in the early seventies, and a lobby filled with good intentions. The half-moon-shaped desk against the wall served as an unkempt command center, complete with a sweating iced coffee cup and the remnants of a midmorning snack. A few waiting room chairs with wooden arms and faded geometric patterns were positioned near the entrance. Two hallways branched off to the left of the desk, in perpendicular fashion.

"Yeah, hey, I'm Tom," he replied. He stretched out his hand.

"Beth, nice to meet you," she replied. "So Pinegrove duty, eh?"

"Yup," Tom said, laughing. "I heard it isn't too bad, though—we just play a bunch of games and listen to war stories."

"Yeah, I'm sure it'll be fine," she said.

A man with a clipboard rounded the corner, shaking his head. He dropped the clipboard onto the command center, which startled them. Tom raised an eyebrow to Beth, who stifled a giggle. The man went behind the desk and picked up the phone. Pained lines emerged on his forehead. His fingers jabbed at the buttons, and while he waited for an answer, he covered the receiver and said, "Five minutes, guys, I've just had to deal with a shitty situation. Literally—you don't want to know. Yes, hi, hello, is this Dr. Johnson?"

Tom and Beth looked at each other. Beth covered her mouth to stifle more giggles.

"A literal shitty situation," Beth whispered. "That can only mean one thing, right?"

"Sure hope Dr. *Johnson* can relieve that somehow," replied Tom.

"Yeah, he better get up here quick!" said Beth, wiping tears away from her eyes.

"So," said Tom, catching his breath. "So, you and Mags have hit it off, huh? How'd you do it?"

"What do you mean? She's cool," Beth shrugged.

"It's just that she's not the easiest person to get to know— it takes awhile to get in with her."

"Really? We started talking during our first activity at camp, and that was that."

"Huh, interesting. At home she mostly runs with the guys—it's always been that way. There are one or two girls that she hangs with, but ever since she was little, she always picked tree forts over playing dolls. It's pretty cool that you were able to connect with her so easily," said Tom, shoving his hands into his shorts pockets.

"Yeah, I like her. We have fun," said Beth. The phone receiver slammed into its cradle, followed by a dramatic sigh.

"Are you the Kinross campers? I mean, I assume you are with your polos," said the man. "Follow me. I'll take you to the Playroom. One of your counselors will come get you when the bus is here—probably like an hour or so. Anyone need the bathroom? I don't want any more accidents today…not on my shift!" The man let out a weak laugh. Beth offered a sympathetic smile, and they fell in step behind him.

"Playroom? Sounds like we're going to a room full of toddlers," said Tom under his breath to Beth.

"You basically are," interjected the man, pushing through a set of swinging doors. They walked by rooms with half-open doors. A cacophony of beeps and coughs filled the hallway. Trays of half-eaten breakfast sat on carts outside bedroom doors: fruit cups with grapes floating in peach juice, toast crusts, lukewarm instant coffee, unopened pats of butter wrapped in little gold foil squares. The sour tang of medicine seeping through aging skin, the aggressive spritzes of cleaning agents, and the warm, moist air made it feel like they were walking through a rotting jungle of human sadness.

"Here we are," said the man, turning to his left and holding his arm out in a welcoming fanfare. "There are board games in the corner, but they mostly like to play what's already on the tables. And don't get on them for cheating; most of them have some form of dementia. They'll argue you till you're blue in the face—you'll never win."

"Thanks," said Beth, pushing through the door. Turning to Tom, she said, "So, where do we start?"

"Good question," he replied, looking around the room. The walls were pale green, with thin curtained windows that let in some daylight. A few men in bathrobes had their wheelchairs grouped together, but weren't saying much. A cheery woman wearing bunny slippers shuffled over to Beth and Tom with her walker. Her lips were smeared with bright pink lipstick.

"Oh boy," said Beth, as the woman inched closer.

"Hi, dearies! I haven't seen you in so long!" squeaked the woman.

"Uh, hi!" Beth returned her exaggerated smile. Tom instinctively took a step backward.

"I was wondering when you two would come back! See

what I'm wearing?" She leaned all of her weight forward onto the walker and lifted up her right foot, wiggling it.

"Those are...nice?" replied Tom.

"I should think so, you gave them to me, dearie. Did you think that I'd forget? No, sir! I love them! They are so snuggly and cute!" She returned her posture to an upright and locked position. Beth saw more movement in her peripheral vision.

"Another one is coming," she murmured.

"It's like night of the living dead," Tom commented under his breath.

"Harriet, why are you hogging these lovelies? You do this every time! Sorry about her—she never remembers," said a sallow-faced woman, smacking her lips when she talked. She inched closer to them.

"I do, too, remember! I remember lots of things! Who do you think you are?" replied Harriet.

"See? You don't even know who I am!"

"Psst, hey, you two—you, campers—come over here, quick while they're into it," said a voice to their right.

Tom and Beth turned and saw two men in wheelchairs at a table by the window, beckoning. They were playing cribbage, each with a large plastic cup of water with a straw sitting on the table.

"Eh, pull up those chairs over there," said one man as he pointed, his whiskered face gaunt, but lit up by bright blue eyes.

Tom grabbed two folding chairs, and he and Beth joined their table.

"Death traps, those are," growled the other man, motioning to the chairs. His partially opened bathrobe revealed a white ribbed tank top stained around the collar. He lowered his glasses to survey the two campers.

"So," he said. "You got stuck with Pinegrove duty, did ya? Lucky you."

"Yeah, we're here for an hour if you want to talk or play a

game or something?" said Tom, finding it difficult to maintain eye contact.

"Hah! Kid, you haven't seen half the shit I've seen in my lifetime. 'Do I want to talk?' he says," cackled the man.

"Don't mind Clarence," said the man with twinkling blue eyes. "A lot of times the local high school will bring in history students, to try to get firsthand accounts from war vets. It doesn't sit well. I'm Andy." He jangled the dog tags around his neck.

"Goddamned book reports, that's what they'd have us become," muttered Clarence.

"Nice to meet you both," said Beth quickly. "So, what street are you on?"

"What's that, sweetheart? You're at Pinegrove," replied Andy.

"No, your game," she replied, pointing to the cribbage board. "Are you on third street, or are you in trouble?"

"Ha! Very good, very good. Third street, indeed! You know the game, then?" The skin around his eyes crinkled when he smiled.

"Sure do," said Beth. "My grandfather taught me when I was very young. It's how I learned a lot of math. Variations of fifteen, anyway."

"Let's test your knowledge, then! What do you reckon I have in this hand?" asked Andy. He held up his cards for her to see.

She leaned over and thought for a moment, and then grinned. "Well, I reckon you have nineteen."

"And you? What do you think?" he asked Tom, flashing his cards at him.

"I don't really know the game—I mean, it's fifteens? Okay, so hang on. Um…" stalled Tom. Clarence let out a knowing chuckle.

"I'm not seeing anything that adds up to fifteen," he replied, defeated. Andy fanned his cards out for the table.

"That's because nothing does," said Clarence.

"That doesn't make any sense," said Tom.

"That's the joke: if you have nineteen, you have zero," said Beth, grinning.

"Nil, nada, zero!" Andy laughed.

"It's impossible to have a cribbage hand add up to nineteen," explained Beth.

"Huh," said Tom.

"It's sarcasm, kid. How are you ever going to keep up with this pretty little thing if you don't know sarcasm when it bites you in the ass?" growled Clarence.

"Oh, it's not like that," said Beth quickly. Tom rubbed his eyes and looked at the clock. The bus couldn't get there soon enough.

"Sure it isn't," smirked Clarence.

"So, you're from Camp Kinross," said Andy. "We get a lot of you kids in here. Week after week, all summer long."

"That must get old, from your perspective," said Tom.

"Yep," stated Clarence, shuffling the deck of cards. One slipped out of the pile onto the floor. Tom picked it up and handed it back to him. Clarence grunted in reply.

"Do they let you guys go outside at all?" asked Beth.

"Not much, but it's not the worst thing," said Andy.

"No? I don't think I could stand being trapped in here day after day," confessed Tom. Beth nudged him under the table and shot him a warning glance.

"You're thinking about it all wrong," said Andy.

"Yeah, when you've been laid up in a jungle trench for ten days straight, with your toes rotting off your foot from walking through swamp after goddamned swamp, not knowing if your buddy next to you is going to get blown to bits in the next thirty seconds by the Japanese, this is a goddamned paradise," said Clarence, shaking his head.

"Where were you stationed?" asked Beth.

"Guadalcanal. Marines. Andy was at Bastogne. Go look

that one up in your history books," muttered Clarence. He handed the deck to Andy. "Your deal."

"It was literally hell frozen over," chattered Andy. "So yeah, this place isn't so terrible."

"That makes sense, sorry," said Tom.

"Don't apologize! You kids are too soft nowadays—always apologizing for everything under the sun. 'Sorry it's cloudy today!' 'Sorry I have an opinion about something!' 'Sorry I looked at you funny!' Knock that crap off," said Clarence. "And be happy you'll never be drafted."

"Do you guys know anything about the camp? Or the history of it?" asked Beth.

"Not too much," said Andy. "The way we ended up here was through relatives—we aren't from this area.

Clarence counted his cards. "Fifteen two, fifteen four, pair is six, and three makes nine."

Andy looked expectantly at Beth and Tom. They exchanged confused looks, until Andy spoke up. "Well, aren't you gonna ask?"

"Ask you what?" said Tom.

"The last camper who visited asked us all sorts of questions about the camp, and if we knew about the grounds being haunted." He grinned wide, bobbing his head from side to side. Clarence rolled his eyes.

"That's ridiculous," said Tom.

"I agree," said Clarence. Tom waited for more affirmation in their newfound solidarity, but Clarence ignored Tom and reorganized the cards in his hand.

"Wait, someone from our camp asked you about it being haunted? When was this?" said Beth.

"That's right, miss. It was maybe a year ago now. She said she didn't have any proof, but she thought something was going on over at that camp that warranted outside help of some sort," replied Andy.

"Something going on—like what?" asked Beth, lowering

her voice.

Andy leaned toward her. The silvery flecks of hair protruding from his face were illuminated in the sunlight. "She seemed to think there was something going on, because she said a few campers were sent home for strange reasons."

The color drained from Beth's face. Tom looked at her and the men, half grinning.

"Well, Kinross runs a tight ship," said Tom. "That has happened a few times during our week, too, but the staff has their reasons. This camper sounds crazy."

Beth looked at Tom in disbelief, but quickly realized that he hadn't been privy to what she, Maggie, and Ryan were trying to uncover. She smiled politely and replied, "Let's hope it's all sorted now."

"Hey, Tom, Beth! The bus is here," Counselor Adah stood at the door to the Playroom, motioning to them.

"Have a great day," said Tom. He folded up the chairs and stacked them back against the wall. As he did this, Beth felt a soft hand tug on her wrist.

"You take care," whispered Andy. "I saw the look on your face—I know you know what I'm talking about. That other girl wasn't lying to me, you know. Two weeks later her photo was in the papers—missing. Turns out, she was from a few towns over. I think the whole thing was covered up by local law enforcement. Whatever it is, it's bigger than you and your friends. Be careful."

Beth squeezed his hand in thanks and gave him a sad smile.

"Nice to meet you both," said Beth. Clarence nodded. As she walked toward the door, she felt the weight of Andy's piercing blue eyes follow her out.

Tom slid into a seat on the almost filled bus, making room for Beth to join him. "That was something, huh?"

"Sure was," agreed Beth. She fixed her hair into a messy bun on top of her head. "They were pretty interesting though...when they weren't harassing you." She turned to

Tom with a wry grin.

"Oh, yeah, that was great. Really fantastic," he said, shaking his head. "Why do old people always get a verbal free pass?"

"I dunno, it seems like a generational thing. They fought in all of those wars, their best friends were dying left and right, and you're going to tell them that saying something is culturally insensitive now? You think they're going to instantly change, after all they've been through?"

"It still doesn't make it right," winced Tom.

"It doesn't," agreed Beth. "They seemed decent enough, though, overall. Sorry you got picked on."

"What? I'm fine—I don't care," said Tom. He stared out the window.

"No, I just—eh, sorry," said Beth, shifting in the seat and looking across the aisle.

The bus drove through the intersection on Main Street. Tom saw two figures sitting close together on the street. The bus slowed. As they approached, Tom could make out Maggie and Ryan. Tom's face puckered as if an inescapable bitterness was on his tongue. Honestly, what did she see in him? Everything that Becky had relayed made him out to be a pretentious prick. But Alex hadn't said much about him; if he was really bad news, he probably would have. Why Ryan, though? What was so great about him, that she wanted to spend all of her free time holed up with him and Beth? Beth was fine, but she wasn't even a Lifer. It should be me sitting out there, thought Tom. He watched her push her hair behind her ears and do her patented half smile, before she stood up to board the bus.

39

"Great work at community service today, everyone!" exclaimed Kate to the ravenous campers in the Mess Hall. A hush fell over the room at the sound of her voice. She and Greg stood by the entrance, surveying the crowd. It was quiet, expectant. A mixing bowl clanged to the ground in the kitchen, resulting in giggles and a cautious applause from the campers.

"You sure have earned your lunch today, so eat up! This afternoon there's open swim, and after dinner tonight we have a special activity planned for you!" boomed Greg.

Joey leaned across the table, his polo grazing Liv's plate of spaghetti. She made a face. "Manhunt!" His face contorted into a demonic grin. Becky pushed his forehead away with her palm. Alex grabbed his shoulder to sit him back down.

"What exactly is…Manhunt?" asked Liv.

"It's hide-and-seek for teenagers," said Corey, rolling his eyes.

"Oh what, you're too cool for Manhunt now, Cor?" said Becky.

"Yeah, he's too cool ever since Penny had to leave," whined Joey.

"Sure," said Corey, shaking his head.

"So, is it like teams or something?" asked Liv.

"Usually," said Tom. "At least that's how we've always played it at home."

"Oh, you've played?" said Joey, swiveling toward Tom.

"You just stirred the bee's nest, man," said Alex, rubbing his forehead.

"So you've played Manhunt back home? With your friend Maddie? You guys, uh, ever on the same team?" asked Joey.

"Maggie, and yeah, sure, why?" said Tom, his stomach tightening.

"Find any good places to...hide? I can think of one in particular..." Joey snickered. Liv looked down at her plate, twirling her spaghetti into an endless circle around her fork.

"You're such a pig, Joey. Why did they let you become a Lifer? Seriously, someone had a severe mental lapse on the night they tapped you." Becky tossed her balled up napkin onto her tray.

"Joey, Becky, guys—big picture, come on. What Joey's driving at, Tom, is that Manhunt is sort of like...Bonfire Night," said Alex.

"But you play at night? What about the night bell thing? I don't want to get...kicked out," said Liv, the color draining from her face.

"Aw, are you afraid wittle Tommy here is going to—" started Joey.

"Shut it," said Alex, punching him in the arm. Joey slouched in his chair like a deflated balloon.

Becky patted Liv on the leg. "They make an exception, sweetie. Don't worry about it."

Tom glanced over at Maggie's usual spot. Sure enough, her, Ryan, and Beth were deep in conversation, oblivious to the racket of the Mess Hall. Becky caught him looking at them and said, "So, Tom, how was community service today—I saw that you were with Maggie's friend, Beth? How was she? Where were you guys assigned?"

"Oh, uh," said Tom, turning back to the table. "She was fine. We were at Pinegrove. It was pretty depressing."

"Yeah, it can be heavy there," agreed Alex. "Good of you to do it, though. Those guys need people like us around them."

"I don't know," said Tom, his mind cycling through the insults from earlier in the day. "The guys we 'entertained' were kind of dicks."

"Well, Liv and I could have used your help—we were at the Abbottsville Episcopalian Church helping set up for a yard sale this weekend. We had the absolute worst time with the folding tables, didn't we, Liv?" said Becky. "Just look at my hand!" She held out her freshly bandaged wrist.

"Yup," agreed Liv, twirling away at the remnants of pasta on her plate.

"Were they really that bad, Tom?" pressed Alex. "Because if they were, that's something to bring up at the next Lifer meeting. Kate and Greg want that kind of feedback."

Tom thought it over. "Yeah, they were jerks. I mentioned it casually to Counselor Neal earlier—I bumped into him and he asked me how community service went. I figured I should be honest? I'll bring it up to them, too. When is the next meeting?"

"I'll find out. Probably before Manhunt. You know, to welcome all the new Lifers, that sort of thing. They usually like to have one pretty soon after initiation," said Alex.

"Liv was telling me that your friend made the cut, too," said Becky, smiling sweetly.

"Yeah, she seems nice," added Liv.

"Why haven't you invited her over here to sit with us, Tommy?" pressed Becky. "She's one of us now, after all."

"I dunno. She seems fine doing her own thing," said Tom. The thought of Maggie sitting over here, with him…

"Nonsense," said Becky, standing abruptly. "Back in a sec!"

"Becks, hang on," said Alex, but Becky pretended not to

hear him and walked over to the corner table.

***

"Look alive," said Beth, her eyes tracking Becky as she snaked through tables and chairs toward the head of their table.

"So," she said, arriving to their table with hands on hips. "It looks like I may have misjudged you. Congrats on becoming a Lifer." Becky extended her hand to Maggie. Maggie blinked a few times and stared at her hand before reluctantly shaking it.

"Thanks," she replied slowly. She withdrew her hand and glanced at Ryan in her peripheral vision.

"How about you guys come join us?" said Becky, smiling and gesturing to their table in the center of the Mess Hall.

"We're good," said Ryan.

"Oh, Ryan, let's put it behind us for the greater good or whatever, hey? We have three extra seats, just come over. If for no other reason than to see if we can hit Joey's breaking point?" She forced a laughed.

Ryan sighed. "Why, Becky? Why do you want us sitting over there so bad? We're fine here. Why are you trying to force—"

"No agenda, I promise. I just thought we should bury the hatchet. Your friends seem cool, and I admit that I jumped to conclusions. I messed up and want to live my best Lifer life by making this right. Cross my heart!" declared Becky with pleading eyes. "Besides, I heard that the dance hinges on our girl here, and I want to hear about this mix she's made." She smiled warmly at Maggie, folding her arms across her chest. "I'm not taking 'no' for an answer."

Maggie sighed. "Okay, fine, yes, let's just go sit over there, who cares." She pushed her chair backward to stand. Becky smiled with the satisfaction of winning first place in a local beauty pageant and sashayed her way back to her table.

"This is going to end well," muttered Beth.

"No kidding," said Ryan, raising his eyebrows.

"Scooch over, you animals, we have company!" sang Becky.

"Scooch isn't even a word," muttered Ryan.

Maggie squeezed into a chair between Ryan and Corey. Beth opted for a seat next to Liv.

"Well, isn't this cozy," quipped Joey. An awkward silence fell over the table.

"Way to make it weird, Joe," said Germ, chewing on a crust of garlic bread.

"What? What'd I do now!" said Joey, raising a disgusted hand in the air.

Maggie looked over at Tom but couldn't get his attention. With everything they had uncovered at the library, she felt a natural gravitation to tell him. Or maybe he would be able to just tell by her face that she had to talk to him? Whatever was happening at Kinross, she had to let him know, so they'd at least have a chance of getting out of here, Lifers or not. But he wouldn't even look at her. What was his problem? It's not like she wanted to infiltrate his little camp clique. She only wanted Becky to be less annoying, especially if she, Beth, and Ryan were going to figure this whole thing out. She sighed and turned to Corey.

"So what were you guys talking about before we made it awkward by coming over here?"

"How we're going to be playing Manhunt tonight probably—the 'special activity' Kate mentioned," he replied.

Under the table, Maggie thought she felt Ryan's foot press up against the side of her sneaker. Maybe he thought her foot was the leg of the chair—they were all sitting pretty close together. Still, she didn't move it.

"So is it teams? Is that how they play it here?" She asked, looking around the table.

"Basically, yeah," said Alex.

"So, you've, uh, played before, huh?" asked Joey. Corey shot him a look of contempt.

"Yeah, my team usually wins back home. Isn't that right, Tom?" said Maggie confidently. Tom nodded and looked away. Alex put his face in his hands as a preemptive measure.

"Joey—" warned Becky, gritting her teeth.

"Oh, I bet your team wins!" said Joey. Garlic bread crusts flew from all angles.

"What, I don't get it," said Maggie, bored.

"Everything is a euphemism with this perv," said Corey.

"Hey, no one's perfect! They told me that at initiation!" yelled Joey.

"Every crowd has one," said Germ.

"That's the best you've got, Joey?" challenged Maggie, smirking. "A weak joke about me hooking up with a bunch of dudes playing hide-and-seek in the woods at night? Do better."

The table oohed at Maggie's comeback.

"Getting called out stings way worse than the babbling nonsense you spew, Joe," teased Alex.

"That's not what your mom said last night!" retorted Joey.

"Reduced to 'your mom' jokes. I'd say that's a victory, Maggie," smirked Alex.

"So, Maggie, tell us about this dance mix you've made," said Becky. She stabbed a few green beans on her fork and chewed slowly.

Ryan casually leaned backward and over toward Maggie. She could only just make out his barely audible "Tell them nothing" over the din of the cafeteria. His breath was so close to her face it sent a shiver down her neck.

"It's, uh, it's gonna be good. But I don't want to ruin the surprise," said Maggie, shifting in her chair.

"The Lab is such a creepy place. I can't believe you've been holed up in there!" said Becky, scrunching up her nose.

"Nah, it's cool—I was in there a few weeks ago," said

Germ. "Tons of crates of old records and stuff."

"Yeah, pretty much. The equipment has seen better days, that's for sure," said Maggie.

"Hate to interrupt you guys, but wrap it up—swim is in twenty," said Mark, walking by their table. "And Kate and Greg wanted me to pass along that the next Lifer meeting is at the end of dinner tonight—so eat fast and get there. We don't want you guys missing out on the special activity."

"Oh come on, Mark, we know it's Manhunt. It's always Manhunt," said Corey.

"Hey, don't be such a wiseass." Mark grinned and walked away.

40

When the campers returned to their cabins to change for swim, they found a neatly folded pile of dark clothing sitting on their beds. A notecard resting on top of the clothes simply read, "Dinner Attire."

"Seriously?" said Maggie, holding up army fatigue pants. She spun around to Beth, who was coming out of the bathroom.

"Wow, they go all out, huh?" Beth replied.

"It's a pretty intense game of Manhunt," added Becky, draping a beach towel over her forearm.

"I-I'm not going to be very good," said Liv. "Maybe I can help keep score or something?"

"Nonsense, Liv, you have to be out there because Tom—" Becky caught herself and shot a quick apologetic glance at Maggie.

"It's fine," reassured Maggie, sliding into her sandals. "I really don't like him like that. Honest."

Becky smiled and continued, "You have to be out there because you'll get to team up with Tom, if you know what I mean."

"Yeah, but how do they keep track of the campers—what if someone goes missing?" argued Liv, wringing her swimsuit in her hands.

"Oh, sweetie, stop being a Nervous Nelly. I think you're just worried about Tom, and trust me, you have nothing to worry about."

Liv shifted her glance to Maggie and then back to Becky. "Right, okay," she said, and went into the bathroom to change.

Becky leaned into the communal mirror on the wall and fixed the strands of hair falling around her face. "You know, Maggie, I have to admit, I didn't like you at first. I was threatened by you; the way Ryan was fixated on you from the very beginning. I'm a jealous creature...but aren't we all?" She let out a shrill little laugh.

"But now I see that he was really embracing his Kinross Lifer duties by recruiting you. He has never taken such an interest in anyone—well, except for me—sorry! But it's true. He's usually like Corey—sitting back, all broody, drawing or writing or whatever in that little notebook of his. But anyway, what I'm trying to say is that you actually seem pretty cool. The way you threw it back in Joey's face in the Mess Hall earlier—that was great. I hope we can bury the past, and maybe...be friends?"

Becky capped her tube of lip gloss and pursed her lips at her reflection. She spun around and faced Maggie, smiling.

Uneasiness simmered in Maggie's stomach. Was Ryan really just using her to further the goals of Camp Kinross? She thought they had great chemistry, but maybe she was only feeling what she wanted to feel. Did he really care about the camp that much? And if he did, why did he bother researching all that stuff about the weird Kinross history and the Bennington Triangle—they were trying to expose something about the camp, not keep it a secret, weren't they? He did mention that he had something to tell her. Maybe he was going to come clean? None of this made any sense. And why did she care so much anyway? She was now tangled in the very kind of social web she despised. She also couldn't escape the constant nagging in her brain—a little voice that, despite all of these uncertainties, still wondered when she'd see Ryan next. Was Becky's fireside chat a subtle way of trying to make her steer clear of him? She didn't seem as catty as before, but maybe it was to keep her enemy closer? Is she so narcissistic that she could be going out with Alex, but still want the rest of the camp to want her? She weakly smiled and nodded at Becky.

Hannah came out of her room. "You lovelies ready? Let's go give those boys something to chase tonight, shall we?"

"Can she really say that?" Beth asked.

"You're gonna have to be more specific with the 'she' you're referring to in here," muttered Maggie, following the rest of the girls out of the cabin.

41

The afternoon sun beat down on the campers as they descended to the beach. It was a scorcher of a day. Horseflies barred their teeth and flew in a fury between ankles. Feet stepped gingerly, but quickly, over sand that had been baking in the sun all morning. It was an obstacle course from hell; most of the campers made a beeline for the cooling relief of the lake.

Maggie and Beth dropped their towels on the beach and swam to the far edge of the dock.

"I hate swimming in this," confessed Maggie, motioning to the murky lake.

"Oh, me too," agreed Beth, dunking her head back under the water to fix her hair.

"You can't see what's lurking beneath the surface. It's not right," said Maggie.

"You know there are snappers in here somewhere. Maybe it's better we don't know," said Beth.

"It's just too hot out to not be swimming." Maggie treaded water and swiveled her head around, surreptitiously scanning the crowd for Ryan. "Hey, can I ask you something?"

"Yeah, sure, anything," said Beth, holding on to the dock

with one arm. "Jesus, that wood is hot." Maggie splashed a little water on the dock. The puddle sizzled on the planks. The girls hoisted themselves up and sat, dangling their legs in the water. Counselor Adah sat at the other end of the dock, twirling a whistle in her hand.

"Do you think—agh—this is such a weird thing to ask. You know what, never mind, forget it," said Maggie, taking a section of her wet hair and squeezing out the water.

"No, what is it? I mean, I know we've only been friends for a few days, but you can talk to me," assured Beth.

"It's not that. I don't know. I'm more afraid that if I put it into words, it's going to make it real, or change something." Maggie bit her lower lip.

"It's Ryan, isn't it?" Beth gave Maggie a sympathetic smile. Maggie scrunched her face and looked back at Beth without answering.

"It's obvious there's something there," said Beth.

"See, I kinda thought that, but I dunno, I didn't want to jinx it, I guess. I mean, there's so much stacked up against us. Plus what about all that stuff Becky just said in the cabin?"

"Becky sucks. I don't care if she's being fake nice or real nice, she always seems to have some underlying agenda. Don't let her or her games mess with you."

"Yeah, no, I know. You're right," said Maggie, staring down at the water. "I just don't know where I stand with him. I can't tell. He's so crass, but also guarded. It feels like we've been best friends for thousands of years, but there's more to it. I can't wrap my head around it—it's just one huge mindfuck."

"I get that," said Beth.

"And then there are his super subtle moves," continued Maggie, shooing a dragonfly from her leg. "Like, is he touching my foot with his foot on purpose under the Mess Hall table, or is it nothing, and I'm completely overthinking it? Because it's not exactly obvious. Which is nice, in a way; it means he's not a jerk. But I wish he'd just give me some unmistakable indicator that I'm not making up this entire subtext in my head."

"Yeah, like you want one clear signal that he's into you, even if nothing comes of it," said Beth, swatting at a horsefly circling her head.

"Yes!" exclaimed Maggie. "I don't get why I even feel this way, I barely know anything about him. And what's with these dreams I'm having?"

"You mean the creepy ones?" asked Beth.

"Oh, man, I haven't even told you the half of it, because he's been around every time I've mentioned them." Maggie recounted the beginning half of her dreams to Beth—the amusement park, the walk by the river, the bar, the game of Scrabble.

"Woah, I had no idea," said Beth, whistling a little.

"Yeah, and it's not like I'm thinking about him right before bed in hopes that he'll be in my dreams—I promise! But he shows up, night after night. It's maddening."

"That's pretty weird. And you haven't mentioned any of this to him? Not even when you guys were hanging out at the library?"

"Nope. I mean, how do you approach someone that you have somehow unintentionally developed massive feelings for in a very short period of time, and say, 'Hey, so about those dreams I've been having...by the way, there are also these really intense scenes in them, prior to the weird stuff I've told you about, and they all have to do with how we're totally attracted to each other.' That conversation is going to be a homerun."

"You know what this whole thing reminds me of? Have you heard of the band Weezer? This is just like the last song on their album," said Beth.

"Yes! 'Only In Dreams'? That song is like my whole life right now. I just got that album through Columbia House—

it's so good," said Maggie.

"Yeah, it really is," agreed Beth. "There are so many songs on that album that are better than their radio hit."

"'Buddy Holly'?"

"Yeah."

"Agreed."

They sat there for a few moments in silence, taking in the placid scene. From the dock, they could see Becky and Liv lying on their towels, next to a few girls from Cabin Four. Other campers were scattered throughout the swimming area, lounging in black inflatable tubes. Maggie spied Ryan on the edge of the beach next to Corey, the lake's water lapping against their ankles. Maggie watched Ryan's lips move. She fought the urge to entertain the idea that he could be talking about her. That's just ridiculous, she thought. Across the pond, Tom and Alex paddled a canoe back to shore.

"Did I tell you I had community service with Tom?" said Beth.

"No! How'd that go?" asked Maggie.

"It was okay. The nursing home was kind of sad and smelled like expired milk, but the two guys we ended up talking to were pretty decent. They didn't take to Tom too well, though. It was weird. He seemed pretty cool and funny while we were waiting in the lobby, but once we were in the room with them, I don't know, he fell flat."

"He's not great with old people. Actually, that's not fair. He's just uncomfortable around them. He lost his grandparents pretty recently," she sighed.

"Ahh, I'm sorry, that sucks," said Beth.

"Yeah, Grampa Dunne was in a nursing home, and Grandma Dunne was at home. It was pretty sad. They went within two months of each other." Maggie frowned.

"That's tough. Were they close to him?"

"Oh yeah, they lived in our town, not far from us," said

Maggie, swirling her toes in the water.

"Well, I guess it's comforting to know that he had them for so long…so many kids don't get to have their grandparents around when they're teenagers," said Beth.

"True," agreed Maggie, "that probably explains why he seemed out of sorts."

"Speaking of out of sorts!" said Beth, turning to Maggie suddenly. She lowered her voice to a whispered exclamation. "I forgot to tell you! One of the old men that we talked to said some odd stuff as we were leaving."

"Really? What?" They paused their conversation while a camper walked past them to jump off the dock. The splash sent water everywhere, but unlike the first day of camp, the residual damage was a welcomed refreshment in the heat.

"First, one of the guys asked us if we were going to ask them about the camp being haunted."

"Like ghosts opening doors—"

"No, no. He said about a year ago, one of the campers who had Pinegrove duty started asking him if he knew about the camp being haunted, or about weird things going on at Kinross in the past. He told her he didn't know, but then a few weeks later he saw her picture in the paper because she was missing, and—and!—he thought the police covered the whole thing up. She was from a few towns over, but I guess the story just disappeared."

"Woah," said Maggie. "What if that camper was the same girl from that article I saw—Penelope? Corey's Penny? I mean, it might not be, but still."

"Yeah," said Beth, "and as we were leaving, he pulled me aside and said whatever my friends and I might be up to, to be careful. It gives me goosebumps to think about how he said it. It's like he knew we were trying to uncover something, even though I didn't say anything about it."

"Yikes," said Maggie. "I don't know how we'll be able to tell Ryan, now that we're sitting at the cool kids' table."

"Get him alone during Manhunt maybe?" said Beth, winking.

Maggie kicked water at her.

"I just want one sign from him. Just one," said Maggie, shaking her head and looking back over at Ryan sitting on the beach.

42

"Make the call."

Greg sat behind the camp office desk and passed the receiver to Kate. He held down the switch hook so the line wouldn't disconnect.

"How much longer can we let this happen?" Kate whispered, clicking a retractable pen over and over. She stopped clicking to accept the outstretched receiver from Greg and flipped through an open file on the desk.

"It's not really up to us, is it?" said Greg, keeping an eye on the screen door for any stray campers.

"Have you called Rick yet?"

"Yeah, I talked to him about ten minutes ago. He said he'd let the rest of the station know."

"What about Gerry at the paper? And Bob at Channel 4?"

"Gerry won't let a repeat of last summer happen, trust me. Besides, that story disappeared. And Bob has never been a concern, you know that."

"It's just...it's just getting out of hand, don't you think?" said Kate, pulling her finger down a list of names. It stopped briefly and then moved horizontally across the page.

"It's not for us to decide."

"But, Greg, someone is going to catch on. Someone is going

to realize that these kids aren't really running away, going home, or forever missing. At some point, some parents are going to request an outside investigator or send in the state police." She looked hard at Greg.

"We'll cross that bridge when we get to it."

"How can you be so calm about this?"

"Look, it's been what—two years since the Incident. Our methods are working, are they not?"

"They're working, but campers are dying, Greg. The numbers are increasing. It's not being kept at bay. I think some of the counselors are starting to feel uncomfortable about the whole thing."

"Uncomfortable?" Greg laughed. "Uncomfortable?! Are they uncomfortable about losing their life?" He slammed his fist on the desk. "God, this place! You'd think they would remember that they were all campers not so long ago. They pledged an oath, dammit!" He swiped the phone from Kate's hand and slammed it back into the cradle.

"I know, I know," said Kate, trying to appease him. "I just think they could use some reassurance, that's all. They work really hard to make sure the rest of the campers don't suspect anything, and it's harder with the more kids we have to dispose of."

"Fine, okay, yes. We'll have a special counselor meeting before Manhunt. But I swear to you if one of them falters, they're next."

"Understood. I think that will be a significant motivator to get their heads back in the game," agreed Kate.

"Have we selected the next...candidate?" asked Greg, sighing and looking at the list.

"Well, this one is from western New York, and she's not a Lifer, though I sort of thought she should've been..."

"Western New York, hmm," said Greg. He spun around in his chair and examined a map of the United States pinned to the wood-paneled wall. There were tiny red marker dots pressed into the map, scattered throughout the Northeast. He stood up and leaned in to have a better look.

"Then there's always this one from Frederick, Maryland," said Kate quickly. "He might be more suitable becau—"

"No, we had one from Maryland last summer, see? Right here." He pointed. "But we haven't had one from western New York ever. I think that's our go-to."

"She hangs out with a lot of the Lifers," Kate argued, staring at his back.

"That shouldn't be a problem, as long as the counselors do their job. Everyone has a role to play," said Greg. "It worked with Penelope."

"Corey was close to uncovering something after Penny," said Kate.

Greg ignored her. "I think western New York will do just fine."

Kate let out an inaudible sigh. "Okay, who do you want to take care of it?"

"Um, why don't you have Mark and Hannah take this one? Give Delilah and Adah a break."

"All right."

"And we'll call the parents in a day, like we always do."

"Okay," said Kate slowly.

"You good?" said Greg, annoyed.

"Yeah, fine," said Kate. "I'm just not sure about this one. I feel like it may come with repercussions."

"Eh, it'll be fine. You thought that about Penny, too. Now, here," said Greg, picking up the receiver again and letting go of the switch. "Make the call." He handed it to her.

"Right," said Kate. Looking at the list, she punched some numbers on the phone. The phone rang several times before a tinny voice answered.

"Hi, is this June's mom? This is Counselor Kate at Camp Kinross. Are you sitting down?"

43

The afternoon sun was sinking behind the tips of the pine trees, as Maggie and Beth walked up the path toward their cabin. Ahead of them, Hannah was relaying glory days to Adah. Behind them, Becky was passing bits of relationship advice to Liv. Other campers could be heard bubbling over with excited chatter about the much anticipated game of Manhunt.

"I think I have an idea," said Beth.

Maggie glanced at her out of the corner of her eye. "Yeah?" said Maggie quietly.

"I *definitely maybe* do," replied Beth. She thought a moment, before speaking again. "What if during Manhunt, I go look for...an Oasis?"

"How?" whispered Maggie, picking up on the code. "There are so many...uh...in there."

"Yeah, but it's one of my favorite albu—erm, getaways? I know exactly what it looks like."

"It's the one in London, right? The picture on the street?" asked Maggie.

"No, that's *(What's the Story?) Morning Glory*. This is the one where Liam Gallagher's lying down on the floor like a dead person," whispered Beth anxiously. "I'll be able to spot it super quick."

"It's risky," winced Maggie.

"It'll be fine. It's our best chance—it's our only chance, really! Tomorrow is the dance. Campers and counselors will be everywhere. Someone is bound to ask questions if they see us both creeping around the Lab. I'll go back to look to see if Woody stuffed the envelope in that record sleeve."

"If that album is even there. Yeah, I guess you have a point?"

They continued their walk in silence, while conversations pinballed around them. A cool breeze blew off the lake; an appreciative sigh of relief emanated from the girls, happy to have the slightest reprieve from the day's relentless heat. In the twilight, the shrubbery between the trunks of the tall pines changed from green to muted blue hues. The horseflies retired for the day, while the mosquitoes floated gleefully through the air around the smorgasbord walking through their territory. On her left, Maggie noticed a dense patch of briars. A jet-black bird with a snowy breast sat perched atop the thorny bush.

Maggie stared at the bird, unable to place its familiarity in her mind. It cocked its head and looked directly at her. Maggie glanced around, at Beth and the other campers, but no one seemed to notice the bird.

"Hey, Beth, look at this," nudged Maggie.

"Huh? What's up?" replied Beth.

Maggie motioned for her to look at the thicket, but when she pointed to the spot, the bird had disappeared.

"That's weird—I just saw this cool looking bird sitting on top of those thorns, but it—it must have flown away…" said Maggie. Her voice trailed off as she tried to make sense of what she saw.

"Um, neat? I didn't know you were a birder," giggled Beth.

"No, I've just seen it before—that type of bird. I can't remember where, though. I think—I think it…looked at me," said Maggie.

"Okay, yeah, you've definitely had too much sun today." Beth laughed.

"Yeah, probably," agreed Maggie, gradually pulling her eyes away from the thorns.

"Maybe it was a magpie," teased Beth.

"Funny," replied Maggie. "What does a magpie even look like?"

"No idea." Beth shrugged. "I always thought it was the British equivalent of cow manure."

"I think you're thinking of mud pies." Maggie laughed.

They reached their cabin just as the glow bugs began to noticeably flicker through the atmosphere. Dampness hung in the air like a soaked towel. The girls filed into the cabin and rushed to form a line for the shower.

"Easy, my lovelies, everyone will have a chance to rinse off before dinner, deep breaths!" assured Hannah. "You each get five minutes—I'll time you. Oh, and make sure to put on your special evening attire."

Maggie leaned against the wood-paneled wall with her towel over one arm and closed her eyes.

"Make sure you save some hot water!"

"Who's using hot water after a day like today? You want a cold shower. It's better for your skin."

"You're going to want a cold shower after tonight's game of hide-and-seek!"

"He doesn't even know I exist!"

"Becky, are you going to finally hook up with Alex tonight?"

"What makes you think I haven't already, sweetie?"

"Did you know that rinsing your hair with cold water makes it nice and shiny when it dries?"

"No one's going to have time to dry their hair tonight, sorry, girls!"

"I hope we have more than five minutes to get ready for

the dance tomorrow night."

"Maggie, how's that mix coming? The whole dance rides on you, you know."

"Good, I think?"

"Ew, God, there's a spider in the corner of the shower!"

"Kill it!"

"I can't reach it! It's up in the corner!"

"Use your shampoo bottle!"

"Nope, I'm getting out."

"Hannah, tell her to kill it! I can't go in there knowing that thing is in there watching me shower!"

"As if it wants to see you naked!"

"Hannah, dooooo something!"

"Is it moving?!"

"No, it's not moving! Not right now, anyway!"

"It's not going to hurt you, just let it be! It's only nature, my lovelies."

"What if it's one of those freakishly fast spiders? Those are the worst!"

"Don't spiders eat mosquitoes or something?"

"Yeah, you should be thanking that spider for keeping the mosquitoes from whining in your ears while you're sleeping."

"I heard that you swallow four spiders a year while you're sleeping."

"Ew, shut uppp! That is so disgusting! Why would you say something like that!"

"I wonder what's for dinner tonight?"

"Who's next—hop in!"

Maggie hung her towel on the hook outside the shower and pulled the curtain. She scouted the four corners of the stall, and sure enough, a small, plump spider clung motionless to one of them. She turned the water faucet to cool and leaned her head under it, letting the cold water spill over her. Tonight could be interesting, she thought. Hide-and-seek, in teams.

Would she be with Ryan? Would he want to hide with her? Would he want to hide with her because they had so much to discuss and figure out about what was going on at Camp Kinross? Would he want to hide with her for other reasons? Would he kiss her? Funny, not even in all of her crazy dreams had her subconscious allowed that to happen. Aren't dreams supposed to be filled with all of the things that a person longs to happen? Aren't they supposed to be a place where you can have all the things that can't be had in real life? And yet, even in her wildest dreams, dreams filled with an incomprehensible longing for him, paired with terrifying monsters and freak weather patterns, actually getting with Ryan never registered. Maybe she should just kiss him. Maybe she should tell Ryan about the weird bird, although, judging by Beth's reaction, maybe she should keep that one to herself. Beth was a good friend. It was a shame she lived so far from Bradford; Elmira, New York was at least six hours away. It's funny how living in close quarters for a week can really make a person connect with someone. It was nice to have someone else in on the supposed Kinross conspiracy, too. Sure, she could have told Tom, but at this point, there's no way he'd believe any of it. Hopefully Beth could get into the Lab tonight. Maybe Ryan could offer a better suggestion at dinner. But they were sitting with Becky and the cool kids at dinner, which posed a problem, and then there was the Lifer meeting at the end of dinner. There was no way they'd have time to hash out a plan between now and then.

She quickly rinsed off and reached for her towel on the hook. She wrapped it around her body and stepped onto the dampened bath mat. Beth was still waiting in line for the shower. As Maggie walked by her, she tried to convey with her eyes that they needed to talk. Beth smiled, sweetly unaware, and moved forward in the queue.

Maggie pulled on her night fatigues—an army-green V-neck T-shirt and dark cargo pants. Under the pile of clothes folded neatly on her bed was an army-green bandana. She stared blankly at it for a moment, then wrapped it around her wrist and tied a knot with her teeth. She towel dried her hair and brought her small makeup bag over to the mirror. Becky was already at the mirror and stepped to the side to share the space.

"Just because it's dark out doesn't mean we can't look good, right?" she grinned.

"Yeah," said Maggie, a small smile forming on her lips.

"Here, let me help you," said Becky, holding an eyeliner pencil expertly between her fingers. She leaned in and drew a thin black line across the edge of Maggie's eyelid.

"But I thought, you know—Ryan?"

"It's fine. Just because I want every boy to like me at camp, doesn't mean that I can actually have every boy like me at camp. Besides, I think Alex and I are getting more serious. I should know better after tonight. Ryan's all yours. I'm just jealous by nature," replied Becky, shrugging.

"Really?" Maggie's eyes narrowed.

"Scouts honor, or whatever," said Becky. "It's better this way. He and I had too much friction, and not the good kind. We looked great on the surface, but deep down we never connected. Plus, it's better for Kinross, too. Especially now that you're a Lifer."

"What do you mean?"

Becky lowered her voice and leaned closer, her face nearly touching Maggie's. "It's not really public information, but camp attendance is down this year. And the counselors don't always find Lifers. Sometimes they don't even hit their minimum number of Lifers for the summer. They don't just pick anyone, despite the rumors that fly around camp."

"I haven't heard any rumors about that," said Maggie.

"It's a thing, trust me," assured Becky, dragging a tube of lip gloss across her lips. She held it out to Maggie. "Here, put this on."

Maggie took the tube and gave it a few test squeezes. She copied Becky, blotting her shiny lips together.

"Put your hair up in a high ponytail," instructed Becky.

"But it's still wet. I don't think that's—"

"Just do it. It's sporty and cute. Do you wanna make out with Ryan or not?"

"I, uh, hadn't given it much thought?" Maggie shrugged.

Becky turned from the mirror to face her. "Sorry?" she said, shaking her head as if she had inadvertently walked into a spiderweb.

"I, um, well, I can't really tell what he thinks of me," said Maggie, biting her lower lip.

"Have you seen how he looks at you? Why do you think I was all in a tizzy at the beginning?" Becky laughed.

"I mean I catch those looks once in a while, but then he goes cold on me. I don't think it's a game, either," argued Maggie.

"Honey, put your hair up in a high ponytail and stop being your own biggest obstacle. You're a Lifer now. You need to jump."

"Why are you being so nice to me?" Maggie blurted out.

"You're a Lifer now," Becky repeated. "We have to take care of each other. We have to put aside all the petty bullshit for the greater good. This camp will never survive if we can't get along. It's bad enough with the missing campers."

The words fell out of her mouth. Becky immediately scanned the cabin to see if anyone else had caught her slip.

"Wait, what did you say?" asked Maggie, her eyes wide.

"I—I didn't say anything," Becky said quickly. "What I meant to say was the campers who were sent home."

"Yeah, but you didn't, you said 'missing campers'—what do you know?"

"Shhh! Keep your voice down! I don't know anything," Becky hissed.

"Becky, tell me." Maggie's eyes narrowed.

"Look," said Becky, her eyes scanning the cabin. The din of

the shower and giddy chatter made their conversation mostly inaudible. "I was walking to the Infirmary after lunch to get another bandage for this stupid cut from setting up those tables at community service. When I was near the door, I paused because I heard Greg getting loud at the camp nurse—Counselor Eve. He sounded pretty fired up, but it was mostly muffled. All I could make out was 'Well, we have to do something about it, or there will be more missing campers!'"

"So you're thinking that the Lifers should stick together because..."

"Oh, I don't know! I mean, what if a Lifer goes missing? Then what? We need to stick together. Maybe we have a better chance at not going missing—with our higher status. All I know is from the little rumblings I've overheard from Kate—that camp attendance isn't what it used to be, and then to hear Greg freaking out about missing campers—something isn't right, you know? But I'm not about to put my head on the chopping block to find out. Because in all honesty, it sounds crazy."

"I believe you," said Maggie quickly.

"What? You do?"

"Yeah, I believe you," repeated Maggie.

Becky's eyes narrowed.

"No, I do," Maggie said slowly. "I think more may be going on than any of us realize. Do any other Lifers know?"

"Oh yeah right," said Becky. "Like I'm going to throw all of this at someone like Joey."

"Why me, then? We barely know each other, and we've pretty much hated each other since the beginning of this week. Is this some sort of trap?" Maggie asked, stepping back from the mirror.

"No trap," she replied shortly. "Honestly, you...you seem like one of the smarter Lifers we have here. I mean, I think Ryan is probably the smartest, plus you're in with him, so I don't know, I thought—"

"Ohhh, you thought you'd use me to get to Ryan, since he won't give you the time of day," finished Maggie.

A sheepish grin crossed Becky's face. "Maybe? I mean, what would you do if you were me?"

Maggie scoffed. Both girls stood for a moment, staring at their dewy militant reflections in the mirror.

"We need to get the others in on this," Maggie said after a few moments.

"Okay, but how?" asked Becky.

"I dunno. Divide and conquer?" suggested Maggie. "Maybe during Manhunt?"

"It's going to be hard. Especially given the format."

"What do you mean?"

"For Manhunt, it's usually campers versus counselors."

"Seriously?"

"Yep. And they play to win. It's like a dozen college-aged gym class heroes."

"That's...that's not what I expected you to say."

"Oh yeah, totally, just wait until you see them in their gear. They do the eye black, sweatbands, the whole bit."

"Wow."

"Yeah," said Becky, her eyes glazed over in thought. Creases formed on her forehead. "And now...now that I think about it more, in the three summers that I've been a Lifer, we always lose one or two campers because of Manhunt."

"Lose..."

"They get sent home, for misbehaving or something," said Becky.

"Oh, man," said Maggie.

"Yeah, now that I'm thinking about it..."

"Right?"

"It doesn't make sense, though," argued Becky. "The counselors really care about the kids at this camp. There's no way they'd let them go missing on purpose. They'd call the cops, wouldn't they?"

"It doesn't add up," agreed Maggie. "We should probably be careful who we tell about this. I, for one, don't want to go missing."

Becky stared at her, worry spreading across her face like an allergic reaction.

"Okay, so what are we going to do?"

Maggie shifted uncomfortably in her unrequested newfound authority.

"Well, let's sort this out—Ryan is in, I'm pretty sure Liv will be in, Beth isn't a Lifer, but she's in, and I don't know—maybe Corey knows something about it? Ryan's been talking to him a lot. What about the rest?"

"How do you know that Liv is in?"

"We were initiated together, remember? And she saw—well, something, in the woods. I'll let her fill you in."

"Really? Okay. I think it'll be pretty hard to persuade Alex, but if we can get him, Joey will be in. Although I'm sure he'll screw this up somehow—whatever 'this' is. Germ seems reasonable, though."

"Yeah, we have to keep this as contained as possible. If rumors start flying, we're dead."

"Hopefully not literally," said Becky, shivering.

"So what if…what if I talk to Ryan, you connect with Liv, and then we figure out a way to fill everyone in at breakfast?"

"What about Tom?" asked Becky.

"He's not going to hear it from me—it'll be better if it comes from you and Liv, being that he's so starstruck."

"Did you ever…with him?"

"Not that it's any of your business, but no," huffed Maggie.

"Ah," said Becky. She paused. "So yeah, divide and conquer is great and all, but we don't have an actual plan."

"Well, we have a few things in the works. We found out some stuff at the library and are trying to piece it all together. Beth's looking into something tonight—hopefully during Manhunt."

"Okay, good. You talk to Ryan and Beth. I'll talk to Liv. And we'll come up with a way to tell the rest at breakfast tomorrow morning."

"Should we say anything at dinner?"

"Probably not. All of the counselors will be eating tonight."

"Carbing up before the big game?" said Maggie sarcastically.

"I'm not even kidding about them—you'll see," said Becky. "But we should probably play nice during dinner."

"Play nice..." repeated Maggie.

"Yeah, like leave your snarky 'I'm better than you attitude' at the door," replied Becky.

"I don't think I'm better than anyone!" insisted Maggie.

Becky raised an eyebrow.

"And you're going to drop your sugary sweet fake act with me?" retorted Maggie.

"I don't have a fake—" started Becky.

"Ladies! Unplug those hair dryers! I told you there wouldn't be time for that. Speaking of time, it's time for dinner!"

The girls of Cabin Three turned to see Hannah standing in the hallway, dressed head to toe in black, gloved hands on her hips. Her hair was tied in a low bun, wrapped with a black bandana around the crown of her head. Eye black was smeared under her shiny eyes. "Game on!" she smirked.

"Sweet Jesus," muttered Maggie.

"Told ya," replied Becky.

The other girls murmured disbelief as they filed out the cabin door. Maggie and Becky exchanged looks and nodded in mutual understanding.

The greater good.

44

Woody stood over the sink armed with a scouring sponge and a bottle of blue soap. A pile of pots and bowls were stacked on the counter next to him—an endless task, but he didn't mind. Washing dishes was meditative. And today, he needed the extra time to think. He didn't like to get involved with camp politics, but this summer was proving to be an inescapable divergence. He only wished he hadn't overhead that particular conversation—when he brought the delivery invoices to the camp office for processing. Up until then, all of it had been mere speculation.

Nothing but stories to scare youths around a campfire.

A hunch.

But as he approached the office, Greg had gotten loud, and Kate was making a phone call she didn't want to make. So he paused outside, curious, and listened. The counselors never told him anything. To them, he was simply background filler, another behind-the-scenes cog cranking out memorable summers for kids year after year.

Well, this one would be memorable, all right.

A chef's knife clattered to the floor, narrowly missing the toe of his work boot. That was a freebie. Another freebie was when they didn't do a background check when they hired him. Maybe if they had, they would've learned that he was more than a war vet. Maybe they would've learned that he was on the run. Maybe that knowledge would've alerted the authorities.

After receiving an honorable discharge from the whole Vietnam debacle, it was strongly suggested that he participate in a classified governmental program to assist in interrogation methods. MK-Ultra, they called it. But the joke was on those crackpot scientists pumping pills and tabs into bodies. Those pills and tabs didn't have the effects they were hoping on old Forrest Pemberton. His brain waves morphed into something they weren't prepared for: "heightened intuition," they murmured among themselves. He called them hunches and didn't see what the big deal was. They wanted to do more tests—they threatened to shock his brain into scrambled eggs if he refused—but he had had enough with the hazy film floating behind his eyes. He was tired and wanted out.

He escaped their sterile labs and set off to find a quiet hole in Vermont to settle down. It was messy, his departure from the facility, but he had no regrets. Especially after 'Nam. And by now, with the program defunct, they had probably stopped looking for him. Probably. He bent down to pick up the knife and sighed as he casually tossed it into the cloudy dishwater.

Funny, as invisible as his role was at camp, he sure heard a lot. He knew where campers were from, who had crushes on who, the cliques, the fights—all of the incessant teenage minutia that ran rampant through the camp like an incurable bout of verbal diarrhea. A constant white noise. He had his favorites—the campers he was most interested in. He derived this from the chatter fragments that hit him like shrapnel while he served the campers, masked in a stoic glare. It was always a passive interest—he rarely engaged. No sense in it. First it's a nod, then it's a conversation. Next they're asking for an extra scoop of tater tots. Demanding butterscotch sauce at the ice-cream social. Begging for a moratorium on meatloaf night. His mother's own recipe, the ungrateful sots. And then they leave, whether it be after a week or a summer.

Or permanently. Never to be seen again.

No, staying out of their lives made the most sense.

Only now he couldn't stay out of this.

Something was brewing. Something big. He had felt it for a while now.

He sprayed down the inside of a pot encrusted with gravy and frowned. Should've deglazed it when he had the chance. He jammed the scouring pad into the pan's depths and pressed hard into the metal, the hot water scalding his hand. There was one camper in particular that he had taken a liking to over the years—a Lifer—one who seemed to have similar curiosities—hunches—of his own. And now, with that other one—the new one he ran around with—the girl—things had become even more curious. She was an integral part of this. One after another, his hunches flared up like a bad case of hemorrhoids. These two campers were different, but connected, and he wasn't sure how.

He had been seeing things at night. Terrible things. He saw the kid. He saw the woods. He saw burning white fire. He saw something dark.

When he overheard that phone call outside the camp office, he also knew the next camper they were talking about. He scrubbed the pan vigorously, erasing all evidence of his cooking transgressions.

This summer, he might not be able to stay out of it.

This summer, he might have to follow his hunches.

This summer, he might have to get his hands dirty like he did after 'Nam.

He might have to help save them all.

45

The Mess Hall teemed with camouflaged, competitive excitement, resembling a mealtime for new recruits after their first day of boot camp. Even Woody wore army-colored threads, making him all the more menacing when serving mashed potatoes from an ice-cream scoop.

"Are those Woody's real army fatigues, from when he was in 'Nam?" whispered Beth.

"Probably," replied Maggie.

They giggled as they moved toward him in the food line.

"Hey, Woody, are you playing tonight?" asked Maggie, nodding at his clothes.

"I'm always playing. But it's not a game," muttered Woody. He scraped mashed potato from his scoop. Beth started to slide her tray down the line, but Woody said, "Wait. You—hold it. Bring that back here."

"No, really, I'm fine, Woody, but thanks." She started to slide the tray again, but Woody reached over the serving window and grabbed her tray with Mr. Miyagi dexterity.

"Wait," he repeated, glaring at her. He reached under the counter and pulled out two energy bars. "Take these," he said, placing them on her tray.

"Woody, these aren't really my thing," said Beth, looking

at the tray and then back at him.

"Don't be an idiot," he said evenly. "Take them. Put them in your pockets and move along."

Beth took the bars and shoved them into her pockets.

"Woody, any word on—" started Maggie.

"No, there's no dessert tonight," replied Woody.

"Do I get any bars?" asked Maggie. Woody stared at her with a blank expression. He slung more mashed potatoes and, holding the ice-cream scoop, beckoned Maggie to move along in the line.

"Why is he so weird?" exclaimed Beth.

"I feel like he's a dead end. Maybe he just says and does bizarre things to everyone," said Maggie. They carried their trays to the center of the room, where Becky and some of the other Lifers were already sitting.

"Hi, girls, sit down!" said Becky cheerfully. Maggie winced at her, and Becky quickly steered the conversation away from them.

She polled the table. "Who's ready for Manhunt?"

"Did I see Greg with night vision goggles?" asked Tom.

"It wouldn't surprise me," said Alex. "They're in it to win it."

"But what's the prize?" asked Liv.

"I'm not sure what the criteria will be this time. Last session the losers had to scrub every bathroom before the dance."

"Seriously?" Liv replied.

"Yeah, it was disgusting," added Becky.

"But if they don't make the stakes high, campers won't take it seriously," said Alex.

"Yeah, like last summer—I think it was during one of the August sessions—they said something like 'If you guys don't win, there won't be a dance' or some bullshit like that," said Germ.

"They can't do that! What about my mix?" complained Maggie.

"The thing about that, though, was that the campers didn't care. They were like, 'Fine, yeah, we don't want to sit around in the lame-ass Rec Hall for a few hours anyway.'"

"Oh god, that's right, I remember that week!" exclaimed Joey.

"Yeah, it was the closest the camp ever came to a mutiny. Greg was furious," said Alex, pressing a pat of butter into his mountain of mashed potatoes.

"I bet he was," said Maggie.

"So what they do now is use the fear of gross chores to make us play," sighed Becky.

"What's the strategy? How do we win?" asked Tom.

"Yeah, do the campers ever win?" added Liv.

"Once in a while," said Corey, "but that also comes at a price."

"What do you mean?" asked Beth.

"What Corey means is, sometimes players get booted for not adhering to the rules," explained Alex.

"Like cheating?" asked Liv.

"I'm pretty sure Penny wasn't cheating," said Corey, staring at Alex.

"No one's accusing her of anything. We don't know the whole story," argued Alex, sipping his bug juice.

"And we never will," said Corey, gritting his teeth.

Ryan patted his arm. "Easy, man. We gotta focus."

"Christ, what is Greg wearing?" spat Joey. Maggie choked on her drink, and Ryan laughed, slapping her on the back. Becky shook her already lowered head.

Greg walked to the front of the Mess Hall, black long underwear shrink-wrapped to his body. The fabric squeezed against his bulging thigh muscles as he reached the center of the room. He cracked his knuckles through black running gloves and surveyed the room. A bandana was tied over his normally flowing hair, with night vision goggles resting on top. The room erupted into waves of howling laughter.

Greg turned on his game show host smile and cupped his ear, mouthing, "What's that? What are you saying now?" The rest of the counselors weaved around the tables of campers, leaning in to shush them. The din lowered to the clinking of dishes and low murmurs. Greg laughed a hearty laugh and clapped his hands together, like he was sitting down to a hot Thanksgiving feast. One oblivious camper was still jabbering away in the corner. The room collectively followed Greg's line of vision and stared at the unknowing offender.

"Hey, champ, keep on yammering away. No, really, go ahead! I'll wait," said Greg.

The camper's face turned beet red; he stopped mid-sentence and slouched in his chair.

"You guys can laugh and chat all you want, but it's not going to help you win when you're out there tonight!" He pointed to the Mess Hall doors. Kate sidled up next to Greg and gave the campers a taunting, dancing smile.

"Tonight, for those of you who don't know, we are playing a game called Manhunt, which is pretty much self-explanatory in its title. The teams aren't by cabin; it's counselors versus campers."

The campers responded with jeers.

"But there's more of us than you guys! That's an easy win!" shouted Joey. Alex shoved his forearm into Joey's stomach.

"Joey, you've played before, you idiot," whispered Becky.

"They love getting riled up!" Joey whispered back.

"How perceptive, Joseph!" replied Greg, smiling wide. "We do need to level the playing ground somehow, don't we. Hmm…" Greg scratched his head, pretending to be deep in thought. After a minute, he looked at Kate, whispered something in her ear, and turned back to the campers.

"The rules of the game are simple. You hide. We hunt you. But you must hide with a teammate. Two to one ratio. That will make it more fair. Sound good?" asked Greg.

"That seems less fair!" someone shouted.

"That's what we are doing!" replied Greg, in a tone that suggested that the matter was closed.

The campers eyed each other for matchups. Maggie looked down at her tray. She felt a hand lightly brush her arm. She looked at Ryan. "Partners?" his eyes suggested. Maggie nodded and turned her head away to hide the smile forming on her lips.

"And no funny business out there!" barked Kate, wagging a finger across the Mess Hall.

"Oh, come on now, Kate, let 'em have a little fun!" said Greg, jostling her shoulder. "But don't be stupid, get it? That means you, Joseph."

Joey stood at attention and saluted Greg before Corey and Ryan could pull him back down into his seat. Becky rolled her eyes and twirled a straw in her fingers.

"What are the boundaries?" piped up a camper.

"Good question! You can't go into the main parking lot or inside any of the camp buildings. Otherwise, fear is your only boundary."

Liv exchanged a look with Maggie and shoved her trembling hands under the table.

"You should also be aware that the great outdoors is not your domain—it's Mother Nature's...especially at night. She's a fickle beast and not to be taken lightly. There are wild animals in these forests—fishers, wolves, coyotes, opossums, and sometimes even bears. They will not give you a free pass just because you're a Kinross camper. So go as far as you choose, but remember, we may not find you first," warned Greg.

"Oh, and we need just a quick word with the Lifers before we get this game underway—Lifers! Quick meeting outside in five minutes," said Kate. She clapped her hands to signify the end of the announcements.

Chairs scraped against the floor. Campers hurried to dispose of their refuse and to piece together strategies outside the Mess Hall.

The Lifers sat at their table for a moment longer. Liv and Tom, Becky and Alex, Maggie and Ryan were all paired, leaving Beth, Corey, Germ, and Joey at odds. They surveyed one another.

Becky tapped her fingers on the table impatiently. "Okay, guys, we need to hurry. The meeting is in a minute. How should we divvy these guys up?"

"Um, I'm sitting right here," huffed Beth.

"No, honey, it's not you. It's nothing personal. We need to figure out who is the best suited to be with loudmouth over here," said Becky, gesturing at Joey, who blew Becky a kiss in return.

"She's right," said Ryan, "and we need a strategy." Alex looked at Ryan with faux astonishment. "Well, well, well, look who's a team player again. Welcome back, man!"

Ryan grimaced. "Yeah, we just have to figure out a way to beat them this time."

"Don't they already know all of the hiding places, though? Don't you guys play this every week all summer, every summer?" asked Maggie.

"We play a lot, but not every week. Maybe once every three weeks. They like to switch it up with Capture the Flag or a movie night if it rains," replied Alex.

"Yeah, they know most of the spots," sighed Corey. "Also, it's really a game of Counselors versus Lifers. Because the newbies pick the most obvious places to hide. Obvious to us, anyway."

"There must be a way to outsmart these try-hards," offered Beth.

"Haven't found one yet," Germ said, shrugging.

"Okay, but wait—some of the newbies must find good spots once in a while," argued Tom. "Like at home, Mags and I used to climb trees to—"

"Used to, huh?" snapped Maggie.

"That's all well and good, Tommy, but open your eyes! There's nothing to climb around here," said Becky.

"Yeah, no idyllic trees for you to build a fort in, buddy," said Joey, patting him on the back.

"Come on, guys, we better get to the meeting," replied Liv, her eyes darting around the emptying Mess Hall.

"Right, okay, how about it's Beth and Corey, and Germ takes Joey," said Alex.

Beth breathed an audible sigh of relief.

"Smallest straw, goddammit," said Germ. He hung his head and stood up from the table.

"Like hell I'm the smallest straw! We're gonna win because of me!" retorted Joey. "Game on!" He winked at Liv.

Maggie and Ryan cleared their trays and met Beth in the doorway. "See you in a few, okay?" said Maggie.

Beth nodded, a knowing smile creeping up her lips.

Ryan led her to the small secluded clearing where the Lifer meeting was being held, behind the Mess Hall.

"Hey, Ry," said Maggie. "I gotta tell you something…about Beth."

"Oh, so you're allowed to use nicknames, but I'm not?" joked Ryan.

"Shut it. This is serious! Beth is going to try to find that envelope tonight."

Ryan stopped walking. "What? Tonight? She can't. You can't go into buildings."

"She doesn't care. She said she thinks she can risk it."

"That's pretty fucking stupid," said Ryan.

"Jeez, calm down! I don't think it's a great plan, either, but what choice do we have?"

"Uh, plenty. Like she shouldn't go. We'll figure something else out. And anyway, that envelope might not even prove anything. It's dumb to think that one little envelope will hold all the answers. It's not worth her life. No, call it off."

"Worth her life? Really?" hissed Maggie.

Ryan squared his shoulders to her but remained silent.

"Okay, fine, but she was pretty determined. And how are we going to call it off now, anyway? We have this meeting and then the game starts!"

"Let me think, just let me think," said Ryan, closing his eyes and rubbing his forehead. They continued their walk to the meeting in silence.

"Ugh, it didn't work," said Ryan, punching his hand lightly.

"What didn't?"

"Nothing, forget it."

A few Lifers stood on the outskirts of the huddled group, patrolling the woods for eavesdroppers.

"Sorry for the impromptu meeting, and I know it's not our usual spot, but we'll keep it brief," said Kate. Her voice was subdued.

"First, a quick welcome and congrats to the new Lifers! You've made the decision of a…lifetime!" Greg flashed a smile and laughed through his teeth at his corny joke. Kate rolled her eyes and swirled her fingers in a circular motion beckoning Greg to get on with it. He cleared his throat and continued.

"Okay, the only order of business—has anyone noticed anything off? Anything weird or inappropriate from your fellow campers? Anything during your interactions with people during community service? We are responsible to Abbotsville, so we need to hold people accountable if there was poor behavior, on anyone's part."

Tom glanced around at the other campers and scuffed his foot against a patch of crabgrass in front of him.

"Anyone? Something unbecoming or distasteful? Insulting? C'mon, guys, I'm sure there was something," pleaded Kate.

Maggie and Ryan stood on the fringe of the group. She leaned into Ryan and under her breath said, "Seems like they want to find something."

Ryan leaned back into her, so close that she felt his lips brush against her hair when he whispered, "Yeah, they always want someone." A pop of electricity surged through her. Was this a sign?

Alex nudged Tom. Greg witnessed their exchange and took a step toward Tom.

"Hey there, sport! Got anything for us?" His grin was so wide it seemed to stretch to his earlobes.

"Well, sort of? It doesn't seem like much, though. I'm not sure it's what you're looking for," replied Tom, avoiding Greg's intense stare.

"No! Speak! Please!" exclaimed Kate, a twinge of desperation in her voice.

"Uh, okay. So I had Pinegrove duty for my community service, and the guys we ended up talking to were rude." A few snickers floated through the air, but Greg and Kate slowly descended upon Tom.

"Go on. Rude how?" asked Greg.

"Well, they were mostly ragging on me, not on Beth, like I wasn't tough enough because I didn't fight in a war. I didn't say anything back to them, though, I tried to take the high road."

Liv, who was standing next to him, took a step closer to Tom and gave his hand a quick squeeze.

"Interesting. Okay, do you remember their names?" asked Kate.

"Uh, yeah...Clarence and Andy. They were playing cribbage when we arrived. I'm guessing they usually do," said Tom.

"Thank you Tom, for coming forward and being so honest. We tend to have a lot of issues with the folks over at Pinegrove. I'll put in a call."

Tom breathed a sigh of relief at the end of the impromptu interrogation. Greg stepped back and motioned to the Lifers, extending their chance to offer up any more names. After several uncomfortable moments of silence, Kate uttered, "We better move this along," to Greg, who nodded twice before rubbing his hands together.

"Okay then, but be on the lookout tonight, will you? There's usually one or two who try to push the limits. Stay focused. The integrity of this camp depends on it."

"Oh, we're focused...on beating you tonight!" said Joey.

"In your dreams," Greg sneered, sliding his goggles down over his eyes and adjusting the strap.

"And if we pull it off? If we win, what's in it for us?" demanded Corey.

Kate's face transformed into one of patronizing adoration.

"Oh, Corey, honey, that never happens—you know that. But I like your spirit! Hopefully you picked a better teammate than last summer!" winked Kate.

Corey flared his nostrils and balled his fingers into a tight fist.

Heat spread across Maggie's forehead at the thought of Penny. She blurted, "In the off chance that we do win, what do we get?"

Greg cocked his head and looked up at the star-strewn sky. His cheeks ballooned, and he let out an exaggerated sigh.

"Well, Katie, what should they get if they defeat us somehow?"

"You mean besides bragging rights? Besides the pride of being a winner?"

"Yeah, that seems like enough to me, too," decided Greg, smirking. "But what we will give you is five minutes to strategize. Be at the bell in five." With that, Greg and Kate jogged back to the Mess Hall.

The rest of the Lifers dispersed, while the core group stood around looking at one another.

"I've got nothing," said Alex after a few moments of awkward silence.

"So, we can't go indoors, and we can't go too far into the woods because a bear might eat us..." said Maggie, glancing at the other Lifers.

"Thanks, Captain Obvious!" muttered Joey.

"Save it, Joey, she wasn't finished," snapped Becky. Maggie shot Becky a look, which Becky returned with a sweet, encouraging smile. "Go on, Maggie."

"Okay, is there anything we can hide in? Maybe that would throw them off, for a minute anyway," suggested Maggie.

"You mean like a trash can, for Joey?"

"Funny, Germ. Real funny."

"I thought so."

"That might not be a bad idea," said Ryan. "There's all sorts of stuff around camp—the bus, that rusted-out Chevy behind the Infirmary, canoes, the dumpster..."

"I am not hiding in a dumpster," huffed Becky.

"How do we know when the game is over?" asked Tom.

"They ring the bell. Anyone left hiding is supposed to come out when they hear it."

"So our strategy to win is to hide in some shit? Haven't we tried that like a million times?"

"Have any better ideas, Joey?"

The Lifers threw expectant glares at Joey. "Okay, fine. Fine! But this isn't much of a plan. And it's not like the newbies won't try this, either."

"It's worth a shot." Alex shrugged. He put his hand on the small of Becky's back and steered her toward the bell.

Maggie raised her eyebrows at Ryan. "Where should we go?"

"You're the one with the plan."

"Not really." Maggie hesitated, pushing a strand of stray hair behind her ear. "But we should try to find Beth before the game starts."

"Right, good idea. Let's go."

46

The Lifers joined the rest of the campers at the front of the Mess Hall. The counselors stood stoically on either side of the bell, with hands positioned on their hips. Hannah slapped at an incessant mosquito, then promptly returned to formation.

"Are—you—campers—ready?" shouted Greg.

The campers whooped and trash talked in reply.

"Bring it on!"

"You're going down!"

"Say your prayers!"

"It's on like Donkey Kong!"

Maggie rolled her eyes. She weaved her way through the crowd, following Ryan. He turned back and yelled, "You see her?"

"No! Not yet—what if we don't?"

"I don't know, but I do know that it's almost—" A loud clang interrupted Ryan. The bell swung back and forth. The game had begun. Campers fled from the Mess Hall grounds like hunted gazelle. Maggie and Ryan stopped and looked at each other for a moment, their eyes exchanging the same thought—run.

"Good luck!" sang Hannah as the campers ran by counselors, who were bouncing on their toes and stretching their arms.

"Follow me!" Ryan took off through the underbrush. Maggie's arms flailed as she jumped over rotting logs, trying to keep up with him. They skated through pine needles on the forest floor. Briars ripped at their legs—a feeble attempt to slow them down. Maggie's heart pounded in her ears. She had played Manhunt hundreds of times at home; granted, the games were never this big, and nothing was ever really at stake, but since when did she care about winning this much? So what if they get stuck cleaning bathrooms or washing dishes for Woody? Ryan ran ahead of her. He clawed at the air, batting away invisible cobwebs.

"That—was—gross!" he huffed. They took a hard right— the Infirmary was up ahead. The area was quiet. The lights inside the Infirmary were off.

"That's...weird," spat Ryan.

"What?"

"Lights...are...out."

They ran behind the building. Stranded in a ditch was a rusted out Chevy Celebrity. The wheels were flat and missing hubcaps. The windows were shrouded in dust, and a crack spanned the entire windshield—a permanent spiderweb glittering in the moonlight. Ryan and Maggie slowed as they approached the car.

"Dreamy," said Maggie, pulling at the front door handle. It didn't budge. She moved to the back-seat door. With some effort, it creaked open. Maggie jumped back.

"Wanna go for a riiiiide?" sang Corey in his best Billy Corgan voice, leaning across the back seat through the open door.

"Jesus, Corey, you scared me!" said Maggie. "Beth! We were looking for you!"

"Slide over, quick," said Ryan. They squeezed into the back seat of the car. Maggie shut the door tightly and slammed her palm down on the button lock. The rotting upholstery from the ceiling ballooned downward.

"Yeah, the front doors don't work. We tried them. And the passenger side window was open when we got here, so the seats are pretty gnarly."

"Smells great," commented Ryan.

"Beth, thank God we found you! You can't go to the Lab. It's not worth it."

"Yeah, Maggie's right," said Ryan. "We can find a better way."

"What are you guys talking about?" asked Corey.

"Don't be stupid. I'm going," insisted Beth. "It's our best chance of recovering that envelope. We're pretty close to the Rec Hall—it'll be easy."

"Yeah? You're going to sort through a ton of records without turning a light on?" Ryan leaned over to look directly at her.

Beth clicked on and off a small flashlight in reply.

"Shut that off!" he exclaimed. "We can't draw any attention to ourselves."

A twig snapped. They froze.

Ryan slowly slid down in the seat. The rest copied him. Their heads were level with the door.

Another snap.

Then another.

Each snap drew closer to the car.

"Shit," exhaled Corey.

Fear pulsed through Maggie's veins. She was sure that everyone could hear her heart trying to bust through her rib cage. Her arm rested on top of Ryan's arm and pressed into his chest—she could feel his heart racing against it. She tried to look at him with her peripheral vision, but feared even the slightest twist of the neck would draw attention to their hiding spot.

The twigs stopped snapping.

A scratching noise grazed the hood of the car.

It stopped, then a rhythmic tapping started.

Tap, tap, tap.

A pause.

Tap, tap, tap.

Pause.

Without warning, the tapping became a slamming, as if a maul ax was punching holes into the metal hood. Maggie squeezed her eyes shut. She could feel Ryan's pulse quicken. Her palms were on fire. The fabric of his pants was at the edge of her fingertips—well worn and soft from weeks of night games at camp. She opened one eye and looked at the windshield. The moon's glow was a hazy sparkling residue through the cracks in the windshield. Maggie could just barely make out a shadow looming over the hood. Maybe it was the angle in which she was sitting. Or a visual distortion from the broken windshield. Or perhaps the positioning of the moon. The silhouetted figure appeared to be as tall as a flag post, but the shadow didn't stretch more than two feet wide. A familiar, sickening feeling brewed in her stomach. Seconds felt like hours. Maggie opened her other eye and squinted, trying to get a better look. If she could only lean forward just the slightest bit...but the moment the thought appeared, she felt her head shout, "No! Don't move!"

Only it wasn't her inner monologue.

She distinctly heard Ryan's voice. But there's no way he yelled out loud—and that loud. Beth and Corey would have said something. Someone would have hit him to shut him up. The stranger outside the car surely would have heard it.

And then, as quickly as the assault had started, it stopped.

Twigs snapped as the attacker moved into the distance.

After a moment, a shriek emanated from the woods.

"Jesus Christ, what was that?" whispered Beth.

"No idea." Ryan turned to Maggie, then Corey. "You okay? You guys good?"

"I think so," said Maggie, wiping the sweat from her hands

on her pants. She took a breath and sighed. "So, that was, uh, a counselor?"

"Possibly," said Ryan. He exchanged a glance with Corey.

"Did you guys see it through the windshield? It looked bigger than a person." Maggie shivered.

"Do you think it's gone, whoever or whatever it was?" Corey rubbed his forehead. A cloud passed in front of the moon. The four were cloaked in darkness.

"Probably," said Ryan. He leaned forward, his fingers brushing across Maggie's leg. "Maybe it was Greg with his stupid war game props."

"Yeah, they get off on scaring the shit out of us during Manhunt." Corey shook his head.

"But why wouldn't they have tried to open the doors?" asked Maggie.

"Beats me," said Ryan.

"All right, I'm going to go try to get that envelope now." Beth reached for the door handle. It groaned as the lever released. She pushed open the door with her foot.

"What? You can't be serious! Shut that door! Were none of you here for what just happened? I don't think that was a counselor! It couldn't have been. I felt that same sickening feeling from…from my dreams—no, you're not going!"

"Cor, why don't you go with Beth? She'll fill you in on everything I haven't, and if she gets into trouble trying to get into the Lab, then at least you'll be there to diffuse," said Ryan.

"You guys are out of your minds!" said Maggie.

"Yeah, I can do that," said Corey, climbing out of the car after Beth. He closed the door carefully, lifting the latch handle to avoid being heard by whatever lurked in the shadows.

Maggie and Ryan sat in silence, in darkness, for a moment. Despite the freed up space in the back seat, he didn't slide away from her.

"I can't believe they left!"

"It sounded like whatever it was, it moved away. They should be okay."

"So Corey knows?"

"He knows a lot. Not everything."

"Think he'll be able to help Beth?"

"He'll keep her out of trouble."

"So, what happened with his girl—Penny?"

"Oh, that. That was last summer. He's still pretty fired up about it. Penny was like you—well, I mean, she was a cool girl, though she didn't have your…uh, she was smart and sweet—she slid right into the Lifers circle as if she'd always been there. She was infectious. Even Becky liked her from the get-go."

"But then she was kicked out?"

"That's just it. She was picked to make a mix for the dance—like you—and then the next morning after Manhunt, she didn't show up to breakfast. No one, and I mean no one, had any idea—not Mark or Hannah—none of the trustworthy people, so to speak, knew what happened. We were all shaken by her absence. Greg and Kate took our table aside and explained that she had been caught stealing from the Lab."

"But that doesn't make any sense—there's nothing to steal in there! What are you going to shove a Simon and Garfunkel record under your polo?"

"Exactly. It didn't add up. Corey was real tight with her, so when he heard this, he freaked."

"Was she a Lifer?"

"That's the other thing—I'm not sure if anyone has told you, but Lifers don't get bounced from camp. Ever. They get plenty of warnings and reprimands—counselors can make your life hell if you abuse your privileges—but they won't kick you out. It's just how it's always been. But she was a Lifer."

"If she was so well liked, kicking her out seems to go against what the camp is trying to build, with this whole Lifer thing."

"Yeah. Plus, Corey knew her. He knew she'd never steal anything. So he snuck around. He tried to uncover the real reason. And he didn't give up—still hasn't. He spent the rest of last summer skulking around cabins and eavesdropping on counselor conversations."

"Has he found anything?"

"Some stuff, yeah. Which is why I knew I could trust him. He wants the truth as much as we do."

"So what did he find?"

Ryan paused. His eyes shifted over each of the fogging windows before answering.

"He thinks that campers are being murdered for sacrificial purposes. He thinks that local law enforcement is involved somehow. He doesn't know who is doing it or why, or how, but he knows the counselors choose their victims."

"Murdered?" hissed Maggie. She winced and looked out the window. "That can't be right—that's just, that's impossible. What about the parents?"

"He suspects they have a way around the parents. One afternoon he went to the Infirmary for a bee sting, and on his way back he walked past the camp office. He hid underneath one of the windows, and he heard Kate on the phone, telling someone that she had some 'unfortunate news' about their kid."

"Wait, wouldn't the parents drive up here immediately? Do an entire search of the camp and the woods?"

"They do. Corey thinks they do it at night, so as not to spook the campers. It's partly why we can't be out past the night bell."

"There's no way—a missing kid, and they're not going to search the camp during the day? That doesn't make sense."

"I didn't say his theory doesn't have holes in it."

"So what about Penny?"

"What about her? She's gone."

"But he thinks she's dead."

"Yes."

"What makes him think that, specifically?"

Ryan sighed. "When Penny was 'sent home,' Corey refused to believe it. He skipped activities and meals and wandered the woods. The counselors let it slide and gave him a lot of space; they thought it was a good life lesson or whatever. Anyway, on one of his walks through the forests, he went pretty far—farther than he probably should have gone. He was somewhere near the base of Mount Kinross, I believe. He came across a bunch of boulders and a cave. He took a few steps toward this flat rock and threw up—like his body knew without him actually knowing yet. He said when he wiped his mouth, something shiny, sort of near this big flat rock, caught his eye. He knelt down and pulled a silver heart-shaped locket from the dirt. It had a 'P' in script on the front. It was hers. She wore it every day."

Maggie hugged herself, her shoulder pressing into Ryan's even more than before the four of them were in the back seat.

"Did he tell anyone?"

"Not really. He told Mark, me. It had blood on it, Mags, the chain of the necklace. Dried blood."

"Jesus. What did Mark say?"

"It's hard to get a read on Mark—he didn't say much. He might be our closest thing to an ally out of all of the counselors. He wavers, but he's cool. I doubt he'd ever see us as a threat to the point where he'd want us murdered. That's what Corey and I were talking about on the beach earlier, by the way." He raised his eyebrows at her and smirked.

"What? I didn't care—ugh—you're so annoying." Maggie blushed.

"Yeah, most people either love me or hate me," said Ryan.

"Wait a second—no! You didn't even see me looking at you

during swim the other day! How did you—"

"Hey, that's the other thing I wanted to say," said Ryan. He sat up a bit. Maggie looked at him from the corner of her eye. His face was so close to hers that the tiny hairs on her cheek stood on edge, as if lightning was nearby. If she turned her head, her lips could touch his. Energy coursed through her body and buzzed at the tips of her fingers. Maybe he'll kiss me. Maybe he wants to kiss me. What harm could one kiss do? It had to mean something, this sudden electrical storm surging through her. It's not like she willed it to happen; it just materialized, like a tornado ready to wreak unexpected havoc. There was no place to take cover. Please just kiss me.

"This isn't going to be easy," he said.

Maggie bit her lower lip. "No?" Her eyes twinkled. She turned her head slightly.

Ryan closed his eyes and sighed. "It's not like that."

"Not like what?"

"It's the thing I tried to tell you the other day while we were waiting for the bus."

"Oh, the family thing? Sure, go ahead," said Maggie, deflating.

"Only it's not a family thing. It's something about me."

"Ryan, just tell me. It's not a big deal."

"It will be," he resigned.

Maggie let out an exasperated sigh and faced him. "Talk," she insisted.

"I have this ability," he said quietly, "to see things."

"Uh, hey, genius, most of us have that ability," she replied.

"No, dummy. I can see shit in people's heads."

"You can...what?"

"I can see what other people are thinking. Well, sort of. Sometimes. And I can make people see things. I can pass along ideas and thoughts to them...just by thinking."

"Stop it," Maggie laughed. "Like Professor X? I thought you were being serious."

"I am," said Ryan. He looked down at his hands.

The car fell silent. Outside, barred owls hooted, sounding more like rowdy monkeys in a dense jungle than any bird of prey on the prowl.

"Ryan, hold on a sec. You—you think you're telepathic?"

"I don't think...I know."

"Oh my good God. Of course! I don't fall for the kid who secretly still plays with G.I. Joes, or has a hidden stash of Beanie Babies with all of the tags intact—no! I fall for the guy who thinks he can read people's minds. This is just brilliant! Really." Maggie buried her head in her hands.

"You...fell for me?"

"Seriously, right now?" Maggie shook the muffled words out of her head. Then she sat straight up with daggers in her eyes. "Okay, hotshot, if you can read my mind, what am I thinking right now, huh?"

"It doesn't work like that," he replied quietly.

"What do you mean 'it doesn't work like that'? You're going to drop some batshit crazy sci-fi nonsense on me like this, and then tell me that there are specifics as to how this 'superpower' works?"

"It's complicated, like with your dreams," said Ryan.

Maggie's eyes widened with accusation. "What about my dreams?" she said evenly through her teeth.

"Just let me explain, okay? This isn't easy, you know," he replied, leaning away from her.

"I'm all ears."

Ryan ran his fingers through his hair and sucked in a big breath of air. "So I can't, like, plant things in your head. Well, I can, it's just—there are certain things I wouldn't. And I can't make you like me or anything like that. I can just set up scenarios, paint pictures, pass along information..."

"So my dreams—all of these awful nightmares I've been having with that horrible monster, were put into my head by—by you?" Maggie set her jaw.

"Not entirely. It's hard to explain."

"Really? Is it just me? Do you do this to others, too?"

"Listen, there's just some stuff I'm never going to be able to explain to you, and you're just going to have to deal with it!"

Maggie looked up. "How am I suddenly the bad guy here? You're the one who dropped this on me! I can't control my dreams...but apparently you can?"

"Shh." Ryan held his hand in the air. "Someone's outside."

Suddenly, the back-seat door flung open, and Greg yelled, "Aha! Caught ya!" He reached inside and grabbed Maggie's wrist, dragging her out of the vehicle with Ryan following closely behind. "Two more POWs!" he cried gleefully. He marched them through the woods and back to the bell. "Line up with the others, alongside the Mess Hall," he barked, before bounding off into the woods.

Maggie's head spun. "So hold on—you're saying—" she started.

"Not here," murmured Ryan.

"Then where?" asked Maggie, clenching her fists. "You can't just unload that on me and—"

"Follow me," he said. They hurried back to the Mess Hall and quickly slid behind the line of the Manhunt prisoners. Ryan ducked underneath the latticed ramp running alongside the building. He motioned for Maggie to follow him.

Cobwebs were thickly strung across the little alcove, as if woodland creatures had decorated for a Halloween party. The ground was dank, with decaying leaves piled up against rusty cans stacked near the lattice.

"Lovely," said Maggie.

"This buys us a few minutes," he said. "Okay, so the only thing I have been trying to convey to you in your dreams is the thing—the monster. I promise."

"So you can see it?"

"Yeah, I can see it. I've seen it."

"What?!"

"Shh, not so loud."

"No." Maggie paused. "No. No, no, no. That's not real. It can't be real. You're insane. You've lost it!"

"I didn't say it's real. I said I've seen it, but I've only seen it in my dreams, just like you. It's the second summer I've seen it, and I don't know where it came from. So I passed it along to you."

"Gee, thanks," replied Maggie, brushing a cobweb away from her mouth.

"I was able to pass it on to Corey, too," Ryan continued, "and, well, you know his deal. He's been trying to find information on it, but I think he was getting too close. The counselors suspected he was up to something, so they took him off library duty for community service."

"Those missing pages in that book we found, was that…?"

"No. He said he had also come across that book, and the pages were already ripped out. The next week he was reassigned."

"That's weird," said Maggie, wiping her eyes.

"Yeah, that's what tipped him off that there might be some sort of counselor conspiracy."

"You're not suggesting that he may be onto something with his sacrificial offering theory…"

"I don't know what to think anymore. I hadn't given it much thought until you came along."

"Huh?"

Ryan winced before turning back to Maggie. "There's more."

"More?"

"Okay, so I have this—let's call it 'telepathic' ability, but when you came along, something happened. It's really hard to—"

"Hard to explain, right, yes, I know!" persisted Maggie.

"When you came along, something got messed up. This week I've been having more dreams with that monster.

Normally if I had an out of the ordinary dream, I'd pass it on to Corey, thinking maybe it would help him somehow in figuring out what happened to Penny, but I couldn't take them to him anymore. I could only take them to you."

"Take them?"

"I see a door—in my mind. I open it, and I can share stuff from my head with you."

"So you're a lucid dreamer?"

"Something like that, I guess. Sometimes it's called dreamwalking, but mine doesn't happen only at night. It can happen while I'm awake, too. But not often."

"How—how did you figure out that you could get into my head?"

"A door showed up when I met you. When it didn't appear for Corey anymore, I figured I'd try you," sighed Ryan, scanning their whereabouts before continuing. "But every time I opened your door, I woke up feeling like I was on fire."

"Like sweaty? That's normal, isn't it? Like some sort of subconscious panic attack?"

"No, I felt like someone was holding a flame to me, but all over my body. I've never felt anything like that."

Maggie sat motionless, looking at the wet, rotting leaves. She met Ryan's eyes. "In my dreams, I felt really hot, too—I remember that distinctly. I felt like my tears were wax and that my insides were combusting. Do you mean like that?"

"I guess? But it was when I woke up. What I think is…"

"Yeah?"

"Maybe there's something different about you, too."

"What? No, you've lost your mind." Maggie laughed. "I mean, I think it's cracked that you think you have this secret power of mind control, but to suggest that I have my own X-Men ability is insane. I'm out of here." Overwhelming waves suddenly crashed over her. Maggie crawled back toward the alcove's entrance.

"Maggie, seriously, hear me out, will you?"

"Nope, I'm done," said Maggie. Her blood boiled and hot tears welled in her eyes. How could she let this happen to her? Why did she let herself get so close to him? Why did she let her guard down? Wasn't she happy enough with her regular life? She had Tom, and when they got home, things would go back to normal—movie nights in his basement, bike rides to Pluto's Pizza, Capture the Flag with the younger neighborhood kids, pool days at Brendan's house. Why did she need any of this? This was all stupid drama that wouldn't mean anything the second she got back home. I don't need to be a Lifer, she thought. I don't need Ryan or his stupid charm—so what if it felt like they had known each other since the beginning of time… He probably planted that thought into my head anyway, she thought dejectedly. Telepathic? Dreamwalking? Come on. This guy wasn't worth her tears. Campers may have gone missing, but it's not her business. I'll just survive the rest of the week and get the fuck out of here. I'll bury my feelings for him and patch up the hole that he created in my defenses.

"Maggie," Ryan said, reaching for her hand.

"Don't…touch me," she replied coolly, a tear slipping down her cheek. She climbed out from under the ramp and weaved away from him into the mass of campers waiting for the game to end.

With eyes forlorn, Ryan watched her go. He felt a tap on his shoulder. Corey looked like he had been visited by the ghost of Christmas past in the shadowy moonlight.

"Corey, what's wrong—what happened? You look like you're going to be sick."

"It's—it's Beth," he spat.

"What? What happened? Where is she?" Ryan asked, quickly looking around the crowd.

"She's—she's gone. I don't know how it happened. But I think they took her, like they—like they took—" Corey coughed to cover the sob escaping from his throat.

"Shit, okay. Okay. Come with me. We have to find Maggie." He grabbed Corey's shoulder and dragged him through the crowd.

"Maggie? Maggie! There you are. Maggie, listen—" said Ryan, out of breath and exasperated.

"No, Ryan! You listen! I'm done! I said I was done! Get out of my life! What don't you understand—"

Ryan dodged the sting of her words and pressed on. "Maggie, it's Beth," he said. Maggie looked at Corey, who was biting his lip to keep from breaking down. Their eyes met, each a reflection of anxiety and horror.

"What? Where is she?" Maggie asked, bewildered. Ryan shook his head, trying to find the words. Corey squatted, resting his elbows on his knees. He covered his face with his hands.

"Not again," he moaned. "I can't go through this again!"

"We have to do something! Tell someone!" Maggie said, her anger growing shrill.

"They'll just say she's probably still hiding, or that she wandered too far," moaned Corey from the ground.

"Why don't you just put it in some counselor's mind, huh?" snapped Maggie, looking directly at Ryan. "No, seriously! If you have the power to do it, why don't you just fix the whole damn camp, huh? Why don't you save all of these alleged missing campers? What's your problem? You can't tell the missing campers how to get back to camp before they're killed by whatever goddamned monster you've conjured up in your insane imagination? Save them, Ryan! Send them a MIND MAP!" Maggie's hands pushed against his chest, knocking him off his footing. The campers around them started to take notice of the scene. "Come on, Ryan! Save them! Why don't you mess with them instead of me, huh?"

"Easy, Mags, easy," said Ryan, his eyes pleading with her.

"You suck, you know that? You really suck. You're a jerk, and you led me on, and you devised this stupid fucking story as your out!" she screamed, her eyes no longer able to harness her flowing tears.

"Where is she, Ryan? Where, huh? Where is she? Why isn't she with Corey? Find her with your MIND!" screamed Maggie, hysterical.

Ryan grabbed her and pulled her into his chest. Her body heaved in sobs. Corey stood up and made quiet jokes to the campers around them. "She just really hates losing?" he said with a shrug. The other campers raised their eyebrows but resumed their conversations.

"We'll find her," Ryan whispered to Maggie, picking a cobweb from her shoulder. "And it's not my out...I don't...want an out."

Maggie wiped her eyes and blinked a few times. "I don't even know why I care—this is so dumb," she said, sniffling.

"Yeah."

"You still suck," said Maggie, "and I'm still mad."

"Obviously," replied Ryan, laughing a little.

"How are we going to find her?" Maggie looked from Ryan to Corey, both distraught and ashen. They continued to scan the ever growing crowd of campers. Maggie spotted Becky and Alex, both slightly disheveled with flush grins on their faces.

"C'mon, let's go," said Ryan.

Maggie followed them as they moved through the crowd of camouflaged campers, bored and irritated at their imprisonment. Ryan stopped next to Becky and Alex.

"Hey, guys," said Alex, and threw them a defeated grin of sympathy and a shoulder shrug. Maggie moved next to Becky and asked under her breath, "Did you talk to him?"

Becky hesitated. "I was, uh, preoccupied?" She smoothed her tangled hair down.

"Seriously?" said Maggie, raising her voice. Ryan shot her a look.

"What's up? What did I miss?" asked Germ, appearing on

the outskirts of the group.

"Where's Joey?" asked Corey.

"No idea. We split up when Greg charged at us by the Rec Hall. Jesus, he takes this game seriously—it was like we were running for our damn lives." Germ shook his head.

"You may have been," mumbled Maggie.

Alex rolled his eyes. "Come on now, guys, it's all in good fun. We were designed to be competitive. It's in our blood. When you think about it, Kinross is just trying to expand our potential within our species—"

"Oh, cut the crap, Alex," spat Corey. "How can you be that oblivious? Maybe you should be hanging out with the other Lifers instead of us."

Alex's eyes narrowed. "What's your problem, man? Ever since last summer you've been a moody little—"

"Guys, now's not the time for this—the counselors will be back any second," said Ryan.

"Why are you defending him, Ryan, huh? You two are always skulking around together. If I didn't know any better, I'd think you were trying to undermine the camp," Alex accused.

"Wait, where are Tom and Liv?" asked Maggie.

"Haven't seen them since the start," Alex shrugged. "I'm sure they're just fine."

"Well, Beth isn't," retorted Maggie.

A silence fell over the group.

"Wasn't Beth with you, Corey?" accused Alex.

"Alex, stop—" said Becky anxiously. Her eyes fell on Corey. "What happened to Beth?"

"She's missing."

"She'll probably come wandering out when they ring the bell, you'll see."

"She's not going to," said Corey evenly.

"What's that supposed to mean?" demanded Alex. He looked around at the silent Lifers. "Why am I getting the feeling that I'm the only one who doesn't know what the hell is going on with you guys?" He turned to Becky, who averted his eyes.

"Something is going on here, at camp," started Ryan.

"Oh, not this again," said Alex, throwing his hands in the air. "You need to bury this shit. Your crazy conspiracy nonsense is going to get us all kicked out of camp. You gotta stop!" He pointed at Ryan and then Corey. "And for you to rope these other Lifers into this—wait until I tell Greg—just unbelievable."

"No! Alex! You have to listen!" said Becky, grabbing his hand, her eyes pleading.

"I thought this stupid story was dead. I humored it last summer. I kept quiet, but now I'm done with it. It's toxic, and it's going to poison this camp—I can't let that happen. As a Lifer, I swore an oath—"

"What good is an oath if you're the one dead?" hissed Maggie. "What good is defending an oath that is killing people? What does that say about you, and using all of your goddamn potential to set a murdery example for others?"

"How do we know Corey isn't the one making these girls go missing, huh? If you want to talk about conspiracies…" Alex retorted.

"Look at him, man," said Germ. "There's no way he's doing that. Just shut your mouth and let's listen to this."

In the distance, white lights bobbed in unison through the woods. The counselors were on their way back.

"Alex, just hear us out, okay? We need you. It's going to take all of us. We can't stop this without you."

"Stop what?" said Alex, sighing.

"The…Wendigo," said Corey.

Maggie stared at Corey. The floating puzzle pieces in her mind rotated into place. The monster she had been seeing in her dreams, it had to be. The Scrabble game, the teeth, the screams. She looked at Ryan for affirmation. He nodded slightly. Maggie took in a big breath and exhaled, rubbing her temples.

"What—the—fuck—is a Wendigo?" said Alex, rolling his eyes.

"It's literally your worst nightmare," said Maggie without hesitation.

"Jason Voorhees is my worst nightmare." Alex laughed. He looked around, but the other Lifers weren't laughing. "You can't be serious," he said. The bobbing lights were closing in. They could make out Tom and Liv being dragged from the woods by two counselors. Becky caught Liv's eye and nodded for them to come stand with the rest of them.

"Hey, guys, they caught you, too, huh?" said Tom. When nobody replied, he said, "Did we miss something? Why are you guys so tense?"

Alex set a steely glance on Ryan and Corey before turning to Tom. Ryan returned the stare. Corey dismissively raised his hands in front of him and dropped them.

"Well, Tom, glad you asked! Ryan and company here seem to think that there's some sort of beast in the woods that is killing the campers who are getting 'sent home' from camp."

Liv's eyes widened. She grabbed Tom's hand and bit her lower lip.

"They're right," said Liv quickly.

Alex's eyes widened. "Jesus Christ, they have you believing this, too?"

"No, I haven't talked to them. I saw something when we had our blood drawn, during initiation. I saw it outside of the Infirmary," replied Liv.

"Saw what?"

"Something awful. Something that wasn't human or animal."

"Why didn't you say anything before? Why didn't you go to the counselors?" Alex demanded.

Corey jumped in. "Lay off her, man. What the hell is she

supposed to do with that kind of information on her own?"

"Why wouldn't she do anything with that information? I'll tell you why—because it sounds crazy!" argued Alex.

"The counselors are in on it. They're dropping the campers off to be eaten by this thing," said Corey.

"A sacrificial offering? Don't be so naive—why would they do that?"

"How should we know? All we can do is guess. Maybe it keeps the evil away from the camp?" added Becky.

"This is ludicrous."

"How about this, Alex. How about you go along with us, see it through, and if it's a complete fabrication, we'll all be sure to absolve you in front of Greg and Kate before we get kicked out of camp," said Maggie.

"Campers! It's time to tally up the victims!" Greg boomed in front of the crowd outside of the Mess Hall.

The group looked at Alex expectantly. He rolled his eyes and said, "Fine, okay, but I'm going on the record as thinking that you're all out of your minds. Do you even have a plan for this idiotic escapade?"

"Not yet," said Corey. "We needed to have you on board first. We'll come up with something tonight and hash it out over breakfast tomorrow."

"Is Joey really not back yet?" said Germ, scanning the crowd. An uneasy silence fell over them amid the sea of grumbling campers awaiting the outcome of their loss.

"Campers! Attention!" yelled Kate. She looked at Greg, who stepped forward.

"Your effort was valiant, though if we're being honest, in vain," bellowed Greg, surveying the crowd. "Even with teams, it seems you guys couldn't get the job done."

"This is over the top," Germ said, yawning.

"That being said, since you couldn't pull off the big W, we have a special twofer punishment—no, no, punishment is the wrong word." He chuckled. "We have two consequences for you!"

"Seriously?" said Corey. Ryan nudged him.

"Quite serious, I'm afraid, Corey," replied Greg. "See, this morning, Woody received an extra bulk order of onions. We don't want these onions to go to waste, but we have no need for them. So, you're each going to eat one! Raw." He snickered.

The campers exchanged confused looks.

"Just throw them out or donate them," said Ryan. He looked at Mark, who wiped his face and shrugged.

"Nah," said Greg. "This is easier than transporting the bulk bags to the Abbotsville food pantry. And we don't want rotting onions sitting in our dumpster—trash pickup isn't until Monday."

"This is stupid," said Becky, her face souring.

"This is hazing," Maggie said under her breath.

"What kind of onions are they? I hope Vidalia!" asked Joey, walking out of the woods. His shirt was mangled and leaves were caught in his curly hair. The Lifers looked at him sideways.

"Nice of you to join us, Joseph!" exclaimed Greg, giving him a slow golf clap.

"Nice of you to not find me," he retorted. "So, I won, right?"

"Sadly for you, they are not Vidalia. They are the standard yellow variety, and no, you didn't win," smirked Greg. The other counselors busied themselves by picking up orange mesh sacks from the picnic table and distributing onions to the campers.

"But the dance is tomorrow night—we're all going to stink!" whined Becky, holding an onion in the palm of her hand.

"It'll be over a lot faster if you just peel it and eat it like an apple," said Germ, letting flecks of the papery skin float to the ground.

"Wait, hold up, what's the other punishment? You said there were two," Joey pointed out.

"Ah, yes, thanks for the reminder, Joe! Litter duty, after breakfast tomorrow," replied Kate. She scrunched her nose as the wafting acrid aroma of onions dispersed into the air. The sounds from the humming insect nightlife were overpowered by the crisp skins crumpled and tossed aside, the soft crunch of the onion's dense, spicy interior, and the disgusted groans from campers.

Maggie bit into her onion. Her taste buds absorbed the slow burn as they came to terms with its pungent flavor.

"It's bad enough when onions are in salad and you taste them for the rest of the day," she complained to Ryan, who looked unaffected by it.

"This is so gross," she continued. "My mouth is on fire, and I'm pretty sure everyone is going to be oozing onion from their pores for the rest of the week."

Ryan tilted his head and took another bite.

"Wait a second," she said, distastefully picking a stray piece of onion skin from her tongue. "Are you...are you enjoying your onion?"

Ryan shrugged. "I dunno, I kinda like it?"

"Oh my GOD, seriously? Well, maybe I should go let Kate know, I mean I'm sure they have extra—" Maggie pretended to look around for a counselor. Ryan yanked on her shoulder to stop her. "Nah, one is plenty. I'm good."

"You sure? Because she's just over there," said Maggie, her face feigning concern.

The campers spat and moaned. A few stumbled into the corners to wretch the spicy vegetable out of their system.

"Those jerks just ruined onions for everyone here, probably for forever," huffed Alex.

"Yeah, except for this guy," said Maggie. "He's eating his like it's a piece of chocolate cake."

"Really, man?" implored Alex.

Ryan shrugged again.

"Hey, Ry, I shouldn't have freaked out earlier. Sorry, man. Your theory is insane, but you know what? I'll go on your little monster chase. I doubt it will resolve anything, but for the sake of camaraderie or whatever, especially after this bullshit onion stunt…I'm in. But we definitely need a plan," said Alex.

"Okay, great. Can you get Joey on board? Whatever we plan to do, we should execute during the dance tomorrow night," said Ryan.

"Yeah, I'll get Joey on board, though he's gonna be a weak link," sighed Alex.

"You never know," said Ryan.

"Wrap it up, campers!" chimed Greg, surveying the clearing. Onion peels rolled through the clearing like tumbleweeds over the plains.

Ryan turned to Maggie. "We'll find her. It's going to be all right."

"You don't know that," she said, her face falling.

"Gotta hang on to hope. Otherwise, what else do you have?" he replied.

"Can you look into her head, to see where she is?"

"I tried. It doesn't work on some people. It only worked once for her." Maggie's mind flashed to Bonfire Night and Beth's weird "you're meddling with powers you can't possibly comprehend" comment.

"What's our plan then?" asked Maggie, averting her eyes from his gaze.

"We take off after the dance. Find where they're bringing the missing campers. Find this thing—wherever it lives. Corey has a pretty good idea."

"You mean *if* it lives. And if it does, how are we going to kill it? With what weapon? A stick? We don't have anything," Maggie argued.

"We'll think of something. The first hurdle is to get

everybody out during the dance."

Disappointment seeped into Maggie's thoughts. Great, now he won't even hear the mix I spent hours making for this thing. All I wanted is for the stupid stars to align just once, so we could have that one dance, she thought. Even if I'm still mad at him right now. Even if I think he's completely crazy with his telepathic nonsense. Even if he suggested that I have some unfathomable superpower. Even if we get kicked out of camp by sneaking off to kill an imaginary monster in the bug-infested woods of Vermont. All I wanted for three and a half minutes was the chance to dance with him to Tommy James. Dammit, dammit, dammit.

"Yeah, whatever, sounds good," said Maggie. She glanced at him to gauge his reaction, but he was busy observing Greg and Kate, who ushered retching campers to their respective cabins.

Ryan turned back to Maggie. "Sweet dreams!" He winked. "Too soon?"

Maggie raised her middle finger to eye level at him. Ryan half laughed and joined the crowd headed to the boys' cabins.

47

They were surrounded by lockers. Row upon row of cream-colored, square lockers.

"Where are we?" asked Maggie.

"No idea," replied Ryan, looking around.

"Are we at your high school?"

"I don't think so; are we at yours?" Ryan looked at the ground. Instead of linoleum lining the hallway, the floor was covered with matted, dried out grass.

"No, but we're not at camp, either," said Maggie.

"I have to tell you something," he said.

"Oh, from earlier? About your family?"

"Not exactly. Focus."

"Huh? Wait—am I awake in my dream, actually talking to you in real life, except not?"

"Shh. Listen."

Voices could be heard echoing down the hall.

Unfamiliar faces began to crowd the aisles.

The volume increased.

The rows became jammed with ambling bodies, all trying to get to their lockers.

The din of laughing, shouting, and metal doors slamming reached hysteria.

The narrow hall was squeezed to capacity, with kids shouting, "I just gotta get my stuff, move over!" Maggie found herself pressed against Ryan. She looked at him, the crowd becoming tight, encroaching on any personal space left in the hallway. Her eyes must have reflected panic.

"Hey, it's all right. We're fine right here," he said.

Her smile was shaky, she could feel it.

She looked around. Others were hanging out in the packed area, not needing anything from inside their lockers, but laying claim to the space they had managed to carve out.

There wasn't anywhere to go—no bathroom stall to hide in, no nearby classroom to escape. A lone opening at the end of the hall could barely be seen through the congealing mass of kids. Outside, it was pouring.

Her arm pressed into Ryan's. She could feel the smoothness of his fingertips touch the fringe of her cutoffs, then her leg. She didn't move a muscle. It was the one time in her life that she didn't want this mild claustrophobia to subside. Should she touch him back? What if he pulled away? How much closer could she get to him? She held her breath, paralyzed.

A large figure in dark clothing made his way down the hall. "You have to leave," he barked, pointing a baton at a group of kids. "You don't belong here. You don't have a locker. Get moving, now!"

"Shoot, we don't have a locker!" said Maggie, turning ever so slightly toward Ryan. If he kissed her here, like this, she was sure no one would notice—like hiding in plain sight. Like his fingers on her leg.

"Sure we do," he said. He turned to the locker behind him; Maggie followed suit. They pretended to fidget with the dials.

"You ever have that dream where you can't remember your combination and you're late for class?" asked Maggie.

"Yup," replied Ryan, turning the dial. "Let's see, we can start at the beginning. One for sorrow, two for joy, three for a girl, four for a boy."

"Isn't that a nursery rhyme or something?" Maggie laughed.

Ryan ignored her and continued. "Five for silver, six for gold, seven for a secret, never to be told." He lifted up on the latch, and the locker opened.

"Are you kidding me? That's not possible—this can't be real life. How did you do that?" said Maggie, her eyes wide.

The man with the baton neared them.

"Maggie, look," said Ryan, taking a step back. His eyes were glued to the inside of the locker.

Maggie peered around the door. Inside sat a black bird with a white breast—a magpie. It hopped a few steps toward freedom, cocked its head at Maggie, sprung from its feet, and flew down the hallway over the swarming students.

"That's the bird I saw in the woods with Beth! How did it—" Maggie started, but words failed her when they both looked back into the locker. Maggie recoiled.

"It has to be you," said Ryan.

"What? No. No! I'm not going without you! I don't even understand what I'm supposed to be doing! I want to wake up! Wake up!" she insisted. Hot sparks tingled at the edge of her fingertips.

Ryan put his arm around her shoulders and pulled her closer to the open locker.

"Get off me!" Maggie screamed.

Anger welled in her stomach. Her hands burned.

The man with the baton approached them.

Ryan stood behind her and held her shoulders firmly in front of it.

"Go!" he screamed, and pushed her straight at the locker.

Maggie braced herself, but her face didn't smash into the locker—the scene fell away completely.

She was falling through space.

She landed in a clearing in the woods. Disoriented, she stood up and looked around. Her stomach dropped; bile burned in her throat.

A bludgeoned beyond recognition camper lay on a large, flat rock. An arm hung limply over the side. Counselors Greg and Kate leaned over the body. They looked up. A blinding white light shot out of their eyes; blood-smeared mouths chewed methodically. In the distance, a murder of magpies swirled above the lake. A gangly shadow crept along the opposite shore. A screech echoed across the water.

"Hungry, Maggie?" asked Kate, grinning. Veins bulged from her neck with every chew. Maggie raised her scorching hands, white light whirring around them, and shrieked.

She snapped awake. Her heart raced, and sweat dripped from her temples. She looked around the cabin and took a deep breath, then noticed the empty bed next to hers.

Nightmare blurred with reality.

Beth.

48

The campers dragged their feet into the Mess Hall the following morning, dreading the upcoming task they had earned during Manhunt the night before. Maggie bumped into Tom as they got on line for breakfast.

"Oh, hey, Mags," he said, looking distracted.

"She's not here yet," Maggie replied coolly. "She was still getting ready when I left."

"What? Yeah…oh no! No, it's not that. It's your friend. The one I had community service with. Beth?"

Maggie swallowed hard. "Yeah, Beth—what about her?"

"It's nothing—I just—I know she's missing and I'm just—"

"Spit it out."

"I just hope that what I said at the Lifer meeting the other night didn't impact her getting kicked out of camp."

"Is that what Greg and Kate are saying, that she's been kicked out? She's missing, Tom!"

"They're not saying anything that I know of." Tom gazed out the window of the Mess Hall.

"What's going on with you?" Maggie said.

"What do you mean?" asked Tom.

"You're acting weird. And I don't mean about the whole Liv thing. That's just—whatever. Fine. But you don't seem right."

Tom went white at the accusation. "You don't know what you're talking about."

"Don't give me that crap, Tom. I've been over your house every day since the third grade. You look the same way you did the time you were playing dodgeball inside your parents' house with Jeff Branard, and you fell through your mother's glass coffee table. What gives?"

Tom half smirked at the reference. "Yeah, that was a disaster, wasn't it?"

"Yeah, you were scared shitless of your mother coming home from work that day, and you have the same look now. Did you see something?"

"No," said Tom, scrubbing his forehead. "It's just that—I'm worried that whatever I said at that Lifer meeting had an impact on Beth getting kicked ou—I mean, going missing."

"I'm sure it had nothing to do with it," said Maggie, softening.

"No, you don't understand! I think it could have. Those guys at Pinegrove were really nice to her."

"So?"

"What do you mean, 'so'? Don't you see?"

"I'm not a mind reader, Tom," said Maggie, and immediately cringed at the relevancy of her sarcasm, with what Ryan had told her.

"I think because of what I said, maybe the counselors thought she was siding with those old guys, or whatever. Maybe she should have defended me, instead of sitting back?"

"Defend you? Defend you! Please, Tom, you can stick up for yourself. But why would you say anything to begin with? Can't you see that they use that sort of information to weed out the weaker campers? How are you not seeing this?"

"Well, you bought into it, too," argued Tom.

"Not really—"

"Yeah, you definitely have, just so you can stay here longer to hang out with what's-his-face—"

"You know his name is Ryan, and you have no idea what you're talking about," said Maggie, her cheeks reddening as anger brewed in her stomach.

"Sure I don't. Anyway, there's something else you should know." Tom reached into his pocket, his hand trembling. He pulled out two mangled dog tags and handed them to Maggie.

"What the hell are these?"

"When Liv and I were trying to find a spot to hide during Manhunt, we went out past the Infirmary, into the woods. Probably deeper than we should've gone."

"Spare me," scoffed Maggie.

"No. God! Stop. We ran forever. We stopped to catch our breath, and I saw something shiny on the ground reflecting in the moonlight. I walked over to see what it was, and it was…it was these."

"Yeah, okay, so what are they? Or better question, whose are they?" Maggie asked, but looking at Tom's face, she already knew the answer.

"Those guys?"

Tom nodded.

"Well, maybe they—"

"Maggie, there's blood on them. When we were at Pinegrove, one of the guys was wearing a bathrobe and a tank top, and these were around his neck, intact. The tags say 'Clarence.' I—I don't know what to think, but…" Tom looked away and closed his eyes. "I think something really terrible has happened because I said something…I feel sick."

Maggie stared at Tom, unable to find any words to console him.

"Something is definitely going on here, don't you think?" he continued. "What do we do?"

Maggie looked around. Ryan walked through the screen

door and scanned the crowd. Was he looking for her? Their eyes met, and instant electricity sparked through her body. She gave a brief smile and turned back to Tom.

"I think we're going to try to sort it out this morning—you missed some of it last night when you got back late from Manhunt. Also, you should probably eat something."

Tom sighed and walked to their table empty-handed. Maggie rolled her eyes and stood on line. Burned cinnamon and the unmistakable pungent scent of scrambled eggs overpowered their nostrils. When they reached the serving station, Woody eyed Maggie with particular interest.

"Where's your friend?" he grunted under his breath.

"Huh?" said Maggie, taken aback by the question.

"Your friend," he said, coughing. "Where?"

Maggie stared at Woody, searching for an appropriate response. What if Woody was in on the whole missing camper thing? What if those energy bars he gave her were actually poison—something to drug her? How could she trust him, when all he had ever been to her was super weird and cryptic?

Woody rubbed his forehead, impatient for a response. He leaned forward over the vat of scrambled eggs and whispered, "Is she gone?"

Maggie stood frozen on the sticky linoleum. She nodded slightly.

"Make sure you're out picking up trash near the boathouse after breakfast," he said gruffly, flashing her a nearly undetectable sympathetic smile. Maggie continued to stare at Woody, pushing her tray through the queue.

She joined the rest of the Lifers at their table. Everyone was quiet, even Joey. They had plates full of food, but were fidgeting with their silverware instead of eating. Maggie took the empty seat next to Ryan. She became transfixed on the syrup spilling from her French toast and how it pooled around her pile of scrambled eggs.

"Any ideas?" asked Becky, breaking the silence. Her eyes

fixed on Ryan.

"Woody just told me to be by the boathouse during litter duty today," blurted Maggie.

"What does that even mean?" asked Corey.

"I dunno. But he also asked me where my friend was...Beth...asking if she was 'gone.' And then he told me that."

"Jesus, that's ominous," said Germ.

"I know, right? I mean, can we trust him?" Maggie asked, turning to Ryan.

"I'm not sure. I think so?" Ryan replied.

"Well, it's not like we can trust just anyone on the staff," said Liv quickly, looking around.

"Stop looking so shifty, Liv. Someone's going to see you. We have to act normal. All of us. We have to put on a real show as Lifers. You know, 'all in' kind of stuff. Set an example. We can't let anyone suspect anything, whatever that 'anything' may be," said Alex, wiping his mouth with a napkin.

"Alex's right," said Becky confidently. "That means, Joey, you still have to be a dipshit."

"You say that like it's a hard thing!" Joey smirked. He broke the tension with a few laughs.

"Seriously, guys, what's the plan, though?" asked Corey.

The laughs turned into uncomfortable coughs.

"Liv and I found these last night," said Tom, tossing the dog tags onto the center of the table. The unsuspected clatter caused them all to sit up straight. Ryan lunged to cover them up and drew them to his body, his hands acting like the snout of a hungry hippo desperate to eat a marble.

"What are they?" asked Becky quietly.

"They're from one of the guys I mentioned at the Lifer meeting last night," admitted Tom.

"That's not possible," said Alex. "We had that meeting and went straight into Manhunt. The information couldn't have triggered those guys to go missing that quickly. And anyway, I'm not sure the counselors would even really care about them…no offense."

"But you said I should mention—"

"Yeah, because it looks good—like you're doing your duty to your camp. Loyalty and all that," replied Alex.

"Yeah, but I mentioned those guys to Counselor Neal, too, earlier in the day. Maybe he put the wheels in motion," argued Tom, his eyes shifting from Alex to Maggie. Maggie glanced over at the food line.

"We're getting off topic," said Becky, tapping her fork against her tray.

"Something happened to those guys," said Tom, leaning forward. "Those tags are mangled and have blood on them."

"Wait…those tags—let me see them." Corey motioned to Ryan. Ryan glanced around before passing them under the table to Maggie. His hand grazed her palm as he placed the cold metal into it and said, "Pass it on."

Maggie switched hands and passed them to Corey. He looked down into his cupped palms for a moment, concentrating.

"Metal," he said after a moment.

"No shit, Sherlock," said Joey, smirking.

"No, dumbass, maybe we need metal. Lots of it," murmured Corey, his eyes lingering on the dog tags.

"For a weapon?" asked Ryan.

"Maybe," replied Corey. "Or protection from whatever the hell is going on. Think about it. Penny's necklace—metal. These dog tags—metal. If it is a monster—a Wendigo—maybe it can't eat metal."

"Yeah, but where are we going to find fucking RoboCop?" asked Joey.

"That could be a coincidence, too," said Alex. The table stared at him. "What?" he said defensively. "I'm just playing devil's advocate! Maybe the counselors are just getting sloppy and dropping shit. Jeez, you guys."

Ryan shook his head. "Alex's right. We shouldn't rule anything out—it could be a coincidence, but it also can't hurt to think there may be something around here that we can use to combat this thing."

"They're also both things worn around the neck," added Germ.

"What about Jonesy's glasses?" argued Ryan.

"And how do we know this whole thing isn't just the counselors killing off campers they don't like, to form a weird unattainable camptopia?" asked Maggie.

"That's pretty dark, Mags," said Tom, grimacing.

"No, seriously! I mean, a few campers get sent home each week all summer long? What if the personal effects are actually just mistakes that the counselors have dropped, trying to get rid of evidence?" Maggie lowered her voice when she caught sight of Counselor Mark making the rounds to each table.

"Incoming," chirped Joey.

"Hey, guys, how's it going? You seem exceptionally tight-knit and broody this morning. Still feeling the loss from last night?" Mark half smirked and stuffed his hand into the pockets of his hooded sweatshirt.

"Yup," said Germ.

"Come on, Germ, don't sweat it. Trash pickup is never as bad as you think it's going to be," said Mark, surveying the table. "You guys have done it so many times, the camp is practically pristine by now." He was met with several sarcastic smiles.

"How long are we out there today?" asked Alex.

"Beats me. Bags and sticks are already out by the picnic tables." Mark shrugged.

"Wanna help?" asked Joey, beaming.

Mark laughed. "Tempting! We have a counselors' meeting while you guys are wandering the grounds looking for litter."

"Why?" asked Corey. Ryan punched his leg under the table.

"I could tell you…but then I'd have to kill you!" said Mark, his eyes growing large as they twinkled. "Eat up—Woody's gonna be pissed if you waste his food," he said, looking from plate to plate. "It's gonna be another hot one out there, too—better guzzle that bug juice!"

"Thanks! We will," replied Becky, flashing Mark a saccharine smile. He rolled his eyes and swiveled to check on the next table.

"Guys, wait a second. What if something is in the bug juice?" asked Tom.

The other Lifers turned to him with skeptical faces.

"Don't be paranoid," said Germ.

"No, I'm serious. Look around." They turned around to observe the Mess Hall. Most of the campers had already finished their juice, their faces stained bright red with Glasgow smiles. Two lines queued with dozens of campers waiting to get at the jugs holding the sugary elixir.

"Maybe they put crack in it this morning," said Joey.

"Sure they did," said Alex. They eyed the untouched plastic cups of bug juice sitting on their trays suspiciously.

"Guys, drugged bug juice? That's too obvious. No way they'd do that. They'd get caught so fast," argued Germ.

"We probably shouldn't drink it, to be safe," said Corey.

"What other options do we have? We'll get dehydrated in this weather if we don't," said Liv.

"Liv's right. We need to drink something. Isn't there usually a water jug out, too?" asked Maggie.

"Yeah, it's right over—" Ryan paused, looking around. "It's not out. What the hell is going on?"

Becky shivered and drew close to Alex. "I don't like this. We need to do something—we don't have a plan, and breakfast is almost over!"

"Okay, okay, here's what we're going to do," said Ryan,

looking at each of them. "Maggie and I will pick up trash near the boathouse to figure out what Woody's riddle is all about. Corey, you and Germ can pretend to pick up trash, but head toward the rusted out cars behind the Infirmary and stack up as much metal as you can, in the off chance that this whole thing is bigger than the counselors. Joey and Alex, we need a way to get to Mount Kinross quicker than skulking through the woods—find a vehicle for us to use tonight during the dance. Steal keys, hot wire—I don't care how you do it, just do it. Becky, Tom, Liv—figure out what this counselors' meeting is about. You can always play dumb if they catch you eavesdropping—you're just picking up garbage."

"What about killing the monster?" squeaked Liv.

"If there is a monster," reminded Alex.

"What about the bug juice?" said Germ.

"Hopefully we'll have more answers by dinner. And don't drink that shit," said Ryan, pointing to the coolers. "Use the hose hookup outside or a bathroom sink or the lake."

"I am not drinking lake water," huffed Becky.

"Have it your way," said Ryan, shaking his head. He looked at everyone. "You guys in? It's not great, but it's something."

One by one the Lifers looked at each other and replied, "In."

Ryan looked at Maggie, and his mind flashed to the field again. She was a picture—her smile glowing in the golden afternoon sun. They were lying next to each other, staring into space. Her dress splayed into the shape of a rustling cotton bell. A breeze blew a few strands of her hair in front of her face. She wiped them away with the palm of her hand, a childhood habit not yet outgrown. She looked at him briefly, under the strands of hair that refused to be tamed in twilight's wild breeze, and then looked away. He caught her grinning. He looked away, too, overcome by the electromagnetic charge of lying next to her—desire warring with the relentless nagging of an ever increasing pit in his stomach. His time with her was inevitably fleeting. She fit him better than anyone else—he suspected that she felt the same. The realization sickened him. It's not fair—this will kill her, he thought. This wasn't supposed to be the way it ended, but it was the only way it could end. It had to be. He had to know she would go on. It had to be him.

He shook his head and blinked twice to erase the scene. Everyone was staring at him expectantly, waiting. "Yeah, all right," he said, coughing. "Let's do it."

Joey jumped onto his chair, raised his fist in the air, and shouted in his best Macho Man Randy Savage voice, "Oh, yeah! Time to take out the garbage!"

49

"Don't drag your bag, dipshit, or the trash we've already collected is going to spill everywhere," said Alex. Joey sighed and hoisted his bag over his shoulder, using his litter stick as a walking pole.

"Any idea how we're going to secure a vehicle for tonight's dance?" asked Joey.

"I'm thinking," replied Alex, wiping sweat from his brow. They hurried through the clearing by the boys' cabins, eager to escape the sun for the shady wooded area of camp.

"I wish Ryan had given us more of a heads-up," said Joey. "We could have rented a limo."

"Funny," replied Alex.

"Seriously, though, this is some dicey shit we're in. We need to figure this out. I may be an asshole, but I don't know how to hot-wire a car."

They stopped walking and took a break under a large maple tree. Alex nodded in agreement. "I think our best bet is to swipe the keys to the camp bus." Joey stared blankly at Alex.

"The bus. You want to roll up to the dance with the bus," Joey repeated. "You outta your fuckin' mind, kid?"

"Got any better ideas, genius?"

"It's not subtle."

"No shit, but it'll transport us all easily. We can nab the keys from the office—they probably hang them by the door. We can't 'roll up to the dance' to pick them up, though. I think they'll have to meet us in the parking lot by the entrance. I don't think any camp vehicle can drive over this shit," he said, kicking a giant tree root protruding from the ground. "No sense in a getaway vehicle if you can't get away."

"Yeah, you're probably right," said Joey.

"Of course I'm right," huffed Alex. "Let's go to the office."

They walked along the pine needle paths, giving brief, encouraging smiles and low-fives to the other indentured campers they passed with litter sticks. The office sat brightly atop a small wooded hill. Joey looked over his shoulder to see if anyone was watching them.

"Think we're good," he said. Alex glanced around.

"Okay, you stay out here and keep watch. I'll be back," said Alex.

He peered through the screen door to see if anyone was inside. He pulled the door handle, the spring hinges creaking as he slipped through. After being in the blinding midmorning sun, it took several seconds for his eyes to adjust to the dim interior. He scanned the room and found it devoid of life. Several key rings dangled from a canoe-shaped key hook on the wall next to the door. Alex flicked through the keys, searching for some hint as to which was for a bus. "Someone should label these," he mumbled to himself, returning a set to the rack. He pulled another set from the wall and noticed a larger key engraved with a bird. He thought for a moment. "This must be it. I've seen that bird logo on buses before." He removed the key from the ring, splitting his thumbnail in the process. "Dammit, I hate these things," he said, biting the rest of his jarred fingernail off and spitting it on the floor.

"Alex, you find it yet?" asked Joey through the screen door.

"Shut up, I'll be out in a minute," Alex replied, shaking his head. What kind of an idiot says something like that on a compromising mission? He looked around the room, but there wasn't anything notable lying around. No murderous schemes hatched on crumpled yellow lined paper, no bloody death instruments. He rolled his eyes. It looked like a completely normal, if not too tidy camp office. The blades of a powered-off box fan spun lazily in the window from the breeze. Two sharpened pencils were lined up on the green writing mat on the desk. A rotary phone sat idle at the corner. A few camp brochures were fanned out on a side table, while binders neatly stood on a lone bookshelf. Even the poster of Smokey Bear hung perfectly in place. Nothing appeared amiss. Their scheme seemed more ridiculous by the second.

The door hinges squeaked again. Alex whipped around, shoving the key into his back pocket.

"Jesus, Joey, go back out there and keep watch!"

"What's taking you so long, anyway? Holy shit, they have a fan in here? Why don't we get fans in our cabins?" Before Alex could stop him, Joey was at the window, twisting the dial to "high." The fan roared to life, blowing dormant dust particles everywhere. They danced in the rays of sunlight cutting across the room through the window.

"That's more like it!" Joey grinned. His face turned to confusion as Alex leaned over the desk, gritting his teeth.

"Shut it off!"

"What? What'd I do?" asked Joey, stepping in front of the fan. The change in wind pattern caused the bottom of the Smokey Bear poster to balloon. The air attempted to billow out the top, but the pressure was too much, dislodging one of the corner tacks. The poster flapped triumphantly at its release.

"Jesus, Joey, we aren't supposed to be in here!" seethed Alex. He switched off the fan. The dust made its slow descent to the floor. Joey knelt to pick up brochures that had blown from the shelf.

"Where were these?" he asked.

"How the hell should I know, Joe? I wasn't planning on creating a goddamned wind tunnel in here!" hissed Alex, stepping over to the askew poster. "Help me find the tack," he demanded, searching the ground.

"Um, Alex…"

"I'm serious, help me find it!" said Alex, anger rising in his voice.

"Alex…"

"Jesus Christ, what!" Alex looked up at Joey, who was staring at the poster. The corner with the missing tack had dropped downward, exposing another poster hanging behind it.

"What…the…hell…is…this?" asked Joey slowly, shaking a finger at the wall. Alex stood up and peered at the wall. Behind Smokey Bear's stern face warning about forest fires was a detailed map of the northeastern United States. Red dots marked random locations across it. Alex leaned closer, pulling the Smokey Bear poster farther away from the wall to get a better look.

"I…I don't know," said Alex finally. "Why would they be hiding this?"

"Maybe they just didn't feel like taking it down? Or they didn't have room in the office to hang both up?" said Joey.

"Look around, moron, the walls are mostly bare. This is weird." He took the corner flap of the Smokey Bear poster and ran his fingers over it. "Hey, check this out. There are tons of tiny holes in the corner. This has been rehung a bunch."

"So?"

"So that means this poster has been taken off the wall and then put back up. A lot," said Alex. "Quick, we gotta find the tack and get the hell out of here."

Joey bent down, and together they scoured the floor and shelves for the tack.

"Got it. It's over here by the bookshelf."

"Great. Here, I'll hold it, you stick it in," said Alex.

"That's what she sa—"

"Don't," said Alex. "Save it for when we get out of here unscathed."

Joey pressed the tack into the wall, and they stood back to assess their work. "Good enough," said Alex. "Let's go."

They moved through the screen door, grabbed their trash bags, and headed to the Mess Hall.

"That's what she said," finished Joey.

50

"I don't think eavesdropping on the counselors meeting is a great idea," said Liv.

"Do you even know where they're having the meeting?" Tom asked Becky.

"Yeah, I think so." She frowned when she stabbed a Hershey's bar wrapper with her litter stick and brown liquid oozed from it.

Tom held open a trash bag for her, and she shook the wrapper from the end of her pole. As they walked, the air filled with dust from the gray gravel. They wandered around the parking lot, picking up stray Styrofoam coffee cups and gum wrappers glinting in the sun.

"So where, then?" asked Liv, raising her hand like a visor to shield her eyes from the sun. She put her stick down so she could put her hair in a bun. Tom squinted and watched her deftly twist the elastic around her fingers and between her hair, like a game of Cat's Cradle. What is it about her, thought Tom, that is so captivating? He's seen Maggie do her hair hundreds of times, but this was different. Liv did it so smoothly—somehow it was sexy, but he was sure that was not her intent. She had no knowledge of just how attractive she was. She glanced back at Tom and shot him a quizzical, wry grin.

"What?" she asked.

"Nothing, just wondered if you're going to do your hair all day just to get out of litter duty," he joked.

"I'm right on top of that, Rose!" she replied. She stabbed a bag of half-eaten Cheetos. A little cloud of cheese dust exhaled into the air.

Becky rolled her eyes and assessed the parking lot. "Guys, quiet for a second." Her face strained as she tried to listen beyond the birds and rustling leaves. After a moment, she said, "I think they're probably out behind where we sat for orientation."

"They don't expect campers to try to clean near that area?" asked Liv.

"I don't know. They probably think they'll easily see anyone if they approach, since it's in such an open area. But there's a small nook off to the right, beyond it. There's a path near that garbage can that leads to it. See?" Becky pointed across the parking lot. Tom and Liv nodded.

"Should we all go?" asked Tom.

"No, I'll go. I can talk my way out of anything with them. I've been a Lifer the longest," said Becky. "You guys keep a lookout. Liv, pretend to be cleaning up near the trash can, and, Tom, pick up stuff on the far side of the parking lot. I'll be able to see Liv from there, should anything happen and we need to abort. You can warn Liv. She can warn me."

Tom and Liv exchanged glances. Liv took a deep breath. "Okay, sounds good."

"Great," said Becky. She bit her lip and said, "Here goes."

She slunk through the underbrush, glancing back over her shoulder a few times to maintain sight of Liv, who watched with her big doe eyes, wide and fearful. As she neared the clearing, she could hear faint voices. She bent down and continued her journey, crawling along the bed of pine needles and through the ferns. A pine cone scale stuck to her knee.

This is just the worst, she thought. She crawled over to the trunk of a pine tree, near the edge of the clearing. Through the brush she could barely make out several counselors huddled together, with Greg and Kate standing in front of them. Becky dusted off her legs and leaned forward to listen.

"It's not my fault!"

"No one is accusing you of anything. Calm down."

"I don't think you understand what we're up against!"

"Seriously? Did she just say that she doesn't think we know what they're up against?"

"All I'm saying is it's not how it used to be."

"Yeah, she's right. Things are unraveling in a way that doesn't bode well…"

"Things are unraveling? Things better not be unraveling! What do you mean 'things are unraveling'?"

"I mean, well, you guys don't see it—you're not out there with us. You don't know how hard it is!"

"What's the alternative, huh?"

"We need to put an end to it. We need to make it stop. It's not right."

"Since when are you the moral police, Mark?"

"We need to tell someone."

"Like who, the actual police? They already know. We bought them off several summers ago."

"Mark has a point. When does this become too horrific to continue? We're already talking mass murders, Greg! How many more weeks, how many more summers can we keep this up?"

"You shut your fucking mouth—never use my name during these meetings, goddammit! And we are not the ones murdering—Jesus! Kate, you were right; I didn't know it was this bad. This is amateur hour."

"Guys, let's focus. What's our immediate problem, and how do we fix it? We can deal with the morality issues later."

"The problem is we cannot confirm that Camper Thirteen

is dead."

"What?"

Silence.

"What do you mean you cannot confirm Camper Thirteen is dead? It should be pretty apparent either way. I'm confused—are you confused, Kate? Because I'm pretty fucking confused right now!"

"We can confirm that the two old guys from Pinegrove are dead."

"So riddle me this: how can you confirm that the two old guys are dead, but you can't confirm that Thirteen is dead? She should have been much easier to handle than those two."

"Well, we found their army tags not far from the spot. They were all bent."

"Good. Let's have them."

"Uh…about that. I think…I may have dropped them. We don't have them now. But we had them."

"Brilliant. That's just great. Well done! Now you get to find them. Did Thirteen not have any leftover effects? Is that why you can't confirm? It usually leaves effects. Did you not find shredded clothes like the others? That's why we go back the next day—it's our way of confirming. You guys fucked it up by dropping number Nine's glasses somewhere around here, and a camper found them—how many times do I need to explain this to you?"

"No, it's not that. It's just…well, she put up a fight."

"Didn't you sedate her beforehand?"

"I tried! I thought it worked, but she came to, just before I got to the cave entrance. And, well, yeah—she put up a fight. I had to sedate her a second time, but the timing for the drop was off."

"Mark, you don't seriously expect me to believe that a fifteen-year-old girl slipped out of your grasp."

"I don't expect you to believe anything! It's the truth. My neck is just as much on the line as yours, so I don't know what you want from me! She escaped into the woods. I tried to chase her for as long as possible. She was still groggy. But I had to go to the drop-off by myself that night—the rest of you idiots were too busy with Manhunt—remember? For all we know, she's dead. If she survived, she would have run. She doesn't have food. The cops would have picked her up on the main road and brought her back here, or at least to the station. She doesn't know they work for us. They would have called it in. She's not getting out of this alive. Have we gotten a call?"

"Not to my knowledge, no."

"All right then, she's probably dead. There's no way she survived the night all the way out there on her own. She probably went back to the cave to seek shelter, and the problem took care of itself."

"This makes me uneasy. What do you think, Kate?"

"I think we need to tighten the fuck up on our protocol. From now on, two people go to the drop-off and take care of it. And two people go pick up the effects the next day. Mark's right—one person isn't enough. Plus, with just one, there's no accountability."

"You're right. From now on, two counselors go to the drop-off and the pickup. Got it?"

Silence.

"Good. But I want to know more about this unraveling. What seems to be the problem?"

"Well, we…a bunch of us…we don't think that the supply is meeting the demand anymore. This thing is insatiable. Didn't you hear it by the Infirmary during Manhunt? It's encroaching on the camp. This can't go on, guys. It just can't."

"It'll go on for as long as it takes."

"What if there were another way?"

"We've been through this—there's no other way. This is all by design. We found a way to make this work, and it works. Let's leave well enough alone."

"Yeah, but what if—"

"It doesn't require anything three out of four seasons of the year."

"That we know of…"

"We've tried other ways, Hannah. Don't you remember two summers ago? That was a bloodbath. You want another one of those? Now that was fucking terrible. What is our goal again?"

Silence.

"Self-preservation. To make this camp the best experience for every cam—"

"Well, that's ironic."

"To make *this camp* the best experience for *every camper*. To give them the purest memories steeped in nostalgia that will last a lifetime. And how do we do that? We surround them with only the best campers to fulfill that experience. If that means we have to weed out some garbage kids who soil our philosophy, then so be it."

"But Beth should have been a Lifer!"

"Don't use her name, and don't put your neck on the line for her, you moron. Sometimes there are other qualifications that factor into our selection for disposal."

"Did you get that type of bullshit rhetoric from the Third Reich?"

"Fuck you! Don't you dare. You're just as interested in self-preservation as I am. I'm starting to get the idea that you let her get away. How short is your fickle memory, huh? Two summers ago? The Slaughter?"

"I remember, I remember, Jesus, stop bringing it up. But couldn't we all just leave?"

"And then what—watch Abbotsville and the surrounding towns burn? Then what?"

"Then it wouldn't be our problem anymore."

"Do you all feel this way? No, really, I'm serious. Do you all feel this way? Do you hate camp life so much that you're willing to give up this idyllic lifestyle that you're living all summer, every summer? You'd rather not protect the other towns in the area from a horrific, inevitable fate? Are you sick of being the unsung heroes?"

Silence.

"I didn't think so. Guys, come on. It's not so bad. This week has been a lot, I know. It's a big ask to do the drop once a week, let alone several times. And yeah, I think you're right—it's getting harder to maintain a level of satisfaction. But it's only during the summer! Weeding out these sullied kids—and this week has had an unusual number of them—is only for the greater good. Really. You'll see. Things will slow down, I promise."

"What about the parents, though? I mean, eventually people are going to catch on. Then we're fucked."

"Yeah, what's our end game?"

"I'll set up another meeting with Officer Leroy down at the station. Walk him through the research again. Assess protocols. Maybe he'll have some more insight—I came across a few things last week. But until then, we need to stay the course, to protect our campers and ourselves. Got it?"

Silence.

"I'll also put a call in to Gerry at the Abbotsville Gazette and Bob at Channel Four. Make sure we don't have another leak like we did last summer. This thing will remain contained."

More silence.

Becky felt the uneasy sensation of a sneeze building. She scrunched her face and pinched her nose as tightly as she could. Her fingernails dug into her skin. She tucked her head between her knees and thought, "No, please God, no." The tingling sensation in her nostrils screamed. She exhaled the tiniest puff of air to stifle her sneeze.

"What was that? Did you hear that?"

Silence.

"No, I didn't hear anything. I think we're good."

"Okay, now, let's really ramp it up. Let's make this dance awesome. Let's find the dog tags. Let's keep an eye out for Thirteen. Keep your ears open around the Lifers. I doubt they'd protect her, but you never know—Ryan and that new Lifer, Maggie, seem to be pretty close to her. This weekend I'll check in with Officer Leroy, and we'll look for a more permanent solution to this nightmare, okay? Sound good?"

Murmurs of affirmation.

Becky quickly backtracked through the pine needles, and raced to the parking lot.

51

"I don't know what Ryan expects us to salvage from this wreck," said Germ, kicking the door of the forsaken Chevy lying in a ditch behind the Infirmary.

"Yeah, the whole metal thing might be a stretch. It's not like we have any hacksaws lying around to cut this stuff up. Plus it's heavy—it'll take forever to carry anywhere." Corey put all of his weight onto the driver's side door. It moaned in protest but didn't budge.

"Yeah, how are we going to smuggle any of this away from here unseen?"

"The thing I don't get," said Germ, peering into the driver's side, looking for the trunk release button, "is if metal is something that could kill this thing, why were the dog tags mangled? Why weren't they untouched?"

"Yeah, you'd think it would be like a vampire or Superman: you can't be around that which can kill you," agreed Corey.

"I think we need a better idea," said Germ, slapping a mosquito feasting on his calf.

Corey sat in the back seat, surveying the rotting cabin.

"We could steal knives from Woody?" suggested Germ.

Corey thought a moment. "If the dog tags were bent, and

the locket was pretty much intact, maybe…maybe the Wendigo can't digest metal."

"But does it digest clothes? Where are everyone's clothes?"

"Beats me. The well?" Germ kicked at the front door, but it remained attached to the car.

"You ever wonder where this hunk of junk came from?" asked Corey, circling the car.

"No kidding. How long has it even been sitting here? Think it'll come to life, *Christine* style?"

Germ leaned in through the front passenger seat and jostled the glove box open. He found a soggy owner's manual and a mildewed handkerchief. "No registration," he commented.

Corey shrugged and circled around to the trunk and tried to pry it open. "Hey, Germ, go to the driver's side and try to pop the trunk on the count of three—maybe there's a four-way in here or something we can use."

"Yeah, all right," replied Germ. He bent down to pull the lever.

"Ready? One…two…three!" Germ pulled the lever, and Corey pushed up as hard as he could on the trunk door. "Quick, come help me—it's moving, but I can't get it to fully open!" grimaced Corey.

Germ rushed over, and together they dug deep into the earth, forcing the resistant trunk to open at a forty-five degree angle.

"Grab something to keep this propped open, just in case," panted Corey.

Germ looked around and found a thick tree branch. He jammed it into the opening. Corey let go and breathed heavy, his hands on his knees.

"Hey, Cor, this might be better than metal," said Germ. He pointed into the darkened cavity. Corey stood up and turned toward the trunk. Inside, laid neatly in rows, were dozens of cans of bug spray.

"Are you thinking what I'm thinking?" said Corey, grinning.

"We need to round up some lighters," nodded Germ.

Corey produced a spare trash bag from his pocket, and the two began filling it with the newfound weapon.

52

Ryan and Maggie casually made their way to the boathouse, so as not to attract attention from any lingering counselors.

"Do you think Beth is…"

"I don't know, Mags. I honestly don't. But if she's alive, we'll find her."

"I keep trying to replay everything in my head—maybe we missed something. I don't know."

"The counselors are always going to have the upper hand—we just have to be quicker. One step ahead. I think once we all meet up tonight at dinner, we'll be just that," assured Ryan.

"Have you ever tried to…tap into the counselors minds with your…thing?" she asked, tapping her temple.

"Nah, once it seemed like something was going on here, I promised myself I wouldn't. It could put me on their radar somehow, and I'd get tossed so fast. Or worse."

"You think they'd really believe that there was a telepathic camper trying to undermine their utopian murder factory?"

"Corey basically said that, too, after Penny went missing. But he eventually agreed, it wasn't worth risking it."

With their heads down, they scanned the brush for litter on the sides of the path leading to the lake.

"I think—" Maggie paused. "I think that Woody has to be our ally. He also gave Beth those energy bars at dinner before Manhunt—but what if he poisoned or drugged her with them?"

"Or what if he is keeping her alive out there because he gave her those bars?"

"They must do something to the campers to be able to take them wherever they are going to be sacrificed."

Ryan stopped walking. "Wait, what did you say?"

"I think that they must give them something, I don't know—a pill, an ether-soaked rag over their mouths—something—before they drag them off to kill them."

"No, no, you said sacrifice."

"Sacrifice, kill, end their lives forever—you get what I mean."

"Maggie, what if—what if it is an actual sacrifice?" he asked earnestly. "Think about what we read in the library, about the weird paranormal sightings in the Bennington Triangle—the evil spirits could be a direct result of cannibalism that happened in this area? What if the evil spirit needs to be satiated?"

Maggie's eyes widened. "You don't think…"

"I think," Ryan continued, "that there's more to thi—"

He stopped mid-sentence; they had arrived at the boathouse. The door was slightly ajar. Ryan looked at Maggie and took a deep breath.

"Here goes," he said, stepping forward to push the door open. Hazy sunlight illuminated a dusty window overlooking the lake. Oars were piled up in one corner; life preservers hung on pegs on the walls. They walked in and scanned the room. A gruff voice from behind them said, "Don't scream."

Ryan and Maggie spun around to the door closing. Woody stood in front of them, arms crossed over his chest.

"We don't have much time," said Woody. "I'll do the

talking."

Maggie and Ryan braced themselves.

"Did anyone see you two come in here?"

Maggie shook her head slightly. Ryan said, "Nope, I don't think so."

"Good. If you want to have any chance at seeing your friend alive, you better accomplish what she was attempting." He stared intently from Maggie to Ryan.

"You mean the envelope that we think is in an Oasis album in the Lab?" asked Maggie.

Woody nodded. "Get to the Lab early and retrieve what you stupidly left behind the last time."

Maggie's face reddened at her earlier infraction.

"Then what?" pressed Ryan.

"What do you mean, 'then what'? That's up to you, kid. You need to decide what to do with what you find. Not my problem."

"Wait, hold on a second—you know that something is going on, don't you? Why won't you help us? We have to put an end to this!" insisted Maggie.

"Look," said Woody, leaning forward and lowering his voice, "I don't know what you have conjured up in that pea brain of yours, but this thing? This thing is much bigger than you, or him, or your little clan, or me. You can't 'just end' it. Trust me. Find your friend and then get the hell out of Dodge."

"We know it's bigger than all of us," argued Maggie. "But we have to try! How can you continue to cook for kids who are being murdered by someone, or something out there? You're an adult! You're the one who is supposed to do something!"

Woody sighed. "Even if I wanted to, kid, which I don't, it can't be me. It has to be you."

"What? Why does everyone keep saying that?" said Maggie, her temper bursting. "I'm not important! I don't matter that much in the grand scheme of this stupid camp, or the universe for that matter! Stop insisting that I'm some sort of magical fix to this nightmare!" Beads of burning perspiration formed on her head.

Woody shot Ryan a look, and Ryan nodded.

"You just might be, so quit your woe-is-me crap. Listen, we don't have time for this—we gotta get out of here. Find it. You know what I'm talking about. And I'll—I'll do what I can," conceded Woody.

Maggie rolled her eyes and stormed out of the boathouse. "Some help he was," she muttered once they were outside.

Ryan fell in step with her. "He was, actually."

"Oh, really? How? Basically, we just told him everything. Greg or Kate probably put him up to it, and we have been too wrapped up in this thing to see a very basic trap."

"You're wrong," argued Ryan. "He told us we needed to find that envelope: that means it was his, which also means that none of the other counselors found it on the night you stuffed it under the cushion."

"Or, it's a way to get me to the Lab so that they can abduct me. That's probably what happened to Penny." Maggie ran her fingers through her hair.

"What choice do we have other than to believe him? He's literally our only hope as far as camp staff is concerned."

"No."

"What's your deal?" Ryan cut in and faced her, his eyes blazing.

"Huh? What? What do you mean, my deal?" asked Maggie, caught off guard by Ryan's direct attack.

"Do you have trust issues or something? You don't let anyone in, you're skeptical of everyone and everything—why?"

"You're kidding, right? You, of all people, are asking me this? You told me to be skeptical of people like Becky, remember?" Maggie shook her head, incredulous.

"This is different. All I'm saying is let's just run with this. What choice do we have…especially in trying to find Beth?"

"I guess," said Maggie.

They walked in silence for a few minutes. Maggie's shoulders relaxed. "You're right—I don't trust a lot of things or people. I'm not really sure why. I think it's probably because I'd rather not trust people than get hurt. Typical, I guess," she admitted. Up ahead they saw campers leaning their litter sticks up against the Mess Hall.

"Getting hurt sucks," agreed Ryan.

"I mean, I'm not an idiot. I know that getting hurt in life is inevitable," she said.

"Yeah, but that doesn't mean you're not going to protect yourself from it if you can," said Ryan.

"I guess. I just have a feeling about this—this place. It's looming over me, like something is going to ruin everything."

"Like, large-scale mushroom cloud atomic bomb ruin?"

"Nah, more like fleeting perfection blowing up because of something I can't control, and then having to live with the outcome for the rest of my life."

"Well, at least you had fleeting perfection. Not everyone can say that."

"But it's the kind you don't realize you're in it, until you're out of it, you know?"

"You lost me there, Yoda," said Ryan, smirking.

"Shut up," replied Maggie, shoving him off the path. They made their way to the Mess Hall.

"Litter sticks over there. Trash bags can be piled behind the Mess Hall," said Adah, chewing on the back of her pen without looking up from her clipboard.

Ryan handed Maggie his litter stick and said, "Here, give me your bag. I'll bring these out back."

"Thanks," said Maggie.

"Well done, campers!" clapped Kate.

"Yes, you really knocked it out of the park—just look at this place!" beamed Greg. He surveyed the crowd of sweaty, irritated faces and flashed a grin. "Why don't you guys go get a drink in the Mess Hall and then hit the lake for a swim. It's hotter than Hades out here, am I right?"

The grumbling campers dispersed, some heading straight for their cabins, while others dragged their feet through the doors of the Mess Hall. Maggie automatically scanned the crowd and duly realized that her eyes weren't going to find Beth…and despite their argument, the other set of eyes she wanted to see were headed to the boys' cabins.

53

Beth's trembling hands tried to quietly peel the metallic packaging away from the energy bar. It was midmorning—the sun cheerfully gleamed through the pine branches onto the forest floor. Birds chirped and swooped from tree to tree with unbridled gaiety. Her eyes darted back and forth. She pressed her back into the boulder behind her to keep her legs from buckling. She hadn't sat down in hours. Her mouth felt like sandpaper. The last beverage she drank was at dinner before Manhunt.

She remembered sitting in the car with Corey, Maggie, and Ryan. She remembered getting out of the car with Corey, and the two of them racing through the woods toward the Lab. She saw something coming at them, out of the corner of her eye. She shrieked, "Corey—Counselor! Run!" But it was all part of the game, wasn't it? She had tripped over a rock wedged firmly into the ground, smashed her knee, and felt someone grab her wrists behind her back. Then everything went black. She swung at someone, or something. Then nothing.

She woke up groggy at the mouth of a dank cave. Her cheek pressed against a cold slab of stone. An ant marched along the outline of her nose. She sat up, slapping the ant away. Her head hurt. Had she hit it when she fell? Where was she? What was that thick, sour smell? What was that dark puddle beneath the stone slab?

She tried to stand up, but the world started to spin, so she sat back down. Maybe she needed to eat something. She reached into her pocket and found the energy bars Woody had forced on her. Well, that was a lucky coincidence, she thought, rubbing her eyes. Or was it? She examined the contents of each bar and noticed a small handwritten number on each one in black marker. She thought of Alice in Wonderland and chose to eat "Bar 1" first. She bit the top of the wrapper to tear it open, but it had already been opened and resealed with a thin piece of tape. She took a bite of the bar anyway. She examined the interior of the packaging and suddenly dropped the bar on the ground. She sat frozen, staring at the wrapper, then quickly picked up the energy bar and scrambled away from the opening of the cave as fast as her weak legs could take her.

The wrapper delivered a warning message to her.

"YOU'RE BEING HUNTED. RUN."

Where could she go? Who was hunting her? What was hunting her? She ignored the pounding dizziness in her head and ran. What about the rest of her friends? Did they know? Could she find help? The police? Maybe if she made it to town she would be safe. But the men at Pinegrove had alluded to the cops being compromised, didn't they? So what now? If the counselors were hunting her, she could hide from them, but if it was something else—the something that they all suspected—well, what then? How do you hide from a monster? How do you make yourself undetectable to a supernatural being that you know virtually nothing about? As far as she was concerned, she was being hunted by Predator, and Arnold Schwarzenegger was nowhere to be found. She was armed with one and a half protein bars and the weak understanding that, given the choice of fight or flight, she would have to learn how to physically fly to have any chance at living through this.

Every snapping twig and rustle of leaves heightened her anxiety. Her eyes swiveled like chaotic marbles over her surroundings. She ran from the mouth of the cave eastward—if she lived long enough and ran far enough, she would eventually hit the ocean. Or at least another town that wasn't near Camp Kinross. Maybe another police jurisdiction is all she had to find to blow this whole thing up. How far did this monster roam? How fast was it? She opened the other wrapper looking for more clues, but the inside was bare. Frustrated, she jammed it back into her pocket.

Then she heard it.

Shrieking.

Bloodcurdling, desperate screams from the depths of what was once a soul. A sound so intolerable to the ears that nails on a chalkboard sounded like a symphony. It was both guttural and high-pitched. The shriek propelled sound waves in a way they weren't meant to travel through the air. It went on forever. It went deep. It ricocheted off trees—a horror-filled cacophony of a woman being tortured with tweezers twisting into flesh by a deranged captor.

Beth convulsed.

She looked around furtively. It didn't sound like it was in the immediate area. Maybe it was a fisher cat—their screams sound like a woman being murdered, don't they? The bile festering in her throat indicated otherwise. This was more than unhinged camp counselors. She ducked behind the safety of the tall pines, desperate to find a tree to climb to gain a better vantage point. She would need to sleep soon. Her heart hadn't stopped pounding against her ribs for over twenty-four hours. Her eyes were heavy, but awake—fueled by fear. She came upon a boulder with a tiny crevice, a tucked away cave. She contorted her body until she was fully in its embrace. She started smearing the damp earth all over her face and body, in an attempt to mask her human scent.

"Please hurry," Beth silently prayed, twisting a macrame bracelet around her wrist. "Please, please, please let someone find me."

54

Joey and Alex were already in the cabin when Ryan and Corey walked through the door.

"Where's Mark?" asked Joey, grinning and tapping an imaginary drum set on his knees.

"Thought he'd be with you," replied Corey, wiping sweat from his brow. He grabbed a bottle of water out of his dresser and crushed the plastic as it emptied into his mouth.

"Nah, he's not here," said Alex. "We were hoping you guys would get back before him. We found something—"

Joey held up his fist and dangled a key victoriously in the air. "We have a ride!"

"Jesus, Joey, put it away! Mark could walk in at any second, you giant moron!" said Alex, throwing an empty can of Mountain Dew at his head.

"What the hell, man? That had soda in it, and now it's all over my bed!"

"And that's how you get ants," chided Corey.

"Go ahead and laugh! By the end of the summer all of our beds will be swarming with those little fuckers, and I guarantee it'll be because of this," threatened Joey.

"So, yeah, anyway, we found the bus key. But something else, too," said Alex.

Germ walked through the door, flicking a lighter in his hand. "What'd I miss?"

"Just Joey's apocalyptic ramblings of how the ants are going to take over our cabin. Same as every summer."

"I thought he didn't start that for a few more weeks," deadpanned Germ.

"You're all a bunch of assholes, and you're going to be sorry."

"Anyway, like I was saying," said Alex, "we found something in the camp office. A map of the northeast, hanging up with a bunch of red dots on it."

"Those dots could mean anything," said Ryan.

"That's what I thought, too, but it was pinned under the Smokey Bear poster hanging on the wall. And the corners of the pin-marked Smokey Bear poster are all ripped—it's like it's been taken down and put back up a bunch."

"How many red dots do you think were on there?" asked Corey.

"I dunno, maybe a dozen or so? I didn't think to count—plus we had to hurry. Someone turned on the fan in the office and blew a bunch of brochures everywhere," he said, scowling at Joey.

"You would've never found that map if it weren't for me turning that fan on!" yelled Joey. "You guys suck, you know that?"

"Was there a dot in Rhode Island?" pressed Corey.

"I don't know, okay? Like I said, we didn't have a lot of time, because this clown couldn't keep watch outside like I told him to," said Alex, clenching his jaw. Joey's nostrils flared as he stood up.

"It's fine, Joey, chill out. Here, have a Snickers," said Germ, tossing a candy bar onto his bed.

"I can't be bought!" insisted Joey.

"All right, give it back then," said Germ, reaching for the candy bar.

"From my cold dead hands!" said Joey, swiping up the candy bar and slapping Germ's arm away with a little too much force. Germ tackled him in response.

"Get off me! You're gonna make it all melty and disgusting! I'm not going to be able to eat it!" he squawked.

"That's what she said," said Alex. Ryan grinned, pushing his pillow up against the corner of the wall. He sat on his bed and pulled out his notebook and pen, watching the wrestling match unfold two beds over.

"Submit!" Germ laughed, pinning Joey's arms behind his back.

"Never!"

"Submit!" repeated Germ, twisting his arms farther. "Or your right wrist will never jerk you off the same way again!"

Joey squirmed and gnashed his teeth. "Nice try, dickwad, I use my left!" he spat.

"Your dick is going to be in a wad by the time I'm done!" said Germ, landing a blow to Joey's gut. He moaned into submission as Counselor Mark walked through the door.

"Why are you guys all in here? It smells like you all just hit puberty at the same time. Go down to the lake and rinse off."

"Isn't dinner in a half hour? There's no time," argued Joey, wiping spit from his cheek with the back of his hand.

"Make time. Go. Get out of here. Now." Mark jerked his thumb toward the door.

Ryan shoved his notebook under his pillow and threw a towel around his neck. "C'mon, guys, we'll just go to dinner straight from the lake—that cool, Mark?"

"Yeah, fine. Just make sure to wear your shirts in the Mess Hall."

They opened the door and met Tom coming up the stairs.

"Hey, buddy, where've you been?" jeered Joey.

Tom stared at him.

"We're going for a swim. Hurry up and grab your towel," said Ryan, annoyed. "We'll wait."

55

Maggie sulked the whole way back to Cabin Three. Off to the side, Becky motioned to her from a shady patch of grass. She was sitting with Liv, both leaning back on their arms with their feet splayed out.

"Hey," said Maggie. "What are you guys doing out here? Isn't it almost dinner?"

"Yeah," said Becky slowly.

"It's...it's worse than we thought, Maggie," said Liv, tapping her foot nervously.

"Did you find out something from the counselors?" Maggie sat down next to them.

Becky glanced around, making sure no one nearby could hear her. She lowered her voice and said, "I overheard the whole meeting. They have a numbering system for the campers they get rid of, I think. They said that they couldn't confirm that Camper Thirteen was dead. Which, like—"

Maggie's eyes went wide with horror. "So this is actually a thing—a real thing? They took Beth somewhere?"

"Seems so," croaked Liv.

"Shhh, and don't use her name. I think number thirteen has to be, you know, her, because no other campers have 'disappeared' that we've noticed, right? Well, except the other

Lifer that declined—June? It didn't seem like they meant her, though. It's good news, in a way, because that means Beth could still be alive," concluded Becky. Her face paled as she continued. "But it gets worse. It sounds like the cops are definitely involved—they mentioned an Officer Leroy—and those two dog tags from the vets—they're uh...well..." Becky looked away.

"I feel sick," said Maggie. She hugged her legs to her chest.

"That makes two of us," said Liv weakly.

"Three of us," corrected Becky. "I feel so stupid. So duped, you know? Like the past few summers I've been coming here, buying into maintaining this image to further an idyllic camp identity. I loved being popular. I loved being the pretty one—the one the boys all wanted! I loved being loved. It felt good. Powerful! I loved making everyone love this place! And all this time, I was just...oh God." Becky sat up and buried her face in her hands. The three of them sat in silence.

"At least now we know. We can use this, right?" said Maggie.

"That's the other thing," said Becky, sniffing. "They said they're going to keep their eyes and ears on the Lifers, to see if we know anything about number thirteen, and if we think she's still alive. They mentioned you and Ryan by name."

Maggie flinched. "So we have to, what—use code or something? Where does that leave us? We don't have much time, and tonight is our only chance to try to find her," she moaned.

"All I know is that we have to be really careful how we interact around them, because if we weren't on a stage before, we sure are now," said Becky.

Liv shooed a moth away from her arm and sat up. "How are we going to tell the guys all of this—at dinner? The dance is only a few hours away!"

"Plus we still have to put on the social performance, get gussied up, and whatnot," said Becky.

"Social performance?" asked Maggie, raising an eyebrow.

"You know, act like we know nothing, and that tonight's all about the boys, the drama…" Becky listed on her fingers.

"The drama," echoed Maggie, sitting up straight.

"You know, hooking up with the guy you want, trying to get kissed—"

"Becky, that's it! We can create a diversion at the dance!" Maggie let her words sink in.

"That doesn't solve the problem of how we relay this info to the guys," argued Liv. "We should be careful."

"Liv's right, and the counselors will be hovering around the Mess Hall tables," said Becky.

"Well, passing them a note is obviously out," said Maggie. "Can we call a special Lifer meeting, or would that be suspect?"

"I'm willing to bet if we did that, they'd have a counselor sit in on it," said Becky.

"Okay, how about this. What if we forget trying to tell them all of the stuff you've uncovered. For now, anyway. If Alex and Joey secured a vehicle for tonight, we can fill everyone in on our ride to Mount Kinross…if we make it that far."

"That's probably safer," said Becky.

Maggie stood up, dusting away the blades of grass stuck to her calves. "Let's go. The guys are probably at the lake. Let's just tell them we have an exit plan for the dance tonight."

"I know just the way to tell them," smirked Becky. Liv and Maggie glanced at each other as Becky's eyes zeroed in on Maggie.

"Why do I have a feeling that this involves Ryan and it's going to be something I don't want to do?" said Maggie.

Becky's smirk grew wider and her eyes twinkled.

"Oh, please. You just have to have confidence." She winked and turned on her sugary voice. "And you will. Yes, this whole thing is bigger than everyone involved, but, honey, it can't hurt to have a teensy bit of fun along the way while this nightmare unfolds. To the lake!"

Maggie closed her eyes and shook her head. She begrudgingly let Becky and Liv take her hands and drag her down to the water.

56

Several groups of campers were scattered along the beach of the lake. The Cabin Two guys sat on the dock, their legs swinging back and forth in the water.

"So, guys, Corey and I found something in that beat-up Chevy," said Germ quietly.

"Yeah, a trunk full of bug spray," added Corey.

"What—are we going to use it as Mace in the off chance that something other than mosquitos attack us tonight?" asked Alex.

"I mean, we could…we could use it as blowtorches," offered Tom.

"That's what we were thinking, too" said Germ.

Tom fixed his eyes on Maggie, Liv, and Becky, who emerged from the woods and walked onto the beach. It was odd, he thought, watching the three of them together. As attracted as he was to Liv, Maggie somehow outshone the other two. It's because he had known her for so long—it had to be. He knew the cadence of her walk. The way she ambled on her heels half a pace slower than them—she was nervous about something. He still wanted to get with Liv tonight, but there was something about Maggie that he couldn't quite place. The way she was biting her lower lip as they neared the dock—the same way she bit her lip during that game of Spin the Bottle. Maybe the bottle would have landed on him. Maybe things would have changed between them, but maybe that wouldn't have been so bad. Why hadn't he chanced it? Her fingers twitched at her sides, like when she was listening to her favorite R.E.M. song. Why did it bother him so much that she didn't even glance at him once as she walked toward them?

"Listen to this guy!" coughed Joey in amusement.

"No, I'm serious! I have friends back home who do this stuff all the time. They get bored, they buy cans of bug spray, grill lighters, and they battle each other by spraying jets of fire at each other."

"Seriously?" said Joey.

"Yeah, they use trash can covers as shields. They see who can hold on to it the longest before the metal gets too hot and burns their hands. Ask Maggie."

"Where'd you say you were from again?" Alex laughed.

"That's it! I can't believe I didn't put this together before!" exclaimed Ryan.

"What?" asked Corey, leaning toward the water to face him.

"Fire! It's fire! The heat, the burning—it all makes sense now," said Ryan, clapping his hands together.

"Fire? You seriously think this is a viable option?" questioned Alex. "How are we going to find lighters? Do any of you clowns have one?"

"I've got one," said Germ.

"Me too." Joey grinned.

"Okay, so that's two lighters—that's not going to cut it," surmised Alex.

"It's better than nothing, for now. Maybe Woody can help us," said Ryan.

"Yeah, how'd that go, anyway?" asked Corey.

"Hey, boys!" cooed Becky, flip-flopping her way down the

wooden boards.

The girls walked the length of the dock and pulled up behind them. Becky nudged Maggie toward Ryan. Tom craned his neck to follow her path and unsuccessfully tried to make eye contact with her. Maggie crouched down behind Ryan. She put her hands gingerly on his wet shoulders and leaned close to his ear, her chest brushing against his back. He turned his head and flinched slightly. "We have a plan to get us out tonight," she said quietly, "but we can't talk about it at dinner. We're being watched." Ryan nodded slowly.

She grinned and then glanced over at Becky with raised eyebrows as if to say, "Is this good enough?"

"Ask Woody for lighters," Ryan murmured, turning his face toward her.

Maggie's heart pounded—she stared at his lips, just inches away from hers. Anticipation flooded her system. If only she…her brain abruptly snapped back with the realization that everyone on the dock was watching her. She slowly stood up, her hair falling over his shoulder as she let go. "Okay," she said. "See you later?"

"Have any secrets for me, sweet cheeks?" mocked Joey.

Maggie turned and walked back down the dock. She stopped behind Joey, pressed her foot against his back, and pushed him into the water.

"You earned that, man!" Germ laughed as Joey sputtered to the surface.

Ryan leaned toward Corey and said, "The girls have a plan, but we're being watched."

Corey nodded. "Any way you can, you know, tap into her head to get the plan?"

"Eh, I dunno," said Ryan. "Maybe?"

"Might be worth a shot," replied Corey.

"Even after she freaked out on me? I don't know. It seems sort of normal again between us. I don't want to chance it." Ryan kicked at the water. "Lately, I've been trying to pass some stuff on to Woody, though. I think he's getting it, but who knows."

"I just want this to be over," sighed Corey. His gaze dropped into the murky lake.

After a moment, Ryan pressed his hands into his knees and stood up. "Whatever it is, it'll be finished this time around, you can count on that. It has to be."

Corey ran his thumb over the silver heart-shaped locket around his neck and stared into the distance.

"I hope so. I hope we find her."

57

"So what sort of 'drama' do you girls think we should cook up tonight?" asked Becky, a coy smile forming on her lips. It was nearly time for dinner. Becky, Liv, and Maggie sat on top of a picnic table outside the Mess Hall, their feet resting on the bench. A few counselors milled on the outskirts of the Mess Hall clearing.

"I think it should revolve around Ryan," said Maggie decidedly.

Liv shot Maggie a questioning look.

"No, she's right," said Becky. "The counselors are already aware of a 'friction' between me and Maggie when it comes to Ryan."

"So, what do we do?" said Maggie, lowering her voice. "Could you, like, get loud if you see me dancing with Ryan? Assuming that he'll even dance with me, that is."

Becky glared at her. "Will you stop it already? He'll want to dance with you. He'd be an idiot not to, especially after your performance on the dock. And he's not an idiot."

"Should I be the one to ask him?" Maggie said, cringing.

"Obviously," replied Becky.

Liv threw Maggie a sympathetic look. "He's going to want to dance with you," she said. "Just because he doesn't show any outward signs of affection doesn't mean he isn't thinking about them."

"Thanks, Liv," Maggie said.

In the distance, they could barely make out the guys coming up from the beach.

"Let's go grab a quick bite, then get all dolled up for the dance," said Becky, hopping off the table and flicked a flirty wave at Alex as the guys neared.

"So, have you, uh, been with him long?" asked Maggie, nodding at Alex.

"Officially, just this week," sighed Becky, "but the chase has been going on for ages. It's a lot of fun. He's very…satisfying."

"I'm never going to get used to this girl talk stuff," said Maggie.

Liv let out a little laugh. Becky stepped between them, linking arms with the girls.

"This is what camp is all about, my lovelies, this is what camp is all about!" She shook her head laughing and steered them toward the screen door.

"Most kids are showering and getting ready before they eat, which is a rookie mistake. Then you're at the mercy of whatever Woody serves for dinner that night. One summer, this kid asked me to dance, but it had been Italian night at the Mess Hall. Not only did he not pass on the garlic bread, but he didn't even go back to his cabin to brush his teeth after dinner! It was less than desirable, let me tell you," huffed Becky. "Shame, though—he was pretty hot. But I couldn't get over the way the garlic wafted out of his mouth when he said, '*Hey*, Becky, *how's* it going?'"

"Ew!" cried Liv.

"I know," agreed Becky.

Maggie surveyed the dinner offerings as they sidled up to Woody's line. Tuna melt with oversteamed mixed vegetables. She turned up her nose and grabbed an extra piece of bread from the basket resting on top of the counter.

"There's no way I'm eating—" Liv started, but abruptly stopped when Woody spun around from his prep counter to face them.

"Hiya, Woody!" said Becky in a cheerful song, "You ready for the dance?"

"Are you?" he replied pointedly.

"Hey, Woody, uh, I have a weird question for you," said Maggie, gripping her tray full of bread. She leaned forward. "Got anything we can use to start a fire? Like lighters?"

"No special orders, who do I look like, Billy Joel?" His eyes simmered. "And lower your voice. What's the matter with you?" He looked around the Mess Hall. Most of the counselors were sitting at their table or hanging out by the door.

"Please, Woody, come on, we have to end this. We have a plan," said Maggie in a hasty whisper.

Woody stared hard at the three of them. More campers piled into the Mess Hall. Woody stroked his chin with his fingers. He gave them a brief nod and yelled, "Next!"

Maggie rubbed her forehead. "Can no one act normal in this whole stupid place?"

Becky tugged on her arm, "C'mon, let's go—the sooner we get out of here, the sooner I get to help you with your eyeshadow."

"My what?"

"Makeup, Maggie," said Liv with a little giggle.

"Honestly, I thought she was joking at first—like it was all an act, you know? But I do believe that Maggie has spent more time climbing trees than reading Seventeen magazine," marveled Becky.

"Imagine that," replied Maggie, rolling her eyes. She watched Ryan move through the food line. What would happen after camp? Would he keep in touch with her? And how did she become so keen on him being around all the time? They were like two puzzle pieces, but not the kind made from weak, paper-thin recycled cardboard. No, they fit together like one of those wooden cube puzzles; finely sanded and grooved in such a way that there is only one perfect way to connect them, and when that connection is realized, it's seamless. Infinite. Would he write to her? Would they try to meet up somehow? Somewhere? She was overcome by the thought that the summer would have to come to an end eventually. These feelings couldn't go on forever, her rational mind implored...could they? Despite everything they had been through in one short week, this was the most fun she had had in ages. It wouldn't be so bad if these feelings hung around a bit longer. Her mind continued to scream questions, but her heart continued to hope.

The guys grabbed chairs next to the girls and slid their trays into the spaces in between. Joey glared at Maggie, water still dripping from his forehead. She grinned. There was a jittery foreboding energy resonating as they picked at their food—they were sitting in the eye of a hurricane.

Germ leaned forward slowly and said, "You guys ready...for the dance?"

The others forced smiles and nodded. Tom caught Maggie's eye, but she looked away. Becky cleared her throat and said, "Well, we really ought to be going—we have to get gussied up and whatnot!" She started to stand up but promptly sat back down when Counselor Greg sidled up to their table.

"You bunch are pretty quiet—pre-dance jitters?" he asked, flashing his game show host smile.

The Lifers didn't answer him. Greg looked at each camper individually before speaking again. He leaned down, planting both hands on the table, his eyes full of fury.

"Look at me, all of you. Look at me! Eyes right here. I don't know what you idiots are up to, but your bullshit attitudes are infecting the rest of the campers who are supposed to be having a once in a lifetime, memorable camp experience. We let you live because you help eternalize this camp and everything it embodies. I don't know how many goddamn times I have to give this speech to you. I'm sick of it. If you think for one sec—"

"You 'let us live'?" interrupted Maggie, her eyes wide, but challenging.

"What?" asked Greg, caught off guard by her question.

Alex glared at Maggie.

"Oh, nothing," said Maggie, ignoring the look. "You just said, 'We let you live because you help eternalize this camp,' that's all."

Ryan kicked her shin underneath the table.

"I didn't say that," said Greg, his eyes narrowing on Maggie.

"You did," said Maggie.

"Maggie, stop!" hissed Becky.

"You obviously misheard me," said Greg, slowly standing up. "I said, 'We let you live here because you help eternalize this camp.'"

"Did I mishear, though? Did I?" asked Maggie.

Germ looked up at the ceiling, rubbing his eyes with his fingers.

"You did," said Greg evenly through gritted teeth. "And you better watch your mouth. All of you better clean the wax out of your ears and make sure you hear this correctly. Tonight is the dance. Don't ruin it for the others. Leave your teenage drama, or whatever the hell is eating you, at the door." He straightened; a grinchy smile returned to his face. "And let's have a great night!" He turned and walked away.

"What the hell is wrong with you?" asked Tom.

"Watch yourself," said Ryan, firing a warning glance at Tom.

"Shut it," replied Tom.

"Guys, enough!" exclaimed Germ.

"What? He did say that—none of you caught that?" said Maggie.

"Yeah, he did, Mags, but you probably shouldn't have called him out on it," replied Ryan.

"I wanted to throw him off his game," said Maggie. "Maybe it'll make him second-guess killing another camper."

"Or maybe he's going to be on high alert now and make our night hell," retorted Alex.

"There's no sense in arguing about this. What's done is done. The girls have to go get ready. We'll see you soon," said Corey.

Becky stood, motioning to Liv and Maggie. She looked over her shoulder at the girls and said, "Okay, forget all this. Let's drum up some excitement for tonight, shall we?"

Maggie and Liv exchanged looks while lifting their trays from the table.

Becky snaked between the Mess Hall tables, speaking in a loud singsong voice. "Tonight is going to be so amazing! I cannot wait! You girls are in for a treat—the first time is always the most memorable!"

"Maggie, you made the mix right?" chimed in Liv, conjuring a smile despite her trembling voice.

"I did. It's, uh…it's going to be a pretty…magical night?" Maggie attempted.

Becky paraded around the perimeter of the Mess Hall and brought her tray to the clearing station. Germ, Tom, and Joey walked by them. "I can't wait! I know I'm a Lifer, but seriously these dances just get better each year—Maggie, you are totally going to hook up with Ryan tonight!"

Maggie blushed and set her tray down. She was unaware of the boys passing when Becky said that, and failed to see Tom's set jaw and steely glare at hearing Becky's proclamation.

58

"I cannot believe the dance is in an hour!"

"I've literally been waiting all week for this."

"Can you do my eyeshadow for me?"

"My boobs look so small today, what the hell! I'm never going to get any with these!"

"Just yank them up more, and tighten your bra straps—that'll give you some lift."

"Like this?"

"Yeah, now squish them toward each other, maximize that cleavage."

"Got it, thanks, Becky!"

"Not my first rodeo, sugar."

"Where's a good place to, you know…"

"The counselors usually let us hang out just outside of the Rec Hall along the building. You can't stray too far, but there are enough dark spots."

"Yeah, but what about that floodlight? No one should be making out under that thing."

"It's not mood lighting, that's for sure. Hey, Maggie, pass me that eyeliner."

"If you get stuck under the light, just keep your eyes closed."

"I hope Ryan, uh…"

"If he doesn't, he's going to have more problems than that thing in the woods, I'll tell you—"

"Shh! Not so loud."

"He looks like he'd be a good kisser."

"Honestly, I wouldn't know. Hey, Liv, is that curling iron hot yet?"

"Wait, but I thought you—"

"Blot your lips, like this. We were together last summer for a while, but we never actually did anything."

"Really?"

"It was mostly a show for the campers—Greg's idea. All-American couple, making chastity look cool and all that jazz."

"Oh. Weird."

"Yep. Turn that way. Thanks. I need to fix a few of these strands."

"Wow, Maggie, that purple eyeshadow makes your eyes look super green!"

"Really? Uh, thanks. I hope that everything goes well for you with Tom tonight."

"Yeah, me too. I hope everything else goes all right tonight, you know?"

"Hey, girls!"

"Oh, hey, Hannah! We're just about ready for the big night!"

"You girls look so dreamy—those boys are in for it!"

"Thanks!"

"Hey, Hannah, is it okay if I run over to the Lab to make sure my mix stuff is all ready to go for tonight? Everything has to be perfect."

"Sure, Maggie, no problem. I think Adah is headed to the Rec Hall to finish setting up the sound stuff and snack table. She'll meet you there."

"Cool, thanks!"

"I'm just putting the finishing touches on our resident DJ—

she has to look perfect for her Kinross debut."

"Her eyes look incredible! Becky, did you do this?"

"She's so talented, isn't she?"

"I haven't even seen what I look like yet."

"Patience! Almost done. Pass me that bobby pin over there, please, Liv? You're up next."

"Here you go."

"I'll let you girls finish getting ready—time for me to freshen up! I'm really hoping this is the week that I finally get with Mark."

"Hannah, you say that every week, and every week you totally hook up with him!"

"Silly girls, it's all about the chase!"

"Oh boy."

"You better finish up so I can get over to the Lab."

"Just one teensy fix right here and…done! Have a look!"

"Woah. You really—how'd you—"

"I know."

"No, but like, how'd you get my eyes—"

"You're welcome."

"Thanks. Is it too much?"

"Shut up and get out of here! Go!"

"Okay, okay, I'm going. See you guys over there?"

"Don't forget—Ryan. Do it."

"Right. Ryan."

59

Flecks of mascara made Maggie's eyes twitch. She tried not to touch her face as she hurried to the Lab, for fear of messing up Becky's handiwork. She weaved along the path to the Rec Hall, smiling at a few counselors along the way, though they all appeared preoccupied and paid no attention to her.

The air was thick and draped over Camp Kinross like a heavy, wet blanket. She pulled open the door to the Rec Hall and was greeted by its warm, but now familiar, stale air. Maggie wriggled her nose and rushed to the Lab.

Adah hadn't arrived yet to set up for the dance. Some of the furniture in the Rec Hall had been removed or pushed to the walls already. A small folding table was in the corner with gold metallic streamers hanging from it.

"DJ booth?" Maggie murmured to herself. She opened the door to the Lab and tugged on the light bulb string. The room looked exactly as it had the night she and Beth had returned in search of the envelope.

"Oasis, Oasis, Oasis," she said under her breath, flipping rapidly through record crates. She moved from one box to the next. In her haste, she pinched her finger between a crate and the metal shelf.

"Shit!" she yelped, sucking on her finger until the pain

subsided. She moved on to the next crate. She flipped past some Stevie Wonder albums and noticed a slightly newer album cover, with Noel Gallagher lying prostrate in a room full of British oddities. *Definitely Maybe*. Maggie's heart leapt. She pressed against both sides of the album sleeve and looked into the opening. The envelope! She peered around the door into the Rec Hall, making sure no one had noticed her, and grabbed it. She folded the envelope twice and stuffed it into her back pocket. She pushed the records back into their resting position in the crate and tugged on the light cord once more.

Maggie walked across the Rec Hall and saw Adah twisting the doorknob to enter.

"Hey there, Maggie!" said Adah. "Wow, cool makeup."

"Oh, thanks," said Maggie. "I was just checking on my mix stuff to make sure, you know, it's perfect."

"Yeah, no, that's cool—want to help me grab the rest of the stuff? Campers should be here pretty soon."

"Sure, yeah," said Maggie, turning back around toward the Lab.

"You excited for tonight?" asked Adah, blowing dust off the top of the stereo before picking it up.

"I guess? I mean, I've never been the biggest fan of dances, honestly."

"Why not?"

"I dunno. I'm not really a part of the 'it' crowd back home. Dances just seem like a social necessary evil in school. And they're always way more disappointing than the hype that surrounds them beforehand."

"I hear you." Adah laughed. "All of my school dances were full of idiot boys who were too chickenshit to ask any of the girls to dance."

Maggie laughed—maybe Adah wasn't part of the abductions or killings orchestrated by Kate and Greg. She seemed pretty cool and clearly wasn't afraid to speak her mind.

"Hey, Adah, can I level with you for a second?"

"Sure, what's up?"

"Well, it's...it's about a guy."

"Which one?" Adah asked point-blank.

"It's, er, Ryan."

"Yeah, he's hot stuff, isn't he?" she replied.

Maggie blushed.

"I just like—I can't tell if he feels the same way as I do."

"Ask him."

"No, I'm serious!" Maggie said, trailing after Adah across the Rec Hall.

"So am I," said Adah, setting a speaker down on the table.

"I can't just 'ask him.' I've only known him for a few days. Plus, I don't think we would ever talk about things like that. It's not our style. And if I did ask him, what if it ruins everything we already have?"

"What do you have, exactly?"

Maggie faltered. "Er, it's hard to explain. It's like a closeness? Physically and, well, mentally I guess. When we're together, it's like we've known each other forever."

"Has he kissed you yet?"

"What? No! God! It's not like that. It's more like...little stuff. It's hard to read if the little things are intentional or not. And then he goes cold. It's maddening."

Adah stood back and sized up Maggie.

"Okay, if I'm being honest, I haven't paid much attention to your interactions, so I can't say whether or not I think he likes you, or whatever affirmation you're after. What I can say is that sometimes guys wrestle with inner demons that we can't relate to. That's probably why he goes cold. But to put it in perspective—there's never a need to touch another person. If it's an accident, most people say 'sorry' afterward because it's an automatic reaction to maintain appropriate social behavior. Get me?"

"Yeah, I get you."

"So if he's touched you more than once, it's likely that it's not an accident, and he's feeling some sort of pull toward you."

"So it's not in my head?"

"Maybe it is. But let me ask you this: is it fun for you, even if it's all in your head?"

"Well, yeah."

"Who cares then?" Adah shrugged and walked over to the Lab.

"I just think it would be better to know, you know?" said Maggie, grabbing her mixtapes from the shelf.

"Well," groaned Adah, hoisting a section of stereo to her chest, "maybe it would be, but what if the feelings aren't mutual, and that changes everything you guys have right now? Or worse, what if the feelings are mutual? You have the rest of the summer with him, and then you go back to your life and he goes back to his. Long-distance shit never works out, not at your age. Trust me."

"Yeah," Maggie sighed.

Adah looked at her over her shoulder. "It's going to be all right. Just enjoy the ride. Don't get hung up on needing classification, or definition or whatever." She put the stereo down on the table and leaned over to plug it in. "If you really want an answer, just ask him, point-blank. But why blow up your whole summer when you're obviously into the little moments? Those little unspoken moments are the ones that speak volumes, anyway, you know? They usually say what a person can't actually bring themselves to say."

"Right, okay. Thanks, Adah." Maggie smiled. She looked around the room, noticing the streamers and disco ball on the ceiling for the first time. "Is there anything else we need to do?"

"Nah, not really—Woody's going to bring over some snacks and set them up on that table over there. You should get your tapes ready—campers are going to start arriving any minute."

Maggie fumbled with the cassette cases. She pressed eject on the stereo and slid the first one in. She had compiled about four hours' worth of music, to account for pre-dance atmosphere when campers would file into the Rec Hall and also post-dance cleanup. She had written out the track listing on the tiny lines of the cassette inserts. The dance would pretty much be on autopilot, she thought, but playing DJ was a solid excuse to not have to partake in the awkward gyrations of teenagers fumbling around in semi-darkness.

Her stomach churned with the anticipation of seeing Ryan. Would he ask her to dance, or would he avoid making eye contact with her the whole night? How would she and Becky cause a scene to distract the counselors? Would it even work? Would they find Beth? Would there be a moment that she knew beyond all doubt that he was into her?

Her thoughts were interrupted when the first few campers entered the Rec Hall. Maggie quickly pressed play on the tape deck. Elvis's voice pounded through the speakers with burning love. Gradually, the room bustled with campers and counselors, all freshly showered, eyes brimming with anticipation. The dance floor filled out faster than dances at home, Maggie noticed. Kinross campers had fewer inhibitions; their camaraderie and encouragement were apparent in the carefree way they swung their arms and hips on the dance floor. Even the counselors were relaxed—they congregated in the corners, laughing at inside jokes and mingling with campers under the strung-up holiday lights.

After what seemed like ages, Maggie saw Becky enter with Liv. Becky squealed and ran across the room to the DJ booth. She threw her arms open and embraced Maggie, as if they hadn't seen each other in over a decade. Maggie braced herself for impact. As they hugged, Maggie whispered, "Found the envelope."

"Perfect!" Becky squealed loudly.

Liv stepped in front of Becky, leaned into Maggie, and quickly whispered, "When you and Becky stir up drama, the guys will sneak out and grab the bus. Then we'll make another scene somehow and run to meet them by the camp entrance."

Maggie stepped back and plastered a calculated smile on her face. "That's excellent news! Congrats!" A counselor walked by and tapped his ear before giving Maggie a thumbs-up. She grinned back.

Her eyes trailed the counselor, but switched paths when she heard the Cabin Two guys walk through the Rec Hall door. Ryan's hair was perfectly tousled, his smile electric. Maggie desperately tried to settle the butterflies dive bombing inside her stomach. His head turned toward the DJ booth. She instantly averted her eyes, turning back to Becky and Liv.

"Guys are here," she said casually. Liv automatically pushed her hair behind her ears.

"Looks like one is headed this way," smirked Becky. "C'mon, Liv, let's see what Woody is setting up over there. Maybe he has something other than cookies."

"Who hates cookies?" mumbled Maggie. She looked down at the tape deck. Shuffled the mixtapes. Smoothed the twisting stereo cords.

"Hey, nice mix."

Maggie looked up, unable to hide her grin.

Their eyes met.

"Oh, hey! Thanks!" said Maggie, flustered. "I could only work with so much—I mean, I only had so much to work with."

"You look good," continued Ryan, his mouth twitched a side grin and he quickly looked away.

"Right—I mean, thanks? So do you," replied Maggie. Her face burned. She quickly changed the subject. "Here's hoping this mix lives up to camp dances of yesteryear."

"I'll be the judge of that," said Ryan matter-of-factly.

"I'd prefer an unbiased judge."

"I'd prefer a little less U2."

"Do you even know what I was working with? Have you seen those music crates? You should be thanking your lucky stars there was any U2 at all. It's a Lionel Richie fest in there."

"You're telling me 'All Night Long' didn't make the mix? Tsk."

"Oh, sorry, I wasn't aware that our parents would also be at this dance."

Ryan smirked and replied, "You can do better than that."

"Get out of here. I'm busy," shooed Maggie, shuffling around the cassette cases some more.

The music transitioned from "Mysterious Ways" to Tommy James's first "Oh" of "Crimson and Clover." Her heart smashed repeatedly against her chest.

"You're not busy; you hit play, and maybe pause."

"I do more than that! I have to make sure the tape doesn't jam."

"Sure." Ryan laughed. "Think the tape is good for a few minutes?"

"Huh? Probably, I mean I hope so, because—"

"Mags," said Ryan, hand outstretched. He was asking her to dance.

Maggie met his eyes. "Um, yes? Yeah, it should be fine," she stammered. Her heart exploded.

Her legs wobbled as she walked around the table. He took her hand in his and led her across the linoleum floor. Surreal waves washed over her. She gingerly put her arms around his neck, afraid he'd pull away at her touch. He drew her waist toward him. She was reeling. They danced in silence for a few moments before he spoke.

"Did you know that Tommy James woke up one morning thinking of his favorite color and flower, and that's how he came up with this song?"

Maggie turned her head to reply, her face slightly brushing his. He smelled like a rainstorm. Her mind was mush. "Really?"

"Yeah. It was after 'Mony Mony' came out. He wanted to change the band's sound, which is why he did all that weird shit with the guitar and vocals on this track."

"Ah," she replied. "I've always loved this song."

"Same," he said.

"I mean, it's no Lionel Richie," she said, grinning.

"Sure isn't," he agreed, and pulled her closer.

The room blurred. Everything melted into the background. But this wasn't one of her dreams, she was sure of it—she was very much awake. They barely shuffled their feet. Maggie's arms draped over him. She felt the outline of his shoulder blades against her fingertips, imagining their smoothness in the absence of his scratchy camp polo. His fingers moved on the small of her back, lightly tapping along with the drum beat. She shifted her arms to move even closer. Maybe he would finally kiss her. Maybe this song would magically keep playing, over and over. She closed her eyes, lost in the hypnotic melody of "Crimson and Clover" and his fingers tracing abstract shapes on her back. She opened them again. Was he turning his head slightly toward her? Was he going to kiss her right here in the middle of the dance floor? She lifted her chin a little and bit her lower lip out of nervous habit. She could feel his breath on her face. His lips were close to hers. It was impossible to stop the pull now.

She felt a tap on her shoulder.

"Hey, Mags, can I cut in?"

Maggie stepped back slightly from Ryan and turned to see Tom standing beside them.

"Huh?" Maggie replied, dazed. The song wasn't even over yet. This wasn't supposed to happen. This was her time with Ryan; Tom was ruining everything.

"Seriously?" Ryan said to Tom, not letting go of Maggie.

"Yeah, I'm serious, man, get out of here," said Tom. "Maggie, c'mon, let's dance."

"What? No! Where's Liv?" asked Maggie, her eyes silently trying to explain to Ryan that she had nothing to do with this.

"You don't need to dance with this clown to prove a point, Mags," scoffed Tom.

"I'm not trying to prove anything! Go away!" hissed Maggie.

"That's enough, man. Get out of here," said Ryan. He let go of Maggie and faced Tom. The other campers around them stopped dancing. Maggie saw Becky and Liv watching from the corner and lifted her hands in exasperation at them. Becky shot her a confused look and whispered something to Liv. Liv moved through the room and tapped Joey on the shoulder. He whispered to Alex; they both turned to watch the dance floor, where a small circle had formed around Tom, Ryan, and Maggie. Alex leaned over to Mark who was standing nearby and motioned to the center of the room. The counselors slowly moved in on the altercation.

"You're making a scene. She asked you to leave. Take a walk," Ryan cautioned.

"Take a walk? Take a walk?" repeated Tom, stepping forward and clenching his fists.

The counselors descended.

"What's your problem, Tom?" cried Maggie.

"What's up, guys?" said Greg, gritting his teeth behind a fake smile. He put his hands on Ryan's and Tom's shoulders. They stared at each other without saying a word. Maggie looked up just in time to see Joey and Alex slide out the Rec Hall doors.

"Nothing," replied Ryan, his nostrils flaring. Greg gave them a once-over, then turned to the other counselors. They shrugged.

"I thought I made myself clear earlier," said Greg, turning

back to them.

Kate jumped in. "How about the three of you cool off? We'll deal with this—whatever this is—later. Don't be selfish and ruin the dance for everyone else with your drama. Figure it out, and by figure it out, I mean drop it."

The other counselors nodded in agreement and faded back into the woodwork.

"You're an idiot, Tom, you know that? Our whole plan might be ruined now because of you!" Maggie whispered harshly.

"This isn't over," said Tom.

"Yeah, it is," said Ryan. "We have bigger issues to deal with."

"How's that?" sneered Tom.

"Well, for starters, you just inadvertently set the wheels in motion. Literally. The bus wheels."

"How?"

"Our plan was to create a diversion during the dance, so Joey and Alex could sneak out and get the vehicle so we can get the hell out of here to find Beth."

"Nobody told me that."

"Maybe pay attention."

"Maybe go fuck yourself."

Maggie jumped in, her voice filled with annoyance and exasperation. "This wasn't the diversion we planned, but now Joey and Alex are gone. We probably have ten minutes to get to the bus, so we need to create another diversion so we can all get out of here!"

"Shit," said Tom awkwardly.

"Yeah, shit," agreed Ryan, shaking his head at Tom.

"So what's the second diversion?" asked Tom.

"No idea!" Maggie threw her arms in the air. "I guess we'll all just have to sneak out? Or make a run for it? But we're running out of time."

"I'm going to find Corey and Germ. I'll be back," said Ryan.

He walked across the room, leaving Maggie and Tom alone for the moment.

"What's wrong with you?" She flexed her fingers.

"I'm sorry, okay? I just can't stand seeing you with that guy. He's a jerk."

"It's none of your business, and no, he's not a jerk. You don't even know him."

"I know him. I've seen his type a million times. He's a pretentious dick and he sucks."

"Where have you seen his type—in our little town of Bradford? In the movies? Life isn't the movies, Tom," chided Maggie.

"Art imitates life," Tom said, shrugging.

"Now who's the pretentious dick?"

"He takes advantage of you because he knows you're into him."

"That's such bullshit! How would you even know? You're barely around us! I don't understand how you can even be bent about this—you don't see me storming over to you and Liv! Is this about that stupid Spin the Bottle game at Noah's? Because newsflash, Tom, the bottle didn't land on you! I kissed Rob that night, and I didn't see you up in arms about that!"

"You just—you deserve better. You're…"

"I'm what?" Maggie challenged.

"Wait—Rob?"

"I'm what, Tom?"

"You're…one of the good ones, that's all. I don't…I don't want to see you get hurt."

"Thanks, Dad," said Maggie sourly, "but I can take care of myself. I need to talk to Becky—we have to get out of here. I don't have time for this."

"Look, I'm sorry, okay? Can we just forget it?"

"Fine," sighed Maggie, looking around the room for Becky. She spotted her at the snack table talking to Woody. "Just be ready to go, okay? Go find Liv."

Maggie moved through the dance floor to Becky, who greeted her with a dazzling smile.

"Hi, sweetie! Great mix! Love the retro vibe," oozed Becky. Maggie forced a smile at her and then turned to Woody, who filled Dixie cups with lemonade.

"Cookie?" he offered gruffly.

"Woody, we have a—"

"Cookie?" he interrupted.

"Uh, sure okay," Maggie said, and leaned in for a cookie. Woody leaned forward to hand it to her and uttered, "Be ready."

Maggie stood up straight and turned to Becky. She nodded.

"So that wasn't the plan—what was all of that?" asked Becky casually. "Was it because you and Ryan were looking awfully cozy?"

"Tom was just being an overprotective idiot," sighed Maggie.

"Looks like you're the belle of the ball," smirked Becky.

"Gross," replied Maggie. "So, what do you think it is that we're waiting for anyway?"

"Not sure. Woody has it covered, though. Maybe we should make our way to the other side of the room near the exit."

"Good idea," agreed Maggie. She scanned the room for Ryan but couldn't find him.

"Hey, did you see where Ryan and the guys went?" asked Maggie. Before Becky could reply, the power to the Rec Hall cut out. Campers shrieked and bodies bumped into each other. They spun around trying to get their bearings as their eyes adjusted to the darkness. Mark's and Greg's voices shouted through the heightening confusion.

"Let's go," said Becky, tugging on Maggie's arm. Maggie looked around again for Ryan, while Becky pulled her to the door. Adah was standing guard next to it, yelling for everyone to stay put and not to exit the Rec Hall. Becky and Maggie pushed to the front of the mass of campers trying to get out.

"Adah! Please! We have to get out!" Becky insisted.

"No, you don't!" said Adah, looking over the heads of the campers trying to get the attention of another counselor to help her.

"No, Adah, she's right, we really do! Counselor Greg was right next to us when the power went out, and he told us to go outside and watch for any campers who try to sneak out, while you guys keep this place under control," said Maggie, the lie rapid-firing from her mouth.

Adah looked at them for a second and then said, "Yeah, all right, fine. Go."

The girls ran out of the Rec Hall. A generator light outside the Mess Hall glowed in the distance.

"Do you think the others got out?" asked Maggie.

"I hope so, but we don't have time to worry about that. We have to get to the parking lot, now!"

They ran into the night, past the bell, down winding paths, past the lightning tree podium, until their feet met the familiar gravel driveway of the camp entrance. No one else was there. Maggie and Becky exchanged glances and spun around looking around for any sign of the others.

"You don't think they left without us?" asked Maggie nervously.

"Maybe they ran into an issue getting the bus?"

The quiet of the evening made them feel even more exposed in the empty parking lot.

Suddenly, Corey, Germ, and Ryan burst through the woods, carrying large trash bags. Maggie breathed a sigh of relief. Her eyes connected with Ryan's for a split second, but he looked away quickly. Was he upset about Tom's scene? Of course, he had to be. He probably thought Maggie was in on it somehow—using him to make Tom jealous. How could she prove to him that she wanted nothing to do with Tom in that way? Maybe before camp she did and hadn't realized it. Things change, though. Before camp, she had no idea that it was possible to feel this way about another person. With Tom, it was comfortable, and he knew everything about her; but with Ryan, something inside of her sparked alive in ways that she couldn't articulate, but she knew with certainty that it had to involve the intricate composition of the universe.

"Sorry we're late—we had to stop for these. Woody left them for us near the Infirmary," said Corey, gasping for air.

"What are they?" asked Becky.

"Dunno, we didn't have time to look—we heard voices not too far off, so we grabbed the bags and bolted," said Germ. He untied one of the bags and jammed his hand into it. He pulled out a can of bug spray.

"Looks like he bagged up more of the stuff we found in the car behind the Infirmary," said Corey, unknotting another bag. He rummaged some more.

"Oh, here we go—he threw in a bunch of grill lighters, too! Check your bag, Germ." Germ pulled out a handful of them and grinned. "This might actually work."

"Where do you think all these cans came from?" Becky asked.

"Maybe personal effects of the dead campers, left in their bunks," said Ryan.

"Jeez, Ryan! Don't say that!" exclaimed Becky.

"He's right," said Germ. "I bet there's shit hidden all over camp. Like in that covered up well. Where's our ride to this nightmare anyway?"

"No idea, we just got here a few seconds before you guys did," said Maggie. She opened her mouth to ask where Tom and Liv were, but closed it again, not wanting to fuel Ryan's fire. Thankfully, Becky intervened.

"Liv and Tom should have been here by now," said Becky, her forehead wrinkled.

"Wasn't Liv with us when we were leaving the Rec Hall?" asked Maggie.

"She turned back to find Tom. I told her to get him and get out," said Becky.

They all turned back toward the camp at the sound of branches breaking. Tom and Liv came barreling through the brush and into the parking lot. "Guys, they're behind us!"

"What?" said Ryan.

"We—have—to—run!" panted Liv. "Greg—and—Kate—"

They scanned the woods and heard more branches breaking not far off. Corey and Germ picked up the trash bags.

"Seriously, we need to go, now!" yelled Tom. Headlamps were bobbing up and down, growing closer to the parking lot. The Lifers exchanged looks and started running down the long camp driveway.

"You little shits better stop running right now!" Greg's voice bellowed through the woods.

"Where the hell is the bus?" sputtered Maggie. The gravel dust kicked up behind them, hanging in the air like a ghostly veil over the road. They started to sprint.

A low rumble could be heard in the distance. "Is that the bus?" yelled Germ. Two glowing lights slowly closed in on them. They couldn't hear Greg and Kate, having put a bit of distance between them down the long and winding road.

"It is!" shrieked Becky. The Lifers waved their arms wildly and slowed to a jog. The bus headlights bounced down the driveway.

"If Joey's driving, we better move to the side!" yelled Corey.

They continued to flail their arms to flag the bus down. The headlights flashed twice. "Definitely Alex driving," Germ said, laughing.

"How are we going to turn the bus around without going back to the parking lot?" asked Maggie, surveying the narrow driveway.

"I have an idea," said Ryan.

The bus squealed to a stop next to them. Alex yanked on the lever to open the door.

"School's in session, kiddies!" Joey said, grinning and hanging out a window.

"Jesus, what took you so long?" asked Tom.

"Settle down, Rocky, I don't want any trouble!" sneered Joey. He raised his fists and jabbed at the air. Tom rolled his eyes.

They scrambled onto the bus. Corey and Germ swung the trash bags over the top of the first bus seat and slid into the seat behind it.

"C'mon, c'mon, hurry up! I can see them just down there!" yelled Alex, jerking the bus door shut and throwing the stick shift into gear.

Everyone found a seat. Ryan sat behind Alex and leaned over the seat.

"I'm not going to be able to turn around without looping through the parking lot," said Alex, his foot increasing pressure on the gas pedal.

"Yeah, I know. You're going to have to put it in reverse to get us out of here," said Ryan.

"You're fucking joking with me right now, right?"

"Wish I was, buddy."

"Drive backward down this driveway? I can't see for shit out these mirrors!"

"Wait until they're right on top of us, okay? That way it'll take them even longer to get back to camp to get another vehicle."

"Unless another counselor picks them up," said Becky, her eyes peering through the dirt-caked windows.

"We're gonna have to take that chance," said Ryan, looking at the back of the bus. Maggie looked at him. He raised his eyebrows, then faced forward again. Through the headlights, they could see two bodies gaining on the bus.

"They're getting closer!" exclaimed Liv, gripping the top of the seat so tightly that her knuckles turned white.

They watched anxiously as the counselors approached. Greg waved at the bus jovially, but Kate was livid. She flexed her fingers repeatedly in the dusty glow of the headlights.

"Not yet," instructed Ryan. "Mags, go to the back of the bus and see if you can help direct Alex out of here."

"Okay," said Maggie. She jumped from her seat and rushed down the aisle, her hands clapping on top of each seat she passed. She squatted down next to the two-seater and peered through the door.

"Ready?" said Ryan, patting Alex on the shoulder. "On three."

"We're all going to die, we're all going to die," repeated Joey.

"Shut up, Joey!" insisted Germ through gritted teeth.

Greg and Kate were at the front of the bus now. The driver's window was open. Greg walked around to it.

"Hey there, Alex, what's going on? Where ya going, champ?" said Greg, looking up at Alex and smiling like Jack Torrance through an ax-shattered bathroom door. Blood trickled down Greg's face, a wound from their nighttime chase through the woods.

"One…" counted Ryan.

"We just gotta go take care of something," said Alex coolly, leaning away from the open window.

"Is that right?" sang Greg. "For a minute, I thought you may have been confused by the camp schedule—we played Manhunt last night. Tonight is the dance."

"Nope, not confused," replied Alex.

"Two…" whispered Ryan.

"Well, it's a good thing you're not confused, because I can't seem to wrap my head around why anyone would need to drive a fucking bus full of Lifers anywhere during a game of

Manhunt or a dance!" screamed Greg, spit flying from his mouth.

"Ryan! Kate's trying to open the emergency exit!" shrieked Maggie. They all turned to the back of the bus. Maggie dug her heels into the rubber matted floor. She pulled the door toward her with all of her might to keep it closed. Corey flew down the aisle to help.

"Open this fucking door right now!" screamed Kate, standing on the rear bumper, furiously yanking on the handle. She smashed her other fist against the door window.

Through the windshield, they could make out more counselors moving down the driveway toward the bus.

"Uh, Ry," said Germ, motioning to the road.

"Three!" screamed Ryan.

Alex slammed the stick shift into reverse and floored the gas. The bus jolted to life, tires spinning dust everywhere.

"Oh my God!" screamed Maggie. Kate's body flew off the rear bumper and into the woods. "Holy shit! Is she...?"

"No, I don't think so," said Corey. He rushed to the side window. Kate was slumped over in a low ditch, her arms maneuvering like crutches to get the rest of her body to move.

"How we doing back there?" yelled Ryan.

"Fine, I think? I can't tell—it's hard to see anythi—"

The bus slammed into a pothole. Alex spun the wheel to adjust. "This is so insane!" he shouted, wiping sweat from his brow. He stared out the dusty side-view mirror, trying to keep the bus parallel with the edge of the dirt road. The counselors grew smaller through the windshield as the bus picked up speed.

"It can't be much farther now," said Germ, hanging his head out the window looking for the main street. Liv whimpered in the seat she shared with Tom.

"Liv, sweetie," said Becky, starting to lose her cool. "Stop whimpering. It's not helping anything right now!"

Liv sat up a little, her hands still shaking. Becky stuck her head out the window.

"Hey! I can see the camp entrance sign! We're nearly there!"

"Yeah, slow down!" hollered Corey.

Alex slammed on the brakes, sending everybody forward.

"Jesus Christ, at this rate, you're never getting your license!" said Joey.

"Fuck off, Joe! This thing is a tank!" cried Alex, breathing heavy.

"All right, back out onto the main road so we can take a right, and then follow the signs for the mountain," said Ryan. He ran his fingers through his hair and sank into his seat.

They headed north, the road corralled by rows of tall pines. The day's earlier clouds had dispersed, and the bus drove through the mountain pass under a blanket of stars. Maggie and Corey joined the others at the front of the bus.

"Hey, Tom, how about you and Liv organize our goodies from Woody?" suggested Becky.

Germ stood up and pulled a cassette out of his pocket, shaking it in the air. "What's a road trip to kill a monster and save our friend without a little...music?" He grinned and pushed it into the dashboard tape deck.

"When did you have time to make that?" Maggie laughed.

"Nah, this one's from back home. But I think it'll be a perfect soundtrack for our situation," said Germ, twisting the volume knob. The opening guitar riffs from Rage Against the Machine's "Sleep Now in the Fire" blared through crackly speakers as they flew down the highway.

"You got the whole album on this tape?" asked Ryan.

"Nah, it's a mix. It's pretty rad, though. I put some Filter on it, Smashing Pumpkins, some STP, little bit of Green Day..."

"Nice," replied Ryan.

"How can you guys talk about music at a time like this?" implored Becky, twisting her wild hair into a sensible bun.

"How can you not?" retorted Ryan. Becky huffed and

turned to look at Maggie, who shrugged and continued to look out the window.

The bus sped down the winding highway carved into mountains. It was early—not yet 9:00 p.m.—but the roads were devoid of other vehicles. The entrance to the base of Mount Kinross wasn't too far from camp. Tom and Liv sorted through the trash bags, separating bug spray from the lighters. Tom pulled out a plastic shopping bag knotted at the top.

"Hey, guys, look at this," he said, holding up the bag. Joey leaned over the seat. "Whatcha got there?"

"Dunno," replied Tom, pulling the knot loose. Inside it was a brown paper bag filled with cookies and water.

"You'd think he'd at least say 'good luck' or something," said Becky.

"Unless he thinks we don't need luck?" offered Liv.

"With the amount of ammo he put in these bags, it's safe to say that he thinks we'll need all the luck we can get," said Germ, sliding back down into his seat.

"Well, what are you waiting for, Tommy? Give me a cookie!" demanded Joey.

"Save some for Beth, in case we find her," said Ryan.

"How can you eat anything right now?" moaned Becky. "This whole thing makes me ill."

Tom stood up and passed the bag to Joey.

"Wait, wait, I have a song for this!" exclaimed Germ, jumping from his seat. He bent over the tape deck and pressed fast forward. It whirred and clicked as he searched for a song.

"Aha!" he exclaimed, and gave the Lifers a knowing nod as the Fun Lovin' Criminals invaded the airwaves.

The others sang along to the chorus while chomping on their cookies, until the Reservoir Dogs sample played.

"Son, I need you cool. Are you cool?" mimicked Ryan with a grin, pointing at Joey. He drummed along on top of the seat.

"I am cool," Joey deadpanned.

Laughter filled the bus. It felt like they were only partaking in a teenage night of debauchery, not on their way to hunt a creature that shouldn't exist in the real world, to look for their possibly dead friend.

"Shouldn't be far now," said Alex as the song switched to Spacehog's "In the Meantime." The night air was cool—the clean scent of pine blew through the open windows of the stuffy bus.

Maggie stood up suddenly and stumbled over Becky to get to Ryan.

"Hey—I almost forgot—I found the envelope," said Maggie, leaning into his seat. Ryan looked up at her and motioned for her to sit.

"I'm, uh…I'm sorry about earlier," said Maggie quietly. "I didn't mean for that to happen with—"

"I know," said Ryan. "It's not your fault."

"So, I found it." Maggie pulled the crumpled envelope from her pocket and lifted the flap to reveal three article clippings. She pulled them out and held them up between the two of them. Ryan put his hand under hers and leaned in to get a better view in the semi-darkness.

"These are hard to make out in this light," he said, pressing his fingers against hers to lift the articles closer to their eyes. Maggie's heart raced. His hand remained.

"It looks like it says something about opossums eating the bones of dead deer that hunters left in the woods? Something about the acrid—no—acid in their stomachs can dissolve bones?" Ryan swung his head around, looking for Joey.

"Well, that's horrifying," said Maggie. Her brain warred between concentrating on the gravity of the situation and not wanting to move her hand away from his.

"That might actually explain some things about the missing campers," said Ryan.

"You don't think—"

"Hey, Joey, bring one of those lighters over here so we can

read these better." Ryan fixated on the articles, but Maggie felt his leg press into hers. Electricity shot through her body.

Joey popped up in the seat behind them igniting a grill lighter in each hand, holding them under his chin. "Are you afraid of the dark?" he growled.

Ryan moved his hand away from Maggie's to swat Joey. "Cut the shit, you're going to give Liv a heart attack," he said. The three of them looked over at Liv, who wasn't paying attention. She sat up straight, mindlessly chewing on her lower lip, her face ghostly white even in the darkness. She stared ahead.

Joey leaned farther over the seat with the glowing flames, imitating the drumbeats during Tre Cool's solo in Green Day's "Longview" that played over the bus speakers.

"Hey, Germ," he said, turning his head away from Ryan and Maggie, "this is a killer mix, man!"

"Joey, watch out with those!" yelped Maggie, pulling her hair away from the flames.

Joey turned his attention back to them and said, "Okay, okay, what do you need?"

"Just hold the lighter steady so we can read these articles," said Ryan, agitated. He held the corner of one of the clippings to straighten it out, but the bus thumped through a massive pothole. Joey fell forward, the lighters jabbing into the papers they were holding.

"Sorry, guys!" yelled Alex.

"Fire!" screamed Maggie. She jumped out of the seat, burning pieces of newspaper fluttering to the floor in the breeze.

"Shit!" yelled Ryan and jumped onto the seat. He tried to stomp on the incinerating pieces of paper. Liv shrieked as smoldering ash flew across her lap.

"Are you kidding me? Look at what you've done!" screamed Maggie. Joey chased a floating ember down a few seats before stomping it out with his foot. Corey looked under the seats. "Did you get them all?"

"There's one up here!" yelled Alex, looking through his rearview mirror at the scene behind him. Germ moved to the stairs and stepped on the last bit of paper.

Ryan bent down looking for any salvageable remains.

"Anything?" asked Maggie.

He held up a charred piece of paper to answer her question.

"You're an idiot, you know that, Joey? A real moron. Those articles could have given us something to help kill this thing! Woody wanted us to find them for a reason, and you had to pretend you were the drummer from Green Day with goddamned lit lighters!" Maggie screamed.

"Mags, forget it, it's fine," said Ryan. "We're nearly there, anyway."

"Just because Billie Joe lights things on fire when he's on stage, doesn't mean everyone should!" exclaimed Maggie, shooting daggers at Joey.

Joey rubbed his forehead and slumped his seat. "Sorry, guys. You're right, I am an idiot. I can't do anything right most times. I'll—I'll make it up to you somehow. Really, I'm sorry."

Maggie looked across the aisle at Joey. A pang of guilt struck her.

"It's—it's fine, Joey. Forget it. We didn't really need them anyway," said Maggie quickly. "Sorry I snapped. It's, uh, easy to get lost in 'Longview'—I get it."

"Something just comes over me when I hear that song!" sighed Joey.

Maggie rolled her eyes and turned to Ryan.

"So, what do we do when we get to the base of Mount Kinross?"

"We ammo up and follow Corey. He knows these woods better than anyone. He'll take us to the cave, where this Wendigo probably lives."

"Yeah, but then what?" asked Becky.

"Then we light that fucker up and find Beth," said Ryan.

"I think we should surround the outside of the cave," said Corey. "If I remember correctly, the mouth of the cave is somewhat wide, but there are several large rocks scattered outside of it. Those could provide us some cover."

"What if it retreats into the cave?" asked Tom.

"Then we close in on it."

"We'll die!" exclaimed Liv.

"You could die choking on a glass of water," said Germ. "Better to go out with a bang."

"What if there isn't any monster?" asked Alex.

"Then we're dead, anyway. So let's hope there is one," said Corey.

"So, we all take a few cans of bug spray and some lighters, and when we find this thing, we torch it," confirmed Alex, flicking on his blinker to take a right into the small dirt parking lot for Mount Kinross.

"That's all I've got. Well, that's not true. I have one other ace up my sleeve, but we'll only use that if absolutely necessary," said Ryan.

"What is it?" asked Liv.

"I can't say," replied Ryan. "Let's just hope it doesn't come to that."

Alex put the bus into park. "We're here," he said, looking out the open side window into the blackness.

"It seems darker here," said Becky, a chill creeping down her spine.

"Yeah, I don't love this, either," agreed Maggie, looking around.

"If you don't love it, imagine Beth out there," said Ryan quietly.

Maggie nodded and stood up. "Let's go, guys," she said, smoothing her hair.

One by one they filed out of the bus. Corey and Germ carried the bags of ammo and set them down next to the tires.

"Hey, guys, look what I found in the glove compartment," said Alex, waving around a flashlight and two road flares.

"Nice, we're going to need all the light we can get," said Corey. "We should carry a can or two of bug spray and a lighter—in case we come across something along the way."

The Lifers exchanged uncertain looks but nodded. They each picked up a few cans and a lighter.

"We'll carry the rest in these bags, and then put them behind a rock or something once we get there," said Corey.

"Are we going to hike without a light?" asked Liv.

"Of course not, Liv, we're going to each carry a torch, but not before we put a giant 'EAT ME!' sign on all of our backs!" sneered Joey.

"Joey, don't," said Becky, looking at Liv, who was visibly shaking.

"Why'd we bring her, anyway?" asked Joey.

"Enough. Guys, we're all in this together. Let's stick to the plan and get it done. You ready?" asked Ryan, looking at each of them.

"Should we, like, put our hands in or something? Do a little 'Go Team'?" Joey grinned.

"Seems unnecessary," said Becky. They shifted their feet in the dirt and looked around.

"Let's just bring it in anyway," said Alex, thrusting his hand forward.

"What should we say?" asked Maggie.

After a moment, Germ spoke up. "Burn, motherfucker, burn?" They laughed to themselves, and one by one piled their hands on top of one another.

"This is so nerdy." Maggie shook her head.

"This is camp," replied Germ. "On three."

"But should we scream it? Is that safe?" asked Liv.

"Liv!" they shouted in unison. Liv cowered and smiled a little. "Okay, okay, right, scream it then, screw it," she replied.

"On three!" repeated Germ.

"One.. two..."

"Burn, motherfucker, burn!" they shouted into the night, throwing their hands in the air.

"Let's go—the counselors can't be too far behind us," said Corey. He ushered everyone to a trail off to the side of the parking lot. They fell in line, glancing up at the looming mountain in front of them and began their journey into the darkness.

60

"What took you so long?" demanded Greg. "I thought Neal and Eve told you to bring this car to us fifteen minutes ago!"

"Sorry, Greg, we were trying to maintain order—the campers were panicking—we had no idea the Lifers were behind it!"

"That's not good enough!" shrieked Kate. "Those little assholes stole the bus!"

"Why would they want the—"

"Why do you think?"

"They can't know. It's just not poss—" started Hannah.

"I told you that camper was the wrong choice, Greg, I told you! Those little brats have snooped around and have somehow caught on to what we're doing and now they're trying to stop us!" Kate said, her voice becoming more shrill with every word.

"Well, there's nothing we can do about that now, is there? What's done is done. Now we just have to deal with it," said Greg matter-of-factly.

"What do you mean by 'deal with it'?" asked Mark, his eyes narrowing. "You don't mean…"

"Don't question me!" screamed Greg, slamming his foot down, causing the gravel around his loafer to ripple. "We are going to take care of them, end of story!"

"But what about the rest of the campers?" asked Hannah.

"What about them? Adah can divvy up responsibilities between the rest of the counselors. They can combine bunks—whatever. I don't care what happens, as long as we take care of this situation before it gets out of control, understand?" yelled Greg, trying to tame his unruly hair by pulling it down in his fists.

Mark and Hannah exchanged looks.

"It will ruin everything, don't you get it?" said Kate, looking at them while wringing her hands. "If they blow this up, we're finished. We're all implicated. All of us! There's no way anyone gets out of this clean."

"You don't know that for certain," said Hannah calmly. "Be reasonable."

"You swore an oath, it's as simple as that," Greg said, shrugging. "An oath to protect this camp and its secrets at all costs, or else you're next. Funny how you so quickly forget the fate of Counselor Andrew."

"Andy was in love. How can you even—"

"Andrew was distracted, and that tart he fawned over was a blight on this place," sneered Kate.

"Why, because she spoke her mind? Because she questioned your motives?" said Mark, raising his voice.

"We don't have time for this. Give me the keys," said Greg, holding out his hand.

"Greg, let's just think about this for another minute, yeah?" pleaded Hannah.

"The time for thinking has passed. You're either with us or against us. If you're against us, get out of the fucking car so we can hunt them down. Now!" screamed Greg.

Mark turned to Hannah and she nodded. He opened the door and stepped out of the car, tossing the key to Greg.

"It's all yours. You're making a big mistake," said Mark.

Hannah exited the vehicle and walked behind it to stand

with Mark. Kate shook her head wildly.

"You're next. You're fucking dead!" she screamed, slamming the passenger side door shut. "Let's go, Greg, we're wasting time!"

Greg looked hard at Mark and Hannah. He wagged his finger at them. "Not only is this the right thing to do, but it's the only thing to do. You're both weak. We'll talk about this when we get back."

He jumped into the car and slammed on the gas pedal before pulling the driver's door shut. The car sped down the winding driveway at breakneck speed, its headlights zigzagging through the darkness.

"Fat chance," said Mark. He looked at Hannah, who was bewildered and looking around at the trees.

"What do we do now? How do we help the kids? Greg and Kate are coming for us next," she said, her voice shaking.

"Not if I can help it," said Mark. "Let's get back to camp. We have to talk to Woody and make some calls."

"This is a nightmare," replied Hannah.

Mark stepped closer to her, putting his arm around her shoulders as they walked back to camp. "It's going to end this summer, though. It has to."

"I hope you're right," she said, sniffing and leaning into him.

61

The Lifers stepped carefully through the woods at the base of the mountain, the only noise being the occasional murmur escaping their lips or a stick cracking beneath their sneakers. The darkness was dense and unwelcoming—spiderwebs stuck to skin and mosquitoes feasted on exposed flesh. Dread seeped from their pores. The trees loomed over them like menacing soldiers, standing at attention for the grotesque creature they were hunting. Fear infected each of them—a poison swirling in their minds, heightened by every rustling leaf and hooting owl. They kept their eyes ahead, unable to muster the courage to see what animals might be lurking around them. The trail had a few switchbacks and was padded with pine needles, providing them with the stealth movement they needed to reach the cave.

"We only ascend a bit—it's not too far from here," murmured Corey. "The cave is only a little ways up the mountain."

As they walked deeper into the forest, they could hear a faint tapping sound. They exchanged looks.

"Do you think that's Beth?" Maggie asked Ryan in a low voice.

"Dunno," he replied. They walked toward the tapping.

As they neared, the tapping became a crunching. The air was hot and carried a metallic scent. They closed in on the source of the sound.

It was the snarls that stopped them in their tracks.

"Hey, Alex," said Corey, slowly beckoning with his arm to get Alex's attention. "Give me that flashlight." They scanned the side of the darkened trail.

The crunching and snarls increased.

Corey took a deep breath. The sound was industrious, intensifying. He clicked on the flashlight and waved it over the side of their path. Liv, Becky, and Maggie screamed.

"Jesus Christ!" said Germ.

"What the fuck is that?" said Tom, turning away from the light.

"The article wasn't wrong," said Ryan, repulsion overtaking his face.

"That's so fucking disgusting. Shut the light off, man!" yelled Joey.

Corey stared at the scene a moment longer, rage shaking through to his core.

In the warm glow of the flashlight, dozens of shiny beady eyed opossums stared back at them, while the rest were busy feasting on the remains of several large bloody carcasses. Their cablelike tails whipped back and forth excitedly at the discovery of each new meaty morsel. Mouths gnawed on what looked like human rib bones jutting skyward. Two were engaged in a battle, tugging back and forth on a mangled piece of flesh.

Maggie gagged. She dropped her can of bug spray and held on to Ryan's shoulder to steady herself. Behind her, Joey retched into a bush.

"There are so many of them," said Becky, horrified. "Hundreds!"

"Let's keep moving before they get any ideas," said Alex.

"I can never unsee this," whimpered Liv. They continued

to stare, unable to look away at the bloody nightmare in front of them.

Corey shut off the flashlight and flicked his lighter. He seethed. Maggie looked at him and knew his thoughts. Was this how it ended for Penny? He raised his arm, held the can of bug spray outward, and pressed down on the button. A giant cloud of fire erupted, sending the opossums squealing and scattering into the woods.

"Goddamned disgusting rodents," said Corey. He flicked off the lighter and shoved the can back into his bag. "We need to keep moving." A rogue opossum scurried across the path in front of Corey. He pretended that he was going to chase it by stomping his foot on the ground. It turned its blood-stained face to him and hissed before scampering off.

***

They moved through the forest, stepping over gnarly roots bulging like unruly varicose veins from the earth's skin. Jagged stones obstructed the trail. The deeper they walked, the more suffocating the path became. Darkness closed in.

"How are we going to find Beth? We can't exactly call out for her," whispered Maggie.

"If she's alive, she's probably hiding and won't come out until she knows it's safe. Think we gotta slay the beast first," Ryan replied.

"What about Greg and Kate?" asked Liv.

"Yeah, I almost like the idea of dealing with the monster over them," said Tom.

"We can't worry about those assholes right now," said Germ. "Let's just find this thing and kill it."

They arrived at a large bend in the trail where a boulder forked the path. They stopped walking. Corey swallowed and nudged Ryan. "This is it. This is where—where I found—"

"It's all right, man. We're gonna get this thing. It's as good as dead," assured Ryan.

Corey looked at Ryan and then the rest of them. He coughed. "The cave is just a few hundred feet to the left."

"I can't believe you wandered all the way up here last summer," said Germ.

"It's not that far from camp, if you cut straight through, behind the Infirmary. Besides, they were probably happy about it. I bet they figured I'd turn into a free meal," said Corey bitterly.

"Joey and I will sneak down that way to get the lay of the land," said Alex.

"Joey will *not*," said Joey, crossing his arms over his chest and shaking his head.

"Come on, dipshit, we're going," said Alex, grabbing the arm of his shirt. He begrudgingly agreed, and they disappeared down the path.

Germ rummaged through the trash bag. "Take as many as you can carry," he said, handing out bug spray cans to the rest of them. Corey and Ryan took off their shirts and tied them into satchels to carry the ammo.

"You guys are going to get eaten alive," said Maggie.

"Uh, let's hope not," winked Ryan.

"I meant by bugs, not the Wendigo! Jesus! How could you say something like that?" replied Maggie.

"You said it," argued Ryan, smirking. Maggie threw her hands to the sky in exasperation; he laughed.

"Keep it down! What's so goddamn funny?" hissed Joey, ducking out of the path and into the clearing.

"That was quick. What's the good word?" asked Ryan.

"We saw the cave. It's pretty quiet right now," said Alex, wiping a cobweb from his arm.

"Yeah, and Corey was right—there are a few big rocks that we can use to take cover, but—"

"But?" prompted Maggie.

"But a lot of the smaller trees in the area have been snapped in half like matchsticks."

"Meaning?" prompted Becky.

"Meaning that the edge of the clearing isn't easy to move around. Some of the trunks are leaning against each other, or splintered," said Alex, looking uneasy.

"And tell them about the rock," said Joey.

"You already mentioned the rocks," said Tom.

"No, Tommy, not the 'rocks', the 'rock'," said Joey, making a face.

"Okay, what's 'the rock'?" sniped Tom.

"Guys, come on!" implored Becky.

"Now's not the time to take a tone, Thomas," said Joey, wagging his finger.

Alex spoke slowly, letting each word sink in. "There's a large, flat rock sitting about a hundred feet from the cave entrance."

"Yeah?" said Liv, biting her fingernails.

"It—it looks like it's a place where—where bodies are dropped off," said Alex.

Corey nodded. "Yeah, I remember seeing something like that in the daytime. It was sort of brownish on top." Maggie shuddered, recalling her dream that ended with Greg's and Kate's faces buried in the stomach of a kid lying dead on a flat boulder.

Ryan knelt down, wiping the pine needles from a sandy patch of ground. "Give me some light," he urged. He leaned back and grabbed a few sticks and stones. Germ clicked on the flashlight and held it above Ryan.

"Okay, so the cave is here," he said, drawing an arch into the sand. "We are currently over here, right, Cor?"

"Yeah, that looks right," he replied.

"Joe, put the stones where the rocks and 'the rock' are located." Joey knelt down beside Ryan and pushed them into the sand. He took the flatter stone and placed it in the middle of the map.

"Great, okay. Alex, where are the worst of the splintered trees?" he asked, handing Alex a bunch of twigs.

"Well, the two bad areas are off to the left, about here," he said. He snapped the twigs and planted it into the ground.

"Got it. Okay, Germ, you set up behind this rock with all of the supplies, and we'll scatter around the perimeter, behind these rocks and this area with splintered trees. But we have to assume that the trees aren't going to matter to the Wendigo."

"I'm not sure anything matters to this human-eating freak show," chattered Joey.

"At least it'll provide some cover," said Corey. "I'll take the trees."

"Cool, bring Joey with you," said Germ.

"I can't even get a rock to hide behind? Why do you guys hate me so much?"

"We're just setting you up to be the hero, buddy," said Corey, patting Joey's shoulder.

"Fine, yeah. Whatever." Joey shook his head, glaring at Ryan.

"Alex and Becky, you take this area next to the cave," continued Ryan, pointing at the map, "and Liv and Tom, you set up next to them. Maggie and I will attack from the center. Germ will fight from all over while he keeps us loaded with spray. Sound good?"

They nodded. The sickly sweet scent of ferns was suffocating. Overhead, shrill cries from bats echoed as they swooped between the trees. Maggie bent down to double knot her sneakers.

"So we just take turns blasting this thing?" asked Germ.

"Yeah, but wait until it gets sorta close. You're only going to get so much range with these cans," said Tom.

"He's right," said Maggie. "Back at home our friends had to sort of lunge at each other, spray, and then retreat."

Tom smirked. "Remember that time Smitty stutter-stepped by mistake during his retreat and singed his eyebrows off?"

Maggie gave him a quick smile. "Yeah, a cautionary tale for sure."

"Okay, so we lunge at the Wendigo, light up, flame thrower its ass, and then get the fuck back," said Corey, gripping a can tightly in his hand.

"Rinse, repeat," added Germ.

"Yeah," said Ryan, running his hand nervously through his hair. "Anything else? Are we missing anything?"

"Let's do this thing," said Corey.

"Wait! How are we going to know if it's dead?" asked Becky.

"Beats me." Ryan shrugged.

"How are we going to draw it out from wherever it's hiding?" asked Liv, looking nauseous.

Ryan thought for a moment, and smirked. "We're going to do what kids do best. We're going to make some noise."

They moved down the path. Germ gave them a thumbs-up as he got into position, dropping the bags of ammo behind his rock. The others split off to take their spots around the cave entrance.

Ryan tested his lighters. Maggie stood next to him biting her lower lip. A thousand thoughts swirled in her mind. What if this was the end, and she never had a chance to say everything she wanted to say to him? Like how she wanted a redo on their dance. How she didn't mean for them to get into this mess in the first place. How she wanted to be with him more than anything, even though it was pretty much impossible—the odds were incredibly, almost magnificently, stacked against them. It was as if tiny particles somehow escaped an alternate universe, one in which they were happily entwined without consequence. A universe she could only dream about in her current existence. The particles had traveled through space and time to forever infect her thoughts with him, and hope. Couldn't this be fixed? Couldn't they find a way? There had to be a way! But now wasn't the time to bring it up—not on the brink of fighting a supernatural nightmare. There might not ever be a good time to tell him—a classic case of words and bravery strung together perfectly in her mind, but paralyzed by fear when they reached her lips.

"You ready for this, Magpie?" Ryan adjusted his shirt satchel and flashed her a half grin.

"Oh, sure, yeah. Who wouldn't be? This doesn't feel crazy at all," said Maggie, grabbing her cans of bug spray.

"I know, right? But it's the best shot we've got," replied Ryan.

"Yeah," said Maggie quietly. She tested her lighter and looked at him expectantly.

"And now we're gonna go stand on that flat rock and make some noise," he said, pointing to the center of the clearing.

"Wait—the bloody sacrificial rock?"

"Yup."

"We?"

"Yup."

"And what, just scream until something comes out of the cave?"

"Just follow my lead, okay?" said Ryan, his eyes twinkling.

"Oh God," cringed Maggie.

Ryan jogged over to the rock and hopped up. He turned and offered his hand to Maggie. She accepted and clambered onto it. She looked around and raised her hands questioningly.

Ryan grinned. "Ready?"

"That grin suggests I really shouldn't be."

"How's your singing, anyway?"

"Wait, what?"

Ryan spun around on the rock, making sure everyone was in place; the others watched from their hideouts. He gave them a thumbs-up and looked back at Maggie. He took a deep breath, leaned backward, and bellowed:

"Look into my eyes, you will see

What you mean to me
Search your heart, search your soul
And when you find me there, you'll search no more!"

"A Bryan Adams song? Really? If the monster kills us, this will be the last song we hear before we die—you singing Bryan Adams? Of all the songs?!" Maggie stared at him as if he had completely lost his mind.

Ryan grinned and continued. He held out his hand to Maggie as if serenading her. She squeezed her eyes shut, mortified.

"Don't tell me it's not worth tryin' for
You can't tell me it's not worth dyin' for
You know it's true
Everything I do—I do it for you!"

Maggie peeked out of one eye. Her cringing slowly turned into a grin. The whole thing was completely ridiculous—summer camp, superpowers, monsters, and now, Bryan Adams. He motioned for her to join in. She sputtered out lyrics between breaths of incredulous laughter. Ryan clutched his heart and shouted:

"Don't tell me, it's not worth fightin' for
I can't help it, there's nothing I want more
You know it's true
Everything I do—I do it for you!"

He grabbed Maggie's hands. They spun around on top of the bloody rock, their voices carrying through the clearing.

"There's no love
like your love
And no other
could give more love
There's nowhere
unless you're there
All the time
All the way, yeah!"

Maggie's eyes danced with amusement, her hair flying

wildly in their centrifugal breeze. The others came out of their hiding spots. One by one they joined in, belting out the lyrics.

"I can't help it, there's nothing I want more!
Yeah I would FIGHT FOR YOU
I'D LIE FOR YOU
WALK THE WIRE FOR YOU
YEAH, I'D DIE FOR YOU—"

A piercing shriek reverberated through the depths of the cave.

Their spinning slowed like a merry-go-round ride wrapping up. Maggie teetered, trying to regain her balance. Grins faded. Fear set in.

The shrieks grew nearer.

"Get back to your spots!" yelled Ryan, pulling Maggie down from the rock. They ran behind their boulder.

A muggy stench of sour milk and decay wafted through the clearing. Ryan stifled a gag. Maggie's stomach lurched. They peered around the side of the rock. Waiting.

The shrieks were on top of them now.

They turned, thinking the noise was behind them. It was cacophonous, splintering. The whine of a thousand circular saws grating through metal. Joey puked behind a tree. All eyes were on the mouth of the cave.

A single translucent leg emerged from the darkness.

Quickly followed by another.

It leaned out of the cave, its gnarled antlers scraping against the edge. Thin, ropey arms gripped the top of the entrance. Too thin, like stretched out Silly Putty. Only ashy. Its emaciated body was draped with saggy, see-through skin. Machete-size teeth flashed in the moonlight. Deep black eyeballs darted around sunken eye sockets.

Desperation and bloodlust spewed with every shriek.

Ducking out of the cave, it rose over the clearing. Loose skin flapped as it swayed around, searching for the source of the noise.

"Holy shit! Look at that thing!" gasped Maggie, instinctively grabbing Ryan's arm. Her breath quickened.

Moving swiftly into the clearing, it leapt onto the sacrificial rock with unsettling agility. Maggie looked down and saw Ryan's hand trembling.

The shrieking stopped.

The monster slowly scanned the perimeter. Vertebrae popped loudly as it twisted back and forth. Rotting air from its snakelike nostrils puffed into the clearing. Ryan reached for Maggie's hand. Her heart kickstarted.

A commotion from the matchstick trees made them both turn. Corey was trying to hold Joey back, but he struggled free. Corey lunged after him.

"Get back here!" he yelled.

Joey ran toward the monster. It zeroed in on him. Crouching slightly, the Wendigo's joints crackled and popped like a fresh bowl of Rice Krispies.

"Fuck off, you Ridley Scott wannabe piece of shit!" shouted Joey. He whipped out a can of bug spray and flicked his lighter.

"Joe, it's faster than you think!" screamed Ryan. He dropped Maggie's hand and sprang to his feet.

"Ryan, no!" she shrieked.

Before Joey could press down on the aerosol can, the Wendigo was inches from his face. Rancid puss particles spattered onto his nose. Its jaw creaked open like a rusty hinge.

Wider and wider.

Dimples lined its throat. They pulsated and bloomed into small bumps.

The creaking continued.

Joey stood inches from death, frozen. Tears dripped down the sides of his face.

"Burn him, Joe!" screamed Corey.

The creaking stopped.

The bumps spawned hundreds of white barnacles, each with a razor-sharp tooth sticking out.

It closed in for the kill.

Ryan jumped at the Wendigo. He pressed the nozzle and ignited his lighter. A stream of fire illuminated the clearing. The blast was brief, hitting the Wendigo in the leg. Distracted, the monster snapped its mouth shut and immediately reopened it to shriek. It swung its antlers at Ryan. Joey scrambled back to his spot.

"Go! Go! Go!" shouted Ryan.

They all sprang into action. Acidic pine-scented fumes engulfed the clearing. The makeshift flamethrowers singed the Wendigo. Disoriented, the monster spun around, lashing out and swatting its gangly arms through the flames.

Maggie ducked a blow and lost her footing. Her head smacked against the earth.

The world started to spin.

Her vision blurred. She pushed up on her hands, desperate to get back into the fight. The ringing in her ears muffled the noise around her. A horror movie without the score. Blasts of fire exploded in every direction. The beast writhed and lunged at them. Her friends' faces were ablaze with fear and fury, clothes soaked with sweat. Maggie scraped her foot against the dirt, trying to stand. Her ankle wobbled in protest. Germ hurled cans of bug spray to the others. He grabbed Maggie's arm, yanked her to her feet, and screamed at Ryan, "Is it working?"

"Maybe? It's hard to tell!" Ryan yelled back, catching a full can of spray in the air, tossing the empty one behind him.

"We're gonna be out of spray soon!"

"Already?" yelled Corey. He grabbed another lighter behind a shattered tree trunk and ran back into the fray.

The clearing was consumed by a stifling heat. Alex threw his empty cans at the Wendigo's head. "Just die already!" he screamed.

The blasts were too brief to penetrate the creature's thick, saggy skin.

"Shit! I'm out!" shrieked Becky, shaking the can she held and pressing on the nozzle impatiently. The flame sputtered, then fizzled.

"Here, take one of these!" yelled Liv.

Becky did a double take. Without taking her eyes off the fight, Liv picked up an extra can and threw it to her.

"Thanks!" said Becky, bewildered and grinning. Liv stole a quick glance at Becky, returning the grin.

The Wendigo showed little sign of weakening.

"Didn't you say you have a plan B?" Germ yelled to Ryan.

"I don't think this is working, man!" screamed Joey, his voice cracking.

Tom cheated in closer to the Wendigo. He flicked his lighter. Pressed down on the bug spray. The blast was strong, striking its lower torso. It recoiled, letting out a guttural shriek that shook the surrounding trees.

"Maybe a few more hits like that!" Corey shouted over the Wendigo's pulsing screams. The monster's arms swung wildly, knocking Becky into the underbrush.

"Somebody help her!"

"It's retreating! Don't let it go back into the cave!" yelled Maggie. She ducked another blow from the monster's rubbery arm. Its hand landed on a boulder, shattering its overgrown, brittle fingernails.

"Mags, come here, quick!" replied Ryan.

She turned away from the monster. "What?" she replied, scrambling to meet Ryan behind the boulder. "We have to keep fighting!"

"It's not enough. I think it's time," said Ryan, giving her a weak smile.

"Time for what?" she asked, confusion and exhaustion smeared all over her dirt-caked face.

"Plan B," said Ryan, and without hesitating for another

second, he put his hand on her shoulder and closed his eyes.

62

Her mind flashed white. She was in a breezy field. The sun stretched its last golden rays across the tips of tall grass. Wildflowers lazily waved their goodbyes to the day. Crickets told stories from the shadows. The air carried the rich scent of deciduous trees and dried grass. Earthy and clean. It was the kind of air that was insatiable. It smelled like childhood. It felt like home.

Maggie looked up at the sky in full hypercolor as twilight descended. She squinted, in search of the first stars—or were they planets? She could never remember.

"Hey!" a voice called out in the distance.

Maggie spun around. Across the field Ryan pulled a door closed behind him, blanket over his arm. Her eyes grew wider than her confused smile. She furrowed her brow and walked over to him.

"What are we doing here? I wasn't asleep, so—so this can't be a dream. Wait—shouldn't we be trying to kill that thing? And did you just walk through a door to get into this field? What's going on?"

Ryan grinned. "Finally, I was really hoping you'd get it this time."

"Get what?"

"Get what this actually is—being able to be in your head. Believe me now?"

"Wait, so this is a part of your superpower?"

"Basically. And you can actually talk back now—about time."

"But I talked back in my other dreams, didn't I?"

"You did, but you weren't fully aware in them. You typically just freaked out," he smirked.

"Shut up," she said, punching him lightly on the shoulder. They surveyed their surroundings.

"So what is all of this? Where are we? Where'd I get this?" Maggie tugged on the fabric of her sundress. They walked to a part of the field where the grass was matted. June bugs defied the laws of aerodynamics with their quirky dips through the air. A dilapidated white screen rose a few hundred feet away. At the edge of the field, a faded wooden 1960s "Drive-In" sign swung in the breeze.

"Did you dream this place up? I've never actually been to a drive-in," said Maggie.

"Sort of," said Ryan, "but you did, too." He motioned with his head for Maggie to look at the screen. It flickered to life. A pool, a dolled-up lifeguard, and a bunch of kids watching their nerdy friend hatch a crazy plan to get mouth-to-mouth.

"Sandlot—I love this movie!"

Ryan shook the blanket out and said, "You gonna sit and watch, or what?"

"Oh! Yeah, sure," Maggie replied, her face aglow in the dusk. She kicked off her sandals and sat down, leaning back on her arms.

"I love the scene when the kids run through the Founders Day celebration in this movie! I wish I could be there."

"You mean you want to be chased through town by 'The Beast'? Given the night we're having, you may want to rethink that."

Maggie laughed. "No kidding. But the whole classic

Americana-ness of it, you know? It's pretty perfect. Like all of this," she added, motioning to the field around them.

"Mags, we don't have much time," said Ryan, looking at her out of the corner of his eye.

"Right, but we'll defeat the Wendigo with whatever your plan B is, and then we can, I don't know, hang out, or whatever, if they shut the camp down. Right? Road trip?" She grasped at straws.

Ryan bit his lower lip and looked away. "Yeah, we'll defeat the Wendigo," he said quietly, "but we are going to have to go back soon." Glow bugs twinkled above patches of grass.

Maggie turned from the movie and slid down onto the blanket to look at the stars. She cradled the back of her head in her hands. Ryan slowly lay down next to her. They were as close as could be without touching. The din from the movie faded. They watched night descend, lying side by side in a comfortable silence—so much being said in nothing at all.

After a while, Ryan pointed to the sky and said, "There's Cassiopeia, right there."

"Where?" asked Maggie, though she had picked it out moments before. He leaned closer to her and pointed to the constellation. His arm grazed her face. "The one that looks like a funky E or a sideways W."

"Ah, I see it now," she said, smiling. "Do you see the Seven Sisters?"

"Is that the one that looks like a tiny dipper?"

"Yeah." Maggie giggled.

"Yeah, I see it."

"It's so peaceful here," said Maggie, her eyes trailing a satellite.

"Yeah, no one to fuck it up."

"So, this—all of this—you're going to remember it when I wake up, or come out of it?"

"Yeah, I will. You will, too. I know, it's a little creepy. And I can't fully explain it, but it's kinda cool in some ways, right?"

"It's like a secret clubhouse, but in my mind."

"Our minds."

"Right. So I could say or do anything in here, and it wouldn't have any impact on the outside world?"

"Well, except that I would know, so I guess it could have some impact."

"But this isn't real."

"Reality is what you make of it. It's as real as you want it to be." Maggie felt his hand flinch by her fingers. She sat up and faced him. He gave her a questioning look and sat up beside her.

"Okay, so if I take your hand, like this," she said, trying to ignore the sudden surge in her chest, "this feels real. Your hand is warm and—and yet this is somehow all in my—our—heads? Like, will you remember how this feels?" Electricity tingled in her fingertips.

Their eyes met. In the distance, a muffled shriek echoed across the field. They both turned. Ryan scanned the tree line.

"Ah, fuck it, let's go," he said finally. He stood up, tugging on her hand. "C'mon, let's get out of here for a minute."

Maggie got to her feet. Before she had time to grab their blanket, her arm jerked forward.

"Wait, Ryan, my sandals!"

"You don't need them. Let's go."

They walked fast. Then they were running. They ran with hands entwined. Maggie's bare feet could barely keep up with her heart smashing against her chest. They ran through clouds of bobbing glow bugs, their light streaking the air as if they were running at hyperspeed in an '80s outer space movie. They weren't running from something, but toward; they were just kids, they were invincible. They sped between the trees, without inhibition.

"Are we—are we being followed or something?" gasped Maggie, turning to Ryan. "Because I'd never add that to our dream world!"

They neared the edge of the woods, distancing themselves from where they had heard the shriek.

"Beats me," said Ryan. They stopped running for a moment to catch their breath. He glanced at her and said, "Let's go a little ways farther, though."

They ran deeper into the forest, swerving around darkened trees and jumping over roots. They closed in on a silhouetted beech tree with an unusually large trunk. Slowing as they approached it, Ryan let go of her hand. Out of breath, Maggie grabbed at a stitch in her side and grinned in the aftermath of his touch. She looked around the dense wood—they had only been running for a few minutes, but the forest had completely swallowed them.

Ryan looked around. "I think…yeah…I think we're alone now."

Maggie leaned her arm against the tree trunk and rolled her eyes. "Uh, you mean there doesn't seem to be anyone around?"

He stared at her.

"Get it? Like the Tommy James and the Shondells song? You know, we were talking about them earl—I was just making a bad jo—?" she stumbled, but stopped.

He closed the gap between them.

Maggie bit her lower lip. Unable to finish her sentence. Unable to look away from him.

Her mind short-circuited.

In the next moment, she felt her back against the tree and his lips against hers. No hesitation. She pressed into him. Wrapped her arms around his neck. She kissed him back with a fervency that could only come from the cosmos. His lips were warm and soft and familiar and new all at the same time. Her fingers trembled as she traced them down his face. His mouth moved to her neck. Her shoulders curled up and she laughed a little. He found her mouth again and kissed her through his grin. Her fingers tugged on his belt loops. His hands slid under the hem of her dress, up her smooth thighs. He pulled her closer. Enveloped her completely.

Time stood still.

Ryan leaned his forehead against hers, his breath warm on her face. They stared at each other, eyes wide and alive in the moonlight. Dizzied by unhindered affections racing through her mind, Maggie looked at the ground to steady herself. Looked back up at him. His eyes were still on her. Her face burned in the dark.

"We really gotta go now," breathed Ryan.

"Or—or we could just stay here for a bit…"

"Don't forget the Wendigo—we have to stop it. That's what that screech was. It'll end this whole thing if it attacks one of us while we're here."

"Ah, right." Maggie circled around, not really knowing where to go, not knowing what to do. An inescapable magnetic pull drew her to him. "Okay, so what now? How do we get out of here?"

"Well," Ryan said, "I can usually just snap out of it, which should break the connection, and we'll come out of it."

"But we need a plan first," said Maggie.

"Obviously," said Ryan. "Plan B. When the connection breaks, you're not going to like what happens. Like, not at all."

"Jesus, what's going to happen?"

"I can't tell you. It'll only work if you don't know ahead of time."

"What will work?"

"Your fire."

"My—fire. Wait, what?"

"Yup, I've figured you out."

"You…you have, have you…"

"I did. You're pyrokinetic, dummy, and it's triggered by things that infuriate or hurt you."

"Did we really just kiss and now you're calling me a

dummy?"

"We don't have time for this. The Wendigo is going to start eating up all of our friends. Focus, Mags."

"Fine, fine. So the plan is for us to snap out of this, I'll see something horrific, and my alleged rage-fire superpower will magically ignite and incinerate the Wendigo?"

"Hopefully. But what you see will cut you to the core—and I'm—I'm sorry for that. I wish it didn't have to—"

"Right, okay, I'm sure it'll be fine. Hey, one more thing?"

"What's tha—"

Maggie threw her arms around him and kissed him again. His hair tangled with her fingers. His hands were all over her. Her heart exploded like a firework, crackling like radio static down the side of the night sky.

She pulled back and met his eyes.

"I just—" she started.

"Shh. Let's leave it like this." He held her face and pressed his mouth to hers once more. "You ready?" he said quietly.

They were out of time.

"Think so."

"Okay."

Ryan pulled his lips away. His fingers dropped to his side. He found her hand. They stood side by side, silently catching their breath, staring into the trees. He gave her hand a squeeze. They looked at each other. His eyes burned into her memory forever, and all went black.

63

Maggie blinked. In a split second, the serene twilight vanished and she returned to the supernatural hell on earth.

"Hey, Ry?" said Maggie, turning to look at him. His hand was no longer in hers. He was gone. She looked around. Sprinting with a stick, Ryan headed directly for the Wendigo.

"What? No! NO!" she shrieked.

In one horrifying moment it all made sense.

The Wendigo had its back to Ryan. He jumped up onto the sacrificial rock and smacked it with the stick. The creature whipped around instantly, shrieking in outrage. It snatched Ryan up in one of its gangly hands.

"RYAN!" Maggie shrieked again, tears burning down her face, her blood instantly boiling.

The monster let out another shriek. Gripping him tightly, it flipped him on his side. Ryan struggled and sputtered. He kicked at it, but the Wendigo's loose, doughy skin easily absorbed the blows.

Heat seethed throughout Maggie's body. It coursed through her veins. Emanated from her pores. Stretching forward, her arms started to shake uncontrollably. Her mind was consumed by the scene in front of her. All emotion melted away.

Her brain ignited. She couldn't escape it but didn't want to, either. Specks of dust lit up in the air around her, as if a swarm of glow bugs closed in on her. Tiny lights spun around her fingers and around her body. They rapidly accelerated until they blurred around her fingertips.

The Wendigo raised Ryan to its mouth. The others looked on in horror—shouting, pleading, throwing things—but the monster was fixated. Maggie looked at Ryan. He nodded and smiled weakly at her.

A sickening snap echoed through the clearing. Ryan's eyes went cold, his body limp. The Wendigo opened its creaking jaw and bit through Ryan's torso. Blood gushed down the sides of its saggy face and onto the rock.

Maggie's world went silent.

A pause.

And then, without warning, her mind exploded into yellows and oranges. Her body was on fire. She screamed, but couldn't hear anything. Scorching embers dripped from her eyes down her cheeks. The whirring glow in front of her had concentrated into a white-hot fire.

"KILL IT!" her thoughts screamed, staring through the burning white light. The fire stopped whirring and shot directly at the monster. It lashed out, screeching its ear-splitting scream, as she buried it into the side of the cave.

Maggie stepped closer. Walking past the sacrificial rock, dark and wet with Ryan's blood, she faced the Wendigo. A large hole oozed black puss from its side. Gasping for air, the monster clutched Ryan's lifeless body under its arm. Maggie couldn't take her eyes from Ryan. He looked like a rag doll. His limbs hung by a string, like a loose tooth dangling from a sliver of gum. His floppy hair was matted with sweat and blood. She would never again be close enough to feel it. His eyes rolled into the back of his head. Rage flooded her system. Her body shook. Again, the tiny flames started to circle around her hands.

"NO!" her mind screamed, the white light whipping around her. She looked at Ryan's body. She looked at the Wendigo's snarling mouth. The fire shot at Ryan. His body burst into a thousand twinkling bits of light and dust. The monster let out a guttural gasp as it tried to stand, using the cave wall for support.

"DIE!" shrieked Maggie. Before the Wendigo could swat its blood-soaked arm at her, she used the fire to bury it into the side of the cave again. Its rubbery body burst into flames, flailing wildly as it roasted. The stream of fire continued to incinerate the creature, its face contorting into caricatures of horrific design as it melted into oblivion. Razor-sharp teeth clattered to the ground, landing on top of the smoldering pile of ash.

The whirring lights around Maggie dissipated as quickly as they had manifested. She collapsed to her knees.

Tom immediately ran toward her. "Mags, you okay? Jesus Christ what was that?" The others came out from their hiding spots, visibly shaken. Maggie breathed heavy but didn't speak.

"You just—you just made fire! From the air!" exclaimed Germ.

"It's dead right? Is it dead?" said Liv. She looked around for confirmation from the others.

"It's over," said Maggie, choking back a sob. Tom put his arm around her for comfort, but she shrugged him off. "Stop. I'm okay, I'm okay."

Tom stood up and backed away. Silence fell over the clearing. They looked at each other, stunned and unsure of what to say. Ryan was alive only a few moments ago, and now, he was gone.

"We gotta find Beth," the words caught in Maggie's throat. Dusting off her knees, she straightened up and looked at them. "That's what all of this was for—that's why we're all here, right?" She furiously wiped the tears from her eyes and looked around. The others nodded.

Alex grabbed a nearby flashlight off the ground and scanned the perimeter. "Where do we start?"

Corey motioned to a path off to the side of the cave. "Maybe down that way."

The others murmured in agreement and followed Alex across the clearing. They slowed as they passed the spot where the Wendigo was destroyed, where Ryan went to the stars. They were unable to turn away from it. Becky and Liv held onto each other, whimpering as they walked by. A stream of tears silently flowed down Maggie's face.

Joey walked beside Maggie. He looked at her with his own tear-streaked face and said, "Well, I sure as hell won't ever mess with you when you're on your period!"

"Jesus, Joey!" yelled Becky. The others stopped walking. Alex and Corey turned around, exhausted and annoyed. Maggie looked at Joey for a moment. Initially incredulous, her eyes crinkled and a grin slowly appeared on her face. She exhaled a barely discernible laugh through her nose. But that wasn't enough. The flood of emotions she buried during the battle had to escape, and Joey had been the tipping point. She let out a laugh that echoed through the woods. The others exchanged looks and slowly started to smile. Her laugh went on for what seemed like an eternity. It was infectious—they all started laughing. Howling at the sky.

Maggie turned to Joey. "You know what? I'm really glad you were here for this."

Joey grinned at her and wiped his eyes.

"I HATE you!" he mimicked, assuming a power stance and throwing his arms out in front of him, pretending fire was blasting out of his hands. Pyrotechnic sound effects exploded from his mouth.

"Imagine?" exclaimed Germ. "Wait, did you know you could do that, Mags?"

"Not really," said Maggie, catching her breath. They

resumed walking. "Ryan knew, I think. He kept trying to tell me, but I refused to believe him. I didn't want to listen."

"Yeah, he had a hunch—he told me," said Corey. They walked through the forest, the flashlight methodically bouncing off the pine needles and roots in their path.

"We should start shouting for Beth," said Tom.

"Yeah, good idea," replied Alex.

"Beth! BETH! Beth, can you hear us? It's safe!" hollered Becky. She was met with silence. They continued to shout for Beth, but only received replies from the crickets and owls.

"What if she's too weak to shout back?" said Maggie, wiping the sweat from her brow.

"That's a good point," said Corey. "Maybe we should split up."

"We should NOT!" yelled Becky and Liv at the same time.

"What if there are other freak creatures out here?" argued Becky.

"Don't forget the opossums," Liv shuddered.

"Hey, guys, what are the odds we run into Greg and Kate out here now?" asked Tom.

"We'll have to deal with that if it happens," said Corey. "Our priority is to find Beth before…" His voice trailed off.

"Beth? Beth!" Maggie shouted. She stopped suddenly, holding up her hand to silence the others. She veered quickly off the path and marched through the brush.

"Maggie, you don't know what's out there. What are you doing?" Tom hollered after her.

"I thought I heard something!" Maggie replied, moving deeper into the woods. "You guys, come quick! Bring a flashlight!"

They high-stepped over ferns and swiped at cobwebs to catch up with her.

"Shh, did you hear that? It sounded like…like coughing, didn't it?"

"Beth?! Beth can you hear us?" Corey yelled.

A quiet moan emanated just beyond where the campers stood. Corey took off instantly toward the noise.

"Beth? Beth! Beth! I've got her!" screamed Corey. "Over here, you guys! By these rocks!"

She was barely conscious, wedged in a crevice between two boulders. She gripped a pointy rock shard in one fist, crumpled protein bar wrappers in the other.

"I…I just tried to…" Beth whispered, her voice shaky. The others looked on, helpless and horrified.

"Shh, don't say anything. We need to get you to a hospital," said Corey.

"Let's get her out of there," said Alex. The guys knelt down on either side of her and pulled from her shoulders. When she was freed, she collapsed into Corey on the ground, draping her arms around his neck and shaking uncontrollably.

"It's over. We killed it. Maggie killed it," repeated Corey, rubbing her back and pushing her hair away from her face. He looked up at the others and said, "Guys, we gotta go, right now—I think she's in shock. Let's get back to the bus."

Maggie knelt down in front of Beth and put her hands on her shoulders.

"You're going to be okay, okay?" Maggie choked back another sob. Beth nodded. She squeezed Beth tight and then moved aside to let Alex and Corey help her to her feet. They walked carefully, Beth's arms around Alex's and Corey's necks to support her atrophied legs.

They wound their way through the paths leading back to the trailhead in silence. As they neared the entrance, red and blue lights danced between the trees.

"What the…" said Alex.

"It could be a trap!" warned Becky. She held on to Alex to steady herself. "We should be careful."

"Becky's right," agreed Tom, "the local cops were in with the camp."

"I'll go scout it out," said Joey, cutting ahead of the rest of them. His silhouette threaded between the flashing lights. The rest of the Lifers waited, bracing themselves. After a few minutes, they could hear Joey hustling down the path toward them.

"Hey, guys—it's all good! Come on out! It's the state troopers! We're safe!" shouted Joey.

The parking lot at the base of Mount Kinross was a spectacle. State police cars had cordoned off the entire lot. Two ambulances were positioned next to the bus. A firetruck wailed in the distance. Three additional cop cars surrounded another car off to the side.

"Is that Greg's car?" Liv pointed.

"Looks like it," said Corey.

"Hey, they're over here!" yelled a gruff voice. Woody motioned to the police.

"Woody!" Maggie yelled. They rushed over and surrounded him.

"This one needs medical attention!" Woody shouted, pointing at Beth.

Two EMTs hurried over to the campers and assisted Beth to the back of the ambulance.

"Woody! Why are you here?"

"How did you know?"

"Did you know about the Wendigo all along?"

"Did you call the cops?"

"Did they catch Greg and Kate?"

"Where are the corrupt cops?"

"What about the other counselors? Have they been arrested?"

Woody held up his hands, and the barrage of questions immediately stopped.

"Where's Ryan?" he charged. They turned to Maggie. She looked at Woody, tears welling in her eyes. Woody didn't ask again but pulled her in for a hug. She cried into his flannel shirt, holding on to him longer than he had anticipated. He coughed a few times and cleared his throat. She let go and looked at him expectantly.

"Mark and Hannah knew that you guys took off. Greg wanted them to help catch you, but they weren't having it. Mark found me in the aftermath of the dance chaos, and we made some calls. Staties picked me up to come help look for you before Greg and Kate did something…well…regrettable. Fortunately, the troopers intercepted them as they arrived at the trailhead." Woody took a deep breath and looked at each of them. "I'm glad that you're all—well, most of you—are alright."

"Maggie saved us from the Wendigo," said Becky.

"No." Maggie shook her head. "It was Ryan. He sacrificed himself to save us. It's the only reason we survived."

"It was a nightmare," said Liv.

"It really was," agreed Alex.

"Is it done?" asked Woody, lowering his voice. "Is it dead?"

"It's a pile of ash by the cave," said Corey, looking over Woody's shoulder at Beth sitting in the back of the ambulance.

"Wait—if you knew about the Wendigo all along, how come you've never tried to kill it? Or tell the army?" asked Tom. Woody stared down Tom before replying.

"I have tried to kill it, pea brain. Many times. You think I'm going to just sit back, turn a blind eye, and let kids die? And why didn't I call the army? Gee, I don't know! On second thought, you're right, they'd probably jump at the chance to listen to a vet requesting tanks to decimate a creature that doesn't exist in the natural world. Yeah, in fact, I'm sure they'd come running."

"Fair," croaked Tom.

"Where's Mark?" asked Joey.

"He's back at camp—he and Hannah and the rest of them are calling parents, getting all of that sorted out. Keeping campers calm, you know? State police are there, too, ripping the place apart for evidence."

"Are they going to get in trouble? I mean, they helped Greg and Kate, right?" asked Liv.

"Does everyone know what really happened?" asked Corey.

"No, and it's going to stay that way. None of you should ever mention that thing in the woods to anyone, you got that?"

They nodded.

"Ever," repeated Woody, staring hard at each of them.

"Mark is telling the parents about the deceased campers, as well as the local authority cover-up," he continued. "The state police know everything and are prosecuting. Your parents will be here tomorrow. It's over."

The campers stood in silence, stunned.

"So, what now?" asked Becky finally. They were interrupted by a scuffle near one of the police cruisers. Greg lashed out at the cops trying to handcuff him. Kate was already in the back of the car, leaning her head against the window, her eyes unfocused and weary.

Greg continued to thrash while the cops restrained him; they finally slapped handcuffs around his wrists. His hair dripped with sweat and spit flew from the corners of his mouth while he demanded his constitutional rights. The cops flipped him around and threw his chest against the police car. Greg stopped struggling when his eyes landed on the campers a few hundred yards away.

"You! You little pieces of shit! This isn't the end, you idiots! You think it's over, but it's not over! You don't even know what you've done!" he spat.

They looked at each other, then at Woody who shook his head. A cop grabbed Greg's shoulder and pulled him away from the car, while another cop opened the rear door and jammed him into the seat, slamming the door with a satisfied grin.

"What if they say something about the Wendigo?" asked Becky.

"They'll try, no doubt, but it's unlikely that anyone will believe them. They'll argue that they weren't the ones doing the killings, but the state won't see it that way," said Woody, staring at Greg's maniacal face, plastered to the window of the cop car as it circled out of the lot.

A state trooper wearing a hat walked over to them, carrying a notepad.

"We're going to have to get statements from all of these kids," he said to Woody. Woody nodded and looked at Maggie before motioning for her to go with him.

"Just tell the truth," said Woody slowly, letting each word sink in. Maggie nodded and looked at the others. Everyone nodded and seemed to understand what that meant.

"I'm going to check on Beth," said Corey. "I'll be over there if anyone needs me." He walked toward the ambulance before anyone could reply.

Maggie walked with the cop to his car. He motioned for her to sit against the bumper.

"So, what happened?" he asked gruffly.

"We were looking for our missing friend, and the counselors went nuts."

"What reason do you have to believe that your friend was missing?"

"Well, Greg and Kate kept telling us that campers were being sent home for breaking camp rules, but we never saw them leave."

"I see," replied the cop, making a note. "You realize that stealing a bus and driving without a license are punishable offenses, even in Vermont," continued the cop, not looking up from his notebook.

"We thought our friends were being murdered!" exclaimed Maggie.

The cop stopped writing and looked at Maggie. "That's a

serious accusation; what made you think that?"

"We found things at camp that used to be our friends' stuff. Things they wouldn't have left behind."

"Such as?"

"Glasses, with blood on them."

The cop scribbled in his notebook.

"So we wanted to investigate. We thought the local police might be compromised."

"Why did you think that?"

"Because if campers kept going 'missing,' it didn't make sense that parents weren't coming up here and demanding search parties to look for their kids." Maggie's voice became irritated at having to justify herself.

"I see," replied the cop.

"I don't understand why I am being questioned like this— we found our friend—how much more proof do you need?"

"Listen, kid—Maggie, is it? Listen, Maggie. It's not that I don't believe you. I need to gather everything I possibly can so that we can present it all to the state. It's a huge undertaking and not one to be taken lightly. People are going to go to jail for a long time. So I need to make sure that my information is as accurate as possible, so I can sleep at night knowing that I did the right thing by putting these sick fucks away. Capeesh?"

Maggie was taken aback by the trooper's candor and nodded. She started over, retracing the last week of camp. She recounted Petey and Stacey, Jonesy's glasses and disappearance, June rejecting her initiation, the mistreatment of campers during Manhunt. She carefully stepped over any interaction with Ryan or finding the monster. She went as far as to mention the opossums in the woods and how they may be responsible for getting rid of the bones. The cop raised his eyebrow, but said nothing.

When she was done, she breathed a sigh of relief and said, "And now, I'm talking to you." She smiled weakly.

The cop looked at Maggie, closing his notebook. "Thank you, Maggie, this has been very helpful. You may go back to your friends now."

Maggie walked back over to Lifers, automatically scanning the crowd for someone she knew wouldn't be there. She fought back the tears welling in her eyes, by looking up at the sky flashing red and blue.

The others took turns giving similar statements. Corey rejoined the group, nodding knowingly at Woody. He stood next to Maggie and put his hand on her shoulder.

"I told Beth not to mention the Wendigo...or him," he murmured.

"Ah, okay, that's—that's good," said Maggie, looking away.

"Yeah. I'm really sorry, Maggie," said Corey, kicking the dirt in front of him. He opened his mouth to say something, but then changed his mind.

"Yeah," said Maggie, her voice trailing off. "Thanks, Corey." She caught Tom's eye, but looked away immediately. She couldn't stomach looking at him right now or talking to him. It was too much, after everything that had happened.

A state trooper started the bus; it roared to life. Diesel exhaust poured into the clearing. He hopped out and motioned to Woody.

"All right, you guys, get on the bus," said Woody. "That trooper is going to take you back to camp. Mark and Hannah will take care of you. I'm going to stay with Beth. They're going to take her to the hospital."

The campers filed onto the bus and slumped into their seats. Germ's mixtape played "Under the Milky Way," but no one seemed to notice. The trooper boarded the bus and surveyed the seats.

"We ready?" he asked. No one replied. He punched eject on the tape and turned off the radio, annoyed.

"What is this garbage?" he asked, waving the tape in the

air.

"It was The Church, man," replied Germ, sighing heavily.

"Sure it was," said the trooper, and tossed the tape to him. "You keep it." He sat down in the driver's seat and shut the door. "Here we go," he said, shifting the bus into gear and backing out of the lot.

Things were never going to be the same. The realization leveled Maggie like a sucker punch. Tears streamed along the outline of her cheek pressed against the bus window. She wiped her nose with the back of her hand. Her bleary eyes could barely make out the trees flicking by. She had to focus on something else. Anything else.

She felt something digging into the back of her leg. Shifting in her seat, she found a flip top pocket notebook. Ryan must have left it on the bus, before they went out to find the Wendigo. She picked it up and traced her fingers over the springy spiral spine. The cover was well worn and soft; the corners of the cover battered. She tugged at the elastic that bound it shut, but changed her mind and let it snap against the cover.

Not yet.

Instead, she held the notebook in her hands and pressed her cheek back against the window. It felt cool and wet, the night's condensation transferring to her skin.

Headlights bounced up and down along the road. The bus slowed through an intersection—the traffic light steady and green. Maggie stared at its glow and thought about the famous green light at the end of Daisy's dock, illuminating the promise of a future that could never be realized by Jay Gatsby. She had pretty much made it to her green light. She found her counterpoint—or he found her—it didn't matter. If serendipity was behind the melodic weaving of lives, it composed a perfect symphony when it connected them. She had felt it instantly with him—that indescribable "it" that might only come around once in a lifetime, if you're lucky enough to recognize it.

And in a blink, it was gone.

Or was it?

She stared out the window.

Fuck it. She had to know.

She slid the elastic from Ryan's notebook and flipped it open. Her eyes ran quickly over the first page. She closed the notebook, looked up, and grinned through her tears.

EPILOGUE

∗∗∗

"What took you so long?"

"Sorry, I had to grab the rest of the vials. The police were prying open the well when I snuck away from the Infirmary."

"Which police, Eve?"

"The state police. Do you think they'll find us?"

"Way down here? Unlikely. Did you seal off the entrance?"

"What do you think? Honestly, Neal, I'm not an idiot."

"Of course not, dear, of course not. I'm simply making sure we've taken all of the necessary precautions, same as always."

"How long do you think we'll be down here this time?"

"I suspect a fair amount of time, my love. They've taken away Kate and Greg, and if it's the state police, they're probably tearing the place apart."

"But they're not going to find the Lab?"

"We've gone to great lengths to preserve our subterranean bunker, my pet. We've been doing this for decades. No one has ever peeled back the linoleum or moved the shelves holding those dusty old record crates. Now, the vials?"

"Right, right, here you are." Eve walked over to the bench and handed Counselor Neal a small plastic bag. He pulled the vials out, examining them in the fluorescent light, one by one. "Beautiful, just beautiful. You did well, as always, my dear." He clasped her hands and pulled her down for a kiss.

"I need to get these beauties into the centrifuge right away, so that we can start extracting the DNA—it's time to rebuild. Speaking of which, why don't you go check on the kids?"

Eve nodded, leaving him to his blood spinning. She walked down a long hallway, the generator lights tripping on each time she passed a motion sensor. The walls were lined with floor-to-ceiling glass cylinders. Inside, human life in various stages floated in liquid. Numerous tubes and monitoring cords were attached to their mouths, noses, and chests. Eve ran her fingers along the cylinders as she passed them. An overfilled white pushcart sat at the end of the hall with a blanket covering its lumpy contents. Well, we'll have enough meat to get us through this transition, she thought. She glanced at the cart and wondered who they had lost while she was busy with camp duties.

Eve tutted and pushed through the double doors. The hall light flickered to life, revealing several locked doors with small windows cut into the center of them. She stopped at the second door and rapped on it. "Knock, knock!" she said cheerily. Inside, a teenage boy was lying on a cot reading a book. When he saw Eve, he smoothed his wild hair and flashed her a game show smile.

"How are you today, Gregory? How was your day?"

"It was great! I've been reading this book on outdoor activities, and this game called Manhunt that kids play—it sounds fantastic!"

"Indeed, it is." Eve smiled. "Soon enough, you'll be able to play it."

"Really?"

"Really!"

"With other kids?"

"Yes. And what's more is that you'll be in charge! You're going to be in charge of everything."

"Oh, Evie, that sounds great. I can't wait!"

"Soon enough. But you know, with great power comes great responsibility."

"I'd do anything for you, Evie! You know I would!"

"That's music to my ears, Gregory, music to my ears. Get some sleep now, my boy."

A satisfied smile slowly crept over Eve's lips. She pushed through the double doors and walked back down the corridor. She sat at her desk and tapped some papers together into a neat pile. She pulled open her bottom desk drawer, and her eyes caught on three torn book pages. *Wendigos: How They're Created, and Incantations Used to Permanently Destroy Them.*

Her eyes danced as she shut the drawer. Yes, thought Eve, smiling wide, everything was going to be just fine.

THE NOTEBOOK

* * *

Scribbled in tiny, scrawling script, on the inside cover of Ryan's notebook was the following:

7/95

Magpie!

If you're reading this, I'm gone.

But that means the monster is dead… and we've probably made out…

Anyway, there's so much more that you need to know—about me, about the camp, about how this isn't over yet…

Are you ready?

—R

THE MIXTAPE

***

Here are most of the songs and artists referenced in Camp Kinross (in no particular order), along with some songs I couldn't shake while writing. Check them out!

Crimson and Clover—Tommy James and the Shondells
Save Me—Remy Zero
Fire Water Burn—Bloodhound Gang
At My Most Beautiful—R.E.M.
Light My Fire—The Doors
Molly (16 Candles)—Sponge
Got You (Where I Want You)—The Flys
Only in Dreams—Weezer
Slide Away—Oasis
Scooby Snacks—Fun Lovin' Criminals
We Didn't Start the Fire—Billy Joel
Electrolite—R.E.M.
Sweet Dreams (Are Made of This)—Marilyn Manson
Magpies on Fire—Red Hot Chili Peppers
Morning Mr. Magpie—Radiohead
Longview—Green Day
For What It's Worth—Buffalo Springfield
Breezeblocks—alt-J
I Know Places—Taylor Swift
Uncertain Times—The Raveonettes

Blow Up the Outside World—Soundgarden
E.S.P.—Buzzcocks
(Everything I Do) I Do It for You—Bryan Adams
I Think We're Alone Now—Tommy James and the Shondells
Under the Milky Way—The Church
Again—Janet Jackson
Eat, Sleep, Wake (Nothing But You)—Bombay Bicycle Club
The Sounds of Silence—Simon and Garfunkel
Don't Drink the Water—Dave Matthews Band
Sleep Now in the Fire—Rage Against the Machine
Acquiesce—Oasis
Slide—Goo Goo Dolls
We Could Run—Beth Ditto
Sherry Fraser—Marcy Playground
Ring of Fire—Johnny Cash
All Over You—Live
Space Oddity—David Bowie
Live Forever—Oasis
Zero—Smashing Pumpkins
Mysterious Ways—U2
Onion—Shannon and the Clams
A Murder of One—Counting Crows
Burning Benches—Morning Runner
In the Meantime—Spacehog
Murmurations—Ben Howard
Apocalypse—Cigarettes After Sex
Grey Cell Green—Ned's Atomic Dustbin
Dream World—Growlers
Unchained Melody—The Unrighteous Brothers
*Crimson and Clove*r—Joan Jett and the Blackhearts

https://open.spotify.com/playlist/36RyFFY5oMg4nL8Pbsh
9HR?si=eKHd_rNXTbWQtznrd6XSFQ

THANK YOUS

This book has been a long time in the making, and it wouldn't be where it is today without the help and incredible encouragement from some exceptional people.

Thanks to Joan Millman for teaching me how to "show, not tell" in my writing; Stephanie Miller for co-authoring countless stories with me in seventh grade and sparking my love for writing; Stephen King for always unabashedly pushing the supernatural envelope, and murdering his darlings; Sarah Dessen for writing an incredibly nice reply to my fan mail in high school, insisting that I "keep writing"; and my grandparents, for letting me lay around their house on Cape Cod as a kid, listening to oldies on the radio, watching the 1961 version of *The Parent Trap* over and over and over, and giving me lots of space to dream.

Thank you to my most excellent friends and family, who have not only cheered me on over the last number of years, but have given me invaluable feedback on my drafts and advice, minus any sugar coating (which I appreciate so much): Jonathan and Marcie Naumowicz, Liz and Jeff Einhorn, Brad and Alissa Santarpia, Chris and Betsy Nardone, Aaron and Melissa Amara, Lauren and John Kougias, Beth and Dave Anderson, Rachel Goodrich, Franzi Drummond, Heather Roberts, Audrey and Bharat Battu,

Amanda and Loren Decker, Holly Noelle Perry, Melody Perry, Erin Perry, Lydia Perry, Tiara Perry - you are amazing, and I couldn't have made this happen without you!

To my transatlantic music soulmate, Matt Gully, thank you for continuously sending me inspiring tunes, your relentless positivity, and all the witty banter that never fails to make me laugh. I'm so happy you decided to pop into that pub in Plymouth all those years ago.

Thank you especially to Lily Goodrich, my first reader and fan, who propelled me to finish this story after I had stalled out. I hope you enjoy it even more in its final state.

An extra thanks to Jonathan Naumowicz for your first pass of edits, invaluable insight, and excellent conversation about all things literature.

Thank you to Elie Perler for your second pass of edits, as well as all of our phone chats to discuss wonky sentences and plot points.

Thank you to my wonderful editor Sandra Ogle, who tightened everything up and provided fantastic feedback, and thanks to Dean McKeever for the unbelievably excellent book design and artwork that I couldn't have dreamt up in a million years - I'm completely in love with it.

A special thanks to Jon Michael Darga for your constructive feedback and kindness during my querying process.

Thank you to my mom for always encouraging me and insisting that I should write a novel, and also for not sending me to traditional summer camp, thus fueling my obsession with it - I love you!

Thank you to my brother, Derek Pearl - I love you!

Thank you to Brandon for all of your "Shouldn't you be writing instead of watching TV?" motivations, and for being the most accommodating and excellent husband anyone could ever ask for.

And last but certainly not least, thank you to Jasper and Violet - you are my whole heart. I cannot wait for you to read this someday.

ABOUT THE AUTHOR

Holly Louise Perry grew up in Carver, Massachusetts,
and now resides in a small town in Connecticut.

When she's not writing, she's probably
on a roadtrip with her family,
listening to The Beatles,
or thinking about where she should get her next ice cream.

This is her first novel.

For more information or to contact Holly,
please visit perrylanepress.com

Printed in Great Britain
by Amazon